The Misfit

by

Ralph Alcock

Copyright © Ralph Alcock 2024

ISBN: 979-8321633205

First Edition

The author asserts the moral right under the Copyright, Designs and Patents Act 1988 to be identified as the author of this work.

All Rights reserved. No part of this publication may be reproduced, stored in a retrieval system or transmitted, in any form or by any means without the prior consent of the author, nor be otherwise circulated in any form of binding or cover other than that which it is published and without a similar condition being imposed on the subsequent purchaser.

My thanks for the advice and encouragement from Cherry Alcock and Paul Forrester-O'Neill, as well as the support from my literary agent, Darin Jewell.

Chapter 1

1972, South Yorkshire

Patricia Byrne knew she was in trouble. Her body seemed intent on announcing to the world she was pregnant. She had no siblings she could whisper to, collude with, confide in. Theirs was a small, dark, terraced house sitting in the shadows of coal-black slag heaps. It had dull-green painted walls and a black mantelpiece that dominated the front room. Patricia wished she lived in one of the bright, new homes on the council estate which had encroached ever closer as if to taunt those living in the shoddy terraces. That's where the cool, edgy kids lived. The ones that smoked menthols, wore the shortest skirts, had lacquered hair, took rides on motorbikes and snogged in the park.

Her mother seemed to like the idea of her going to the youth club with her friend, June Tiplady, as if it were nothing more than a milk-bar with soft music from a jukebox serving shakes and burgers. The youth club was a far cry from her mother's imagined 'have a nice time, enjoy yourself' gathering, it was a loud, raucous din-filled place supposedly run by a youth-worker from the council. He was a native himself and knew the score. He managed, somehow, to keep it sufficiently under control to not worry the council or the police. They wanted the kids off the streets and turned a blind eye to most of what went on. The two teenagers always waited until they were round the corner before June took a fag from the crushed packet in her jeans and shared a menthol.

There were some from the estate who scared Patricia with their sudden threats and taunts. Those from the Fisher clan were the worst, but she'd stood her ground; she could hold her own. And her nervous excitement was like a drug. At times she tingled with fear, but her feeling of exhilaration was like awakening into another world.

Patricia retched into the bathroom sink, the sound echoing, unmuffled by the thin walls. She trod warily down the stairs and into the front room. Her mother was sitting at the table by the front window, her elbow resting on a pile of Patricia's school exercise books.

"You're pregnant!" she shrieked, her voice rising into an unfamiliar register.

Patricia felt her stomach heave. The clock on the mantlepiece ticked loudly as if adding a mechanical note of exclamation. There was nothing she could say.

Her mother's shrill voice filled the silence, "You stupid, stupid girl!" She stared out of the window for a few moments and then slowly turned back to Patricia. "You can't keep it," she said in a measured tone. "I dread to think …"

Before she could finish, there was the sound Patricia had feared: her father's heavy boots in the hallway. She could smell the reek of the man as he opened the door, the waft of sour milk from his stained apron and an acidic, earthy smell from the cloth he used to wipe the batteries on his milk cart. He placed a bottle of milk on the table,

"Give us two rashers, Ethel." He looked at them both as if suddenly aware of the tension in the room. He slowly followed his wife's eyes to his daughter. "What's up? Is she sick?"

"No, George. Worse."

"What do you mean … worse?" His eyes roamed over Patricia. "Nowt wrong with a bit of weight," he said.

"She's pregnant; in the club, up the duff."

Patricia trembled, waiting for the rage brewing in her father's puce face to explode. His arm flew across the table, sending the milk bottle scudding across the floor. The thick glass smashed against the tiled hearth, milk hissing against the embers in the fireplace. She instinctively lifted her arms as her father lurched across the room.

Her mother screamed, "Don't you dare hit her! That's not going to solve anything!"

He kicked out at the shards of glass crunching under his boots. "You stupid bitch! Whose is it — that skinny runt from round the corner? I'll get the bastard." He leaned towards her, stretching his thick neck, "What's he goin' to do about it?"

Patricia found her voice. "Wasn't him."

"Who, then? Don't tell me you don't know!" He wagged his finger at her. "What are you, a tart?"

Ethel stared at her daughter, "Well — who was it?"

"From the barracks ..."

"A pimple-faced squaddie!" her father exclaimed.

"Where is he now?" Ethel demanded.

Patricia hung her head, "Dunno ... gone ..."

"Gone! ... Gone!" her father shouted. "What the hell do you mean 'gone'?"

"He ...he ... left the army," Patricia stammered. "He's gone back to Sunderland."

Her mother gasped, "Don't tell me he's married?"

Patricia gave a reluctant nod.

Her dad slapped the palm of his hand against his forehead and sat heavily on his chair. "What's to be done Ethel? She's brought shame into this house, shame on our family. God knows what the neighbours will think ... and the family. There's your sisters to think of, and my brother. He always said she'd come to no good."

"He's a pervert!" Patricia screamed. "He's always trying to get into my knickers."

Her father lurched towards her, his hand raised, ready to strike. Patricia stood erect; her feet planted on the brown linoleum. Her Mother leapt to her feet, as nimble as a cat, and pushed herself in front of Patricia. George's hand caught her on the side of her head.

"Sorry, Ethel," he pleaded, his voice shaking.

Ethel straightened herself and glared at her husband. Her face was reddened where her his big hand had clipped her cheek. "Your brother has been in trouble before," she said, fiercely. She turned to Patricia, "Wasn't him, was it? Tell me it wasn't him?"

Patricia shook her head. "Not him," she said.

Ethel exhaled rapidly, a swift snort. "Thank God." She touched the side of her face and glared at George.

"There's only one thing we can do," she replied. "It'll have to be adopted. Better get her into Beech House."

Her husband nodded, as if relieved there was a solution, of sorts. "I've seen 'em leaning out of the windows. The nuns will sort her."

"You deliver there, right?" Ethel said.

"Not anymore," he replied. "I don't want to see her heaving her belly around."

A week later, Patricia was bundled into the back of her parents' Austin A40 clutching the suitcase she'd packed that morning. The local priest had agreed, with just a few formalities, to arrange for Patricia's admission to Beech House. He'd also had a word with the school's head teacher where he was chaplain. They'd both agreed, having one of their girls heavily pregnant would be in no-one's best interests. Patricia had spent the week in near isolation, confined to her room for most of the day.

Her parents hardly said a word. They were suited, grim-faced and stiff-necked, intent, it seemed, on ignoring not just the stifled sobs of their daughter, but also the twitching curtains and furtive glances from their neighbours. Her father drove as carefully and cautiously as he might with a full load of milk bottles. Patricia wished he'd pick up speed instead of the slow, excruciating amble. She leant against her suitcase and stared out of the window. After a few minutes, they left the last of the terraces in the 'pit village' and drove along a road lined with trees and large semi-detached houses. They had front gardens, bay windows, a driveway and a garage. To Patricia, they were homes, like those in magazines, where families were always happy, the mothers were well groomed, and their husbands didn't work down the pit or operate a milk float.

It took twenty minutes or so to reach the large gates that fronted 'Beech House'. It had a discreet brass plate on the entrance pillar, that simply said, 'Private Home'.

A stern-looking nun opened the door. She ushered them into a vestibule off the hallway. The tiled floor shone, and the dark furniture smelled of beeswax and polish. The nun beckoned them over to a large desk with a ledger opened at a blank page.

"This is our admission form," she said, uncapping a fountain pen. "No father, as I understand." Patricia was ignored. The nun asked her parents to confirm their daughter's name, address and date of birth. She then took an envelope from the desk drawer and handed it to Patricia's father. It was marked 'Donation'.

"We prefer if you don't contact your daughter until after the baby is adopted."

Patricia stifled a sob, "No ... no! It's not what I want!" she exclaimed in a voice that didn't sound like hers.

"It's for the best, Patricia. You'll see," her mother replied, her voice quivering. She stepped towards Patricia and gave her a reluctant hug as if some demonstration of affection was an expectation. "It'll be over soon enough."

"We'll be off then," she heard her father say. She watched as he turned awkwardly, shepherding her mother towards the door.

There was such a deep hush about the place that Patricia wondered if she was on her own. The nun gripped her elbow. "Come with me." She led Patrica to the main stairs. "The laundry's in the basement. Sheets are to be changed twice a week and soiled bedding changed immediately. You will of course be responsible for the cleanliness of your undergarments and night clothes."

Patricia heard the whispered gossiping as the nun pushed open the dormitory door. There were four girls; one looked about her age, not yet sixteen, the others a couple of years older. They were huddled around the window overlooking the drive. Patricia realised they'd been watching her arrival. They turned — vexed, alarmed, frightened, Patricia couldn't tell — and then hurried over to their individual beds.

"What have I told you about staring out of the window," the nun said, sharply. "If this happens again, I will see you are all on extra duties. This is a Sunday — the day for you to pray and reflect on your sins." The nun moved Patricia forwards, a gentle nudge as if she was an object to be displayed,

"This is Patricia. She's to have the bed next to yours, Claire."

The nun turned to Patricia. "Unpack your things, there's a locker next to your bed and a bible in the drawer." With a swish of her habit, she was gone. Patricia exhaled the sickly breath she had been holding in her lungs and slowly surveyed the others. Claire's bump had just started to show. Two were more obvious. One looked very close ...

"That's Monica," said Claire, following Patricia's stare. "How long, now?"

"Couple of weeks, I think," Monica replied in a dull tone.

"What about you?" Claire asked. "When are you due?"

"It's three months since …"

"You were shagged," one of the other girls said, laughing. Patrica gasped. It was an experience stitched in her memory, coarse and ugly.

"ENOUGH!" exclaimed Claire. "None of that."

"Didn't mean any harm," the girl replied. "Sorry," she said, quietly.

"Always says the wrong thing, does Noreen, ain't that right?"

The girl laughed. "Known for it." She produced a pack of cigarettes. "Fancy a fag? Don't worry about the nuns, this is their quiet time."

Patricia nodded. She wasn't a smoker, but it seemed the right thing to do.

"This is the one afternoon they give us a bit of peace," Claire told her.

"Yeah, thank God for Sundays!" Monica quipped. They gathered round a half-open sash window and shared a cigarette, wafting at the tell-tale fumes.

Janine was the other girl. Little about her suggested she was pregnant. She was very pale, her arms were skeletal thin, and her hair was close-cropped and spiky. She was wearing a smock dress, hung like a tent, enveloping her breasts and belly. She stood apart from the others, but reached eagerly for the cigarette when it was her turn.

"Janine's had it rough," Noreen said, speaking as if Janine wasn't there. "Tried to 'ave an abortion, didn't you Janine?" The girl nodded.

"Some backstreet slag," one of the others remarked. "All she managed to do was make her bleed. They brought her in here last week." Janine's hand shook as she passed the cigarette onto the next girl.

Patricia took a deep drag and gulped the smoke into her lungs. The nicotine hit was immediate. She coughed violently, holding the cigarette in her outstretched hand. The others laughed; cackling, high-pitched laughter that had them all giggling. Patricia felt as if she was back in the gang at school, hitching their skirts high, calling out to boys they fancied.

She slept soundly that night. She stirred and stretched as a gap in the curtains ushered in the morning light and then retreated into the warmth of her bed. A deep-sounding bell boomed, like a warning — a foreboding of what the day might bring.

"Patricia, get up ... get up. Breakfast ..."

Patricia felt herself wretch at the thought. "I don't want food," she said.

"Tea and dry toast then. You've got to eat something."

Claire nudged Janine in the bed opposite. Patricia stared as the girl struggled to lift her head. Her reddened eyes were large and pained.

"I'll tell the nun," Claire said, as if reading Patricia's thoughts.

The day followed a routine; breakfast, washing up, mopping the floors, then morning prayers with the priest. Patricia took an instant dislike to him. His eyes roamed from one to the other, fixing on their breasts, and then tutting as he watched them walk back to their seats after taking the sacrament.

That night, Janine died.

Patricia would never forget the sight of the blood-soaked bed. One of the senior nuns told them to get out, in a matter-of-fact tone that suggested she'd seen it all before. One of the younger nuns rushed past carrying a bundle of clean sheets, her normally serene look blotched by the tears running down her face. It was a strange feeling, something Patricia had never experienced, not even when she'd seen her grandmother collapse, twisting the hearth rug in her gnarled fingers. She felt an acute sense of guilt that someone, just a short distance away, had died in agony without any of them realising. Her stream of tears had blurred the scene, her brain numbed by the shrieks of the others. There was suddenly silence, as if their collective anguish was too much to bear.

That night, they pinched flowers from the vases in the church and laid them on the mattress that was still damp and reeked of bleach. One of the nuns replaced the flowers when they started to wilt.

The following morning, immediately after the bell had sounded, they were ushered into the room that served as a chapel. As she raised her head from her prayer, Patricia saw, with a sense of relief, that it was a different priest — younger, taller, with a shock of dark hair.

He introduced himself, "I'm Father Carey," he said. "I want to pray with you in our grief at the tragic loss of Janine. I never met her," he confessed. "I wish I had. Her short life ended in such pain and misery. She was mistreated and abused." He took a deep breath, "It saddens me there was no-one she could turn to — not even the church. I hope, indeed I am sure, she found comfort in the friendship you provided in the last days of her life, and for that you deserve our thanks." He stepped forward and clasped his hands, "I'd now like you to offer your own prayer in the silence her passing deserves."

Patricia, like the others in that small room, sobbed loudly, as if given freedom to express their grief.

It would be several years before Patricia encountered Father Carey again.

Patricia's baby — a boy, 7lbs 1oz — was born in the afternoon of the 13th of October. She loved the warmth of his skin, the doll-like fingers that gripped hers, the tiny mouth that suckled so readily, and the sweet, milky smell that she inhaled, like a narcotic. He had a fluff of dark hair which she smoothed over his soft scalp, wetting her fingers to make it shine. Hesitant at first, she soon learnt to hold him firmly over a plastic bowl and rinse his body with warm water. She'd pat him dry and then dust his pink skin with talcum powder. She reveled in the attachment she felt, as if her umbilical cord had never been severed.

It took a few moments before she realised something was wrong. She was suddenly wide awake, wild eyed, frantically looking round the room. A sickening feeling gripped and grew in the pit of her stomach. The basket next to her bed had gone. She knew this was going to happen, but she hadn't expected it'd be this soon. It was just five days since she'd given birth.

She felt a desperate, uncontrollable urge to find her baby son. She moved too quickly, the room swimming round as she attempted to get out of her bed, and then the vague sense of being helped back into her bed by two of the nuns.

"Try not to upset yourself," one of them told her. "It's all for the best."

For the best? For the best, Patricia repeated in her head. There was nothing about any of this she could see as being for the best — not for her, not for her baby boy. Maybe for my parents, she thought. Maybe for the people who'd adopted her baby. Who were they — these baby thieves?

Patricia watched from the bedroom window as often as she could, peering, furtively, an ear cocked for any sound of the nuns. Later that afternoon, she heard a car on the gravel drive. She sneaked to the window and watched it pull up close to the entrance. The woman, in particular, looked far too old to have her baby. She had a thought they might just be visiting. About fifteen minutes later Patricia heard the crunch of gravel. She leaned on the edge of the window and watched. The woman was carrying a bundle, a baby, holding it close. It began to cry as one of the nuns opened the passenger door and helped her into the front seat. The man followed. He suddenly looked up as if aware he was being watched. Patricia caught his gaze and instinctively lifted her hand as if to wave.

He knows, was Patricia's immediate reaction. He knows I'm the mother.

He looked up again as he opened his car door, a look that Patricia took to be one of guilt. She felt herself shudder and then ran out of the room and screamed. She ignored the nun holding a finger across her lips and grabbed one of the half-full buckets lined up in the washroom.

Patricia didn't know how long she'd been on her knees scrubbing the tiled floor in the entrance hall. She hardly noticed the nuns stepping past her as if she was now a person of no importance. One of the other girls persuaded her to stop. She placed a hand on her shoulder,

"Patricia ... leave it. You must be shattered."

She left the scrubbing brush and bucket of dirty water in the middle of the hall floor and let herself be led up the stairs and into their dormitory. There was a plate of cheese sandwiches and a glass of milk next to her bed. Patricia ate, devouring the bland food as if it was her last meal.

Late the following evening, she was called to the mother-superior's office.

"Your parents will collect you tomorrow, Patricia. Please strip your bed and empty your locker before you leave." She lowered her head and returned to the ledger on her desk.

"That will be all," she said.

Chapter 2

Her mother became increasingly exasperated at having to tell Patricia there was no way she'd ever know who'd adopted her baby boy.

"Look, Patricia, just accept it. The baby's gone to a good home. He'll be well looked after. The nuns make sure ..."

"How can they possibly know!? All they want is rid of it!"

Not for the first time, Patricia stormed out of the house and ran across the road to her best friend. June Tiplady had given birth three months earlier. The father had scarpered as soon as he found out she was pregnant. June's family had insisted she keep the baby. She'd had it at home with her own mother there in support. Mrs Tiplady was well experienced. They were a family of three girls and four boys.

Mrs Tiplady reached out and placed a hand on Patricia's shoulder, "I'm sorry, pet," she said, "It shouldn't have happened. It was horrible what they did." There was a warmth in her voice, a warmth Patricia hadn't experienced for some time. It was a noisy, cramped house, more so with nappies and baby clothes draped over the fireguard. Patricia looked, enviously, at the family photographs crowded on the mantlepiece, and the pile of magazines in the corner next to an old sewing machine. A doll-like dress was pinned, waiting to be sewn. There was often a loaf of bread on the dining table, slices disappearing into the toaster as if picked off by sleight of hand. A teapot was filled and refilled on a regular basis and home-made soup simmered on the stove. June appeared, a baby's dummy in her mouth, carrying a near-empty feeding bottle, the baby perched, nonchalantly, on her hip. She lifted her into the air and rubbed noses with her giggling infant. It began to hiccup and cough. June's mother laughed, scooped up her granddaughter and lifted her against a muslin cloth that seemed to be a fixture across her shoulder. With just a few taps of her fingers, the baby burped, a dribble of regurgitated milk slipping down its chin. Mrs Tiplady wiped the baby's mouth and handed her to Patricia. "Here, Pet" — it was her name for almost everyone — "you hold her." Before she realised, Patricia was nursing the baby. She'd been given the name Amy, after June's mother. She rocked Amy in the crook of her arm, smiling at the cooing infant.

"She's wonderful," she said. "Just wonderful." Amy began yawning and rubbing her eyes. Mrs Tiplady laughed and reached over, gently holding the palm of her hand against the baby's forehead. Within seconds, its breathing had slowed and its arms had gone limp. "She's asleep," Patricia said in a hushed tone. "That's amazing."

Mrs Tiplady lifted the baby from Patricia, cinched the shawl that had loosened, and popped her into the cot in front of the window.

"It's lovely to have a baby in the house, again," she said. "Brings the place to life."

Patricia smiled. "Certainly does," she remarked, not that she'd ever thought of Mrs Tiplady's house as needing anything to enliven the place.

Patricia was determined to get out of her parents' house as soon as she could. The atmosphere was tense, noises seemed amplified in the long periods of eerie silence. They talked at her, perfunctory sentences that were specific, sharp and cutting, often prefaced by a hesitant cough, like a warning. Her father had taken to stamping his boots on the front step and shouting to her mother that he was 'home'. He invariably plonked his fat arse into his armchair and hid behind his paper.

It all happened in a weekend. She'd gone with June to a dance. It was a popular venue, and that evening was no exception. They joined the queue to pay and get their wrists stamped so they could come and go. It was packed. There was a bar along one wall, a crush of people shouting orders and waving their arms in attempts to catch the attention of the besieged bar staff. A good-looking man held out two bottles of pale-ale, "You'll have no chance getting served ... on me," he said. "I got these in early, just in case." Patricia didn't care much for his name, not at first. It was her Uncle Vince that had bothered her with his long slippery arms and searching hands. But Vince Harrison made her laugh. He was from Liverpool and had a fund of stories and a good smattering of one-liners.

"A crowd pleaser, that one," June told her friend. They were in the women's loos, sharing the mottled mirror. "You be careful." Patricia had her father's wide mouth and strong nose that had a turn at the tip like the end of a ski-jump. She was blessed with her mother's thick, voluminous, dark hair. She'd had it styled; a cut just above her shoulders and a low, curtain fringe. She had a slim, strong, build, and her pregnancy had rounded her figure, giving her curves something like June's. She'd always envied her friend's well-filled figure, which always attracted attention and seemed to complement almost every item she wore.

June winked in the mirror at her friend. They'd spent time in the kitchen applying their make-up. She pouted her lips, "Don't we look good!"

It turned out Vince was 'between jobs'. He'd last worked in the summer on an amusement arcade in Bridlington.

"Not much call for that kind of work round here," he remarked, a broad grin emphasising the dimples in his cheeks. It was his eyes that captivated Patricia, as much as his dark, swarthy looks and quiff of jet-black hair. They were bright blue and seemed to sparkle the more he got into one of his stories.

"Got a job lined up on a building site," he explained. "Guaranteed," he added, as if needing to reassure them of his financial status. Patricia wouldn't have cared if he was a pauper. She was besotted. And what she wanted more than anything else was to get out from under her parents. Living with them was a constant and painful reminder of what they'd made her do.

They offered no resistance when she announced she was leaving home to marry Vince. They went to the registry office, her father signing the consent form with a slow scratch of the ink pen, and then quickly ushered Patricia's mother out of the office building with just a glance at the newlyweds. He'd given them fifty pounds in an envelope the previous night. Patricia told Vince they should give it back.

"Don't be so bloody daft," Vince told her. "We need it for the rent."

Things went well, at first. They got a council flat in a tower block on the Marshbrook estate and Patricia found an office job with a firm of solicitors, on the understanding she went to night-classes for shorthand and typing. It took a bit longer, but Vince eventually got a job as a labourer on a building site. Patricia was pleased at having a new name, Patricia Harrison. And then she realised it would give an even greater sense of having made the break from her parents if she used her middle name. From then on, she was Maggie Harrison; and she took June's advice. "You've lovely hair. It's so thick and glossy. Let it grow — and easy on the hair spray."

"If I must," she told her friend with a grin.

It was soon clear Vince liked to drink. The money he earned on the building site was never enough. "Just 'till I get paid," he told her, when he hadn't the cash to see him through one of his long sessions at the pub. Maggie had gone with him when they'd first moved into their flat, just a short walk from 'The Crown'. It was a new experience; nothing like the laughter-filled nights out with June, drinking rum and coke and nattering about lads, pop music, clothes, and especially June's little Amy. Too many rum-and-cokes with Vince and the talk became slow and melancholic. Vince downed pints and bought rounds for his mates, eventually sliding along the bar, leaving Maggie standing alone wishing she were somewhere else. He got nasty when he was drunk. The worst was when she didn't have any money to spare. He sometimes grabbed her handbag, holding up any money he found,

"What's this, you lying bitch!?"

She gave up trying to explain it was for food or the rent. He began to shove her around, smacking her on the back of the head with the palm of his hand until she produced a few coins from the money she had hidden around the house. That particular night, she'd just paid the rent, managed to buy some food from the local grocer and put aside what she needed for her bus fares. Vince was enraged when she eventually produced her small stash of coins.

"I need that!" she shouted. "That's to get to my work!"

Maggie tried to wrestle the money from his fist. He spun round, pushed her against the wall and smacked her across the mouth. Blood gushed from her nose, and she bled heavily from a gashed lip. Vince threw the money on the floor and stormed out, slamming the door in a violent crack. Maggie bent her head over the sink, splashed her face with cold water and tried to staunch the blood with a kitchen towel. She grabbed her bag and rushed down the stairs and into the street, ignoring the stares. And then she ran.

It took ten minutes or so to reach the Tiplady home. She pushed open the door, panting for breath, the tea-towel red with blood. There was a collective gasp from June and her mother. June hugged her friend, ignoring the blood. Mrs Tiplady appeared with a bowl of water smelling strongly of antiseptic. She dabbed at Maggie's lip as she tutted and shook her head, "Bad, that is. Might need a stitch."

June's father carefully folded his paper and lifted himself out of his lounge chair. He was a coal miner, a proud, big man. And a gentle giant.

"Who did this? That fella of yours?"

Maggie nodded.

"Drinks at The Crown, does he?"

Maggie nodded again. He reached for his jacket draped on the back of the dining chair. "I won't be long," he said. "Me and Tony'll go for a quick one."

Mrs Tiplady called after him, "You be careful."

The front door closed with a quiet click of the latch.

Later that evening Mr Tiplady returned, all smiles. The acidic smells of vinegar-soaked chips and wraps of battered fish filled the front room as he laid a bulging string bag on the table.

"Well done, you remembered!" June's mother quipped." She smiled and turned to her daughter, "June, love, get the plates ... and a loaf from the pantry." Plates and cutlery were spread round, together with brown sauce, salt and pepper, a tub of margarine and a half-finished bottle of malt vinegar. Maggie ate carefully, especially after the first sting of acetic acid on her cut lip.

She was still picking at her battered fish when June's dad reached in his pocket and produced a bunch of familiar-looking keys. "He won't be back," he announced, placing the keys in front of Maggie. "I took him round to yours and helped him clear his stuff."

Maggie stared in disbelief. "Thanks," she replied.

"It's for the best," Mrs Tiplady said.

Maggie felt her face relax into a smile. "For the best," she repeated.

"Don't know what you saw in him," June remarked. "Apart from his good looks!"

"I got what I wanted," Maggie replied.

"Oh, yeah?" June retorted.

"A new name, that's what — Maggie Harrison."

Chapter 3

Michael Barrett eased the car into their drive, tensing momentarily as the car jolted over a drain cover.

"Steady, Michael," Barbara whispered. Michael let the car come to a stop and carefully applied the brake. He hesitated before turning off the engine and glanced across at Barbara; she looked exhausted. Her pale eyes were marbled and dull, and the sclera were discoloured and scored by thin, red veins. He was reluctant to turn off the engine. Having Dennis fast asleep in his car seat was a welcome break he hated to disturb. A nurse at the surgery had said they shouldn't worry. All babies cry, he'd soon settle down.

Soon! He was now over two-years old. Barbara had resorted to taking Dennis to her bed, their bed, in order to get the toddler to sleep. He kept telling her it was a mistake, that he'd never go down on his own if she persisted in giving in to his agitated cries.

"What do you want me to do, Michael, leave him to scream his head off!?"

Michael wanted to say yes, that's exactly what they should do. Dennis was ruling their lives, and Lisa, their six-year-old, had begun to shout and run off to her room whenever Dennis threw one of his tantrums.

It was clear to Michael; the adoption had been a disaster. He and Barbara never talked about it, at least not in those terms. They had a child to rear, she sometimes said, as if it was a challenge, a test. Michael prayed that there'd be an improvement in Dennis' behaviour, but every day brought more of the same. "This can't go on," he told Barbara on more than one occasion. "It's got to get better, surely?"

"It will, Michael," was her reply, a reply given with ever weaker conviction.

Dennis started to cry as soon as Michael switched off the engine. It was a soft, sleepy cry which quickly grew in intensity. Barbara heaved herself out of the passenger seat and began unclipping the now wriggling child from his car seat.

Michael gripped the steering wheel and breathed slowly, willing himself to remain calm. It would be another of those nights, his space occupied by an intruder growing ever larger, even more demanding, like some cuckoo invading their nest.

Just short of his third birthday, things seemed to have got a bit easier. Dennis slept in his own bed for most of the night, and he was well beyond that period when he'd tear off his nappy and smear the contents over the adjacent wall. What began to concern them both was the way he turned his head away, avoiding eye contact. Barbara would try and steer his chin towards hers, but he stubbornly resisted, suddenly flinging his face in the opposite direction. He'd taken to running round the living room as if taunting them to catch him, before throwing himself onto the cushions Barbara had taken to placing strategically over the edge of the hearth. Michael would often lay out his toy cars on the carpet, it was the one thing that kept him occupied, at least for a while. It invariably ended when he accidentally disturbed the order he'd created. He was at his worst when Lisa was in the room. He'd wait until she'd arranged her favourite toys — the two dolls that dangled from her arms when she padded down the hall, a tea-set she got for Christmas, and an old teddy bear that had been Barbara's — and then rush over and kick at them. At other times he'd sneak up and push Lisa in the back, sending the sturdy seven-year-old tumbling across the room. She'd stand and glare at him and then swipe at the toy cars Dennis had arranged that morning, laughing at Dennis' screams. Michael was secretly proud, very proud of his daughter. Good for you, he thought whenever she got her own back, often using an old stuffed toy like a club, beating Dennis over the head, sending him scurrying into his room, or finding sanctuary behind Barbara's chair.

Within a few weeks of starting primary school, Dennis' behaviour was different. He became quieter, sometimes sullen, often skulking to his room to re-organise his beloved cars. Michael and Barbara were cautious, wondering why Dennis had changed.

Getting him to go to school was often difficult. That's when he was at his worst, displaying his full range of disturbing behaviour, running off giggling and laughing at their attempts to get him to stand still. His teacher was their saviour. He loved to paint and draw, often producing work that looked as if it had been done by someone several years older.

"He's got a gift," the teacher, Miss Geraldine, told them. Dennis was at his most cooperative when it was an 'art day'. She gave him every encouragement, even when he scribbled over a drawing of his he didn't like. And he began to respond in kind, determined it seemed to elicit a now familiar response; "That's wonderful, Dennis."

Michael studied Dennis; his eyes were glued on the tv, watching the changing of the guard at Buckingham Palace.

"Like soldiers, do you?"

Dennis nodded. He was lying prone, his elbows on the rug, his head cupped in the palms of his hands. He stood and began marching round the room, swinging his arms in rhythm to those of the guards.

Michael joined in, showing him how to salute, stand to attention and follow the command to 'stand at ease'.

Dennis never seemed to tire of marching with his father. Michael bought him a toy gun which Dennis quickly learned to sling over his shoulder and stand as tall as he could, head erect. They'd march, side by side, Michael the sergeant major, barking instructions and telling his recruit to salute the apple tree at the end of the garden, as if it were a statue of a monarch.

It was a drill that Dennis loved, often pleading with his father — "Again, Daddy. Let's do it again."

It was on his eleventh birthday. His mother called him down from his bedroom. Dennis sensed something was wrong. They were sitting stiffly, stern faced. He thought, in the moment, that it might have something to do with his not thanking his cousin, Ricky, for the jigsaw he'd been given. He hated jigsaws.

"Sit down, Dennis," his mother instructed, ignoring the remnants of birthday cake that sat crumbling and curled on a plate in the middle of the table. "We've something important to tell you. It's something we should have told you before now."

Dennis felt a pang of fright. His brain was suddenly on overload.

One of them was dying? Or was he in serious trouble for something — what? Maybe they were all going to live in Australia? He'd love that, it was something he'd dreamt of.

"After Lisa was born," his mother suddenly said, "I found out I couldn't have any more children."

After Lisa, his sister ...?

"We wanted another child," he heard his father say, a voice that sounded as if it came from the next room.

"That's why we decided to adopt," Barbara said, softly.

"You're not my parents?" asked Dennis, his voice quivering.

"Of course we are," she replied. "You are our son and we love you."

"But ... you're not my real parents?"

'We're your legal parents, Dennis," Michael said, in more brusque tones. "We adopted you because, as your mum said, we wanted another child ... and because your birth mother wanted you to be adopted."

"Why? Why did she want me adopted?"

"She was very young, and there was no father to help. She wouldn't have been able to look after you." Barbara was nodding as if to reaffirm what Michael was saying.

"She didn't want me?"

"She didn't have any other option, Dennis. The only thing she could do was have you put up for adoption. And we were lucky enough to find you."

Dennis sat, head bent towards the table, "Will I ever know ...?"

"What, who gave you birth? No, Dennis. They don't tell us."

"And it has to be that way," Michael added.

Dennis sat, staring, blankly, out of the window.

He didn't belong, he wasn't really one of the family, was he? He'd often thought of himself as being different — not big, strong and confident, like his dad. And now he knew why.

And yet he loved them, his mother and father.

His mother was trying to smile. There were tears of betrayal rolling down her cheeks. "God gave us the chance to have you in our lives," she said. It struck him as odd, very odd, that she'd referred to God. They went to Mass very occasionally; Christmas, Easter and sometimes in the holidays.

Maybe it's God's fault? he wondered. God shouldn't let a mess like this happen.

They looked relieved when he announced he wanted to go and read the Captain Marvel comic book he'd been given as a birthday present from his sister, Lisa.

Not that she really was his sister, he suddenly realised. He began to flick through the pages of his comic, his mind filled with thoughts about who is real father might be. Just at that moment it seemed to be more important than knowing who his mother was. He wondered if one day they might come looking for him. He imagined a man and woman, arm in arm, walking towards him, all smiles. They were faceless, their features just blurred images. They could have been anyone.

Dennis was always wary of his uncle, and his cousin, Ricky. A visit from them invariably descended into wrestling in front of the hearth, his uncle pulling him into a tangle of flailing arms and heavy bodies. Dennis especially hated being at the bottom of the pile. Sometimes he pretended to faint or would deliberately bang his head on the corner of the hearth in an attempt to get them to stop. They showed little mercy. His father didn't join in. He sat reading the paper, occasionally flicking it to one side and telling them to be careful or telling them "That's enough." His uncle took little notice. He shouted encouragement to Ricky, praising him for slamming Dennis to the ground or getting him into a suffocating headlock. Worst were the punches aimed with the intention of giving a dead-leg, or a thump to his shoulder. The blows were fierce, often making him limp for several hours. Blood seemed to be the aim. It usually didn't stop until someone got hurt, or blood was drawn from a banged nose or a split lip.

His mother would sometimes appear. She was thin and frail looking, but her voice was sharp and loud. "Stop — right now!" And she'd often reprimand Michael for letting it 'get out of hand'.

There was that time when his uncle had called a halt, shouting 'time' like a boxing referee. Dennis waited until grips loosened and limbs were untangled. He suddenly flung his head back knowing that his cousin was kneeling behind him. The crack of skulls hurt, really hurt. But he had the advantage of surprise. His cousin had cried and bawled like a baby. His uncle got cross, not at him, but at his crying son. "It was an accident, Ricky. Stop blubbing ..."

Michael pulled him to one side after they'd gone. "I saw you do that, Dennis. It was nasty. You could have broken his nose. Your uncle wasn't pleased."

Dennis shrugged his shoulders. "So what," he muttered. Michael appeared not to have heard him. After that incident, his uncle usually came on his own. There'd always be an excuse; "Ricky's sorry he can't come. He's got a football game; out with his pals; gone shopping with his mum ..."

He was nearly twelve when a friend of his sister's began to stay over. They were in the same class and preparing for their GCSE exams the following summer. Lisa was already sixteen, her friend, Jackie was a few months younger. Lisa's bedroom was next door and he could hear them laughing and giggling through the partition wall. Late at night, when the house was quiet, he could hear them talking about boyfriends, teachers, films, clothes ... and sex. He blushed scarlet whenever Jackie spoke directly to him. She seemed to take delight in his obvious embarrassment. Maybe she found it exciting to have a young admirer, even one as young as Dennis, or maybe it was the age difference that meant she could tantalise and tease without any consequences. Or perhaps she just liked to encourage admirers, no matter how young they were. There was the morning she called him into the bathroom to fix his hair, give it a quiff. She took to giving him a peck on the cheek, a goodnight kiss. She asked him to do the zipper on her dress when the rest were downstairs; she even rubbed her hand against his crotch and feigned surprise at his erection. One night on the landing, she kissed him and told him to open his mouth. Her tongue flicked across his and her hand rubbed at the damp spot on the front of his pyjamas.

She stood and laughed as Lisa's heavy footsteps sounded on the stairs.

"Dennis was telling me what he'd like for his birthday," she said.

Lisa looked disapprovingly at her friend. "For Christ's sake, Jackie."

"Jackie giggled, "He's big enough."

"I'm nearly a teenager," Dennis replied, indignantly.

Lisa smirked, "Piss off, Dennis and get to bed."

Chapter 4

In senior school, Dennis began to realise his dad was different, something the smart uniform he wore made abundantly clear. He didn't work in a factory, or a bank, he wasn't an insurance salesman or garage mechanic. He didn't run a shop or work for the council. Michael Barrett was a prison officer, a prison officer in a nearby Young Offenders' Institute in South Yorkshire. Somehow, it seemed worse than having a father in the police. Police officers visited schools, they helped find a lost bicycle, or reprimand teenagers for being too loud. They made people feel safe.

No-one else had a father who worked in the prison service. Some began to tease, saying it wasn't a proper job. It became a source of embarrassment. Dennis took to avoiding his father, finding excuses for not going to the park, enviously watching others playing football with dads who drove vans, or painted houses. He could lie about his mother; tell them she worked in a factory in Doncaster, far enough away that it was unlikely they'd ever find out; close enough to be a possibility. There were times he wanted to tell them he was adopted and invent some story about who his real dad was. But that would mean telling them he was illegitimate, that he was a bastard.

His family lived in a semi-detached house only a short distance away from Marshbrook, a sprawling estate of council houses which was home for the majority of those at his school. Marshbrook was separated from their avenue by a main road and a series of unkempt football pitches which descended into scrub and rough pasture on the fringes of the estate; a no-go area, land-mined with rusting oil drums, burnt-out cars, and emaciated ponies tethered to steel spikes,

There was no escape, not at his school — a huge comprehensive with weeping concrete walls, broken gutters and a maze of narrow corridors. Opened in 1975, the building clearly hadn't lived up to the claim by the then minister for education that it had been designed to equip a generation.

Most of the other fourteen-year-olds were bigger, with deeper voices and the rebellious swagger of fully-fledged teenagers. Worst, he wasn't one of them. He hadn't grown up with a violent father, or a mother who numbed her existence with alcohol. He hadn't had to scrap and thieve, he'd never known what it was like to go hungry. His home wasn't fronted by a rutted lawn, there weren't neighbours with savage dogs barking and howling, there weren't streets with boarded up houses and graffiti-splashed corrugated sheets covering the windows.

It didn't help he was still puny, his narrow shoulders failing to fill the school blazer his dad had said he would soon grow in to. He was elbowed in the corridors, threatened with cigarette stubs that singed the sleeves of his jacket, others crushed the breath out of his thin frame on the jam-packed school bus.

And always the mean-faced ones, singling him out,

"Your dad's a bloody screw. What is he?" Then one of them would grab him by the lapels and shake him, violently, until he stammered a reply,

They'd run off, laughing.

Dennis was shoved as he waited for the bus, trying to blend in, his head bent against a brisk October wind. He found himself being nudged and pushed to the back of the queue. He was suddenly surrounded by five of the school lads he feared most, as if it was an orchestrated plan. They were a couple of years older, school just a holding pen until they could leave. One of them punched him in the stomach. He collapsed, gasping for breath, their snorting laughter ringing in his ears.

"Want anymore?"

He was on his knees, sucking air into his lungs. A boot thudded into his side sending him sprawling. "I'm talking to you, you prick. Well?" Dennis managed a squeaky reply, "No ..."

"I can't hear you."

"No," Dennis repeated, as loud as his airless lungs would allow.

"That's better. We've got plans for you, see." The others sniggered.

Dennis struggled to his feet, clutching his side. "Plans?" he stammered.

"Fetchin'; deliverin'; collectin'."

Dennis nodded. He knew what they meant; everyone knew what they did.

The leader of the bunch, Big Mitch Fisher, grinned and snatched Dennis by the back of his neck. "We've got a new recruit." He tightened his grip, took a drag from the cigarette dangling from the corner of his mouth, and breathed a smoke ring that lingered, halo like.

He held his cigarette close to Dennis' chin. "Nobody'll bother you anymore ... you'll have respect, ain't that right?"

The others grunted in agreement. He thrust his face into Dennis'; "If you ever snitch on us ... "

Dennis shuddered. "I won't, promise."

Big Mitch Fisher patted Dennis hard on the cheek. "That's good, in' it?"

The others took it in turns to punch him on the arm, like an initiation.

That night, Dennis sat on his bed rubbing his bruises. The blue-brown welts felt satisfyingly painful. He knew, from then on, he'd be left alone; no one would dare touch him, not as long as he was with the Fishers.

It didn't take long for the word to get around. For a couple of days, Dennis stuck to the fringes of the Fisher gang as they wandered round the school, taking what was theirs, and what wasn't. Every surreptitious look, every glance, wasn't at the Fishers, it was at Dennis. He began to copy their swagger, scuffing his shoes on the path as if itching to give someone a kicking. A week or so of gathering money in exchange for a few badly rolled spliffs and he had a reputation. Adding a few kicks to those being delivered by one of the Fishers secured his status. He was now one of them; he was protected, he was untouchable. He singled out those who'd bullied him the worst, staring them down, just because he could. He demanded fags, chewing gum, money — anything that took his fancy. Best of all, he liked the nervous looks and the way they stepped aside as he approached.

The heavy rain had stopped half an hour or so before the lunchtime bell. Dennis was relieved. Fridays were never easy, especially in December when it seemed half of them decided to skip. Doing deals when everyone was sheltering in classrooms, corridors and the numerous tiny spaces that hid them from tired teachers, as well as Fisher's gang, was difficult; and there was always the chance some eagle-eyed teacher would want to know what was going on.

Once he'd eye-balled one of his marks, they stood, waiting, as if paralysed by fear and indecision. White faced, they dug into their pockets hunting for coins. Most paid in full. There were a few who pleaded for more time — there were always consequences. Pleased with what he'd managed to collect, he felt the heft of coins in his jacket pocket, slipping a few into a small leather purse he'd pinched from Lisa's room and sauntered across the playground towards the group of Fishers, coils of cigarette smoke signaling their territory.

"Come e'er, Dennis." He strutted over, his arms dangling, his chest puffed out like a fighting cockerel. He nodded an acknowledgement to the five toughs.

"Got yourself a bit of a reputation," said Big Mitch, fingering Dennis' tie.

"Yeah, suppose so."

Big Mitch suddenly grabbed the lapels of his jacket.

"You'll never be one of us, you little runt. We're Fishers, see." The others were grinning. "Don't want you to get above yourself, do we lads?"

"I won't, I won't," Dennis pleaded.

"Think what'd happen if we said you weren't with us."

Dennis shivered. "I'll do what you want ... anything!"

"Course you will." He pushed his face into Dennis', "You've been dipping in already, 'aven't you?"

"No ... honest, just the couple of quid you said I could have."

Big Mitch grinned. "That new teacher is watching out. Don't think he knows about you. Means you 'ave to do more — got it?" He took out a flick knife, the blade springing open with a loud click. The tip grazed Dennis' neck. "Careful you don't get hurt."

Dennis felt his legs tremble. Just for a moment he thought he was going to be cut, even stabbed. His stomach knotted, threatening to spill its contents over the hand holding the knife.

"See these ..." Big Mitch took out a handful of silver foiled wraps. "You sell 'em. Two quid each. Don't get caught. Don't want you ending up in your dad's place!" They all laughed.

Dennis took the wraps and thrust them into his jacket pocket. He felt relieved they hadn't ditched him. He stood and watched them sidle off, sharing smokes. He felt envious — of the club, the gang, the name, their reputation. He wanted their approval. It wasn't just the protection, there was a sense of pride that they'd singled him out. They wanted him, for now. And for now, it was enough.

The Fisher gang was waiting for him at the school gate. It was another Friday, a few weeks after Big Mitch had issued his new demands. Dennis thrust his hand into his trouser pocket, feeling for the plastic bag he used for the money he'd collected. They looked angry. He stopped in his tracks, grit on his shoes, wondering if he dared run. He hadn't managed to push as many of the wraps they'd given him. Big Mitch shoved him into the railings.

"Give ..."

Dennis handed over the bag of coins. It had felt heavy, stuffed into his trouser pocket.

"That it?"

Another lad, small, thickset, was with the gang. He had the new-looking blazer of a first year. He thrust himself in front of Dennis and raised a threatening fist.

"This is my cousin, Billy," said Mitch. "He's going to help you, aren't you Billy?"

The lad grinned and grabbed Dennis by the hair. He could smell the nicotine on Billy's breath. "Yeah, course."

Dennis felt clammy, his body gave an involuntary shudder. Billy Fisher spat in his face: a thick gob of spittle slipped down his nose.

Big Mitch pushed his cousin to one side; "Leave it, Billy. He's one of us — sort of."

Chapter 5

He'd never anticipated the Fisher clan wouldn't be there, occupying their corner of the school grounds. Big Mitch and his mates had left at the end of the year. They would have assumed jobs would be there, just waiting for them. The closure of many of the coal mines had haemorrhaged the lifeblood from the mining villages in South Yorkshire. Jobs were hard to find and the Fishers were opportunists. They fed drugs like sweets, they dangled money in front of desperate mothers trying to feed their kids, they set up gambling dens, sold cheap cider and pimped women who couldn't pay. Big Mitch Fisher slipped easily into his new life. It was work a careers advisor might have said suited his profile.

Dennis was relieved when he heard Billy Fisher had been expelled. He'd attacked a young music teacher, crushing his fingers after seeing his girlfriend and two of her pals leaning against the upright piano as the teacher played Beatles' songs. Being on his own, even if it was his last year, made Dennis very uncomfortable. For a while, it was ok; his reputation and association with the Fishers gave him a sort of false protection. But it didn't take long before other hard nuts became top dogs.

He began to skip school and then simply stopped going. His dad was furious.

"You'll come to nothing, Dennis. You bloody well will go, even if I have to drag you there myself!"

Even his mother had pleaded with him,

"Please Dennis, it's in your best interest. Just take your GCSE's, that's all. You can leave then, get a job. We only want what's best ..."

Dennis took no notice. They knew nothing of the daily hell he faced. Most days, he wandered around town buying a few spliffs with money he'd cadged or stolen from his mother, often finding himself in the indoor market where he could wander from stall to stall, soon realising that no-one there would bother him or ask why he wasn't in school.

There was that night he slinked in very late. He'd been drinking cider in the park and sharing smokes with a couple of lads from the housing estate.

"What time do you call this!?" his dad shouted, flinging his paper across the room. "I've had the school on to me. They think I can't control my own son!"

"And you a screw," shouted Dennis. "That's all you're worried about, your precious reputation!"

He gave a loud belch of stale cider.

Michael Barrett flew across the room and smacked his son hard across the cheek. Blood spurted from Dennis' nostril and dripped off his chin.

Barbara shrieked, "Michael; for God's sake!"

Michael, suddenly as pale as alabaster, reached out with both arms. Dennis shoved his hands away, stormed out of the room and thumped up the stairs. Barbara ran into the hallway and called after him.

"Dennis, Dennis!"

Their cat squawked and fled under the bed when Dennis slammed the bedroom door. A pair of green eyes peered out as Dennis pulled a shirt and a pair of jeans from a drawer. He hurtled down the stairs, swinging his duffle bag like a weapon, pushed past his dad and reached for the front door.

"Please, Dennis, I'm sorry. I didn't mean ..."

Barbara grabbed his sleeve, "Don't go, Dennis. It's late!"

Dennis jerked his arm free. He glared at his mother, flung the door open, and headed off into the dark. Michael ran into the hallway and then turned to Barbara.

"Don't you go defending him," Michael told her. "He deserved ..."

"Deserved what!? He's not one of your borstal boys! And don't you dare say he's not really ours!"

Barbara turned away before he could say anymore. She climbed slowly up the stairs leaving Michael standing in the hallway, his hands clutching the back of his head as if holding it in place, waiting for the glue to set.

Dennis returned late the following night, banging doors as if they were blocking his every move. Michael had left the front door on the latch, at Barbara's insistence.

"He'll be back, I just know he will," she'd said, more in hope than conviction. She'd hardly slept the previous night, listening for any hint of her son. Now, despite the loud noise he was making, she felt relieved.

"He's back," she said to Michael, as if only she had heard the overture of discordant sounds. She listened as kitchen cupboards opened. Plates rattled and cutlery chimed. At least her son was safe. Michael rolled onto his back and stared at the chaotic swirls made by the street light seeping through the fluttering curtains.

That summer, Dennis officially left school. He'd scribbled his name on each of his GCSE papers and left without adding a sentence.

He couldn't hide a look of surprise when his dad told him there might be a job at the indoor market.

"I know the owner. He wants you to go round ..."

Dennis had spent many an afternoon bunking off school and wandering around the market. It had become his sanctuary. He loved the sights and sounds of the market, closeted in its sheet-metal building, and the lingering smells that hung over the stalls. He soon knew every aisle from the fustiness of second-hand clothes, the sickly smell of cheap sweets, the sight of raw meat swinging from the butcher's hooks, the scents wafting from displays of cosmetics and perfumes; they became his markers, his personal map of the premises.

In the far corner of the hall two women sold coffee and tea, always busying themselves, taking it in turns to wipe the red plastic cloth covering a trestle table. When it was quiet, he took to hovering around their stall. Sometimes, one of them would push a mug of tea towards him, heaping in sugar and stirring it vigorously. He developed a routine. A banana from the ruddy-faced man selling fruit, a handful of cashews from the thickset moorish-looking trader and sometimes a slice of balaclava and square of Turkish delight from his wife, a headscarf pulled tight around her head, her dark, deep-set eyes the colour of black olives.

An arrow marked 'Office' pointed up a flight of stairs just inside the entrance to the market. Dennis tapped hesitantly on a door with the name 'Jake Gould' in black letters. The response was immediate,

"It's open."

A round-faced, dark-haired man, tinges of grey ringing his ears like crescent moons, sat at a battered desk. The surface was virtually obliterated by piles of paperwork. Jake Gould stubbed out his cigarette in a stained ashtray and waved his arm at the coil of smoke.

"Shouldn't be doing this," he said, pointing a stained finger at the large 'No Smoking' sign pinned to the wall. "Filthy habit." He swiveled on his wooden office chair, "Michael Barrett's lad, right?"

"Yeah," Dennis replied, his voice pitching into a higher octave.

The man leant forward on his tattooed forearms; "I know you — I've seen you here before."

Dennis nodded. He hoped it wasn't meant as a rebuke of some kind.

Jake Gould grinned. "Better than being at school, eh?"

"I like it here," Dennis replied, pleased his voice had lowered.

"I'll give you a try, lad. I know your dad — good man, your dad."

Dennis took a deep breath. "Suppose so," he said, quickly. There was an oversized perspex window just behind Jake Gould's desk which overlooked the rows of market stalls. A large sheet of paper showing the layout of stalls was pinned on an adjacent wall.

Jake rapped a knuckle on the grimy window. "I want you to keep the place clean; pick up the rubbish, take out cardboard boxes, sweep the aisles, ask if they need any help. Don't lean on your brush, I don't need a slacker." He held out a large hand, "Jake," he said. "Name's Jake ... If you're any good, lad, you can help with the paperwork."

He brushed cigarette ash from his desk and tapped on the partition wall.

"Maggie! ...Maggie! ... " A filing cabinet rattled and heels tapped across the wooden floor. "Got a new recruit," he said as she stepped into Jake's office. "Meet Dennis — Michael Barrett's lad."

Maggie was smartly dressed — pencil skirt, a dark jacket and an immaculately styled bouffant of auburn hair.

"Doesn't look much like him," she commented in a tone that sounded like a reprimand.

"Runs the place, does Maggie."

"If you say so, Jake."

Jake Gould took over the indoor market in 1985. It had been owned and run by the council since the building was erected six years earlier. Within a few months, it was clear the council had little enthusiasm for running the newly erected market building. It became rat infested and was regularly broken into. Hyperdermic needles, charred strips of foil, discarded roll-ups, empty cans of lager and fast-food wrappers littered the floor. There were promises the place would be secured and kept clean. The stench of urine and piles of debris told a different story. Jake had made money renovating rundown Victorian terraced houses he bought for a song using small builders who liked to be paid in cash. He sold them on as soon as he could, often to young first-time buyers, or to older couples fed up with living on increasingly unkempt, feral, council estates.

It was Michael Barrett who'd nudged him to consider approaching the council. They were sharing a few drinks in the local Freemason's lodge reminiscing about the days when the market in the town square was alive with the lure of colours, goods, shouts and the brash banter from the traders.

"They've made a right mess of that indoor market. Pity there's no-one willing to try and make a go of it." Michael balanced his Guinness on a sodden beermat. "How about you, Jake? You're always saying you need something else."

"They'd never sell — not for the right price. I'd be interested, though. It wouldn't take much to improve the place."

"How about a lease, Jake? I reckon they'd be open to an approach," said Michael, giving a quick nod in the direction of the Leader of the Council, his chains of office resting on his ample stomach.

"Goes to bed in those," remarked Jake, grinning.

"He's a proud bugger. I've heard him say the market is a noose round the council's neck. He's sick of the bad publicity it gets —they all are."

The following week, Michael received a call from Jake.

"Michael, guess what? They're going to let me have the market for what I call a very fair price."

"Excellent, Jake. Well done. Just what is a 'very fair price'? Must be good for you to sound so pleased."

Michael could hear him sniggering. "Ten-year lease. No rent, just rates to pay."

"Wow! I told you they'd be keen. They get a functioning indoor market — and you get the building at the right price."

"That's what I told them," Jake replied. "They looked very pleased, as if they'd done the deal of the century!"

"Going to the lodge tonight?" asked Michael.

"Yeah, ok. I owe you a drink or two."

Guinness was their tipple. They both took care, giving the drink the attention it deserved.

"They always pour it well," Jake commented, lifting his glass to his lips. "Cheers."

"Slainte," Michael replied, touching Jake's glass with his own.

They sipped, the thick white head clinging to their lips.

"I'm going to need someone to help run the place — somebody I can trust," Jake said. "Any ideas?"

The Guinness left a white slip on the sides of their glasses as they slowly downed their pints. It was a drink not to be rushed; a drink that gave you time to think.

"I do know there's a young woman at the firm of solicitors off the square who's looking for a job," Michael had remarked. "She's tough, so I hear — Maggie Harrison. She doesn't take any nonsense— and she's itching to leave that job she has. Bored to death, apparently. Wants more responsibility."

"How come you know?"

"They've done some work for me in the past. I sometimes play bridge with one of the partners; he mentioned it. She'd asked him to put the word out."

"Good of him,' Jake remarked. "No catch is there?"

Michael laughed. "That's you all over, Jake, suspicious as hell."

Jake grunted and waved to the barman, holding up his empty glass. 'Two more,' he mouthed.

Two glasses of Guinness were placed carefully on their table; black columns of stout with creamy-white heads, thick as paste,

"Well? ... What about Maggie Harrison?" asked Michael.

"OK. Give me the number. I'll call her ... see if she's interested," Jake replied.

Chapter 6

Jake Gould was quick to revamp the indoor market. The building was gutted of the benches and partition boarding the council had erected. He had damaged sheeting replaced, the roof insulated, new lighting and power-points installed, and added an area enclosed by weld-mesh for the traders to store their items. He was particularly pleased with the fresh coat of pale yellow paint that had brightened the inside and given it the sense he was announcing a fresh start for the market. The outside was also given a make-over, with damaged panels replaced and the main doors fitted with ones that had previously fronted a large department store.

Jake Gould might only admit to himself he'd taken his friend's suggestion to give Maggie the job of running the place. He knew he'd secured a gem. It took very little time for her to stamp her authority making it clear to the traders, and to Jake, what she expected.

June Tiplady was one of the first traders to get a stall in Jake's indoor market. She'd won Morecambe's annual Beauty Queen pageant in 1979 on a cold August Bank Holiday, the bunting flapping and snapping on the brisk sea-breeze sweeping across the promenade. Maggie had gone with her to offer support, wrapping her shivering friend in a sheepskin coat immediately after she'd stepped down from the podium wearing a cheap tiara and clasping a voucher for a year's supply of cosmetics. She'd soon set up a stall on the outdoor market, flogging her free cosmetics.

She'd packed it in shortly after the council had cleared the outdoor stallholders and had taken a job selling make-up in a large retail shop. It was Maggie who persuaded her to give the new indoor market a try.

"You hate working in that store, admit it."

June was charmed by Jake. "I want people like you," he told her. "I'll give you a prime spot. Yours is the type of stall that brings 'em in ... 'specially the young uns." Her new stall was a success. As Jake had hoped, it attracted women of all ages, even schoolgirls spending their pocket money on cheap perfume, kohl eyeliner, and shades of lipstick she knew would sell. June made sure she looked after her older clients, her regulars, with a more subtle range of deodorants, foundation make-up and rejuvenating creams. Her demonstrations and makeovers were just as popular as those she'd given in the large, retail store.

She gave her daughter, Amy, a weekend job when she was just fourteen years old. June knew she'd be a success. Amy was bright and chatty, with a gregarious charm that pulled them in, like a magnet. Her school pals listened attentively as she promoted cheaper products she knew were popular. And it was Amy who suggested they extend their range into lingerie.

"Sexy things," she'd told her mother, without any hint of embarrassment. She was then nearly seventeen and had virtually taken over the running of June's stall. Amy's father came and went with the freedom of a casual lodger. He was, according to Maggie, 'a mixed bag of goods'. A perfect charmer whose eyes and hands wandered whenever and wherever he got the opportunity. His trade was in supplying jewelry to small jewelry shops and the cheaper stuff to a few of the stallholders. It meant he was often on the road doing deals in Birmingham's jewelry quarter and London's Carnaby Street. Amy liked to listen to his stories about the characters he dealt with and the trades he made. But it surprised no one when June finally sent him packing. "This time, it's for good," she told Maggie. He'd been seen on several occasions with a woman running a stall selling cheap bracelets and knock-off watches. Amy had accepted her mother had little choice.

What none of them anticipated was that within a few months he'd take off to Spain with his 'bit of bling', as Maggie called her.

Amy had acquired her dad's eye for a bargain and quickly learned how to strike a deal. She persuaded some of the big stores to let her buy discontinued ranges of toiletries and cosmetics and started advertising in local papers, something that was an anathema to traders in the market. The numbers she brought in were impressive. She ensured she had her best stock for key trading dates — Christmas, Valentine's, Easter, Mother's Day —with the result there were often queues down the aisles. There were features in the local press, even coverage by a local radio station. It also attracted what Maggie referred to as the 'wrong sort' — spivs who thought she'd be an easy target and so-called businessmen who, supposedly, wanted to help expand her business. Amy kept her cool, seeing them off with sharp retorts and a flick of her long hair. It was the boyfriends that caused both June and Maggie the greatest concern. They hung around her stall like moths to the light. Amy went out with quite a few, but there was one in particular Amy seemed keen on — Lee Hogan. He was a few years older than Amy and had been in trouble for stealing cars. Not that he did anything other than take them for a joyride, as far as they knew. June suspected Amy had been his passenger on more than one occasion.

Dennis got on well with the stallholders. He did what Jake had asked, and more. He reveled in his role; helping set up the stalls, sweeping the aisles, clearing empty cardboard boxes, unloading goods from pallet trucks. He seized every opportunity to make himself useful. Some of the women called after him, teasing him with comments about needing his services. There was always a spot of 'good advice' from stallholders, telling him what a lad of his age needed to know. The tea-ladies provided a mid-morning mug of instant coffee, and a sandwich for his lunch, telling him he needed to fill out a bit, before adding a few lewd comments. The dark woman with the headscarf didn't join in the banter; she simply, silently, offered pieces of balaclava with a coy smile that set his heart racing.

He'd seen Amy many times when he'd wandered around, skipping school. Her stall was hard to ignore. Miniature spotlights shone on glass shelves displaying cheap bottles of perfume, lipsticks, deodorants and mascara. There were wrist bangles, headbands and bracelets hooked round a glass curtain rod, thin gold chains, necklaces and scarves dangling from hooks fixed to a wood lathe across the top of the stall, and gossamer-thin bright-coloured lingerie spread over upturned cardboard boxes. Dennis would dare to walk past as often as he could. She was confident and cocky, easily matching banter with the other stall holders. Unlike her mother, she was petite and slim. She had her mother's oval face, large blue eyes and blonde hair which she wore in a ponytail, usually pushed through the back of a blue baseball cap. She usually wore high-waisted washed jeans and a loose sweater over a white shirt. On warmer days, it was a T-shirt and ripped jeans. On those cold mornings when chatter hung on wafts of visible breath, she slipped on an oversized denim jacket which hung shapelessly off her shoulders. Dennis thought it made her look even sexier — vulnerable, somehow.

He felt his face redden whenever she glanced across and smiled. She called out nearly every morning, often commenting on what he was wearing. She'd clearly noticed his new-found sense of fashion.

"Hi, Dennis — nice jeans! Those mine? Look like mine." And then a wave and a big warm smile. He even found a pair of Doc Martens on one of the stalls to match the ones Amy usually wore.

"Like your hair," she said one morning. He'd let it grow so that it curled round his ears and hung over his forehead in a thick dark-brown fringe. "Suits you."

He took every opportunity to help unpack her boxes of goods and collect sheets of tissue paper which she stored in a cloth bag. She often sprayed a whiff of perfume on her wrist,

"A new one, Dennis. What do you think?" she'd say, holding her arm teasingly close, the hairs on her arm sometimes tickling his nose. At night, he imagined being touchingly close, absorbing her heady perfumes through the pores of his skin. Sometimes she was naked, or wearing the brightly-coloured lingerie she displayed on her stall.

Jake spent most of his time at the market. He'd given up renovating houses, it had become a very competitive business with shrinking margins. He still kept a few rentals, houses that were easily let, but his heart wasn't in it anymore. He loved being at the market, ogling over the stalls, sometimes watching intently when it was particularly hectic. It also meant he could keep an eye out for anyone lingering near his private store. It was directly underneath his office and its large metal doors were secured by a heavy combination padlock. The only other person who had access was Maggie.

The commandant, they sometimes called him. "Staring at us from that bloody watchtower of 'is."

"He's alright," another remarked. "Runs a tight ship, that's all."

Dennis was wary at first. The stallholders kept him busy enough, but Jake always had a grumble or two.

"Don't stand there chatting, lad. There's always plenty to do." Dennis took Jake's words to heart. The stallholders loved him; nothing was too much to ask. Jake took to slinging a big arm around his shoulders,

"Doing well, lad. Keep it up." It was said in a hushed tone, out of earshot of the traders.

It was an afternoon in late-September, with the evenings drawing in, when Jake shouted for him to "get in my office!" It'd been raining hard and Dennis had been loading wood crates and cardboard into a skip in the yard. He wondered what he'd done.

"Don't stand there dripping water over my best rug!" Dennis mumbled an apology and shuffled off the threadbare piece of carpet.

"I want you to help in the office, do a bit of paperwork. Maggie will show you." Maggie's desk was in a tiny office boxed off from Jake's by a partition wall. It was well known she took no prisoners. She was all angles; sharp elbows, protruding collarbones and long, bony fingers. Her auburn hair was piled high on her head, not a strand out of place. A can of hairspray always sat on the corner of her desk, next to a bottle of bright-red nail varnish. She often wore a dark-blue trouser suit with padded shoulders and brass-coloured buttons along the edges of the sleeves. She wore plain white shirts, low heel black shoes and tiny pearl earrings. It was a look from which she rarely deviated. It was a commanding, military look, one that she'd cultivated and adopted ever since she'd been employed at the firm of solicitors. It served her well.

Dennis gulped; "Maggie ...?"

"She likes you, don't you Maggie," said Jake, shouting through the door to her office.

"Only if he does as he's told," she shouted back, in her deep, rasping voice.

"Where are you livin', lad? Thought I saw you coming out of that old caravan on the carpark?"

"It's just temporary — 'till I get somewhere better."

"That dump! It shouldn't even be there. It's usually truckers that use it for an overnight."

Dennis shrugged his shoulders, "Ted Bateman said I could."

"That fat bastard. He should stick to selling his meat." Jake leaned back on his swivel chair. It squeaked a protest. "I've got a room you can 'ave. Be better than Bateman's old caravan. Shouldn't be there, anyway. I've a good mind to have it towed away."

"You say that every time someone mentions it," Maggie shouted from her office.

"'Aven't you got work to do!" Jake bawled, making a gesture in the direction of the light bulb hanging from the ceiling. "It's nothing much; a room in a shared tenement I let out. Just round the corner. Got a kitchen, shower, tv room. Twenty-five quid a week."

"Not sure if I can afford it," Dennis replied, desperately trying to work out how much he'd have left.

Jake paused and swung his chair to face the partition wall. "Maggie, you listening?"

"Of course, I am."

"Another ten quid a week for young Dennis."

"If you say so," came the reply.

He turned to Dennis; "Well?"

Dennis smiled; "Thanks, that'd be great."

Jake leant forward, resting his thick, pale forearms on the desk; "Don't let me down, lad. You mess up and it won't just be your job you'll lose."

"I won't ... I won't," he repeated.

"Now, go and talk to Maggie. She'll show you what's needed — checking loads in and out, getting pallets stacked."

"Hope he knows which end of a pencil writes," Maggie shouted in her hoarse, crackling voice.

Jake grinned; "He's an educated lad, ain't you Dennis."

Maggie balanced her lipstick-tipped cigarette on the corner of the glass ashtray. A thin coil of smoke loitered in the still, airless office. She leant back on her chair,

"So, I have to look after you, do I?" Dennis stood in the doorway, wondering if he should answer, not that he could think of a reply. She waved a manicured hand, "Sit down, for Christ's sake." She sighed, "OK, let's get this straight. No nonsense from any of the traders. Don't be a push-over, got it?"

Dennis nodded.

"Right, then." She handed Dennis a clipboard and a sheaf of forms. "One for each trader."

Usually, it was boxes to count and check off. It was his job to keep the pallet carriers busy, moving stuff inside to the various stalls. There were loose items in black bin bags and every Friday, sealed crates of Nokia mobile phones, Game Boys, and MP3 players. Jake was always on hand to supervise when they arrived. The traders cleared their stalls around five, repacking what hadn't been sold and stuffing what they didn't want into bin bags which they flung into a yellow skip in the yard. It was busy; and always the banter whenever things slackened — even an occasional crooked smile from Maggie, her lip curled where her cigarette normally dangled.

Dennis' initial apprehension at working for Maggie was soon lost in the pace of the work. He quickly learned the routine. The traders were happy to cooperate, no doubt grateful that it wasn't just Maggie with her quick, often caustic, remarks. Dennis was helpful in a way that countered and complimented Maggie's style. Jake was clearly pleased. He often winked at Dennis as he left Maggie's office, or gave him a pat on the back.

"Doing a good job, Dennis. That's what Maggie says!"

It gave him a warm feeling that stayed with him for the rest of the day.

And then there was Amy.

Sometimes she'd fix him with a tantalising blink of her eyelashes, heavy with mascara, and hold up a tiny pair of panties and matching bra,

"Which colour?"

Sometimes she'd tease him further,

"I'm wearing these today," she'd whisper with a grin.

And there was the stray cat; a scruffy tabby that had seemingly marked the building as its territory. It appeared at Amy's stall every day, usually in the early mornings. It ate the food they left, ignored the milk in a dish and then curled up in a box Dennis had lined with a blanket. Amy said it was smart. "Warmer than the streets and plenty of vermin to chase — what else does a cat need?" Dennis named it 'Corporal' without explaining why.

Amy had simply shrugged her shoulders. "OK with me ... how about you, Corporal?" The cat had given a particularly deep purr, more like a rattle in its throat. Corporal patrolled the stalls as the traders began to clear up, head low, almost at ground level, ready to pounce.

"Like him, do 'ya?" said Maggie, seeing Amy watch Dennis hurrying to help one of the traders who'd just received a load of goods.

"He's ok," Amy replied.

"Nice to look at," continued Maggie. "He's grown," she added. "Turned out good looking."

Amy's eyes were fixed on Dennis as he jumped down from a flatbed truck. "Suppose," she replied. "Bit young for me."

They giggled, not hearing Jake walk up behind them.

"What are you two looking at?" He glanced at Dennis handing a slatted wood crate to the Turkish man. He and his wife were arranging imported fruits and vibrantly coloured spices on their stall. "Too young for you, Maggie ... and a bit raw for you, Amy."

"What does that mean?" she said, indignantly.

"Nuthin'" he replied, gruffly, as if wishing he hadn't made the remark. He turned and headed to his office. "'Ain't you got better things to do?"

"No!" they shouted, in unison.

Jake shrugged his shoulders and shook his head, laughing. "Women!" he muttered.

Dennis soon began to relax. The routine had a comforting, repetitive rhythm, something he'd never previously experienced. He knew what was wanted, what was expected as soon as he started work. He was supposed to only work half-days on Sundays, but much preferred to be in the market, even if it was just sweeping the floors or cleaning the tables after the traders had left. Sometimes there were a few running repairs; a barrier to straighten, a piece of weld-mesh to be made more secure, a wall to be repainted.

"You still here, Dennis," was the usual comment from Jake. It was said with a chuckle, obviously pleased, perhaps proud, that Dennis had been such a success.

Jake was more like a father than a boss. He paid for Dennis to take driving lessons — need you to drive my van, now and then, he'd said. And Maggie, despite her acerbic reputation, invariably gave him a quick smile before adopting her sterner look for anyone who might be watching. Weeks slipped easily into months. He and Amy often chatted as they worked. The two of them were teased incessantly, especially by the tea-ladies, who referred to them as the 'love-birds'. Dennis longed for the courage to ask her out. But most nights, after he'd helped her clear up, she'd tell him about her latest, as if he were simply her confidante.

A quick two years passed. He'd grown in confidence, he was taller, still bordering being thin, but he looked stronger, his arms and shoulders showing muscle, and he was more mature. He was even shaving. It was the happiest time in Dennis' life.

Chapter 7

"Hello, Dennis."

The voice was deeper, but he knew instantly who it was. He shuddered; a chill arrowed down his spine. Billy Fisher jostled his shoulder as if they were old pals.

"I heard you were working here." He curled his lip. It was the same threatening gesture. "Been a while."

"Suppose," Dennis mumbled.

"Don't look so worried. We're old mates, you and me." He exhaled a curl of blue smoke. It smelled sickly sweet. "Here, want a drag? It's good stuff."

Dennis shook his head. "I'm working," he replied.

"Quite the model employee, ain't you." Billy Fisher took a deep drag; "Heard you're living in Albion Street."

Dennis felt another shiver. "Yeah ... how do you know?"

"Mate of mine lives at the end — number twelve. Seen you coming and going." He sneered, "I might drop in sometime."

Maggie stopped applying nail polish and held her tiny brush in mid-air as Dennis entered the office. "I saw you talking to that Fisher lad earlier," she said. "Bad news, that one. He wanted to work here after he got kicked out of school. One of 'em threatened to torch the place. At least your dad asked nicely."

"He was just saying hi," Dennis replied.

"Don't let Jake see you with him. He'd blow a fuse."

Dennis nodded, relieved that Maggie had returned her attention to finishing her nails.

She glanced up as he walked away. Her mind briefly lurched to thoughts of Brendan Fisher, Billy Fisher's dad, so they said. She felt herself shudder. He was one of the worst.

Dennis had almost forgotten about Billy Fisher. It was several weeks since their encounter at the market and he'd been busy, virtually from dawn till dusk. The first loads arrived before seven; mostly white vans, sometimes a large truck. The worst was a large, refrigerated container that delivered the meat for butcher Bateman. It filled the yard and had to be unloaded quickly, and not just because of the space it occupied.

He'd got back to his room later than usual. The skip was supposed to be collected that night, but the driver had been snared in traffic. Dennis had to wait almost two hours before the truck arrived, and it took nearly half an hour to swap the overflowing skip for the empty. He was grateful for the sandwiches the tea ladies had given him as they cleared their stall.

"Here, Dennis. Cheese and tomato. We'll only have to chuck 'em." He'd shoved them in his jacket pocket; he'd wait until he got back to his flat.

They were a bit stale, but a couple of swigs from the large mug of tea he'd sugared and they tasted exquisite.

Someone thumped on his door. Dennis jumped. It sounded like a boot thudding onto the bottom panel. He spluttered on a mouthful of sticky white bread as he grabbed the door handle, sending wet crumbs in the direction of Billy Fisher's leather jacket. He gulped hard. "Billy ... what do you want?"

"That's no way to greet a mate," Billy replied, pushing past Dennis. "Nice place you've got here."

He picked up a coffee mug from the sideboard, turned it in his hands, and then pretended to let it slip from his grasp.

"Whoops, nearly dropped it." He walked across the room and rubbed his hand across the top of the tv. "Must be nearly new. Pity if it got broken." He turned to face Dennis, "Things get broken, don't they?" He poked his finger into the flesh of Dennis' arm, "Bet you 'ave to be careful, thin bones like yours."

"What do you want, Billy?" stammered Dennis. "Go ... please, go. Leave me alone."

"Please! That's very nice; very polite. I like that." He played with Dennis' shirt collar. "I need a bit of help, that's all. Not much, nothing that'd be any trouble."

Dennis felt the blood drain from his face. His eyes fixed on the knuckle duster Billy began to slip on and off the fingers of his right hand. He instinctively lifted his arm to shield his face and recoiled against the door. The stink of his urine seemed to fill the airless room.

Billy gave a mocking laugh, "You've pissed yourself. You pathetic bastard."

He shoved the knuckle duster hard against Dennis' cheek, rolling it back and forward, as if branding him with a hot iron. "All I want is a few coils of copper pipe. That's not too much to ask, is it? Nobody'll miss it, not if you're careful."

"But ..."

"Just a few coils; that's it. Promise."

It wasn't difficult. There were builders on site and they were much less attentive than the stallholders. He was surprised at what they threw away; saws that looked as if they'd been used just a few times, sometimes a hammer that had been dropped and forgotten, always nails and screws in plastic bags, and, if he was lucky, a few lengths of copper pipe. Dennis waited until they'd left and then shoved the bits of copper he found under one of the skips on the gravelled carpark just outside the security fence. By the end of the week he'd accumulated quite a haul.

Billy smirked when Dennis told him about the stash. "Well ain't you the little thief."

"I did what you asked," stammered Dennis.

"Got another little job for ya."

It was what he'd dreaded. "Just once ... that's what you said."

"Yeah? Don't remember sayin' that." He feigned surprise. "You'll get your share. You can trust me, I'm a pal; right?"

"I can't ... I won't ..."

Billy grabbed him by the throat. "Yes you can, Dennis. And you will."

"They'll notice. A couple of the builders were asking about copper gone missing,"

Billy relaxed his grip, "Not copper, Dennis. I wouldn't want to get you into trouble. No thieving — not this time."

Dennis felt a mixture of relief and dread swirl in his head. "What then?"

"All you've got to do is make sure that side gate is left unlocked, that's all."

Dennis' stomach growled. He swallowed back the acid bile in his throat.

"Jake keeps the keys in his office, there's no way ..."

"We've seen you opening up, so you know where the key's kept, right? My cousin collects the skips, see. Handy that, 'in it?"

Dennis was on nodding terms with most of the regulars; delivery drivers mostly. The skips were collected when they were full; usually after ten days or so and always first thing, before the day got started. It was always the same man, his hat pulled hard over his eyes and never a greeting of any kind. He simply pulled up on the gravel yard, dumped off an empty skip and winched the full one onto the truck.

"I wouldn't want to try that main gate. All them motion detectors, cameras — not stupid, am I? That side gate is just begging to be opened. Looks like tinsel on a Christmas tree — all that razor wire. But nothing else, am I right?"

"Jake ... he'll find out ... he'll kill me!"

"Stop panicking, Dennis. We'll make it look like a proper break in. It's simple — take the key, open the padlock and put the key back."

Dennis felt the blood drain from his face. The big main gate into the fenced yard was alarmed but the side gate had just an old large padlock and coils of razor wire arced over the black steel frame, as if they'd been added as a second thought.

"Oh, I doubt it. We know all about Jake. He's up to his neck in all sorts of stuff. The last thing he'll want is trouble, especially with the law."

It suddenly dawned on Dennis — it wasn't just Billy flogging a bit of stolen copper, this was bigger — it was the Fisher clan. He shuddered.

"You alright, Dennis?" Billy's mocking tone only amplified the fear he felt.

Dennis busied himself sweeping the aisles and helping the traders pack up their boxes. Maggie had asked again about Billy Fisher. He'd wanted to blurt out what was going on, tell her about stealing the copper pipe. He wanted to warn them, get Jake to do something about that back gate — maybe that would stop Billy Fisher?

Don't think so — a voice in his head that refused to leave.

And then the realisation there was nothing he could do, not now. It was too late. And anyway, the voice reasoned, they'll never suspect you of opening the back gate, not if you're careful. Then it'd be all over. Then he'd be rid of Billy Fisher.

But what if he got caught? His head hurt, his mouth felt dry, his hands were damp. He was trapped.

"Wednesday," that's what he'd eventually told Billy. "It's always the busiest day. Jake locks the gates and leaves around six. Maggie lets me out through the office. She's always the last to leave."

Billy Fisher sniggered. "She must love the place."

"She does," was his quiet reply.

Chapter 8

"You've done enough, Dennis," the tea lady told him as she stacked the last of her mugs into a beer crate. "You might as well get off — Jake's gone."

Dennis began lining up some of the trestle tables that had moved slightly off their pitch marks.

"Suppose so," he said. "I'll just finish this ... and see if Maggie needs anything."

He watched the tea lady haul herself up the steps towards the office.

"I'm off now," he heard her shout as she went past the office. In his head, he could see her treading carefully down the stairs and then pushing open the security door onto the street. He had an urge to run after her, as if freedom was just a short distance away.

The broom slipped out of his hands and clattered against one of the stanchions supporting the roof. The sound resounded round the metal hanger like a klaxon. Dennis looked up at the window to Jake's office and wiped the palms of his sweaty hands on his jeans, convinced Maggie must have heard. He held his breath and waited, rooted in indecision. He picked up the broom and carefully hung it on the wall. Treading, as if walking on hot coals, he climbed the wrought-iron steps. He paused outside Jake's office, took a deep breath and slowly turned the blackened knob. The door swung open on hinges that creaked more loudly than he'd ever realised. He stood, his eyes fixed on the inner wall. He could hear Maggie's rasping cough and the screech of the metal filing cabinet being opened and slammed shut. It was Maggie's way. He moved as carefully as he could towards Jake's desk, resisting the urge to simply dash across his office and grab the keys hanging teasingly close. He trod on a piece of crumpled paper lying near the wastepaper bin and flicked it to one side with the toe of his trainer. They were there, dangling on a rack of coat pegs behind Jake's chair. He reached forward and tilted the largest key up towards him with the tip of his finger. His hand shook as he lifted it from the peg and inspected the label attached by a length of twine. He knew it was the right key, but it seemed important to have the reassurance provided by the black scrawl on the tag — 'BACK GATE'.

He left the door to Jake's office open and hurried down the metal steps, grabbing the handrail. His foot twisted and his ankle scraped against the edge of the stairs. He stumbled across the concrete floor, wincing at the pain every time his foot touched the floor. The padlock was fastened to a chain wound tightly round the frame of the gate and looped through a metal ring fixed to the wall. He struggled to open the slide covering the keyhole. It suddenly gave way, pinching the skin on the side of his thumb. He felt a surge of relief when the key slid into the lock.

Dennis hobbled back across the floor of the building, his ankle throbbing and tightening in his shoe. His heart was thumping as he took the stairs, one step at a time. He stood by the door, listening out for signs of Maggie. He held the key out in front, like a pointer, aiming at the coat pegs behind Jake's chair. Just as he reached out, his fingers opening the key's loop of twine, he heard Maggie muttering to herself and the familiar click of her heels on the wooden floor. He froze. Maggie was backing through the door holding a cardboard box overflowing with files. He reached out and dropped the key onto one of the pegs, just as Maggie began to turn.

"Dennis! What are you doing here?"

"Oh ... just off," he stammered. "I thought I'd see if you want anything before I go."

He took of couple of steps towards her, arms outstretched. "Let me carry that box."

"Thanks." She nodded over to a table near the window; "Over there ..."

She shot a look as he stumbled across the office. "You're limping! What have you done?"

"Caught my ankle on the steps ... just now."

"I thought I heard something," Maggie replied. "You'd better get off. Get a bag of frozen peas on that ankle — stops the swelling."

"Thanks," he said, avoiding looking directly at her. "I'll do that."

Jake strode round the upturned trestle tables, kicking at scattered cardboard boxes. Maggie trotted behind him clutching a notebook to her chest, her high heels clipping off the floor.

"Maggie!" he roared as though she was in the next building, "I want a list of damaged goods, missing stock. There's a few of 'em who'll love this. They'll be making claims for stuff they never had."

She sighed. "They'll be upset, Jake. We've never had anything like this. Looks like they were more interested in wrecking the place than stealing anything."

Jake was in no mood to discuss the finer points of the break-in.

"Just get an inventory done, ok!"

"You're the boss. I'd better call the police."

"You'll do no such thing!" thundered Jake. "Not until we've done some checks. I don't want them plodding everywhere. Traders get nervous when they're around."

"The insurance company is going to need a police incident report," replied Maggie. "Otherwise, none of 'em will get a penny."

"You think I don't know that!" Jake took a deep breath and walked slowly over to the storeroom directly under his office. The buckled steel doors sagged limply from their hinges, as if apologising for having given way to the intruders. This was where the more valuable items were stored; jewelry, watches, computers, video players and Sony Walkman recorders.

The shelves were bare: every item had been taken. Jake swung his boot at one of the doors. It wailed in a banshee of noise that echoed throughout the metal shed.

Maggie knew all about Jake's illegal money-making scheme. Not that she'd ever complained when he'd slipped an envelope stuffed with cash across her desk. He stored jewelry and electronic items from supposed dealers, mainly from London and Birmingham — no questions asked. He'd got involved in a new, lucrative scam — VAT fraud. Jake and a couple of the traders were involved. Maggie filled out the forms to claim VAT back on electronic items supposedly imported legitimately and then exported to a fake company. Carousel fraud they called it. She also knew Jake would have a lot of explaining to do, not just to the police, but also to the others involved. They wouldn't be pleased to learn a major consignment waiting to be exported had been stolen. She made a mental calculation of the VAT that would have been claimed and then glanced across at Jake. From the look on his face, she guessed he'd made a similar calculation.

"God, what a mess," Maggie mumbled to herself.

Jake was holed up in his office most of the morning. Maggie had avoided going to her desk and had spent the time making an inventory of the damage and the losses the traders had encountered. Most looked utterly dejected, picking through the mess and the damage. She assured them they'd be fully compensated. Some gave reasonable assessments of the losses they'd incurred, others made exaggerated claims. Apart from those losing items from the 'secure' store, none of them had anything stolen, just damaged and spoiled goods. She bit her lip at some of the claims and simply logged what they said they'd lost.

"It'll be an insurance job, anyway," a few had remarked when Maggie raised a questioning eyebrow.

She took a coffee up to the office later in the morning. Jake barely moved as she entered. He posed a dejected figure. His greasy-looking mobile phone was a fingertip away. Numbers were scrawled on a pad which he attempted to shield, like a schoolboy hiding his crib notes.

"What's the damage?" Jake barked.

"Some wild claims. Mainly spoiled goods, not much else; except for the stuff in the store — jewelry, watches, computers." She paused ... "mobile phones."

"They knew what to look for," said Jake, "and where to look."

Maggie stood, fiddling with her notebook. She'd never seen Jake acting like this; indecisive, uncertain, perhaps afraid. Jake didn't frighten easily. "What do you want me to do? We're going to have to call the police: it's not just a petty break-in. They're bound to find out."

"Think I don't know that!" thundered Jake, swivelling round and staring out of his window at the traders picking through the carnage. They'd righted most of the trestle tables and started sorting some of their goods.

"Ok ... You call, tell 'em there was a break in — nothing much, just a bit of damage — probably kids. Got it?"

"But Jake ..."

"Don't argue, Maggie, just do as I say. Won't be much to see, anyway." He tapped on his window, "It looks nearly back to normal."

"What about the claims, Jake? It'll be at least five grand, and that's not counting the jewelry and stuff."

"I'll make sure they get their money. I doubt if any of them will want some insurance agent snooping around — let alone the cops."

"You sure, Jake?"

"I'm doing 'em a favour." He growled a curse, turned back to the window and scanned the floor below.

"Where's Dennis? He should be busy helpin'."

"I saw him earlier, picking up stuff," Maggie replied. "He's limping a bit; caught his ankle on those metal stairs."

"Tell 'im I want a word. He might know something." Jake paused, "How the hell did they get in, anyway?"

"That side gate," replied Maggie. "Smashed the lock."

Jake peered at the rack of keys hanging next to his desk. Something about it looked wrong. He reached over and lifted the key for the padlock with the tip of his finger.

"It's normally on the next peg." He stared again out of the window. "Those Fishers are involved; I just know it. I can feel it in my gut."

Chapter 9

"I want a word ..."

Dennis breathed hard. "Yeah?" He'd been clearing up all day, working harder and faster than he'd ever worked, as if it was a penance of some kind. He was lost in a maze of black thoughts with Billy Fisher's menacing face etched in his brain. Jake tapped his shoulder. Dennis clutched his broom for support and swung round, his heart thumping.

Jake looked sinister, wild-eyed, "Know anything about this?"

"No ... why should I?"

"Have you heard anything on the street? I've seen that young Fisher lout hanging round."

"Billy Fisher?"

"Yeah — know him well, do ya?"

"Just from school, that's all."

"So, you've never seen him since then?"

"No, not really."

"What does that mean? You've either seen him or you haven't."

"I've seen him a couple of times in the street ... think I saw him in the market."

"When?"

"Couple of weeks ago, I think. Yeah, must have been."

"He's banned from the place! I caught the little sod helping 'imself. Thinks cos he's a Fisher he can do what he likes." Jake moved closer. "Last night; when did you leave?"

"Not late. I saw you lock the back gates, then I left."

"You didn't go anywhere near my office then?"

"Only to see if Maggie wanted anything — ask her ..."

"I did!"

Dennis felt his bladder threaten. "Need to go," he said.

"Where? You're not going anywhere 'till I say so."

Dennis shuffled from one leg to the other, wincing at the pain from his ankle. "I need a piss."

"Something worrying you is it, Dennis? I think you know more than you're letting on."

"No ... no, honest."

Jake shoved him in the direction of the toilets. "Don't want you to stink the place. I'll talk to you later."

"Sorry ... "

"Sorry! What for?" Jake shouted, as Dennis hurried off.

A big hand snatched him as he came out of the toilet. Jake spun him round and grabbed him by the shirt. A couple of buttons snapped from their threads.

"You know something — you know who did it!"

Tobacco-stained phlegm flew from Jake's mouth, stinging Dennis' eyes. Jake pinned him against one of the stalls, bending his back against a trestle table. "You tell me what you know or, God help me, I'll break every bone in your puny body!" He stood Dennis up and pushed his face against one of the steel poles at the corner of the stall. Dennis could taste the tangy metal and sour-smelling grease. The gritty surface rubbed into his cheek like sandpaper.

"They made me," Dennis squeaked.

Jake pushed his face harder against the steel upright. "Who made you? Billy Fisher?"

Dennis nodded as Jake relaxed his grip.

"I didn't think they'd ..."

Jake thumped him in the stomach before he had any chance of continuing. He slumped to the floor, gasping. He felt himself being hoisted by Jake's thick arms. "So, what happened? Let me guess — you unlocked the side gate."

Dennis nodded. "Billy Fisher, he ..."

Jake flung him hard onto the floor; "Get out of here — now! And get out of my flat!" He leant down and glared into Dennis' face. "Don't ever set foot in here again," he hissed.

Many of the traders saw what had happened. So did Maggie, watching from the office window. A couple of stallholders helped him to his feet. The lady selling Turkish foods lifted her hand to her mouth and gasped, "Why, Dennis? Why did he hit you?"

The others waited until Jake had left the building before approaching. "He's mad ... you had nothing to do with this, did you?"

Dennis' glum silence had them shaking their heads in disbelief. Maggie was suddenly there, hands on hips.

"You opened the side-gate, didn't you, Dennis?" He nodded, feeling just as bruised by the disbelieving stares of Maggie and the traders as the beating he'd received from Jake.

"You bloody fool — after all we've done for you!" She reached for a cigarette. One of the traders produced a lighter. "Who was it, Dennis? Who got to you — Billy Fisher?"

Dennis nodded. A lump in his throat rendered him speechless. Maggie stubbed out her barely lit cigarette and took his arm. "You come with me. That face of yours needs attending to. I suppose Jake has told you to go — and leave his flat?"

"Yeah," Dennis squeaked.

Maggie dabbed at the deep scratches on his face. He tried hard not to wince. "I'll pay you from petty cash for the rest of the week. Just stay away, got it?"

Dennis didn't need to reply. Jake had scared him just as much as the threats from Billy Fisher. "I'll have a word with Bateman. He's moved his caravan off site. I think he'll let you kip there for a few days. But that's all I can do."

"Thanks, Maggie."

She cupped his face in the palms of her hands. The strong smell of nicotine on her fingers seemed familiar and comforting. Just at that moment he wanted her to leave her stained fingers on his cheeks for as long as possible.

She stared hard into his eyes, "Stay away from Billy Fisher. He's bad news."

"I will ... thanks, Maggie."

"You'd better go, Dennis," she said, quietly. For a moment, neither of them moved. Just as he was about to leave, she flung her arms round him and held him close. Dennis couldn't help himself; he sobbed uncontrollably.

Bateman's caravan wasn't much, just a cot bed, a battered sofa, a small kitchen table, and a couple of fold-up chairs. The sink leaked from a large crack. There was a toilet that worked and a shower cubicle, a slip of green slime licking the edges of the standing water in the tray and a torn plastic curtain, black with mould. The gas cooker worked, after Bateman had installed a propane cylinder to replace the one that had been stolen. There was a radiant heater fixed high on the wall and a small hot water cylinder above the sink. The door didn't lock and one of the windows was stuck partially open. It was a far cry from Jake's comfortable flat.

Dennis sat at the kitchen table and took the envelope Maggie had given him from his back pocket. He'd struggled to say anything when she'd handed it to him; a stammered "thanks" was all he'd managed. He carefully opened the flap and spread the money on the table. It was far more than he'd expected. He counted it again — £100. There was a scribbled note inside.

'Just a bit of extra to tide you over'.

Then a large 'M' followed by a small 'x'. Dennis slumped onto the cot bed, clutching the money in one hand and Maggie's note in the other.

A week later, Bateman rapped on the window and poked his shiny, pig-shaped head round the door. Dennis was slumped on the sofa, idly thinking about nothing in particular. He shot round with a jump.

"You ok, Dennis? It's not the best place. I'm thinking of having it scrapped in a couple of months. You can use until then if you want."

Dennis nodded, "Thanks, that'd be great."

"Just don't wreck the place," Bateman said. "I might try and sell it."

"No ... I'll look after it."

Bateman stood for a few moments, his arms hanging on the door frame. He grunted and looked round, inspecting the inside of the dilapidated caravan.

"I'll let you know when you've to get out."

"Thanks," Dennis replied.

"You heard what happened to Billy Fisher?" Bateman asked, as he was about to leave.

The name made him wince with a pain that clenched his gut.

"Billy Fisher? No ... Why?"

"He's been arrested. He was heard boasting to his mates, too loud to be ignored —the stupid little fool! Word is he'll be back in the Young Offenders Prison. 'Borstal' I still call it. He did a few months in there last year."

Dennis felt a sense of relief that Billy Fisher wouldn't be around, at least for a while. Young Offenders? His dad's place. He laughed at the thought.

"That's justice for 'ya," he muttered.

It didn't take long for Maggie's money to dwindle. Dennis thought about his warm, comfortable room in his parent's house; his model cars and airfix aeroplanes carefully lined up on a bookshelf opposite his bed, and his posters of Metallica, Iron Maiden and his favourite, Black Sabbath. There were slices of warm toast his mother brought up to his room to 'get him going' in the mornings, the large 'football' bedspread he'd had since he was seven ... And never a care about food or clothes, or money.

Dennis ambled along the familiar street with its semi-detached houses fronted by clipped hedges and trimmed lawns. It was mid-morning. There were few people around; a couple of dog walkers he thought he recognised, and a woman pushing her toddler. She looked warily at the unkempt youth strolling slowly towards her, hands thrust into the pockets of his sagging jeans. Dennis was relieved his dad's old Volvo wasn't in the drive. He opened the door and called down the hallway,

"Ma?"

His mother was in the kitchen. She stood in the doorway and rubbed her wet hands down the front of her floral apron.

"Oh, Dennis! Thank God you're alright. You should have called ... I've been worried sick."

"I'm fine, Ma. I've got a place to stay."

"So we heard. Dad found out from Jake ..." She paused, as if about to introduce a topic that wasn't for discussion. "He was really mad when he found out what had happened; really mad. Why, Dennis? Why did you do it? You liked the job, didn't you?"

Dennis shrugged and looked away. "I had to, Ma. They made me."

"Who, Dennis? Who made you?"

"Doesn't matter ... it's done now."

"Of course it matters! Dad said Billy Fisher was arrested. He'll end up in prison — Is that what you want? These people — they'll never leave you alone."

Dennis spun round. "I didn't come here for a lecture!"

"Please, Dennis! You're talking to your mother, not some street low-life."

"Sorry, Ma. I didn't mean ..."

"What is it you want?" She sighed, "Money, I suppose."

He shifted, nervously, "I don't suppose I can come back — just for a while — 'till I get sorted."

Barbara slowly untied the strings of her apron and let it dangle from the loop around her neck. "I don't think that's possible — not after what you've done. Your dad has made it plain, he doesn't want you back."

"What, just 'cos Jake is his big mate?"

"It's not just that, as you well know. That bag of marijuana in your room. And 'HATE' scrawled over and over with a permanent marker on the inside of the desk. It had belonged to his own father!" Barbara paused, "Worst of all, he found his work uniform in a black bin-liner at the back of your wardrobe, hacked to pieces. How could you!? He thought it had been lost at work. He was sure he'd given it into the prison laundry. He made a fuss, wanted to know who'd taken it. Those poor, young inmates were all disciplined; their visits and privileges were suspended. You've no idea how angry he was."

She lifted the apron loop over her head and hung it carefully onto one of the pegs on the back of the kitchen door. "I never dreamt it would come to this."

"What does he want me to do, beg?"

"No, Dennis; he's angry, hurt, and very disappointed."

"Not the perfect son he wanted!"

"That's not fair. He tried to help — he got you that job at the market as you well know. And look how you've repaid him. It's not what I want, but you have to go. It's impossible for the two of you to live in the same house."

Dennis fidgeted with the collar of his jacket. "I don't know what to do, Ma. I'm broke."

"I thought you might need help. I put a bit of money aside, enough for a month or two. Your dad's not to know …"

"It's your money," Dennis replied.

Barbara shrugged her shoulders. "It's not that easy," she said. "He's a proud man …"

"Him and his bloody pride … sorry …" He leant forward and kissed his mother on the cheek. "I'll pay you back, Ma — soon as I'm sorted." She handed him a jiffy bag. "There's two hundred pounds in here." She pushed it into his hand. "I think you'd better go."

Barbara watched him from the front window, walking hesitantly down the street, just as she'd done when he'd set off for school with the same nervous look — head down, his arms held stiffly by his sides.

She collapsed into one of the lounge chairs, covered her eyes and wept.

It was just starting to get dark, the September sun sinking behind a block of high-rise buildings, when Dennis, flush with notes stuffed into the back pocket of a pair of jeans he'd bought that afternoon from a charity shop, filled his growling belly at McDonalds. Earlier, he'd showered, shaved and sprayed himself with deodorant. Amy had given him a washbag filled with men's toiletries. "These aren't selling," she'd said. "Here, it's yours."

He felt somewhat elated, despite his mother's reaction to him turning up on the doorstep. He wiped his mouth and hands with a paper napkin, returned a smile from the teenage waitress and headed for the Midnight Bar.

He ordered a lager and a bag of crisps. It was early, just ten o'clock. It'd be an hour or so before the place started to get busy. He found a small booth, set his glass of lager on a beer mat, his eyes adjusting to the dim lighting. The place quickly became much busier. He thought he saw her coming in, partly shrouded by a gaggle of her mates. The group headed over to tables at the other side of the bar, giggling and laughing. Their faces were in shadow, just the top of their heads lit by the glow from a lamp hanging over the table. He stared through the throng at the group; three of them were sitting on a bench seat, their backs angled towards him. The one in the middle suddenly stood, waving her hands towards the bar, shouting to one of the waiters. It was Amy! She looked different, not in the torn jeans and floppy tops she wore at the market. He kept looking across, hoping she'd see him. Her high-pitched voice was nearly lost in the buzz and din. She did a double take;

"Dennis! Dennis!"

She was waving, beckoning him over. Her two friends were about to join a group of lads in the next booth.

"You coming, Amy?" one of them said, as Dennis approached. She shook her head. "They're not my type," she remarked.

He slid onto the bench opposite hers. "Now Dennis, tell all ..."

"What do ya mean?"

"Why did you get the sack ... what else? I thought you loved the place?"

"I do ... did. I got mixed up with people I should've stayed clear of."

"Jake was really pissed. Word was he paid everybody off so there'd be no investigation ... something to do with mobile phones taken from his store."

Dennis shrugged his shoulders, "Sounds about right."

"Those phones must have been gold plated!"

He laughed. "Maybe they were, in a way."

"You're a bit of a dark horse, aren't you. How come you know so much?"

"Just stuff I heard, that's all. Maggie told me bits."

"Maggie always knows. She runs the place. It'd grind to a halt without her." Amy leant across the formica-topped table; "She told me you're living in that decrepit caravan of Bateman's."

"Just for a month. He's having it scrapped pretty soon."

"About time. I went in it once, just for a lark. It stank! Put me off my lunch!"

"I won't be sorry to leave it," Dennis replied.

"Have you found a place?"

Dennis shook his head. "Just started looking."

"This may be your lucky day!"

"Oh?"

"I've got a spare room in my flat. I've been thinking about letting it for a while. Me and Lee — that's my boyfriend — could use the money. What do ya think?"

"Er ... well ..."

"Come round and have a look. If you don't like it, no harm done."

"Suppose ... how much?"

"I was thinking about £40 a week. Since I know you, you can have it for thirty-five."

Dennis felt his heart thump. He hoped Amy would assume his flushed cheeks were because of the lager he'd all but drained.

"It's not that big, just a small double bed squeezed in. You can use the kitchen, watch tv …"

"Sounds great," Dennis uttered.

She rummaged in her clutch bag, found a biro, the type used in betting shops, and scribbled on a card she'd produced from somewhere.

"Here — my address. Why don't you come round tomorrow, about four. Lee will be still at work — I hope."

Me too, thought Dennis.

Chapter 10

Amy's flat was above a row of shops on the edge of Marshbrook council estate, separated by a main road from a line of 1930's semi-detached houses. Dennis pressed the buzzer for flat number 2. No reply. He tried a couple more times; the buzzer's muffled sound leaked through an open window above the door. He checked his mobile; exactly 4 pm, no messages. 'She's forgotten,' he mumbled to himself. He stepped back onto the pavement and stared up at the window, wondering if he should call her name. Some of the punters coming in and out of the bookies directly under her flat gave him the 'once-over' as if he was an unwanted stranger in their territory.

"Dennis!" It was Amy's shrill voice. She was at the end of the street, waving. Her blonde ponytail swishing from side-to-side as she quickened her pace, her red bolero jacket flapping against pale denims.

"Hi, Dennis, sorry I'm a bit late. Got held up with a customer."

"Oh, that's what I figured," he replied, his voice leaping into a higher register as it nearly always did when he was nervous.

"Come in," she said. "See what you think."

He followed her pert, swaying figure up the flight of stairs to her flat and into a narrow hallway. Her body pressed against his as she squeezed past and led him into the kitchen. It was painted brilliant white with matching cupboards and onyx counter tops that shone under the glare of ceiling spotlights. It looked sterile after the squalor of Bateman's caravan.

"Like it?"

Dennis nodded, "It's fantastic."

"It's not been in long. Lee has a mate who works in the trade. It all came out of a house that was having a new kitchen. God knows why. There's not a mark on it." She hesitated briefly as if expecting another appreciative comment from Dennis. "I've never cooked or anything," she continued, "just use the microwave. It's quick and easy — and no mess. Love it!"

She took his elbow, "Come on, I'll show you the rest, not that there's much to see!" Her laugh echoed off the plain kitchen walls. "It's open-plan," she said, with evident pride. Set at right angles was an area with a pine table under the front window. A couch and two armchairs were arranged in an arc in front of a large television.

"Nice," said Dennis. "Very nice."

"It's snug," she replied. "Hope you like sport. That's what Lee watches. I'm into soaps."

"Yeah, great," he replied. He liked to watch football but watching it in Lee's company didn't appeal.

"And this is your room," she announced, as if he'd already accepted the offer. It was painted in the same brilliant white as the kitchen. She opened the bedroom door, "It won't go any further. Catches the bed." The two of them were just able to stand between the end of the bed and the large, mirrored wardrobe. Thin Venetian blinds rattled against a small window opposite the door.

Amy pointed to the wall across from the wardrobe. "Our room is next door, and the shower room is at the end of the corridor."

Dennis had assumed it would be bigger. It reminded him of that room in 'One Flew Over the Cuckoo's Nest' with Jack Nicholson playing a man slowly going mad.

"Well? Good in't it?"

"It's very nice," he replied. He wondered about Lee. What would he think?

"That's settled then. You can move in when you like. How about this Thursday? It's my half-day."

"Ok ... that'd work."

"Great! I knew you'd love it. Come round with your stuff about two."

Dennis nodded, "Yeah, will do."

Lee was a scowler. He had a narrow, pinched face, close set dark-brown eyes, and a mullet of jet-black hair, coiffed and quipped. He flung his slim frame into one of the armchairs and reached for the remote.

"Who's this?" He barely looked at Dennis, his eyes were fixed on the tv.

"I told you, Lee. It's Dennis. He's having the spare room."

Lee grunted and flicked through the channels. "I'd forgotten."

Amy moved round the back of Dennis' chair and rested her hands on his shoulders, "You'll get used to him. He likes to show his bad side."

"Oh, piss off," Lee remarked, still playing with the remote.

Amy laughed loudly, as if it was some inside joke. "Just ignore him, Dennis."

Lee hit the off button. "Nothing but day-time stuff." He climbed out of his chair and headed into the kitchen. He reappeared holding a beer and a pack of sandwiches. "Thought I told you to get a BLT."

"All they had was chicken salad— get your own next time! Where' ya going, anyway?"

"Manchester. Got a delivery."

"He's a driver," Amy said. "Takes cars for dealers — mostly up and down the M6."

Dennis was relieved when he heard the front door slam. Amy plumped up the cushions Lee had squashed. "Don't mind him, Dennis.

He's alright." Amy suddenly seemed brighter, as if Lee's departure had freed her, somehow.

"You'll take the room, then?"

He nodded.

"Good." She rummaged in one of the kitchen drawers and handed Dennis a key ring with a fluffy pink heart attached. "The smaller key is for the front door to the flat. The other one opens the door onto the street. Bring your stuff over whenever you like."

"Thanks," Dennis replied.

Dennis didn't have much to bring. He'd spread out his clothes on the bed in Bateman's caravan, thrown away a couple of shirts he wouldn't have wanted to wear in front of Amy and rolled his jeans, tops and underwear into tight bundles he could stuff into the two bags he possessed, a small holdall he'd found in Batman's caravan and a duffle bag he'd had since he was in his early teens.

"That all you've got?" Amy remarked. It was dark when he got to her flat and the bus had been heavy with people traveling home from work. The Friday night traffic had slowed the journey. She ushered him in and gave him a peck on the cheek. She giggled and reached for the half empty wine glass on the counter. "You'd better go and unpack," she said.

"Hungry? I got a beef curry for Lee — he's on another job, It'll be late before he gets back — It'll only go off." Over their heated curry, and what remained of a bottle of wine, Amy talked in the same quick way she sold her beauty products on the market stall.

"It's my mum's stall. I just help out. My dad was in the trade; watches mainly, bit of bling. He's long gone. Took 'imself off to Spain with a woman from one of the fruit and veg stalls. You'll never guess what happened ... he sent me some money for my birthday. Completely out of the blue! Mum was furious. You'd have thought I'd pinched it out of her purse! Anyway, I took no notice. Well, gave her a hundred quid, didn't I — just to stop her goin' off on one. I got five grand! Would you believe it! Five grand! I put a deposit on this place. Still had a bit left to shove in the bank. Got me well set up."

A bit of curry slipped off her fork and onto her front. She grabbed a tissue and rubbed at the stain, smearing her white top.

"First time I wear it and now look!" She held the front out towards Dennis. "I'd better soak it." She stood and in one smooth action, lifted the top over her head. She smiled at Dennis, as if pleased at his obvious embarrassment, "Nothing you haven't seen before!" She giggled, filled the sink with water and splashed the flimsy top in the cold water. "There — won't be a mo'."

She returned wearing something almost identical. "What do you think?"

Dennis felt his face redden.

"About the flat, silly!"

"Oh, it's great."

They watched a film starring Kevin Costner and Whitney Houston. She'd made him sit next to her on the small couch.

"You can't see properly over there, Dennis."

The only light was from the flicker of the screen and a glow from ceiling spotlights that had been left on in the kitchen. "Cosy, this," she said, wriggling over. Their thighs touched. He could feel her warmth as their bodies slid closer, his nose twitching at the cheap scent engulfing the airless room. The love scenes were explicit, the romance was strong — the hero protecting and guarding a beautiful woman.

"Come here, Dennis," Amy said in a low voice, as if someone might be listening. "You want to, don't you?"

Dennis' heart was thumping. "Yeah," he said, staring at her face in the flickering light. She smiled and leant towards him. Their foreheads touched. It was like a structured sequence of smooth events, as if it was something they'd done many times. Her lips brushed his mouth, the tip of her tongue briefly touched his.

And then it was over, the moment gone. The credits rolled, and the ceiling spotlights blazed before he realised she'd moved.

"I'm off to bed. Anything you want, just knock on my door." She giggled. "You know what I mean!"

Dennis imagined, just for a moment ... He returned her smile and laughed.

"Yeah, thanks," he said, suddenly thinking that wasn't the best response.

He lay on the soft, spotless bed. He could hear music playing through the thin wall separating the bedrooms. He thought of her head lying inches away from his ... of that brief kiss ...

Dennis was awakened by the sound of Lee closing the front door of their tiny flat. He heard Amy mumble something inaudible and then a few grunted remarks from Lee and the creak of their bed. Getting back to sleep didn't come easily.

Chapter 11

Dennis was always relieved when Lee got in late from one of his deliveries. Then there was only the odd grunt and the occasional creak of the bed, not the disturbing rhythmical sound of the headboard banging against the partition wall. Most of the time Lee ignored him, as if he was just a part of the furniture. He was helping Amy clear up after breakfast when Lee shouted from in front of the tv.

"Got a job yet?"

"Still looking," Dennis replied, surprised that Lee was remotely concerned.

"Don't suppose you've got a driving license?" Lee called, the tv still blaring.

"Er ... Yeah," Dennis replied. "Jake paid for lessons so I could drive the vans."

Lee slunk into the kitchen, leaned on the counter and held up his empty mug in front of Amy.

"Another coffee."

He looked at Dennis; "I've got more deliveries than I can handle. I could use another driver." His face creased into something resembling a smile. "I'm what you might call 'freelance'."

Amy let the cafetiere she was holding hover over Lee's mug. "Works for 'imself, don't you, Lee."

"That's what I just said. What are you, stupid?"

Amy glanced at Dennis. He thought he could see fear in her eyes.

"Sorry, Lee," she said, quietly.

He spun round, "Sometimes you can be a such an idiot."

Dennis felt sick. He wanted to say something, do something. He sat as if rooted to his chair and stared at the wall behind Lee's head.

"Got a run to Liverpool later — you'll need to come along. You can do a bit of the driving — see if you're any good."

Dennis gave a stiff, reluctant, nod.

"First thing you gotta learn is not to ask too many questions," Lee said, his hands caressing the steering wheel. They were driving south on the M6 in a Mercedes E class. "This motor's nearly new." He sniggered, "Well, most of it. All we got to do is deliver it. There's usually one to drive back up this way."

Lee flicked on cruise control. "Don't drive over 75. Don't need the cops checking it over." He cursed at a driver cutting in front. "Never 'ad a breakdown, yet. If you do, you call me. Got it? These ain't exactly legit."

"Stolen?"

Lee grunted, "That's a mug's game. These are what you might call 'rebuilt' from cars scrapped after a smash up. Bits of 'em get picked over and welded up." He snorted. "Salvage work. A quick respray and they're ready for sale. All we got to do is drive 'em to the dealers. You'd be amazed at the idiots out there who'll buy a quality motor without all the right paperwork — just coz it's cheap." He laughed,

"Some of 'em are legit salvage jobs — keeps it honest!"

'Just for a while,' Dennis told himself as they sped along the motorway in the smooth luxury of the Mercedes. He eased back into the soft leather seat and let his eyes wander over the instrument console.

"Lovely motor, in' it?" Lee remarked. "There's a services in about two minutes. I'll pull in — let you drive."

Dennis felt his skin prickle as he buckled up and adjusted the mirrors. He eased onto the slip road and picked up speed.

"Nice," Lee said, his voice lifting. "Now get past this truck and flick on cruise control like I showed you."

Dennis soon settled. The motorway was unusually quiet and the big car ate up the miles effortlessly, as if being sucked along the smooth tarmac.

"You're a natural, Dennis. Bit of a pro, eh."

"I drove a bit at the market. Did a few runs to Manchester." He patted the steering wheel, "Nothing like this. Mostly vans that weren't exactly new. I got to drive Jake's car a couple of times."

"Like driving, do ya?"

Dennis smiled. "Yeah, like it a lot. 'Specially in a big motor like this."

"Bit easier than those crappy vans you've been driving," Lee remarked. "I thought you'd be useless."

Dennis flicked on the indicator and moved into the outer lane. A truck was making a futile attempt to pass an identical vehicle. Mud flicked up from the truck's tyres, spattering the windscreen. Dennis calmly dabbed the windscreen washer several times until the smeared mud had cleared.

"You're just showing off, now," Lee said. "Good, though."

"Thanks," Dennis replied. It sounded a different Lee to the one who'd scared him with his scowls and abrupt remarks.

"Next junction," Lee said, as they approached a slip road. "There's a lay-by in a couple of miles. I'll drive from there. I know the back roads."

Lee drove down a narrow street of small tenements. Most looked drab and unloved. There was a yard at the end, a large sign hanging from spiked railings.

'Donovan Salvage'.

Three Alsatians rushed towards the car as they drove through the gates. Their heads jerked back as their long chains snapped taught.

"That's the welcome party," sniggered Lee. "I wouldn't go and pat 'em if I were you."

The car inched forward, away from the snarling dogs, and along an alleyway of piled cars, some balanced precariously, like eroding cliffs of twisted metal. Behind the cars was a concrete pad, incongruously clean, and a hanger skirting the length of the yard. Dennis followed Lee's lead and stepped out of the Mercedes. A small, barrel-chested man approached. He gobbed a thick spit, slowly turned and fixed on Dennis.

"Who's this?"

"Dennis, my new driver."

"Don't like strangers. We only employ family," he said.

"He'll be working for me — he's ok, ain't you, Dennis?"

"Better be," the man said, his dark eyes virtually hidden by a well-worn, flat cap pulled down over his forehead. Bits of thread hung from its frayed peak. He took a step towards Lee,

"Two cars," he said, turning as he spoke. He waved in the direction of the hanger. "In't back." He turned, quickly. "I'll get t' keys."

"That's the boss, Gerry, Gerry Donovan," Lee whispered. "Most of 'em are Donovans. Think one of 'em must be his brother. He's in charge when Gerry's away."

The inside of the hanger had two cars on hoists. Both had inspection lights dangling from their raised bonnets and mechanics hanging over the mudguards. Racks of tools hung along one wall above steel workbenches. Sharp, penetrating light lit the end wall behind a partially screened welding bay and bounced off a rack of acetylene bottles chained against the wall. A silhouetted figure, his face lit by a shower of sparks from a blowtorch, was cutting into the chassis of a car similar to those on the hoist.

"This is what's called a chop-shop," Lee said. "They take out parts from scrapped cars and sell 'em on. Some get a new id — vin number — from legit autos. They make a lot of money, the Donovans."

Gerry Donovan shouted from the entrance to the workshop. He was holding two sets of keys and a large envelope. Lee grabbed Dennis by the arm, "He doesn't like to be kept waiting."

Donovan handed the keys and the envelope to Lee. "Liverpool — Maddison's. Get 'em there by ten."

Lee nodded.

Gerry Donovan bawled at the man who'd been cutting with a blow torch. "Dermot! Get that 'effin thing finished, will 'ya." He turned back to Lee,

"What 'ya waiting for?"

Lee handed one of the keys to Dennis. "That's yours, that 'C' class Merc. I'm in that blue Beemer. We'll stop at the Sandbach Services."

Dennis adjusted the seat, then the mirrors. He eased the car forward, following Lee out of Donovan's yard, glancing in his rear-view mirror at the lights in the hanger, half expecting one of the Donovans to come charging after him. Narrow, terraced streets were lined with cars on both sides, their wheels straddling double yellow lines, leaving less than a pram's width on the pavement. It seemed a different route to the one they'd taken earlier. He was relieved when Lee turned onto a wider road, a large sign for the M6 indicating the lane to take as they approached a set of traffic lights. Within minutes, they were on the motorway.

Denis relaxed. He set the cruise control and selected a rock station. He knew it from the first riff. 'Smells like Teen Spirit'. He turned up the volume. Nirvana. He loved their stuff. He sang along ... 'Hello, Hello, Hello ... With the lights out it's less dangerous ...'

"They understand what it's like," he muttered. "They've got the balls ..." He laughed, and then shouted, "It's less dangerous with the lights out!"

He felt lightheaded; flushed with exhilaration.

"This is great," he said, as if there were another person in the car. He let his mind wander to thoughts of Amy, wishing she were sitting in the passenger seat. He wondered if she understood Nirvana? The swish of a car he hadn't spotted overtook in the outside lane, making his heart race. He decided Amy would have to wait.

Dennis felt a wave of disappointment when they reached the car dealer in Liverpool. He'd enjoyed driving much more than he'd expected, and he was good at it, Lee had said as much at the service station.

They'd sat in near silence on the trip back from Liverpool. Lee had simply handed the keys to Dennis and got in the passenger seat. It was an older vehicle — a maroon-coloured Vauxhall with a spoiler fin above the boot and a white flash painted on the sides. It was a manual, with a short, stubby gear stick and a small steering wheel. The engine gave a throaty roar when he touched the accelerator and the lowered suspension scraped on the speed bumps.

"Special delivery for some boy racer," Lee said.

The car bottomed-out in a screech of metal and a thud on the undercarriage. "Watch it!" Lee shouted. "Take 'em dead slow."

"Sorry," Dennis replied, letting the car crawl over the next speed bump. It was quick, very quick.

"The steering's a bit twitchy on these," Lee remarked. "Watch your speed — no cruise control on this thing."

He grinned at Lee as they waited at traffic lights. He held the revs, glanced around at the other traffic, and accelerated hard, the tyres squealing on the tarmac.

"Steady!" Lee shouted. "No need to show off ... And stick to the speed limits. This is a business not a bloody joyride!"

Lee took himself off to the bathroom as soon as they got back to the flat. Amy motioned to Dennis. "Just be careful," she whispered. "I wouldn't want to see you get into any trouble; I know what Lee's like. Some of his mates are mixed up in drugs 'n stuff." She reached over and touched his arm, "I like having you around. This past three months have been great: it's good to have someone else in the place."

"Thanks, I like it here."

"Even with Lee's ways? You've seen his temper. It doesn't take much ..."

Dennis shrugged his shoulders. "We get on ok — money's good. Besides, it won't be for long. I'll get something else."

"Just remember what I said, Dennis. I daren't leave him. I tried ... But you can ..." She stopped abruptly at the sound of Lee emerging from the bathroom.

"Dennis!" Lee's voice echoed down the corridor. "I need you to deliver a package — same place as last time."

"Ok," Dennis mumbled.

It had sounded easy, dropping off a cardboard box to an address; 'just a delivery', he told himself, as if it was a carton of pizzas. This was the third time he'd made similar deliveries to the detached house hidden in a maze of streets on a recently developed housing estate. It had all the signs of young families; a scattering of scooters, footballs, swing sets, loungers, and several sparkling SUVs parked on bricked driveways. It didn't look like a drug dealer's place. But it certainly wasn't occupied by a typical family. It had black wrought-iron gates protecting the entrance with a brick wall at the front and heavy fencing extending around the rear of the property. He'd previously noticed the security cameras hanging from the eaves and the post box built into one of the brick pillars and a warning of a dangerous dog mounted on the opposite pillar. Visitors were clearly not encouraged.

Dennis pushed the intercom button.

A voice crackled from the speaker, "Yeah?"

"It's Dennis. Got a delivery from Lee."

The gate slid back into a recess in the brick wall, just sufficient to allow him to get through. He could hear a dog barking from somewhere at the back of the house as he approached the side door. A thickset man stood waiting for him to approach. His heavily tattooed arms and pudgy hands were looped round his wide belly. He clamped his fingers onto the box, jerking it out of Dennis' grasp.

"Now piss off."

He held up a remote and started the gate. Dennis scooted down the yard and squeezed through, just before it clanged shut.

"Get on ok?" Lee shouted. He was watching the racing on the tv. Dennis nodded.

"Give you the cash?" said Lee, his voice barely audible above the din from the tv.

"What?"

"The money!"

Dennis shook his head. "Must have forgotten."

"That bastard," screamed Lee, flinging a crumpled betting slip across the room. "Wants me to beg for what he owes! Get the dosh first; that's what I told you!"

"Sorry," mumbled Dennis, his voice lost in the noise from the tv.

Lee suddenly let out a 'whoop'. "50 to 1! I had a hundred on that." His thick, angry scowl was gone in an instant. "Come on — you can help me celebrate." He flung a set of car keys across the room,

"You'd better drive." He took out a couple of spliffs from a cigarette packet and handed one to Dennis.

They lit up at the foot of the stairs. Dennis followed Lee into the bookies, ignoring the 'No Smoking' sign dotted with scorch marks from stubbed cigarettes. "I'll take care of that fat bastard," Lee said. "Nobody messes with me." He took a deep drag and grinned as he flicked the wad of notes with his thumb.

"You're ok, Dennis."

Chapter 12

The bar was virtually empty, just a few regulars who looked as though they'd aged much like the dull patterned carpet. They sat in corners they'd made their own, sipping pints, some idly tracing a finger over initials carved into the lacquered tables. Others were squinting at the Racing Post, elbows resting in puddles of beer, arms like props wedged against grey and stubbled faces.

"They'll be here any minute," Lee told Dennis. "News travels fast."

Dennis knew who he meant. They were the other regulars; the cocky hard men, the pale druggies with eyes rimmed by dark patches; and the fast-talking chancers who took odd jobs, cursed the measly amounts they got in benefits and boasted about women they were screwing.

They descended like flies, pulling extra tables towards the large window seat where Lee was holding court.

"There's two hundred on the bar," Lee announced, once it seemed the usual were all there. He gestured, expansively, to the barmaid. "Mary!"

She poked her head over the wooden bar: her pulpit, she called it.

"Twelve, is it?" She laughed loudly, her flushed, fat cheeks jiggling.

A couple of hours later and beer-soaked tables were strewn with empty glasses.

"That's it." announced Mary. "Your money's about gone. I've taken out my tip o'course."

"Thought you might," slurred Lee.

"Just in case you forgot."

Lee laughed. "OK, lads. You heard the lady …"

Some left quickly, as if they'd already decided it was time to go. Others were slower to stir.

Two of them sat watching as the rest blew kisses to Mary and filed out into the bright sunlight. Dennis had met them several times. They dealt in smuggled goods, mostly cigarettes from Turkey and cheap vodka from the Ukraine.

"Need some stuff moved."

"Where?" asked Lee, suddenly brighter and seemingly sober.

"Comes in at Hull. Needs to go to Bradford."

"Just fags," remarked the second man, as if anticipating the obvious question. He took out an envelope. "Five hundred pounds in here. Another five on delivery."

Lee nodded. "When?"

"This Thursday — Hull Docks at nine, just before it gets dark."

Lee reached into his pocket, took out a black notebook and flicked through the well-thumbed pages. "Got to be you, Dennis. I've got a run to Manchester for Gerry Donovan."

Dennis nodded, "Fine with me." It was a better option than working for the Donovan clan.

The pick-up was easy. A quiet area near the Port of Hull. A white transit van flashed its lights as he turned into a road flanked by several warehouses. It was parked near The Anchor, a large hotel, now shabby and empty. Dennis was glad they were there waiting. He was anxious to get on the road to Bradford. The driver got out of the van and motioned for Dennis to reverse up behind their vehicle. His mate opened the rear doors, climbed into the back and began sliding several cardboard boxes along the floor of the van. Dennis helped them lift the cartons into the boot of his car. Three boxes had to be placed on the rear seat of the Mercedes. Dennis covered them with a blanket.

"Fags?"

The driver nodded. "Mostly." He walked round to the cab door and reached under his seat, taking out a package about the size of a shoe box. "This is for Lee." He grinned, "Special order."

It took less than an hour to reach the Bradford turn off. It was a familiar journey. This was the fifth time he'd made a drop to the house at the end of a narrow street of terraced houses. Some of the ethnic shops were still clearing the pavements carrying near-empty trays of vegetables and fruit. He found a space to park his car, checked round in the way Lee had instructed, making sure he knew the quickest way out if there was trouble.

The front door was held slightly open just as he approached. "You Dennis?" The man was dark and thickset. Dennis nodded.

"Where's the stuff?" The man spoke with a heavy accent. He reminded Dennis of the Turkish trader at the market. He pointed across the street to his blue Merc.

"Ok. I help you."

It only took two trips and the transfer was done.

"Good job. You tell Lee, another job next month." He handed Dennis a jiffy bag. "Five hundred. No need to count — we trust each other, yes?" He flashed a big smile of nicotined teeth and slapped Dennis on the shoulder; "You try these — good stuff." He proffered two, battered cigarette packets. "Ten in each — Moroccan." He grinned, "Ok; you go now." The door closed with a soft swish, as if operated pneumatically. Before driving off Dennis counted the money. It was all there, each hundred folded with a twenty-pound note wrapped over four other twenties. Dennis breathed a sigh of relief. Lee had said he could take a hundred for himself. He took out one envelope of crisp twenty-pound notes and slipped it into his shirt pocket.

The brightly lit shop sign beckoned; 'Bargain Booze'. Parking was easy; right outside. He placed the cans of Stella on the passenger seat, tugged open the ring-pull and downed the lager in gulps. He belched loudly, glanced round and lit one of the spliffs. He cracked open the driver's window, wedged another can between his thighs and drove off.

Within twenty minutes he was driving along familiar roads, several miles from his intended route. He relaxed, the alcohol and strong marijuana blending, his mind wandering, the car purring along, his fingers barely touching the steering wheel. The pinprick of red light was suddenly as large as a football. He slammed his foot on the brake, the tyres squealing on the tarmac. The car skidded and shuddered to a halt. The back of Dennis' sweat-soaked shirt peeled from the leather seat as he leaned forward, spilling the opened can of beer. He stared vacantly at the rows of parked cars on either side of the street as if waiting to see what would happen next. The driver in the car behind leant on his horn. Dennis shook his head, looked up at the green light and slammed the gear lever into first. The tyres suddenly gripped, flinging the car across the intersection. He pulled to a stop, switched off the engine and reached for another beer. He drank it slowly this time, letting the cool liquid flush the heat from his brain. He lit another spliff, took several deep drags and then eased the car slowly forward. He felt easier, more in control.

The streets, the roads were now very familiar. He waved nonchalantly at trees lining the boulevard, as if they were old friends. He suddenly realised he was driving down the road leading to his parents' house.

He gripped the steering wheel, picked up speed, and watched the needle climb; fifty, sixty, seventy ...

A car was poking out as if about to cross his path, demanding he slow down. He accelerated hard.

His car ploughed into the other vehicle in a screech of metal, like a prolonged scream, hailstones of splintered glass whipping across his face. His body lurched forwards; the seatbelt lashed across his chest, his head sledge-hammered against the door pillar.

His body wouldn't respond ... he couldn't move ... his mind nothing, a blank. A cold sweat gripped his flesh as he sat, motionless, staring through the shattered windscreen. A trickle of warm, metallic-tasting blood caught the corner of his mouth. Reality returned. He rolled out through the gap where the driver's door should have been. Someone helped him to his feet.

"That's a nasty cut. Are you alright?" He barely heard the shouts of others running towards the smashed cars, just a noise buzzing in his throbbing head.

"I'm ok," Dennis muttered, ignoring the attempts to make him sit. He stared, vacantly, at the familiar semi-detached houses. And then he heard her — Lisa, running towards him, shouting his name.

"Dennis! Dennis! What happened? Oh, my God! What have you done!?"

He belched and vomited, the smell of stale beer filling his nostrils.

Lisa shoved him hard. He staggered against a privet hedge.

"You're drunk ... You bastard!"

Dennis' head began to clear. A woman was sobbing. There were shrieks and gasps. The driver's body was slumped, distorted, a deep head wound weeping blood and brain.

More screams, women running, men shouting, "No, get back! You can't do anything!"

Dennis staggered along the street, focusing on that familiar car; his dad's blue Volvo parked in the drive. Michael ran out of the house and grabbed his arm;

"You alright, Dennis?"

His sister, Lisa was in his ear, screaming,

"You bastard! You bastard!"

Dennis staggered to the porch, his legs suddenly weak, his body shaking. He slid down onto the step, watched the flashing blue lights, and listened to the piercing sirens, as if a spectator. The next thing he remembered was being led to a waiting ambulance.

"He'll be held in custody," the police officer told Michael, once they'd established who Dennis was. "We could be dealing with a fatality."

They found several spliffs in Dennis' car and a number of empty cans of lager. The police report said Dennis had braked hard, turned sharply and lost control, slamming into the driver's side door. The driver was Lisa's boyfriend. She'd refused to budge, staying as close to the wreckage as the police would allow. It had taken some time to get him out. The driver's side had caved in crushing her boyfriend in a concertina of metal and shattered glass.

He died in hospital, his body stuffed with tubes, a respirator feeding oxygen into his lungs, monitors arced around the head of the bed, his mother sitting stiffly at his side, fiddling with rosary beads, her unwashed face stained by traces of dried, salt tears, her bloodshot eyes bulging like coloured marbles.

Lisa managed just one visit.

Michael removed the few framed photographs they had of Dennis, nearly all hanging in the alcove next to the fireplace and placed them in a cardboard box in the attic. Barbara didn't object, she simply wiped away the telltale signs of the missing picture frames.

Chapter 13

Sheffield Crown Court

The Crown Court judge warned Dennis he was lucky not to be facing a longer jail sentence. The other driver wasn't wearing a seat belt, and a motorist approaching the junction in the opposite direction gave a statement stating he'd seen the car pulling out onto the main road. The judge said he had no option other than to find him guilty of Causing Death by Dangerous Driving and imposed a two-year prison sentence. Dennis had expected worse, he'd been warned it might be six, if he was lucky. He couldn't help himself; he grinned, broadly. The judge gave a disapproving look. For an uncomfortable moment, Dennis thought the beak might change his mind and give him a longer sentence. He glanced at the jurors, some of whom were shaking their heads. Someday, he thought, one of you might be standing here. Then you'll know how it feels …

Lisa was in court to watch the proceedings. She leapt to her feet and shrieked,

"What! Two years!" She'd been told he would be convicted of manslaughter; she'd been told he would be imprisoned for at least ten years. "This is pathetic!" A court officer leant towards her and whispered, sternly, for her to calm down. The judge glanced in Lisa's direction with a resigned, apologetic look and quickly left the courtroom.

Barbara was more defensive; "He shouldn't have been given a prison sentence; it wasn't just his fault." It was said without conviction, as if it was something she had to say, something any mother would say in defence of her son.

The smell of stale body odour hit Dennis as soon as they opened the back door. A hand in the small of his back shoved him forward and into the van that would take him from the crown court to jail. Lee had warned him: 'sweatboxes' he said the prisoners called them. There was a corridor down the centre of the van with a row of cells on either side, each with a bench fixed to the floor and a small window at head height. No toilet, just a couple of empty water bottles rolling around the floor.

By the time they moved off, there were four other prisoners locked in the individual mini cells. One of them was shouting and banging his fist on the metal side of the van. A guard in the driver's cab slid open a window grill.

"Cut it out, will ya."

Someone vomited. The acrid stench filled the vehicle.

"You filthy bastard!" exclaimed the guard.

Dennis sat on the plastic bench, gripping the edges as the van jolted over speedbumps. He rocked backwards and forwards, humming something his mother used to sing when he couldn't sleep.

There was a sudden loud shriek from one of the prisoners.

"This is a madhouse," he mumbled. His arms began to tremble and the fear he'd fought to suppress gripped him in the pit of his stomach.

It took over an hour for them to reach the prison gates. Dennis felt a sense of relief that his journey in the stinking sweatbox was over, and trepidation about what was to come. The van inched through several security gates, finally coming to a halt to the sound of a metal gate clanging shut. The rear doors were slowly opened. A beam of bright sunshine lit the dark interior of the van, dust motes dancing as they pleased.

One of the guards stepped up into the van and splashed a bucket of water over the floor. Dennis could smell the disinfectant in the spreading grey water. His cell was opened first;

"Out," shouted a prison guard, brandishing a pair of handcuffs.

He was led through a series of doors, placed into a holding cell with the other prisoners and told to stay calm. A stifling blanket of rank odours filled the air.

It takes a long time to get into prison.

The wait in the holding cell was eventually followed by two guards marching the prisoners, one at a time, to a small room. Two more prison officers were snapping on rubber gloves.

"Get undressed."

"Everything?"

"Yeah, everything."

Dennis had tried to convince himself it'd be just a strip search, nothing invasive. The rubber gloves confirmed his worst fears.

He was being led into a world he wanted no part of. Not that he put up any resistance, quite the opposite. He was compliant, as if sedated, letting the processing procedures carry him inextricably closer to the heart of the jail. The long corridors were painted in a pale green gloss and the concrete floors were matt red. It looked to Dennis like a long tongue emerging from the mouth of a large lizard.

"This is yours," the guard said, pointing to a cell door. He slid back a small hatch and peered in. "New mate for ya."

A thin, grey-faced man was sprawled on the lower bunk reading a magazine. He was wearing prison clothes: a well-worn dark-blue shirt and faded blue trousers. Dennis' outfit was barely worn. It marked him out as a 'new boy'. "Not as nasty as some, are ya, Dave?" said the guard.

The man grunted. "If you say so."

Dennis noticed his nicotine-stained fingers and the Rizla cigarette roller on the edge of his bunk.

"Make yourself comfortable, Dennis," said the guard. "This is as good as it gets. Just remember, make sure you keep your prison tag with you at all times." And with that last piece of advice, he was gone, closing the door with a loud slam.

Dave said little, other than he'd been in the same prison since his conviction for robbery with GBH five years earlier. It was said with a smirk, revealing stained teeth and a missing front incisor.

Dave was more talkative in the evenings after the last meal of the day, when they were lying on their bunks smoking one of his roll-ups. Instructions mainly, on what to do, who to talk to, who to avoid.

"You take my advice, stay away from the Fishers. They run the place. Drugs, fags, special treats. You heard of 'em? They come from your way."

Dennis shuddered at the revelation. His skin prickled. "Yeah, I know of a few."

"Just keep your head down, that's all I'm saying. One of the Fishers is the main man — Danny Fisher. But call him 'sir' if you want a quiet life. 'King Fisher' some call him. And watch out for the 'screw-boys'."

"Screw-boys?"

"They keep the peace, as much as is possible. They're the ones who have special links with some of the screws. It's a dangerous game. If they play it the wrong way they can end up in hospital, or worse. Some of them are snitches, giving the screws too much information. Most of 'em report back to Danny Fisher. Trading information, that's what they do. Parole comes easy for them, if they can make it that far."

"That it?"

Dave snarled. "Don't get stupid. This ain't the place to play the tough guy."

"Sorry," Dennis replied.

"Don't ever say that!" he hissed. "Not a word you use in this place, not if you want to be left alone. There's even a few screws who'll take the piss. Most of us just want to do our time. Some poor bastards are never left alone; nerds, grasses, spice heads, nonces. Stay well away from them. Last thing you want is to be picked on. And look out for the foot soldiers. Nasty bastards. They do Fisher's dirty work. Gives 'em status, see."

Dave's warnings had scared Dennis. He only felt comfortable when he was in his cell with the door closed.

"Got to show your face," Dave told him. "You can't hide, not in here. Put your name down for a job.

He was put on cleaning duties, mopping the floors in the main corridors usually alongside two, sometimes three, other inmates. They said little; whispered remarks about a guard, nods and sniggers at a couple of punks —those that sell 'favours' — a gesture, a flick of the hand, towards inmates they did deals with. It passed the time, but more importantly, it got him noticed. He began to relax. "I can deal with this," he told himself. "I'll make it ok." He began to take his meals and his breaks with a couple of the black prisoners also on cleaning. Over the next couple of months, they told him about their parents coming over from Jamaica in the early fifties. They talked about going back, as if they too had stepped off one of those migrant ships. Their sing-song accents became stronger whenever they talked about the 'old country'.

"You been to Jamaica?" Dennis asked.

They'd both laughed; deep resonant laughter that rumbled down the corridors.

"Nah. We're British, man. Just like you. T'is where our brothers live."

Dennis never felt easy. There were shouted threats, flare ups, fights between prisoners. Worse were the searches by prison guards looking for drugs, makeshift knives, mobile phones. It wasn't unknown for something to be planted in the cell of a prisoner who 'needed sorting'. He managed to escape any serious intimidation. His two black 'minders' were big and muscled, spending much of their time pumping iron.

And then it happened. Someone let it be known his dad was a prison officer at the Young Offenders Institute. Life became a living hell. Even the Jamaicans kept their distance, telling him to piss off whenever he tried to join them. No friendly slaps on the back, no big laugh echoing down the corridors when he walked towards them carrying a mop. Other prisoners kicked his bucket, sending grey water spilling across the floor. He was pushed, shoved and punched. In the canteen, he was forced to wait at the back of the line. Nearly every day he was made to scoop up food they'd tipped on the floor. They spat onto his plate and shoved knuckles into his mashed potatoes, wiping their hands on his prison shirt. The guards stood by and waited until the prisoners had done their worst before stepping in, shouting and tapping their batons on one of the tables.

"That's it, had your fun."

Dennis couldn't take much more. It'd gone on for over a month. It wasn't just the physical intimidation; it was the way everyone ignored him. They wrapped silence round him, like a tourniquet. It was at breakfast when he finally broke. It had been particularly ugly. The prisoners had taken it in turns to spit on every item he placed on his tray. Even the prisoner serving fried eggs stuck his finger in the yoke and tipped it over the edge of his tray. One of the guards pointed his baton at the trail of yolk dripping onto the floor,

"Clean up that mess!"

Dennis scooped up a fistful of egg and flung himself at the guard, managing to shove the palm of his hand into his face before he was grabbed by two other guards. Dennis scrapped as if his life depended on it, kicking, screaming, biting. He could taste blood as his teeth sank into the hand of one of the guards. Several prisoners joined in the fight, flinging Dennis around like a rag doll, elbowing guards, smashing chairs and tables. A klaxon alarm had prison guards cramming into the canteen, cracking heads with their batons and tossing cans of pepper spray.

It was suddenly over. Some of the prisoners began straightening tables and picking up chairs. Others stared at Dennis curled on the floor, rubbing his reddened eyes.

One of the guards poked him with a baton, and bawled,

"Get up! You're pathetic!"

As Dennis staggered to his feet, he was grabbed and pinned against the wall, his face rubbed against the rough block as handcuffs were snapped onto his wrists.

He was taken to an isolation cell — punishment cells the prisoners called them.

The heavy door slammed shut; steel-on-steel echoing in the bare, sterile room.

For most of the next day, Dennis refused to come out of his cell, lying on his bunk with a blanket pulled over his head. The guards gave him time, and then insisted he move. They provided an escort to the showers and the canteen. Prisoners hissed, even gobbed as he walked past, his head fixed on the floor. That night, Dennis lay face down on his cot, his hands gripping the angle-iron frame. His fingers snagged against a sharp edge at the end of the frame. It felt good, rubbing his wrists against the metal — carefully at first, and then more forcefully. He stopped to examine his wrist. The grazed, reddened flesh was smeared with blood. It felt satisfyingly painful. He sucked at the skin, pulling the oozing blood into his mouth. He waved his scarred wrist in the air and shouted at the cell door;

"Look at me!" He sucked harder, blood now seeping from the corners of his mouth.

A guard peered through the grill. "What the! ..."

Keys rattled, the cell door was flung open, the prison guard reached back and hit a red emergency button above the cell door.

Dennis could hear boots clattering down the corridor. He continued shouting, wailing loudly. One of the guards grabbed his wrist. Still holding Dennis' wrist, he turned towards the other guards; "Get the medic — quick!"

They trussed him in a restraint vest, pushed him onto his cot bed and told him to lie down and keep still. Dennis stared at the ceiling, wide-eyed.

The medic ordered the restraint vest to be removed.

"Not on my watch," he said in a bitter tone. "That thing is only for absolute emergencies." He waited, impatiently, for the vest to be removed. He lifted Dennis' arm and examined his wrist;

"Just superficial," he remarked letting Dennis' arm flop back on the bed. "I want him on 24-hour watch; he's not in a good state. I'll get the doc to look at him. It won't be until tomorrow, though."

"Suicide watch, I suppose?"

The medical orderly nodded. "You know the drill."

Dennis was lifted and half-dragged into a larger cell on the same corridor. It had two beds, a cot bed in the corner and a larger bed opposite.

I'll take the first shift," one of the guards said. "You stay calm, Dennis. You'll be here overnight." He turned to the other guard; "I think he's ok. I'll buzz if there's a problem. He's not the violent type."

"I want no trouble from you," the guard told him as he stretched out on the bed opposite. "Try and get some sleep."

Dennis closed his eyes. He felt strangely relaxed, safe, the frightening prison routine no longer filling his head. As if drugged by some narcotic, images swirled in his head;

He was back in the market, standing next to Maggie. They both looked across at Amy and then began kissing, snogging. Amy was screaming ... Dennis! Dennis! Maggie whispered in his ear ... forget her, Dennis. Forget her ...

He woke with a jerk and looked vacantly around the room — no Amy, no Maggie, no market, just his cell.

"You ok, Dennis?" he heard the guard say.

He nodded, and rolled over onto his side, too scared to let his mind search for any more images.

He was barely awake when he heard the cell door close.

"How's he doin'" the new guard asked.

"He seems ok," was the reply. Dennis didn't think that was the right answer. He thought about putting them straight but let the moment pass. The new guard was an old hand. He'd watched high-risk prisoners many times throughout his long career. He talked almost constantly, despite Dennis lying still and uncommunicative.

"What out about you, Dennis?" he suddenly asked. "Must be someone out there."

It took Dennis by surprise. He was answering before he realised.

"Amy. She writes sometimes."

"Girlfriend, is she?"

"Uh ... No, just a friend."

"Sounds like someone who cares."

"Yeah ... suppose."

Dennis wished now he'd replied to just one of her letters. It had seemed so pointless.

Chapter 14

Dennis had slept well: he felt secure and safe. Breakfast was brought to his windowless cell. He devoured it eagerly, soaking up the last of his fried eggs with a bread roll.

The guard laughed, "Enjoyed that?" Dennis nodded. "The doc will look at you later, probably after lunch. If he says so, you'll be able to go back to your cell."

Dennis hung his head, "Didn't think it'd be that quick."

"Look, Dennis. This isn't a bloody hotel. The longer you spend here, the tougher it'll be when you go back. I shouldn't be saying this, but you starting that fight in the canteen like you did will have got you some respect."

The prison doctor shuffled as much as walked. He had a shock of wiry, grey hair that looked as though it had been left to its own devices and dark staring eyes supported by crescents of crinkly flesh. He looked old and tired.

"This him?"

The guard nodded. "Yeah, doc. Prisoner Dennis Barrett."

He took out a pencil light from his inside jacket pocket and shone the thin beam towards Dennis. "Just want to have a look at your pupils." He leant forwards, lifting Dennis' chin, "Eyes wide …"

Dennis could smell coffee on his breath and see stains on the lapel of his jacket.

"Any headaches?"

Dennis shook his head.

"How are you feeling?"

"Ok, I suppose."

The doctor turned to the prison guard; "Is he eating?"

"Yeah, had a good breakfast. He just finished lunch."

"Good, good. Let me have a look at that wrist ... He's fine," he remarked, as if Dennis had a mild cold.

Dennis was escorted back to his cell shortly after the doctor left.

Dave was lying on his bunk. He lowered the magazine he was reading just long enough to catch Dennis' eye.

"You're back," he growled. The cell was stiflingly hot and rank with the stench of sweat, and unwashed clothes. Dennis stretched out on his bed trying to ignore the clanging noise of cell doors and the shouts of both prisoners and guards.

Dave aimed his magazine at the table fixed to the wall. It skidded over the formica surface and onto the floor. Dennis reached, instinctively, and picked it up. Photos of glossy, expensive cars filled the cover.

"Got a message for you," Dave snarled. "Fisher wants to see you."

Dennis felt a cold sweat in the small of his back. "Fisher? Why?"

"No idea." He chuckled; "I didn't ask. One of his minders will come for you before lockdown."

Someone gripped Dennis' elbow as they filed into the canteen. The line parted as they approached the counter. Mashed potatoes, grilled fish and peas were carefully placed on his plate with a mug of tea. No jostling, no spitting in his food, no-one threatening to snatch his tray.

He followed the thickset man who'd gripped his arm to a table well away from the food counter and the steam-filled kitchen.

Prisoners tucked in their chairs and leaned forward as they walked past.

"Eat up. Mr Fisher doesn't like to be kept waiting."

Dennis struggled to eat; his chest felt tight and his throat ached.

"Leave it," ordered the 'minder'. "Let's go." He was taken to the top floor. Most of the cell doors were open, not a guard in sight. The minder leaned round the door of a cell at the end of the corridor,

"He's here, boss." Dennis was shoved forward. He knew it was a Fisher as soon as the man turned to face him. The same eyes as Billy Fisher — pale, like washed-out denims. The same broad nose, and a deep knife scar at the corner of his mouth that stretched across his face.

"Take a seat, Dennis." Fisher pointed in the direction of a lounge chair squeezed between the cell wall and a card table with a faded, green baize top.

"Heard about your bit of trouble." He tutted. "It shouldn't happen. It's not your fault your dad's a screw, is it?"

Dennis tried not to stare at Fisher. He was stockily built with rounded shoulders and the thick forearms of someone who'd spent time lifting weights. They looked alabaster smooth; veinless, bloodless.

He sat on a wooden chair, his eyes wide and wild. "You know what pisses me off, Dennis? Thugs. Violence is something to be used sparingly — when it's needed —otherwise it's meaningless. Loses its punch." He took a pair of wire-framed spectacles from his top pocket, and wrapped them across his face, stretching the loops behind his ears. "I dislike random acts of violence. Too many thugs in this place, as you well know. That's why I wanted a little chat. If you like, I'll have a word — put a stop to all this nastiness."

Dennis' weak bladder wasn't helping. He squirmed in his seat.

"The problem with this place is it's full of violence — stuffed in, bottled. It doesn't take much to set it off. That's not what I like, Dennis. It interferes with business. We all get tarred with the same brush. Lockdowns, searches — and all because there's been a spot of violence. Oh, don't get me wrong, I'm all for a bit of violence when it's needed."

'Violence, violence ...' Dennis shuddered. Fisher seemed to be deliberately repeating the word. 'Is he blaming me?'

"Knew Billy, didn't ya? Heard you were a mate. Anyone who's a mate of a Fisher deserves protection. You'll be left alone Dennis, I'll see to that. One of the Jamaican lads will mind you. You sit with them, nobody else. Course, I'll need you to run a few messages. It's business — I help you, and you help me."

Dennis nodded, not sure if he should say anything. His eye caught sight of a large spider centred in its web in the corner of the ceiling. It was devouring its prey.

Fisher leaned forward, his squat nose almost touching Dennis'. "I've a good memory — a very good memory," he said, tapping the side of his head with his finger. "It's like a filing system. I'll keep a mental note and my lads will keep a watch. You'll have no trouble, not as long as you work for me." He leaned back on his chair and smiled. "That ok, Dennis?"

"Er ... yes, thanks, Mr Fisher."

"Good. Oh, just one more thing. I won't forget your dad is a screw. It's my memory, see." He smirked, "It won't let me."

A prisoner stepped into the cell waving a mobile phone, "Message for you, Boss."

Fisher grabbed the phone and began reading a text.

"We'll keep in touch, Dennis," he said, his eyes fixed on his phone.

No-one touched him, not now he was in with the Fishers. Even the prison guards treated him differently. Dave wasn't as deferential.

"You watch yourself. He'll want you in ways you haven't dreamed of. Sold yourself to the devil you have."

"Don't need your advice. I know what I'm doing."

Dave shrugged his shoulders. "Just don't get me involved."

It was in the canteen when he received his first job. Two of Danny Fisher's acolytes plonked themselves on the bench opposite.

"Mr Fisher wants you to collect. A late payment. Wants his money and a reminder to pay on time. Someone you know — your mate, Dave."

"I'll ask him ..."

"Ask him! We don't ask, Dennis. We tell."

Why Dave? He's been ok to me, was the thought in Dennis' head. I can't do this. Another thought arrived in his brain like an urgent message. He realised, in that instant, that all he wanted was to get out of the place still sane, and in one piece. Friendship meant nothing: friendship was dangerous. Friendship was his enemy. He allowed himself to smile. He'd found the solution; it was obvious.

The two minders stayed just outside the cell door. "Ok, Dennis. He's all yours."

Dave was lying on his bunk. "What's up, your pals left you?"

"I'm collecting, Dave. You owe Mr Fisher."

"What, for that scraggy bit of tobacco? It was rubbish stuff."

"Look, Dave. If you know what's good for you ..."

"Quite the little hard man, ain't ya?"

The two minders were in the cell before Dennis realised.

"Problem is there?"

Dave jumped off his bunk and reached under his pillow for a battered tobacco tin. He prized it open, almost spilling the contents onto the floor. One of the minders grabbed the tin and emptied the tin.

"I owe fifty quid; there's seventy in there."

"Tough." He handed Dennis a crudely made knuckle duster. "Pop him one. Needs a reminder, don't you Dave?"

Dennis' hands trembled as he pushed the knuckle duster over his fingers. It had been made for a man with much larger hands. He had to grab it with his other hand to stop it falling to the floor. Dave, his face blanched white, instinctively ducked as Dennis swung his fist. The blow caught him on his shoulder. One of the minders snatched at the knuckle duster, wrenching it off Dennis' fingers. "For Christ's sake! ..."

He swung at Dave. The blow sent him spinning against the wall, blood streaming from his mouth. He turned to Dennis; "Got to leave a mark, see. Always leave a mark."

The other minder threw a small plastic bag onto Dave's bunk. "Mr Fisher sent your next stash."

"I don't want anymore ..."

"Course you do. Just don't be late. Oh, this'll be sixty."

"Inflation," added the other minder. They both laughed. Dennis stared at Dave as the minders headed off down the corridor. "Sorry," he mumbled, immediately regretting his remark.

Dave swiped at the blood round his mouth. His nose was bleeding heavily, and his lower lip was beginning to swell.

"Piss off."

Nobody asked what happened or who'd rearranged Dave's face. The word was circulated in calculated, knowing whispers. The only hint of surprise was that it was Dennis.

"That runt?" Only the stupid took it any further. The usual reply told them all they needed to know. "Yeah — him and Fisher's goons."

Two of Fisher's men sat across from Dennis. It was a week since Dave's panic-filled face had been left battered and bruised, his lip less swollen and the side of his face now a pallet of colour. Chat had gone. The silence that filled their cell was punctuated only by the sounds of Dave's restless sleep and occasional sighs as he padded carefully round the cell. Dennis had taken to getting to breakfast early, just as the kitchen started at 6:00am. He sat at the table Fisher's cronies used; always left empty, as if it had a 'reserved' sign a permanent fixture. One of them took several deep-fried chips from Dennis' plate and took a slurp of tea. His mate shoved Dennis' mug to one side, as if it was a barrier of some kind. "Got a job for you," he whispered, pushing a piece of paper into Dennis' shirt pocket. "He's all yours."

"Do a good job this time," his pal said. "We'll be watching."

Dennis waited for them to leave the canteen, looked round to make sure there were no screws watching and took the scrap of paper out of his pocket. There was a scribbled name and cell number. He knew Jimmy McCann. A small man, a Glaswegian, with a thick accent, squashed face and a lightning temper. He was someone to avoid. McCann had singled him out, not that he'd ever touched him or spat in his food, he'd simply stood in front of Dennis and fixed him with a threatening glare, his fists in front of his barrel chest, like a boxer. The word was he'd crossed Fisher, adding his own brand of extortion, demanding additional payments.

Dennis had imagined it would be some other old lag, someone like Dave who hadn't paid for his last pouch of tobacco, not one of the toughest, hard men in the prison. This was a test, he knew that. If he couldn't deliver, there'd be no protection. He clenched his fists and gritted his teeth. Jimmy McCann deserved a thumping.

Dennis saw Jimmy McCann swaggering down the corridor heading towards his cell, arms held wide, like a gun slinger. He suddenly reached out and grabbed a prisoner by his lapels. He tried to pull away, but there was no escaping Jimmy McCann's grasp. The man's jacket stretched as tight as an elasticated bandage and his body arced, bending like a straw. Dennis watched, his legs uncertain, as if on weak, swaying springs. He wished he'd taken a piss. McCann tilted his head as though he was about to inflict a 'Glasgow kiss' and then laughed, letting his victim move back, hesitantly, as if genuflecting. The prisoner walked quickly away without looking back, McCann's laughter echoing after him. Dennis took a deep breath and shouted, surprising himself with the strength of his voice.

"McCann ... Need a word."

Jimmy McCann spun round; "What the hell! ... Are you talking to me?"

"Yeah."

"What business has the likes you got with me?"

Dennis willed his legs to take him closer. "Fisher business."

"Oh, yeah?" McCann's voice didn't carry the same threat. He glanced over Dennis' shoulder at a couple of Fisher's loyal heavies standing at the end of the corridor.

Dennis nodded towards McCann's cell. "It's private, Jimmy."

Jimmy McCann had been given his own cell. Fisher had fixed it. It was what he did for his top band of enforcers.

McCann slowly closed the cell door. "This better be good," he said. "Can't believe Fisher is using someone as pathetic as ... What's it about, anyway?"

Dennis breathed hard, exhaling slowly. "You've been on the take."

"That it? We all take a bit of a cut, Fisher knows that."

"You've gone too far, Jimmy. Mr Fisher warned you before."

McCann sprang forward and grabbed Dennis' shirt collar. "You think I'm going to take orders from you!" They both turned as the cell door was flung open. The two huge minders grabbed Jimmy and pinned him against the wall. McCann's chest seemed to deflate. His battered face looked worn and ugly.

Dennis glared at him. "Don't you ever speak to me like that again!"

McCann glanced at the minders. "Ok ... ok." His voice was softer. The hard edginess had gone. "You've given your message. I'll go and tell him ..."

Dennis stabbed his finger into McCann's chest. "No, Jimmy. You're on your own now. You don't work for Mr Fisher anymore."

The minders released their grip. McCann sank heavily onto his bunk.

"Get up," Dennis ordered.

McCann got slowly to his feet.

"Put your ugly head against the wall." He was enjoying it. McCann was his for the taking. He grabbed the back of his neck and smashed his face against the block wall.

Dennis strode down the corridor smiling, feeling elated. Other prisoners moved quickly out of his way. The word was out.

Although he never felt comfortable beating up someone like Dave who wanted little else than a few smokes, maybe a joint, banging on the cell door of a prisoner who'd made his life hell gave him a sense of exhilaration. They were the ones who showed the most fear, they were the ones for whom it was payback time. Prisoners knew all too well about the damage Fisher's gang could do. They controlled the supply of almost every illegal drug, as well as access to mobile phones. Then there were prison guards who were willing to turn a blind eye to Fisher's activities, some even willing to take payments which at first seemed just a perk of the job, before they realised they were snared. That's when they became paranoid that they'd lose their jobs, or worse, end up on the wrong side of a prison cell.

Dennis was virtually free to wander round as he pleased. He relished his status, quickly establishing a reputation as an enforcer, although he always ensured he was accompanied by a couple of the Fisher heavies. It gave him the freedom to inflict his own style of physical beating. Cracking heads against the block wall of a cell was his modus operandi. He even acquired a nickname — 'the blocker'. There was no mistaking a prisoner who'd been 'blocked'. A rough, deep graze and blue-black contusions that resembled weeping plums on the forehead. He'd seen them tremble as he, and a couple of minders, pushed their way into a cell.

"I'm surprised at you, Dennis." Fisher's gold tooth flashed as his lip curled into a mocking smile. "Quite the hard man ..." He laughed, "Not that I'm complaining. How long have you got left in this palace of mine?"

"Next month, Mr Fisher. About that."

"That's what I thought. Heard you were given a 'gold star' by the parole board." He leaned forward, "Just remember what I've done for you in here. This last year or so might have been ... different, shall we say?"

Dennis watched the lip slowly unfurl over Fisher's gold tooth. He nodded,

"Yeah ... er ..."

"That's what I like, Dennis, enthusiasm." He snapped open a newspaper. "Nice to have a chat."

Dennis crept out of the cell, as if treading on hot coals. "Thanks, Mr Fisher," he managed.

Chapter 15

Dennis had marked off the final days to his release in a notebook he kept under his pillow. It became a nightly ritual, staring at his scribbles, and then turning to the next blank page. Slowly and deliberately, he printed, in large capitals;

'OUT TOMORROW'.

It was only eighteen months, but it felt like an eternity, his mind forever scarred by what he'd experienced — by the drugs that helped him cope, and the daily encounter with threats, stares, intimidation, and the vicious violence he'd become a part of. It was the protection from Fisher that had saved him. He thought about his last meeting with Danny Fisher. He'd tried to thank him, but Fisher had dismissed his stuttering attempt with a dismissive sneer. "Just remember, what I've done for you ..." Fisher's words had seemed innocuous enough ... but not now. He shook his head as if making an attempt to dislodge those last words from his head.

"Thank God," Dennis muttered as the first rays of the morning sun began to creep across the white-washed walls of his cell. It was the end of a sleepless, restless night. He lay still, straining to hear the sounds of the jail beginning to stir, watching a spider scurrying across the ceiling and into a crack above his bed. The prison seemed reluctant to face another boring, mundane day. He began to think he might have got it wrong, or the bizarre idea they may have forgotten. Sounds began to club together — the rattle of cell doors, morning shouts from prisoners, orders barked from prison guards — like players in an orchestra warming their instruments, one by one, group by group, in a slow, discordant cacophony.

Dennis heard a rattle of keys first, then the screech of the cell door's twin bolts being unlocked. He sat on the edge of his bed, his heart pounding. It seemed an age before the prison guard spoke.

"Ok, time to go. You ready? Got your stuff?"

Dennis grabbed his bag and followed the guard down the corridor, through a double set of barred gates and then to a cell near the reception area at the front of the prison. He was given a set of clothes; underwear, socks, jeans, a tee shirt, sweater and a jacket. He signed his release form and ripped open the brown envelope the guard had pushed towards him. He pocketed the contents — fifty pounds in crisp ten-pound notes, and a rail pass.

Two prison guards escorted him through three sets of doors and into a brightly lit area near the entrance. One of the guards pushed a buzzer. A thin woman appeared and slid open a screen window,

"He'll need to sign," she said, pivoting a ledger across the shelf in front of the window. She handed a key to one of the guards;

"Locker 5."

The guard returned carrying a cardboard box and a duffle bag.

"Your stuff," he said. "Check it. Sign this sheet."

Dennis shoved the items into the bag; his watch, a belt, his wallet and his mobile phone. He ran his hand around the inside of the empty box, as if wondering why he didn't have more personal items.

"Ok, let's go." He was escorted to the main gates, the prison officers staying close as if they were concerned he might object to being released. Within minutes he was through the main gates and out onto the street. It was still early, still chilly, despite the bright morning sun. He zipped up his jacket and followed the directions they'd given him.

The guard was right, it was only ten minutes to the station. It seemed strange, standing waiting for the commuter train. He suddenly felt lonely. In prison, he knew people; knew their names, knew who to talk to, who to avoid. There were rules; rules of respect, rules of order. He realised, watching the digital clock flick through the seconds like a pack of cards in a riffle shuffle, there are no rules, not out here. Just laws to obey ... or to break.

There were smells, different smells. Aromatic coffee and the yeasty smell of fresh rolls from a small kiosk on the platform, a waft of perfume from a woman who walked slowly past, a whiff from a labrador standing obediently next to its owner. The train eased slowly into the platform, pulling to a halt with a screech from the wheels, steel on steel. Most passengers waited patiently for the doors to open, others were more agitated, hurrying along the platform, pushing impatiently on the door button.

Dennis took a window seat in the second carriage and peered up at the route map displayed above the coat rack. Just four stops. The bus he wanted left from outside the station. It was one he'd taken many times.

He felt his pulse quicken as he stepped off the bus and stood, staring across at the junction where he'd ploughed into the car and killed Lisa's boyfriend. No signs now of the smashed cars; no glass scattered over the road, no twisted metal, no pools of blood. He instinctively touched his forehead, running his fingers along the deep scar slashed across his forehead, his permanent reminder. It had served him well in prison, that scar — like a campaign medal.

He crossed the road and walked slowly up the quiet street of semi-detached houses, wondering if he was doing the right thing.

"I'm their son, right?" he said to himself. The street appeared much posher than he remembered. It struck him as odd that someone like him had actually lived in this leafy, quiet area. He doubted if anyone else from this row of semi-detached houses had served time in jail. He spat onto the pavement and wiped his mouth with the back of his hand. He had the thought that he was, now, more like a Fisher, one of the tough hoods who'd grown up on the Marshbrook estate. He smiled to himself, lengthened his stride and gritted his teeth. I'm a tough bastard, that's all they need to know. If they don't like it, well …

He paused for a moment at the sight of his dad's old Volvo, ran his hand along the side as if to reassure himself it was the right house and rang the doorbell. It took two rings before his father opened the door. They stood eyeballing one another …

"No warm welcome?" he said, curling his lip into that mocking sneer he'd perfected in prison.

"Who is it, Michael?" It was his mother calling from the kitchen. His father filled the doorway, standing erect, defiant. "Go away, Dennis. We don't want you around."

Barbara was in the hallway, legs planted firmly on the hall carpet. Michael pushed past Dennis, "You talk to him …" he said, as he strode off.

Dennis and Barbara stood in silence. The kitchen door slammed shut.

"You can't stay," she said. "Lisa will be home in a couple of hours."

There was an abruptness in her tone he hadn't expected. He suddenly felt very angry. He kicked out at his canvass bag. "You've no idea how hard it's been for me. You try spending time locked in a cell."

"You got off lightly, Dennis," he heard his mother say. It was a voice he barely recognised. She wants me to go, he suddenly realised. He glared at her — It was all his fault; he'd got to her. He heard his mother say something about eating — with them! The hell he would!

He grabbed his bag, swearing under his breath.

"Keep your bloody food. I'll stay at a mate's place."

Before he realised, Barbara was pushing an envelope into his hand.

"You'll need some money."

Dennis slowly reached out and took the envelope in his extended fingers. He felt his lip quiver, "Thanks, Ma."

Dennis knew he had few, if any, options. He daren't call Amy; she'd written several times, but he hadn't bothered to reply. He couldn't see the point. She wouldn't want an ex-con hanging around, would she? He'd kept the last letter she sent, the one telling him she'd finally managed to get Lee to leave — with a little help from Jake and Maggie. She didn't say anything about Lee smacking her around.

Somehow, he no longer associated Lee with Amy. Lee was just another scumbag, but he might let him stay, even just for a week or so. He called his mobile.

"Christ, Dennis, there's not much room in this place. You'd have to sleep on the couch ... Don't know ..."

"Please, Lee. I'm desperate."

"Got any money?"

Dennis paused, "A bit," he replied.

"Ok," growled Lee. "I could use a driver, if you're interested?"

"Yeah, that'd be great. Haven't got a licence," he added as if an afterthought. "Still disqualified."

"That'll be your problem. Just don't get caught."

Dennis paused, as though pondering the implications. "Ok. What's the worst that can happen?" he said, trying to sound lighthearted.

He heard Lee laugh, "You'll be back in jail.

It wasn't difficult to find Lee's place, only a few streets away from the room he'd rented from Jake. It was a three-bed tenement with a galley kitchen and a bathroom at the end in what had once been the kitchen pantry. The lounge was front to back, a window a brick's length from the front door and a larger window overlooking the rear yard. A door in the corner led to wooden stairs and the upper floor. There was a couch along one wall, two battered armchairs and a table littered with crushed cans of lager and several empty pizza boxes. Dennis threw his bag onto the couch, "It'll do," he muttered.

Lee had expanded into the taxi business — two old BMWs with soft seats and loose springs. He kept them parked on a rough piece of waste ground that had once been the site of an end-tenement, the marks of the pitch roof still visible on the gable-end of the adjacent building. Lee assigned one of the cars to Dennis.

"Not as lucrative," Lee explained, referring to the shifting of drugs and fags, "but more regular, and not as much hassle — too many nutters involved now. I still do a bit of delivering cars for the Donovans."

Dennis didn't mind, not at first. It was easy work, usually picking up late-night drinkers in various stages of inebriation. If they looked as if they might throw up in his taxi, he left them to find someone else. It happened just once. It took hours of scrubbing until the tang of bleach was stronger than the stench of vomit. He much preferred taking some old lady to the supermarket. Opening the car door and helping them with their bags made him feel as if he was suddenly, and just for that moment, in a different world, one without the edginess he'd become accustomed to.

"Thank you, young man."

The frailer they were, the more grateful they seemed. The regulars he called by their first names, as if they were personal acquaintances.

He was glad he'd put an umbrella in the car. Rain had been forecast, but not the unpredictable bursts that had started around lunchtime, threatening to drench his shopping ladies. Getting in and out of his taxi and struggling to open his umbrella against gusting rain had left his shirt soaked and his jeans sticking to his legs. The musty smell of wet cloth had begun to fill the car. It was mid-afternoon: he was driving back having dropped off Mrs Arnold, one of his shopping ladies. The wipers struggled to cope with the torrents of water sloshing across his windscreen. He leaned forward, peering at distorted images. The noisy thrum of the thrashing wiper blades didn't help. Shop windows threw light across the wet pavements and streetlights began to flicker.

He took a second glance at the figure running across the street, her meagre-looking rain jacket held up over her head in a futile attempt to protect herself from the sheets of rain now blowing in near horizontal gusts. It looked like Amy ... He pulled over towards the kerb. His tyre ploughed through an overflowing gutter, sloshing an arc of water onto the pavement. It was Amy; thoroughly drenched, glaring at his car as if she couldn't believe what had just happened. He inched forward along the edge of the pavement, lowered the passenger side, window and called after her,

"Amy, Amy!"

She spun round, pulling her rain jacket tight round her head, like a mantilla. Her angry look weakened. She pushed her rain-sodden hair to one side and leant towards his car.

"Dennis, is that you?"

"Yes — Get in!"

She threw her rain jacket through the car window, grabbed the door with both hands and flung herself into the front seat. Dennis lifted the wet coat from his lap and flicked at the water on his legs.

"Serves you right, Dennis — where've you been anyway?"

Dennis glanced across; she was shivering. Her hair hung long and straight, and her lips were blue with cold.

"Not a word! Why, Dennis? I heard you got out over a month ago." She was shouting, pushing her voice against the sharp bursts of rain thudding off the roof.

Dennis gripped the steering wheel and eased the car forward.

"Sorry," he mumbled as the rain quietened. "I didn't think you'd want to see me."

"Why do you think I wrote to you?" she said, her voice now calmer. The wiper blades ticked slowly across the windscreen.

"I should have written," he replied. "I kept your letters."

The rain stopped and a thin sun began to brighten the sky.

"Yes, Dennis, you should have written. What did you expect — that I'd always be here, waiting for you to appear?"

"No... no. I just thought you'd move on. I hated to think you might be with someone else." He paused and stared straight ahead. He was relieved he wasn't having to look directly at her. It made it easier, somehow. He was searching for the right words. "Sometimes I didn't read your letters straight away, in case they told me things I didn't want to know," he said, slowly, carefully, picking through the words. "I read them over and over, wishing I was with you, annoyed at myself for thinking the worst."

In his first few months in prison, they'd taunted him when they heard about one of Amy's letters. They were always opened — checking for drugs he was told — and well thumbed, as if half the prison guards had read them. Once, a couple of prisoners had snatched one of her letters and waved it in the air before passing it to others to read.

"It's from Amy! Sounds like a tart. She'll be getting shagged by some wanker." Someone tore it into shreds, scattering the bits of paper on the floor. A prison guard just stood and watched and then told him to pick up the pieces.

Dennis couldn't tell her he dreaded receiving one of her letters. Someone, one of the guards he guessed, had taken to drawing a heart in red pencil, sometimes adding a woman's breasts and a large penis. The pages were invariably stained with grubby thumb prints. That's why he'd never replied. He wanted her to stop writing. Those prisoners and guards who dirtied her neat writing had violated her, as good as.

Being one of Fishers gang had changed all that. By then her letters were less frequent. They were still torn open and crinkled but that was normal — just some officer who sat like a clerk, opening the mail. He guessed that some of Fisher's men had seen her letters, maybe even Danny Fisher, but none of them said a word. They just accepted he had the right to crack a few heads. As his release date neared, he began to reflect on what he'd done, who he'd become. He winced at the thought; and all because he needed their protection. Would it be always like this? Sometimes he wept, silently wishing he was braver.

He often thought about those few years working in the market. 'It was Billy Fisher's fault,' he repeatedly told himself. Was it? Was it really all Billy Fisher's fault — all this trouble, this life he seemed destined to lead? He wanted to be different. He wanted to be seen as honest and reliable, someone people could trust. He wanted to be looked up to, respected — like his father.

Amy stared straight ahead, her breathing now slow and soft. They were approaching a set of traffic lights; "Take the next left," she instructed. "You can drop me at my place. I need to get changed before I freeze to death."

"You and Lee finished?" he asked as they drove along the shiny, wet tarmac.

"That bastard. He got nasty, very nasty."

"Oh ... What happened?"

"Not now, Dennis." Her voice trembled.

"You ok?"

"Just cold," she replied. "Look, why don't you call me — still got my number?"

"Yeah ... I'll do that."

She leaned over and gave him a quick peck on his cheek. "Thanks for the lift."

He watched her dash for the door, a pink key-fob dangling from her fingers. She turned and waved as he pulled away. He placed his hand on the wet passenger seat and smiled.

Dennis' palms were sweating. His mobile phone felt like a piece of soap. He gripped it firmly, punched in Amy's mobile number and waited, tapping on the steering wheel with the stainless-steel ring he wore on the index finger of his left hand. It suddenly went to 'answer phone'. He paused, and then hit 'redial'.

He hoped he hadn't misunderstood. She did mean it, didn't she?

He almost dropped the phone when he heard Amy's breathless voice,

"Dennis! I couldn't get my phone out of my bag — sorry."

"Hi, Amy." His chest felt tight. Things he wanted to say seemed lodged somewhere in his brain. "You ok?"

He heard her grunt, dismissively. "Is that all you've got to say?"

"No ... no. I'd like to see you ..."

"If I had any sense, I'd tell you to get out of my life. The last thing I want is another man in my life like Lee."

"I'm not like him ..."

"I know that," she replied. "It's just I don't have much trust, not yet."

"Just friends?"

"Maybe ... Yes, I'd like that."

Dennis waited for her to continue. "Amy, you still there?"

"Sorry — I wasn't sure what more to say."

"Maybe we could meet up?"

He heard her laugh. "Just don't stand me up. It's hard to trust a man who's ignored me for so long."

"I won't. I'll be there!"

"Where, exactly?"

"Oh, how about that coffee shop in the High Street, tomorrow ... say around three?"

"Not around three, Dennis. I won't wait."

Dennis felt his chest tighten. "Yeah. See you at three," he said, breathing hard.

She was late. He'd felt compelled to buy a coffee. It was now half-finished and nearly cold. He'd given up watching the door and was aimlessly staring out of the window that looked out over the car park. His heart rate jumped when he spotted her getting out of a blue mini. He stood and waved as she came through the door.

"Hi, Dennis. Sorry I'm late."

He smiled; "No problem. I think you're entitled. Two coffees," he said as a waitress approached.

They sat eyeing one another as if nervous they might say something easily misunderstood.

"You got rid of Lee, then?"

"I told Maggie I wanted him out. She got Jake and a couple of his pals to make sure he left."

"She's ok," Dennis remarked.

Amy laughed. "She sometimes asks about you. I might be jealous if she was twenty years younger."

"Oh ..."

"Don't get your hopes up, Dennis. 'Friends', remember?"

Dennis chuckled, "Yeah, just friends ... What happened between you and Lee?" he asked.

"I told you," she replied, abruptly. "I got him to leave. That's all you need to know."

Dennis paused; he knew he had to tell her. "I'm doing a bit of driving for Lee. He nodded towards the car park. That's his taxi."

"Yes, I know. Just be careful, Dennis. He can get nasty, very nasty."

Dennis looked at Amy. The warmth she'd exuded was suddenly snuffed. "Did he hit you?"

She sat erect and stared across the coffee shop, her eyes flitting nervously. "I told mum I hit my head on the door. She knew, though ... She told Maggie it was Lee ..."

"The bastard!"

She reached across the table and touched his arm; "Forget it, Dennis. He's out of my life now. Don't cause any trouble — please."

"I'm working for him, driving his taxi and staying at his place!"

Chapter 16

Lee had left him a text: 'Gone to Liverpool. PARTY TIME!'

Dennis knew all about Lee's parties. He'd been a couple of times. They'd get pissed in a bar where his mates gathered, then on to a grubby flat with grimy window curtains, take-away boxes piled in the kitchen, bin-liners spewing empty lager cans, and always a fug of fags and a haze of marijuana.

He was glad Lee was away. It gave him time to think, to plan.

Dennis hesitated before phoning the number Danny Fisher had given him the day before his release.

"Think of it as a bit of insurance," he'd said. "Just in case. You call my cousin, Brendan if you need help."

Stay away from the Fishers, a voice in his head repeated, over and over.

Stay away ... don't call ...

The voice weakened.

He stabbed at the green call button. It took several rings.

A gruff voice barked from his phone,

"Yeah?"

Dennis almost dropped his mobile. He'd been a millisecond away from ending the call.

"Brendan? Mr Fisher gave me this number."

"Danny? He's in prison."

"I just got out. He said to call if I needed help."

"You are?"

"Dennis, Dennis Barrett."

"Oh, yeah, he mentioned you. Your dad's a screw, right?"

"Yes," Dennis replied, his voice soft, as if apologising for his father.

"What d' ya want?"

Sweat had gathered in Dennis' armpit. "I need someone to get a warning — something they won't forget."

"Doesn't come cheap."

"I don't have any money ..."

"Not money, Dennis. I might need your help sometime. That's all we need for a friend of the family."

Dennis hesitated. "Thanks," he murmured.

"Who is it?"

"Lee, Lee Hogan. Runs a taxi business."

"Oh, him. Does a bit for Donovan's, bit of deliverin'. What do want with that low life?"

"He was smacking his girlfriend around. She kicked him out of her flat but he keeps phoning her, making threats."

"A friend of yours, is she?"

"Yeah ... I don't want that bastard anywhere near her."

"Is that it? I'd take personal delight in arranging a visit to see Lee Hogan. Where's he livin' now?"

Dennis hesitated; "On Cameron Street. Number 12."

"Who else lives there?"

"Couple of lads drift in and out." He paused; "I've been staying there since I got out."

"Very cosy." Brendan Fisher laughed, "Not a lover's tiff, is it?"

"No ... nothing like that."

"So, you just want him to stop bothering your girlfriend? That it?"

"I'm driving one of his taxi cars. I want to keep it."

"I'm sure he'll be only too glad to let you have it. Take my advice — move out. Sometimes wounded animals can be dangerous, especially if you are too close."

Dennis was glad there was still no sign of Lee. It took only a few minutes to grab his stuff — little more than the clothes he'd been given on leaving prison. He ripped off the lid from one of the pizza boxes and scribbled a note with a thick black marker;

DON'T BOTHER AMY AGAIN.

I'M KEEPING THE CAR.

He cleared the mantelpiece with a single swipe. Lager cans bounced across the wooden floor; several glass tumblers smashed against the hearth. He crushed his heel into a framed photo of Lee standing proudly in front of his three taxis. He kicked it across the room, surveyed the damage, and left, leaving the door wide open and his key on the doormat.

He called Amy. He felt elated, his body tingling with energy.

"Dennis!" She laughed, "You again!"

He sniggered, "Yeah, it's me."

"Are you ok?"

"Never better. Just got my stuff from Lee's place."

There was a long pause.

"Amy, you ok?"

"He left another message on my phone ..."

"When?"

"Last night. He's after me, Dennis, I know it."

"Listen, Amy, he won't be bothering you again. I've seen to it."

"I ... I don't want you involved, Dennis. Please don't do anything stupid."

"It's all taken care of. I left him a message — told him to not to bother you ever again."

"It won't do any good. It'll just make it worse. I know him ..."

"Forget him, Amy. He won't come anywhere near you, believe me."

"I'm scared. He'll come for me; I just know he will."

"I can come round, if it'd make you feel safer." He took a deep breath. His heart was pounding, "You still have a room spare?"

She laughed. "And it's got some things you left."

He saw Amy struggling to lock her front door as he pulled into one of the car spaces. She glanced up, a look of terror on her face. He suddenly realised: he was in a different car. He'd taken Lee's best, one he'd recently purchased, a neat Honda Civic. He unlatched the seatbelt and flung open the car door, calling after her as she ran down the street;

"Amy ... Amy! It's me!"

She kept running — down to the end of the shops and round the corner. Dennis sprinted as hard as he could, ignoring the car door hanging open as if waiting for one of his old ladies to appear with her shopping bag. He saw her crossing the road, running towards a bus that was pulling into a stop. He shouted as loud as his breathless lungs would allow.

"AMY! AMY!"

She tripped on the kerb landing heavily on a grass strip that edged the pavement. He saw her clawing at the ground, her knees pumping against the dog-fouled ground. He caught up with her just as she staggered to her feet.

"Leave me alone!" A man in the bus queue moved towards them, "You alright, love?"

She spun round, panting, as if about to identify her attacker. Her chest was heaving.

"Dennis! It's you!"

The man stepped back,

"It's ok," she said. "I thought it was ... someone else, thanks."

Dennis helped her to her feet and hugged her. She was shaking.

"I thought ..."

He held her until her breathing slowed. "My fault, I should have realised."

She suddenly pushed him back; "Why are you still working for Lee?"

"I'm not," he replied. "I took one of his cars."

"You did what!? He'll come after you, Dennis. He'll come after both of us, him and his mates."

"No, he won't. Like I told you, I've taken care of things."

"I wish I could believe you. And taking his car — it's the worst thing you could do! How stupid can you be! He'll go berserk." She pummelled his chest, "He'll find out about us. He'll kill me!"

Dennis grabbed her and held her by the shoulders,

"Amy, just listen. He won't come anywhere near us. Things have changed, he's not a threat, not anymore."

"What are you mixed up in, Dennis? How come?"

He put his arm round her waist. They slowly walked back to her flat, hip to hip. "Just trust me, Amy. I've taken care of things."

The flat was cold. Amy shivered as she turned up the thermostat. She let Dennis hold her close as if needing his warmth. She suddenly pushed his chest and stepped back.

"Who are you, Dennis? I don't think you really know."

Dennis stared, nonplussed, his mind racing, seeking words, the right words.

"Well? Got nothing to say for yourself!? A lot's happened since those days in the market. You were an innocent, then."

"I ... I don't know what you want me to say ..."

"Something honest, Dennis. A part of me feels sorry for you. Mum and Maggie warned me you'd come out a different person ... and you have ... you're a thug, just like all of them. You are scared of thugs like the Fishers. I can understand that, but you've convinced yourself you need them. You're scared of being yourself." Her face was flushed, her eyes shining. "If you want me, Dennis you've got to live without them. You'll never have a life if you don't."

"I need you, Amy ... give me a chance ... please."

Don't beg, Dennis. It makes you sound pathetic."

"Sorry ... I'm sorry ..." He suddenly laughed.

"What the hell ...!"

"Saying sorry, it's not a word that's said in prison."

Amy smiled, "You better start using it again, and mean it. Learn what it means!"

"Yeah ... yeah, I will ... I will."

"I may be stupid, Dennis, but I want to believe ... You'd better not mess around."

"Trust me, Amy."

"Trust! That's just it, Dennis, I don't trust you, not yet. It's up to you. Just tread carefully. You're not a bad man, I know you aren't ... Your just ...weak."

Dennis stared at the floor. "Yeah, I know," he whispered.

Dennis grimaced when he heard about the beating Lee had suffered. A compound fracture of his right arm. He knew how they did it — a few prisoners had received similar treatment — his arm held down over two bricks and a baseball bat swung hard. A single blow, that's all it took.

It was what he'd wanted, wasn't it?

It wasn't just the broken arm that landed Lee in hospital for almost two weeks. He was almost unconscious when one of his mates found him. Part of his right ear had been severed, a paraffin-soaked rag was stuffed into his mouth, burnt matches were lying on the floor, and blood was streaming from his right eye, The word was he might lose the sight.

There'd been a text from Brendan Fisher.

'Glad to oblige.'

Amy stormed into the flat, slamming the door behind her. "Maggie told me what happened to Lee. Did you have anything to do with it?!"

"It wasn't me. I didn't beat him up," Dennis replied, defensively.

"But you know who did. Who the hell have you got involved with? It's the Fishers, isn't it? Maggie said it had to be them. They're an evil bunch, Dennis. You know that!"

Dennis hung his head. "They said they'd help — that's all. I didn't think ..."

"What, that they'd beat him to within an inch of his life! They've crippled him. I told you, you're in with the wrong crowd, Dennis. They are seriously dangerous. Lee in comparison was an angel!"

"I thought they'd tell him to leave us alone — that's all." He spoke quickly, as if wanting to move on.

Amy flung him a look of amazement; "How stupid can you be!"

"I just wanted him to stop bothering you. He was nasty — you said so."

Amy shivered and sank onto the couch. "Oh, my God, what have you got me in to?"

He shuffled towards her, "It's done now."

"What do you want me to do, thank you? I told you; I warned you. I wanted Lee out of my life — but not this."

Dennis felt a depressing gloom of guilt stifling hopes he might have had for him and Amy. He'd wanted her to be delighted; free of Lee and his threats, free to start again. Free to trust another man.

He stood for what seemed like an age, listening to her sobs and the sound of his own breathing. She slowly raised her head and peeled her fingers from her wet face, her eyes fixed on the window.

"Want me to leave?" he said, pushing out the words in soft ribbons of breath.

"Yes ... No! ... I don't know. I'm scared Dennis, scared to have you around . . . more scared to be on my own."

"I don't want you to be alone."

Chapter 17

1994 ...

A hush descended as the coroner entered the courtroom. He was thin with a bald head that shone like a polished stone and a pencil-thin nose on which balanced a pair of half-moon, rimless spectacles. His skin was white and pale, like those of prison inmates who'd seen little of the sun. He arranged some papers on his bench and cleared his throat;

"Before the inquest starts, I want to say a few words." He waved in the direction of the press. "Everyone associated with this tragic case deserves respect for their privacy. I expect that you will report the facts that emerge and not speculate or draw unfounded conclusions."

Michael Barrett gripped the brass rails of the witness box, white-knuckled, his shoulders hunched. He took a furtive glance at the digital clock on the wall behind the coroner. 10:30.

He barely heard the coroner addressing the jury. His thoughts were dogged by the conviction he should have done something; seen it coming. In his thirty years as a prison officer, he thought he'd seen it all — bullying, taunting, fights, abuse of all kinds, even a stabbing — but never a brutal murder. Billy Fisher had often dished out his own vicious brand of justice. Some would have said he had it coming.

He'd found him slumped naked on the floor of the shower, blood still weeping from several deep puncture wounds. He'd stood hovering over the lifeless body sprawled in a pool of blood and emitted a crescendo of curses, suddenly angry that this had occurred on his shift. Of course, nobody knew what happened, nobody heard anything, nobody saw anything. He knew they were lying. He didn't push it, there was no point. Billy Fisher had made their lives hell for long enough. What they knew was hidden behind well-practised, blank stares.

He smoothed his damp hands down the sides of his trousers, tugged at the inside of the collar of his white shirt and glanced up at the visitors' gallery. They were all there, the Fishers. Billy's mother sat, head erect, looking imperious, disdainful, her eyes fixed on him in a hard stare. Next to her, Billy's father, Brendan Fisher, slumped forward, his tattooed hands hanging loosely over the wooden rail, gold rings the size of knuckle dusters on his sausage fingers. Michael knew enough about Brendan Fisher to feel a chill of fear. He was one of the worst of a bad lot. He was still behind most of the protection rackets and drug trades in the area, administering levels of violence that were ugly and sadistic. They'd never visited Billy in the Young Offenders Institute, not even a phone call. But now, now there was an official inquiry into how he'd died, they'd come, full of anger, intent on finding out who was to blame.

Most offenders of his age were in adult prisons, but there'd been delays. A month later and he'd have been transferred.

The coroner turned towards the jury. "An inquest hears evidence so that you, the jury, can make findings of fact and come to a verdict, a conclusion if you will, about the death of Billy Fisher. Nobody is on trial here. An inquest does not decide matters of criminal or civil liability. We're not here to attribute blame. The purpose is simply a way of establishing facts concerning the death of Billy Fisher. Your role in this inquest is to record when and how he died."

The coroner carefully adjusted his spectacles and took a pen from the inside jacket pocket. Michael Barrett spotted Billy's girlfriend sitting alone, heavily pregnant, ashen-faced, looking like a child. She looked even younger than when he'd seen her on her last visit. That was the time Billy Fisher got nasty, calling her a slag. She'd run out of the visiting room; tears streaming down her face and hadn't taken it well when he told her to forget him. Funny, that, Michael thought. She should've been grateful.

Most of the jurors were looking directly at him, now that the coroner had finished his explanations. There were nine of them — five men and four women. One of the women was young. She looked like Billy Fisher's girlfriend; blonde streaks in her long black hair, artificial tan smeared liberally over her face and arms. His gaze lingered on her talon-like nails. He had a sudden compulsion to peer at Billy's girlfriend to see if her nails were as long and painted in the same glittering colour.

The coroner fingered the pathologist's report and read the summary aloud. "Severe bruising and fingernail marks on his arms and chest. Stabbed several times with...." The coroner paused; "with a screwdriver."

One of the jury members, a black woman, began wringing the ends of the scarf she was wearing. The coroner glanced at her for a moment, and then continued reading from the report;

"The fatal blow was a puncture wound that severed his carotid artery." He coughed, and took a sip of water, before continuing. His words were slow and deliberate.

"The pathologist has reported the spacing and different depths of penetration of the wounds inflicted led him to conclude the blows were made by several individuals."

There were gasps from the public gallery. Brendan Fisher stood and slammed his fist against the balustrade. The coroner frowned, glanced at one of the security officers, and then at Billy's father. "Another outburst and I will have you ejected from the court!" He took his time before continuing, as if letting his words sink in.

"The police investigation found evidence of blood in the adjacent showers suggesting the attackers had scrubbed themselves clean while the deceased lay dying." Billy's girlfriend emitted a loud wail. Her cry echoed round the courtroom.

Standing in the dock under the accusing glare of Brendan Fisher and the dismissive look of the coroner, Michael wished he'd taken the option of early retirement. He held himself erect, staring at the ornate crest on the wall opposite.

"What about the screwdriver?" he was asked.

"It was found in the shower."

"I'm aware of that," said the coroner in an exasperated tone. He stabbed his finger at a folder on the bench. "It's in the police report." He picked up his pen and began tapping the bench as he spoke. "What we would all like to know, Mr Barrett" ... tap ... "is, where did it come from?" ... tap ... "How did such a dangerous weapon" ... tap, tap ... "end up in the hands of those clearly intent on causing serious harm to Billy Fisher?" ... tap, tap, tap.

Michael Barrett knew his answer would seem a pathetic excuse.

"From the woodwork shop. We hadn't realised it had gone missing."

The coroner removed his glasses and held them to one side, his elbow resting on the bench and sighed, loudly,

"Surely you know who had recent access to these tools?"

"They all take woodwork," Michael replied. "We do what we can to prepare them for a job on the outside — give them a fighting chance." He regretted his reply in an instant.

"But not Billy Fisher!" The coroner had adopted an accusatory tone. "Is it not your responsibility to support and protect the inmates, especially one so obviously vulnerable as the young man who died in such horrible circumstances? Weren't you the senior officer? Wasn't it up to you to ensure no one was singled out and attacked?"

The coroner droned on. "Isn't it the case, Mr Barrett, that you receive an additional stipend in your role as officer in charge?" Michael felt the blood drain from his face. He gave a quick nod.

"I'll take that as a 'yes.'"

Michael was seething that the stores had failed to check the tools carefully. It had happened more than once, items secreted in rags and pockets. Drill bits, slips of metal sharpened to an edge, even pieces of swarf from the lathes. They were supposed to have all tools checked back in before anyone could leave the workshops, they were supposed to have random searches, they were supposed to ... to do their job.

The coroner took his pen and tapped the desk several times,

"There were obvious dangers faced by young Billy Fisher, someone who had his whole life in front of him." He turned to look up at the sobbing girlfriend. "The chance to be a loving father has been cruelly denied."

Michael wondered what planet the coroner was on. Had he any idea of the madness and mayhem associated with every aspect of Billy Fisher's life?

'She's better off without him' was the thought itching to get out of his head. He wanted to tell them, make the stone-faced members of the jury understand.

The governor was called to give evidence. He'd only been in post for six months, an accelerated appointment that had astounded the other officers. He wasn't going to take any responsibility.

"I expect my staff to do the right thing."

The coroner seemed to agree with the governor's assessment,

"It seems clear to me that there was a failure of prison officers to discharge their duties."

The governor nodded and let out a loud sigh. "Thank you, thank you," he replied, his head bobbing in a hurried, deferential manner.

The coroner requested Michael return to the stand. "Mr Barrett, I'd like you tell the court who you think should bear the responsibility for this boy's death?"

Michael stood and stretched his six-foot frame. He'd anticipated something like this; the governor lying low, expecting his troops to take the flak. Pride implored him to implicate those at fault. He wanted to shout out and tell the gallery, make them understand; these are tough kids, a mob of misfits society prefers to keep hidden. He'd put valuable time in trying to help Billy, trying to get through the hard shell and tough persona. Some of the other officers had derided him for his efforts,

"That one's beyond help; a wrong 'un; wasting your time."

He couldn't shake off the thought that two of the prison officers in the workshop had deliberately let the lads get hold of the screwdriver. They'd had a few run-ins with Billy, but then who hadn't? He'd also had a few 'conversations' with the lad. Just last week he'd pinned the arrogant sod against the wall wanting to wipe the smirk off his face.

Maybe they wanted to see Billy hurt — badly hurt?

He'd never know, and he really didn't want to find out. "Truth is a slippery little bugger," his grandfather liked to say. How right he was, thought Michael.

Anger threatened to make him tackle the governor for simply washing his hands and protecting his career. Justice wouldn't be the outcome. He'd known that before the hearing took place. Despite the coroner's comments to the jury, blame would be assigned. The coroner had a report to write, conclusions had to be reached. Michael had decided the previous evening he would say nothing that might point the blame at any of the other prison officers. They were all younger than him; they had families, mortgages, credit cards. He was old enough to retire. How he wished he'd never agreed to sign up for three more years. The coroner's thin, whining voice interrupted his thoughts.

"Have you any comments you wish to make?"

Michael shook his head.

The coroner slowly shifted in his seat and directed his attention to the jury.

Members of the jury, I will now ask you to retire to the jury room.

You must decide, based on the evidence you have heard, the cause of death. In this case it is quite clearly the result of several stab wounds. I would advise this is recorded as by assailant, or assailants unknown. You should also include the wider circumstances of his death. What were the likely contributing factors? Was the prison, or the prison staff, complicit in the death of Billy Fisher? You must not, however, name individuals or make recommendations.

The jury took little time to confirm the coroner's suggestion they record death by Unlawful Killing. They looked smug, as if pleased they'd had a role in seeing justice done. The coroner thanked the jury and expressed his appreciation for the way they had conducted themselves. He then sat back on his chair and addressed the entire court, as if preaching from a pulpit.

"It is in the best interests of all concerned if the perpetrators own up to this crime, or at the very least tell the police what they know."

Michael had to stifle a chuckle.

"And as for the governor; I suggest he strengthens the operational procedures within this Young Offender's Institute. Changes must be made." The governor was nodding vigorously.

The coroner paused to adjust his spectacles and looked directly at Michael.

"I am assured that you will be facing a disciplinary hearing." He continued with just the briefest of pauses, "I strongly suggest you consider your position in the service."

Michael felt his face flush. His jaw muscles pulsed as he ground his teeth. He sensed the eyes of the family fixed on him like laser beams. Brendan Fisher suddenly stood in the gallery and shook his ham-hock of a fist in Michael's direction. "You bastard, you bastard!" he bawled. "You're a dead man, Barrett — you hear me? A dead man!"

The coroner appeared to take his time before instructing the bailiffs to remove him from the court. He turned his attention to Michael.

"You may go," he said, returning his pen to the inside pocket of his jacket.

Other members of the Fisher family began shouting abuse. They were calling out, chanting like a football crowd, stamping their feet in a syncopated rhythm,

"Billy Fisher ... Billy Fisher ... Billy Fisher ...

"Clear the court!" the coroner shouted, barely making himself heard above the din.

Their voices echoed throughout the courtroom. An Image of Billy Fisher in a pool of blood pulsed in Michael's head:

Billy Fisher ...

Their chants weakened as they filed out. It suddenly wasn't the bloodied body of Billy Fisher he saw, it was an image of his own son, Dennis, dying, calling for his help.

He shuddered, fighting the urge to shout — Dennis ... Dennis ... DENNIS!

Chapter 18

"Look at this!" Amy burst into the flat waving the local paper. "It's about the inquest into a stabbing at the youth prison. Billy Fisher was murdered! They blame your dad!"

Dennis snatched the paper, which read: 'The inquest into the death of a local man, Billy Fisher, has concluded there were serious shortcomings in the care and supervision of many of the inmates.

Billy Fisher was found in the shower block. He'd been stabbed multiple times and was pronounced dead at the scene. The recently appointed prison governor assured the court there would be a full investigation.

The family of the deceased were in court to hear the outcome, including his heavily pregnant girlfriend. They were clearly angry at the circumstances that led to his death. A number of them had to be escorted from the court.

The Prison Governor refused to add to the coroner's comment that the senior prison officer, Michael Barrett, should consider his future within the prison service.'

Dennis read the article a second time, his eyes drawn to the name of the murdered victim — Billy Fisher. And to the name of the prison officer — Michael Barrett. The death of Billy Fisher would, he knew, result in an avalanche of revenge against those involved. And his dad would be their target. He imagined himself sitting next to a few of the Fishers as they interrogated his father, accusations repeated over and over ...

'You hated Billy ...'

'You wanted him dead ...'

'You hate us, don't you?'

And one of the faceless Fishers asking him the same question every time his father shook his head —

'What are we goin' to do about him? Tell me, Dennis — you're a Barrett!'

He shuddered: it was as if a cold, clammy hand had seized the back of his neck.

There were two of them standing on the edge of the road as Dennis approached The Old Nag, a pub a few miles or so from the entrance to the Doncaster racecourse. Later in the month there'd be plenty of work running punters to the Saint Ledger. One of them waved, flagging down his taxi. He'd received the booking earlier that day. There was something about them that sent a ripple of alarm, a prickle at the base of his spine.

The bright afternoon sun said something different —

'Stop worrying. Just two guys needing a lift home.'

One of them yanked the rear door open as he slid into the kerb. Before he could react, the other man had run round, opened the passenger door and flung himself into the front seat.

"Drive," he ordered.

Dennis glanced at him, "Where to?"

The man in the rear leaned forward. Dennis could feel his breath on the side of his cheek. "Hunters Road."

Dennis felt his throat tighten. These were Fishers' men, he knew it. He gripped the steering wheel and pulled out into the light traffic. A large truck flashed its lights and gave a blast of its airhorn as Dennis swung his car into the outer lane.

"You trying to get us killed?" growled the man in the passenger seat.

Dennis didn't reply. That instruction he'd received in prison had sunk in — 'Never say you're sorry'. Dennis wondered if his two passengers had done 'time'. Probably, he thought.

The rest of the journey was in silence, that is until they reached the turn into Hunters Road. It led to a number of industrial units. He'd sometimes taken customers to Robinson's Removals. He could see a row of their vehicles behind a steel fence.

A grubby finger pointed towards the row of buildings, "That's it, that one at the end."

Its concrete walls were painted flat-grey, and the steel door was pock-marked with blisters of rust. A length of guttering, sagging with the weight of stagnant moss, frowned over a window that had been fitted with a metal grill. The man in the back moved quickly, holding open the driver's door before Dennis had time to unbuckle his seat belt. The other man, much larger than his whippet-thin friend, struggled out of the passenger door, grunting heavily as he hauled his bulky frame out of the car. He was much shorter than his friend but moved quickly in almost balletic, short strides, despite his bulk. Dennis followed closely, leaving the other man leaning on the car. The door opened as they approached. Dennis knew, instinctively, this was Brendan Fisher — round-shouldered, thick neck with a large, clean-shaven face, pale as porcelain, and those eyes, Fisher eyes, almost colourless, as if smeared by a thin veil of mucus.

"Hello. Dennis, we spoke on the phone." It was said as if they were about to have a business meeting. He beckoned them inside. Dennis felt his breath stick in his lungs as they sat at a long table. Brendan Fisher's face was flushed, his jaw muscles twitching. "You heard about Billy?"

Dennis nodded. "Yeah. Shouldn't have happened," he replied.

"Shouldn't have happened! No, Dennis. Nobody deserves to die like that, stabbed to death. Brutal, that is ... brutal!"

The word 'sorry' threatened to escape from Dennis' mouth. Brendan was almost hysterical. He grabbed up one of the chairs and slammed it down onto the tiled floor. For a moment, Dennis thought he was going to be attacked. Brendan picked up one of the splintered chair legs, swung it round like a baseball bat and began pounding on the table. In a sudden violent lurch, he smashed the chair leg against the edge of the filing cabinet, sending a vase of plastic flowers skidding across the floor.

"He was no angel, my Billy. But he didn't deserve to be killed. Those scumbags who stuck him will be taken care of — every one of 'em." He flung what was left of the chair leg at the wall. Seemingly exhausted, he kicked at remnants of the chair, scattering pieces in all directions.

My Billy? Dennis suddenly realised — Billy Fisher was Brendan's son!

"I'm sorry ..." 'that word!' ... "about Billy."

"Sorry! You'll do more than say you're sorry." Brendan smirked, revealing a similar gold tooth to that displayed by his cousin in prison.

"You know who's responsible?" he said, thrusting his face towards Dennis'.

Dennis nodded

"That's good. It's good you know it was your dad's fault it happened." He glared, "But-not-good-for-him." He prodded Dennis hard in the chest with a thick stubby finger, beating a rhythm as he spoke. "Not-good-for-him," he repeated, continuing to stab at Dennis' chest. "Got to be a price to pay — a high price — know what I mean?"

The two henchmen sat in silence, staring at the table.

"An eye for an eye — It's a job for you, Dennis."

"Job? ... For me?"

"You owe us, you owe us big time, remember?"

"Yeah, but I thought ..."

"Thought what? That you'd just help round the office! Oh, no, Dennis. You'll do what I tell you. He's got to pay the price, a big price. My Billy was murdered on his watch. He ain't going to get away with it. You'll do it Dennis; you'll take care of the bastard."

"He's my dad ..." stammered Dennis.

Brendan grabbed his shirt and flung him against the filing cabinet. Dennis gasped as the steel edge stabbed into his back.

"That's exactly why I want you to take care of him!" Brendan smiled, as if they'd struck a deal. He waved his arm in an expansive gesture. "We don't want to rush things, do anything rash, do we now." The two men sniggered, as if it was some shared joke. "Something that keeps him guessing ... shake him up a bit." He patted Dennis on the shoulder,

"Bit of car damage always goes down well," Brendan pointed at his two thugs, "The boys will keep an eye on things as well. Nothing stupid, we don't want anyone hurt ... not yet, anyway. I'll let you know when."

"When?"

"When you've to kill the bastard."

Dennis gulped ... they were all laughing, as if it was a big joke. Maybe it was, he thought. He shuddered, Murder ... murder his father!? He tried to laugh with the others, as if to show he understood what they wanted, and that he didn't care.

It was nearly 2:00am when Dennis slowly edged along the street, his sneakers covered in autumn leaves that had gathered in wet clumps along the pavement. He could see his dad's old Volvo reversed into the drive, the bull-nose grill glinting in the light from a nearby streetlamp.

There was a time when he'd have wanted to do something like this, inflict a bit of damage to his dad's precious vehicle. The intense hatred he had stored and massaged over the years had all but gone. Suddenly angry with himself for being trapped by the Fishers, and angry with his father for getting him into this mess, he grabbed a half brick lying next to a gate pillar and scored a long gouge along the driver's side. He flung the brick into the base of the hedge, clenched his fist around the large screwdriver tucked into his belt and plunged it through the tread. The car looked barely touched. The streetlight left the car in a shadow that hid its scars. The only visible difference was the car sitting lower, appearing to squat on the tarmac drive.

Barbara's car was parked alongside. He stood for some time fingering the handle of the screwdriver. He told himself it was someone else stabbing at the tyres on her car, thrusting the steel tip through the treads. He didn't know how many times he slashed at the tyres. He was suddenly exhausted. He sat on the low wall that edged the drive, flung the screwdriver into the front hedge and gulped to stifle the sob that was aching to leave his throat.

Barbara burst into tears at the sight of her tiny car leaning pathetically, its near-side tyres flattened. She was speechless at the sight of the damage to the Volvo. She turned as Michael approached, her eyes pleading for him to do something.

"What the …!" He strode round his car, running his hand over the large gouge running the length of the car.

"Who'd do such a thing?" Barbara shivered, her voice breaking. "You don't think it's got anything to do with what the coroner said?"

Michael couldn't tell her that's exactly what he thought. A couple of their young thugs, maybe.

"Just kids," he told her. "Bloody kids."

The police were of the same view.

It was late. Michael and Barbara sat in the kitchen silently nursing mugs of sweet tea straining to listen for anything unusual. It was ten days since the incident, but Barbara couldn't relax. She hardly slept, pleading with him to check at the slightest sound.

She became ever more paranoid. She rattled the security chain on the front door every night even though she'd seen Michael slide it in place. She insisted they have additional bolts fitted to the front door and the patio doors and refused to have any of the windows opened. The place felt like a prison. She wouldn't go near her car, even though the tyres had been replaced. She deliberately avoided going any closer than she had to, as if she thought touching it would set off a tsunami of vandalism.

The gusting autumn wind was bending the branches of the tall trees at the back of the house, twigs tapping and scratching against an upstairs window. Barbara gasped, and instinctively reached out and grabbed Michael's arm.

"It's them! I know it is!"

Michael tilted his head in the direction of the noise. The wind had picked up: a storm had been forecast. He wished he'd arranged to have the trees pruned at the end of the summer.

"It's just the wind, love ..."

She suddenly stood, and staggered back against the kitchen cupboard, her right arm twitching. Michael stared in disbelief as she collapsed in front of him, sinking to the floor in an almost graceful way. His legs trembled as he stumbled across the kitchen. He lifted her head as she tried to speak. She groaned, her enlarged pupils set in an unseeing stare.

It seemed to take an age for the ambulance to arrive. They were suddenly there, filling the hallway, moving quickly into the kitchen. He sat at the table watching one leaning close, calling her name over and over. They struggled to lift her onto the stretcher, her body limp, unhelpful.

Michael was alarmed at the speed of Barbara's decline. He'd called Lisa on the way to the hospital. She arrived a few minutes after the ambulance. Almost immediately, she remonstrated first with the nurses, and then with the consultant.

"Can't you do anything!?"

"She won't survive if we try and operate," he told her.

"She won't survive if you don't!" she said, in that manner of hers that bordered on confrontation.

Barbara's temperature soared, her breathing becoming erratic, and the slow shake of the head from the nurse was the signal Michael had dreaded. He was still holding Barbara's limp wrist when she emitted a groan from deep in her chest. Her eyes suddenly opened and flashed at him, like a plea for help.

It was an uncomfortable death.

Michael felt a mixture of guilt and relief; relieved that Barbara's frightening spasms had been controlled with massive doses of diazepam, and guilt that he'd wanted her to die quickly. Their house seemed huge and empty, sounds echoing and amplified in the high-ceilinged rooms, as if they'd been stripped bare.

Dennis let his phone buzz and stared at the luminous glow from the numbers on the digital radio — 06:10. He watched Amy attempt to wrap herself in a towel. It took his mind off things, seeing Amy run half-naked to the shower. "Is that yours?" she called.

"Yeah," he replied, reaching across for his mobile, wondering who might call so early.

He didn't register it was Lisa, his sister — not at first. She sounded anxious and upset.

"Lisa ... what's up?" He could hear her stifling a sob.

"It's mum ... they took her to hospital."

"Ma ... When? Is she ok?"

"She had a stroke, middle of the night."

"Is she ok? ... How bad ...?" He could hear her breathing hard. "Lisa?"

"She's dead, Dennis. She died earlier this morning."

Dennis shuddered. "What! ... She's dead! ... What happened?"

"Someone vandalised their cars; slashed the tyres, damaged dad's Volvo. Dad said she got really upset, what with the threats from the Fishers. She was a mess, he said — not sleeping, shaking with fear every time there was an unexpected noise. I saw her last week — she looked awful. He's distraught. He blames himself for what happened."

Dennis felt the blood drain from his face.

"Maybe he's right," he muttered.

"I can't believe what you're saying! He was doing his job, that's all. If anyone's to blame it's the coroner. The prison governor was pathetic and that report in the newspaper ... Did you read it?"

"Yeah, I read it. He shouldn't have let it happen — that was his job."

"Oh, and you don't think anyone else is to blame! He wouldn't speak out."

"HE WAS IN CHARGE!"

"Don't shout at me, Dennis!"

"Sod off!" He gripped his phone as if trying to squeeze out words, different words. He flung the phone across the room, sank into the armchair, covered his face with his hands and sobbed. He felt cold and alone. He imagined himself standing, tiny, afraid, waiting for someone to claim him.

Amy ran down the corridor, a white bathrobe cinched around her body, her hair dripping wet. "Dennis, Dennis ... what's happened?"

"It's ma ... Dennis rubbed aggressively at the scar on his forehead. She died in hospital early this morning — a stroke."

"Oh my God, that's terrible!!"

Dennis gripped her arm and levered himself upright. "It's his fault."

"Who's fault?'

"Billy Fisher was murdered coz dad didn't do his job." Dennis felt he was reciting something Brendan Fisher had implanted in his brain.

"How can you say that?"

"You read the report in the paper; he was blamed for what happened." Dennis stared at the wall; he didn't want to look directly at Amy. "Lisa said she took it badly."

"Took what badly?"

"Their cars were vandalised — tyres slashed, big gouge in dad's car ..." He suddenly realised Lisa hadn't provided such details. He paused, briefly, a voice in his head... that was stupid.

"Ma got upset ... really upset."

What have I done? — that same voice in his head.

"You think that's what caused her stroke?"

Dennis shrugged his shoulders. "That's what Lisa thinks."

"It might have been the Fishers?"

Dennis stared at the floor, "Who knows? It's dad's fault. He shouldn't have let it happen."

"That's a cruel thing to say, Dennis, very cruel."

Chapter 19

Dennis' phone buzzed. He'd slept fitfully; thoughts of what he'd done refusing to leave him. He blinked several times and rubbed his eyes; it was a text from Lisa:

'Mum's funeral is on Thursday, 10:00 am at the crematorium.

There'll be drinks and a few sandwiches in the King's Arms afterwards.'

He groaned and stared at the screen on his mobile.

She's dead. Isn't that enough? He looked again at the screen. The King's Arms ... that dump.

They knew him there, and not in a good way. The last time, he'd been told to leave after a night of drinking with Lee Hogan and a couple of his mates. He'd never thought of it as a place to have a ceremony of any kind, let alone a place to gather after a funeral — and certainly not his mother's.

He pushed himself out of bed, struggled into a pair of jeans, sniffed at his T-shirt and shoved on a sweater.

Amy looked up from her bowl of cereal, "Rough night?"

"Yeah," Dennis grunted. His throat felt dry, and his voice seemed unusually hoarse. There was another ping on his phone.

"Who's that?" Amy asked.

"Lisa — again. It's about ma's funeral at the crematorium. She says I should go."

"Of course you should go. It's important. You'll regret it if you don't."

"I hate bloody funerals. Neighbours, cousins I haven't seen since I was a kid; they'll just be there to gawk and get free nosh at the King's Arms."

"Gawk? At you, you mean? They'll be there to help remember her —that's what you must do! You're her son, for God's sake."

"I don't want to watch her coffin being wheeled in and pushed through to be cremated like some check-out at the supermarket."

"Well, at the very least, go to the King's Arms!"

Michael thought a service at the crematorium was enough. It was Lisa who insisted they have a 'do' in the King's Arms for the mourners. "To celebrate her life," she told him.

"It wouldn't be my choice," he said, as if reprimanding his daughter for not discussing it with him first. "But if you think it's important …"

"Thanks, Dad." They were words he hadn't heard from Lisa's lips for many years.

There were many more in the pub than he'd expected. The King's Arms had been one of his favourites, the one he and Barbara made their Friday night treat; 'chicken and chips in the basket', a Guinness, and a gin and tonic for Barbara. That was before they'd added a row of slot machines and a carvery which left smells of cooked food permeating the stale air, not helped by the ash trays that seemed never to be completely emptied and the tobacco smoke that accompanied them even when they left the pub.

Dennis had turned up. Still thin as a lath, his dark hair cut short. There was a chain of whispers as Dennis stumbled, spilling his pint glass over best suits and coats. Michael turned away and found a seat in a tiny snug just off the main bar. He needed time to gather his thoughts. A memory flashed; more memories, unfurling like a scroll that hadn't been opened for many years. Barbara convincing him they should adopt ... "Imagine, Michael... a son. It's what we've always wanted." Their arrival at the home, a smiling Sister in a long white habit, a room with dark, subtle lighting.

"He looks beautiful," Barbara had said, peering intently at the infant in the cot.

Barbara picked up the baby nearest the window. It wriggled momentarily and then settled in her arms. "Looks like you've decided!" He remembered helping Barbara and the tiny baby into the car. And another memory that flared into his mind; the young woman, a girl, staring at him from an upper window ...

His thoughts jumped back to Dennis as a toddler, chubby then, still unsteady on his feet, arms waving excitedly, his pink face beaming, squealing with delight when Michael kicked a football across the lawn. And a young Dennis, seven years old, standing by his side wearing an oversized plaid shirt and khaki shorts, erect as a soldier on parade holding that wooden rifle he'd made for his seventh birthday,

He ground his teeth. If Barbara hadn't been so protective, he'd have straightened him out. He'd tried, hadn't he? He'd have made him tougher, he'd have got him sorted, if she hadn't interfered.

Lisa grabbed Dennis' elbow, "Do the right thing," she hissed. "Stop drinking yourself stupid, for God's sake. This is for mum — don't spoil it."

"You look nice," he slurred. "New, is it?" he remarked, eyeing her dark grey outfit and unusually high heels.

"Piss off, Dennis."

"I didn't ask this lot to come. Who are they, anyway?"

"I'm warning you, Dennis, don't do anything stupid. Stop feeling sorry for yourself. We're all upset. This isn't easy, especially for dad."

"Dad! If it wasn't for him, she'd still be alive."

"You are pathetic, Dennis. If you've a shred of decency, you'd go over and see him. Tell him ..."

"Tell him what? That I'm sorry ma died? He dominated her life. She should have left him years ago."

"How can you say such a thing," she hissed. "He always looked after her. He'll be lost without her."

Dennis snatched another pint from the counter and took several large gulps. He belched loudly. "He won't have a live-in maid anymore. That's all she was to him — a bloody maid."

Lisa glared, her cheeks ablaze. "You are disgusting! I wish they'd kept you in prison!" she hissed.

Dennis moved away from his sister and shuffled towards Michael, a nearly full pint clutched in his hand, "Hello, Dad." And then a snigger, "You still here?"

Michael's face turned beetroot red. He glared at his son, shoved him hard in the chest and spun away without saying a word.

Dennis bawled after him,

"Where'y going...? It's your funeral!"

Several people nearby stopped talking, as if the air they were breathing had somehow become tainted. Sensing he might have overstepped the mark, Dennis headed for the loos. They were near the main entrance, down a narrow corridor round the back of the kitchen. The was a smell of old cooking fat from a grill near the ceiling. He shouldered the 'Gents' door, almost slipping on the tiled floor, and stood at an inappropriate distance from the urinal, inhaling the stink of piss as though it were sea air. It gave him a chance to think. He chortled to himself, zipped up and headed outside.

Michael found the door at the rear of the pub that opened onto the car park. He slammed it behind him, brushing past Brian, his bridge partner, and strode off to his car. It looked smart, fitted with new tyres. He'd even made attempts to repair the scored paintwork.

He froze: shattered glass was scattered over the car boot. Someone had smashed the rear window.

Michael brushed the glass from the back seat, his stomach churning at the mess and the damage. Worst of all was a large dent hammered into the driver's door just below the deep gouge he'd attempted to hide with spray paint.

"If I catch the bastard ..." he mumbled to himself.

He drove home, fists clamped to the steering wheel, and turned his car into the drive. It was over 25 years old, but still comfortable and reliable. The house, the one they'd bought a few years after their marriage, had been their home for nearly thirty years. Michael almost missed the envelope on the mat in the hallway. It had been pushed to the side when he opened the front door. He examined it; no stamp, just his name handwritten in uncertain capitals, as if written by a child. He tugged the flap open with his thumb and took out the single sheet of white paper. It had a crude drawing of an emoji with a scowling face. It also had a line, like a neck, drawn at the base of the emoji with a hangman's noose attached.

Michael felt the blood drain from his face. He crumpled the sheet of paper in his fist: his first instinct was to toss it in the bin. 'Might need this,' he thought, smoothing out the sheet. The emoji appeared to stare at him, it's threatening message even more sinister.

He looked out of the window overlooking the rear garden; the neat lawn and borders of shrub roses, and the large buddleia that needed pruning. The flowers and border plants were Barbara's domain. The lawn was his. He could see her, bare-footed, spraying their kids with a hosepipe sending them scampering across the grass in high-pitched squeals and gales of laughter. She had boundless energy, revelling in their games, as if she too was a child. They were good days.

The house seemed bigger, the rooms cavernous, the bed cold and empty. Noises echoed in a way he'd never noticed before. Nights became prolonged, the effortless sleep he'd once enjoyed was interrupted by sounds he'd barely noticed. Every creak of the floor, rustle of a curtain, gurgling of pipes, squeak of a hinge seemed amplified, sinister conspirators in attempts to intimidate him. The image of Barbara's coffin slowly disappearing behind the curtain in its final journey in the crematorium sickened him.

"Why?" he spluttered, his throat tight. "Those bastards!"

'The Fishers, who else?'

It was a thought that wouldn't leave. It nagged, like a raw tooth, its nerve exposed. His sense of fear at what the Fisher's might do was no match for the anger and frustration he felt.

They killed her — as good as.

He balled his fingers and smacked his fists repeatedly onto the kitchen table as if thumping an image of Billy Fisher's father. It served only to inflame his anger. He pictured himself hunting them down in the dirty streets they ruled, camouflaged by the dark, separating one from the herd, a baseball bat his chosen weapon.

Michael was desperately tired. Mornings lifted his gloom providing a reprieve from the torments that nights seemed to bring. He splashed cold water on his face and dabbed at his stubbled face with a towel. Bleary, questioning eyes peered back. He sank into the large armchair next to the fireplace, his eye catching the framed photograph on the sideboard, the one of them all on holiday, sitting on the promenade at Whitby. It was one of those lovely holidays just before they'd adopted Dennis. Barbara in that floppy sunhat with the brim pushed back, white sandals and a striped smock dress and Lisa perched on her knee, smiling into the camera.

He felt a surge of warmth, his mind caught by drifting thoughts. He was on the beach. Lisa was running towards him. He was lifting her up, carrying her laughing and squealing into the water, the waves breaking at her ankles ... and then a sudden large wave that knocked her off her feet. For a horrible moment he'd watched her struggle on her belly, dragged by the undertow. He'd grabbed his child in a tangle of limbs and carried her quickly back to Barbara,

"What on earth! You've got to be more careful, Michael. The tide's on the turn."

He remembered Lisa pushing her little fingers against his legs and him taking a step back, watching as she flung her arms round Barbara's neck.

"I'll get some ice-creams."

"You do that Michael," Barbara had told him, hugging their sobbing daughter.

Dennis seemed to stumble into his thoughts like an unwelcome guest. He could see him now; an image far more vivid, as if it was the first time his brain had allowed him to remember the car smash. Dennis in a blood-soaked shirt stumbling towards the house, a gash across his forehead, his face red and swollen; Lisa a few yards behind screaming at him, tears streaming down her face.

The day suddenly seemed overwhelming.

Chapter 20

Michael turned off the bedroom light and peered from behind the curtain. It was there again, the same car parked about twenty metres down the street, half of the vehicle in the light cast by a streetlight. This was the third night: a dark blue BMW. Two men sat in the front, their faces in shadow. They were dull silhouettes, save for the faint illumination provided by the draw from a lit cigarette, smoke curling into the still night air through a partially open window. His imagination had them thickset, a couple of baseball bats on the back seat, maybe even armed. It was the same routine as on the previous two nights. They sat there for about thirty minutes, slowly moved off, and then accelerated away just as they passed the front of Michael's house.

He rubbed the palms of his hands, alarmed at how hot and damp they felt.

"You bastards!" he muttered.

Early the next morning, he rummaged in a drawer in the lounge where he kept odds and ends. He found what he was looking for hidden under a pile of old birthday cards; a small phone book. He flicked through the pages; Clark, Peter. He was a detective inspector in the South Yorkshire police. It'd been at least four years since they'd last met but there'd been a time when they'd often gone for a drink, sharing names of villains they both knew. Michael called, half expecting his number may have changed.

"Pete, it's Michael, Michael Barrett."

There was a pause as if Peter Clark was gathering his thoughts. "I read about the inquest," There was a hesitancy in his voice that unnerved Michael. "The press didn't hold back," he continued. "That coroner did you no favours."

Michael found himself nodding. He wondered, for just a moment, what the hell he was doing, calling someone who didn't want to be involved. "No, he didn't," he replied. Michael could hear Pete exhaling into the phone.

"Sorry to hear about Barbara," he said. "Very sorry."

Michael felt his throat tighten. "They did it. The Fishers. They frightened her to death. They won't stop, Pete."

"What's happened?"

"They've sent a couple of their goons to park outside my house late at night."

"You sure it's the Fishers?"

Michael felt his anger surge. He forced himself to breath slowly. "It's the Fishers — you know it is,"

"Probably, Michael."

"Probably! You know damn well it's them."

"Look, Michael, as a pal, I have to agree, it's more than likely to be them, or at least, thugs they've hired."

"Then why won't your lot do anything!?"

"You know the answer I have to give …" He paused, as if waiting for Michael to answer. "Evidence, Michael. We've absolutely nothing to go on. I'll try to convince them at this end, but you know how it is …"

"Too many things that are more important, that's what you're going to tell me."

"And resources, Michael. We're under pressure to solve crimes, hit these bloody targets, otherwise we lose even more of our funding."

"Is that it? Is that all you can say?"

"I'll try and have a patrol car swing by more often."

"You do that Pete. Maybe they'd like to drop in for a cup of tea," he hissed.

"I'll do what I can ... but no promises ..." The hesitancy in DI Clark's voice was followed by a long pause. "You've been under a lot of strain. You don't think ...?

"What!" Michael, exclaimed. "You think I'm imagining it? How can you say such a thing?"

"Sorry, Michael, but It's always something we have to consider."

"You mean your bloody superiors and their bloody rules and procedures. I'm not some paranoid freak!"

"Look, Michael ... I'll see what I can do."

There was no sign of the BMW the next night. He'd spotted a patrol car cruising past earlier in the evening, and then again at about the time the BMW had been parked across the street. Pete had done what he promised. Michael just hoped it would continue.

It was Saturday, his usual day for working in the garden. The sun was already streaming through the curtains. He'd found it difficult to sleep and still felt nervous, twitchy, his skin tingling and itching. It was not a condition he was used to.

The beds needed work, the roses needed spraying and the lawn was becoming overgrown. He made coffee, opened the back door and sat at the table on the brick patio. He'd bought it second hand, cleaned it up with a wire brush and emery paper and then spray-painted it in powder blue. It had been a surprise for Barbara; she'd been delighted.

"I thought you were up to something," she'd remarked, her face beaming. "All that paint on your fingers!"

The buzz of a lawnmower a couple of houses away gave Michael a sense of security, as if some semblance of normality had returned. He sipped his coffee and eyed the lawn. The grass needed cutting, a job for later. He thought he could hear the front doorbell. It gave a series of long rings, as if insistent he answer. He groaned, feeling he was being dragged from the sanctity of the garden.

A scrawny young man, a look not helped by straggles of poorly bleached hair, stood, hands on hips, a dirty cloth hanging from the pocket of a well-worn pair of jeans. His t-shirt hung loosely around his waist. It was grass stained and swiped with oily patches.

In his twenties, Michael thought, maybe younger. It was hard to tell.

"Need any lawn work?" he asked, waving an arm nonchalantly towards a small, battered truck parked in the road. A lawnmower splattered with recent grass clippings was held on the flat-bed with several bungee cords. "I've just done number twelve."

"No ... no, thanks," Michael replied, anxious to return to the patio.

"Just thought I'd ask, sorry to disturb."

Michael watched him walk off, keys hanging from a loop on the side his belt. It reminded him of something — those early days; bunches of keys hanging on racks in the main office of the prison. He called out just as the young man started to step into his truck.

"How much?"

The young man smiled and began unstrapping the bungee cords from hooks along the edge of his truck, as if anxious not to let his catch wriggle free.

"A tenner," he shouted, slotting an expanded-metal ramp into a rail at the rear of the truck. Michael's immediate reaction was to wave him off — tell him it was too much — but he hadn't the heart to dampen the enthusiasm of the keen itinerant gardener.

"You could do the back first."

He opened the wooden gate that led down the side of the house. He'd had a lock fitted since the vandalism started. Michael pretended to be drinking the remnants of his now tepid coffee, watching the youth carefully adjust the cutting height. He admired the straight lines made by the lawnmower and the care he took in protecting the edges. He decided to leave him to his task; it was as good, if not better than anything he could achieve.

Michael heard the lawnmower chug to a halt and peered through the kitchen window. His scruffy gardener was carefully emptying the grass-catcher onto a wire-framed compost heap at the far end of the garden.

"That's great," Michael called, as he stepped out onto the patio.

"Haven't finished yet; got to do the edging ... no extra charge," he added with a grin.

Michael smiled. He was enjoying the company, however brief.

"What's your name?" Michael asked.

"Oh, Eddie."

"I'm Michael," he said, extending his hand. "Got some coke in the fridge ..."

"Thanks," Eddie replied, wiping the sweat from his brow with the back of his hand.

"I'll make us a sandwich ... looks like you've earned it."

'Us' ... It seemed such a natural thing to say.

Eddie swigged at the can of coke, his head back, neck stretched. He clutched the chicken sandwich in both hands and ate, hungrily, bits of lettuce and tomato spilling from the sides of the bread roll. He downed the last of his coke, sat back and grinned,

"Missed breakfast," he said.

"Another coke?" asked Michael, who'd hardly touched his own sandwich.

"Nah, thanks. Got to go; need to earn as much as I can."

Michael took a ten-pound note from his wallet and placed it on the table. It hardly seemed enough given the sweat still glistening on Eddie's forehead.

"I could come back next week," he said, pointing in the direction of the borders. "Needs weeding ... I could use the money."

There was a hint of menace in that final remark. He looked sullen; a look Michael had seen on many of the inmates at the Young Offender's Institute.

"This your regular job?" he said, feeling the need to nudge the conversation on.

"Yeah, for now." He looked down at his feet and rubbed at the grass sticking to his work boots. "I got fired from my last job — it was crap anyway — stacking shelves."

"Any family?" The look of menace returned in an instant. Michael regretted asking as soon as the words were out of his mouth.

"Useless they are." Eddie stood and snatched up the tenner Michael had laid on the garden table. "Want me to come next week?"

"OK," Michael replied. "Same time?"

Eddie was still sullen. "Yeah, ok."

The week passed without incident. Patrol cars continued to drive slowly past his house, albeit less frequently. Michael made a mental note to call Pete and thank him. It was Saturday, the day Eddie had promised to return. He wondered if he'd come.

The sound of Eddie's truck pulling into his driveway gave him a sense of relief. It seemed important; a promise made, a verbal contract of sorts — it would have hurt if Eddie hadn't turned up. He heard him whistling and the sound of tools bouncing in his wheelbarrow as he opened the front door.

"Morning, Eddie."

Eddie grinned; "Sorry I'm late ... roadworks."

"Oh, they're always chucking tarmac at the potholes. Never lasts long," Michael replied.

He unlocked the side gate and led Eddie round to the back garden.

"The lawn still looks ok," Eddie remarked.

"You did a good job," Michael replied.

Eddie started scraping his hoe into the hard soil. "This needs watering," he said, as if admonishing Michael for his lack of care. "I'll thin 'em out a bit, water them later."

Eddie was still working his way through the border when Michael stepped onto the patio,

"Tea, Eddie," he called. "I've put two sugars in yours."

"Ta, just right."

"Instinct," said Michael, with a laugh.

Eddie sat on one of the metal chairs on the patio. He took a sip; "Nice," he said, raising his cup.

"Take you long to get here?" probed Michael.

"Nah — it'd be about twenty minutes, with no road works."

"Where from?"

"Marshbrook ... that big council estate."

Michael felt a twinge of alarm. Marshbrook was a Fisher patch. "I know it. I used to have dealings with some families there — long time ago."

"Bit rough there now. Druggies, prossies. I've got a flat on the edge, me and my girlfriend. She's a hairdresser."

"Is that where you were brought up?"

Eddie laughed; "Brought up? Dragged up more like and kicked out. Nothing to do, no jobs. And they wonder why there's drugs, thieving, gangs. Shelia, that's my girlfriend, left home when she was fourteen — went to live with her aunt. Her mother was on the game, see. Not that I'm judging. She needed money like all of us. My mother scarpered a few years back when my dad got out of prison. I send her a few quid when I've got a bit spare."

"You had it tough," Michael said.

"No worse than most. Got into a few scrapes, somehow survived. Doing ok, now."

"Good for you," Michael replied.

He knew he had to ask, "Heard of the Fishers?" It seemed to take Eddie by surprise. His jaw dropped; his eyes narrowed.

"Everyone knows the Fishers," he replied. "Trouble, they are — big trouble." He lifted the front of his t-shirt revealing a vivid scar slashed across his stomach.

"Did they do that?"

"It wasn't a surgeon."

Michael nodded, sagely. "And now?"

"They leave me alone. I'm no threat, see. I just want a quiet life."

"Got to go," he suddenly announced, grabbing his tools and throwing them into his wheelbarrow.

The last of Eddie's tools clattered loudly, bouncing off the sides of his wheelbarrow.

Michael called after him; "Next week?"

"Maybe." His voice sounded hard, edgy.

It was only when Eddie's truck drove off that Michael realised he hadn't paid him for his morning's work.

Chapter 21

The next few weeks were unusually warm. Temperatures soared into the high thirties. The lawn Eddie had mown was a patchwork of yellowing grass and bare areas that looked beyond hope. Sitting on the porch, sipping a white wine, watching the sun sink lower in the sky, Michael's mind slipped back to memories of Lisa, and Dennis as children, playing in the garden. Lisa was like him. In addition to inheriting his frame she also had some of his traits. She liked to be the one in control and had an obvious dislike of being in the wrong. She'd had a few failed relationships, and as for the death of her then boyfriend when Dennis ploughed into his car, it took little time for her to move on.

He looked across at the bare lawn; his mind wandering to those times Dennis seemed to have settled; those games of football, teaching him to march in step, sleeping overnight in a tent ...

And then he remembered that ugly incident when he'd smacked Dennis on the side of his face; blood dripping onto the carpet, Dennis storming out in a temper, and Barbara angrier at him than he'd ever known ...

'Was it all my fault?' he asked himself. 'Did I cause all this?' The threats from the Fishers seemed unimportant — he'd buried his wife, he had only a weak attachment with his daughter, and as for Dennis ... he'd lost him for good. He rubbed at his rheumy eyes and sat waiting for the last hint of the sun to weaken and disappear. He shivered. It had suddenly turned cool.

Michael flung back the curtains and stared out of the bedroom window. It was a cloudless sky and the bright morning sun had flooded the scene like an arc light. It gave him a sense of reassurance and a feeling of lethargy. He could see the Marshbrook estate in the distance, looking calm and quiet as people began to stir. He wondered if single mothers in cramped flats on Marshbrook would have the same feelings about the day? It was a thought that nudged him into gear. He showered, dressed in chinos and a short-sleeved shirt, and then ate a breakfast of toast and black coffee while he scribbled out a list of items he needed from the supermarket.

He recognised him immediately, the tall young man moving his slim frame effortlessly along the shopping mall aisle wearing faded denim jeans and a khaki work shirt; virtually the same outfit he'd worn pushing a mower across his lawn. He saw Eddie wave, turn to the woman next to him and point across, as if he was an object worth viewing. It was Maggie.

"Hi, Michael," said Eddie, all smiles. "Nice to see you. This is ... "

"Maggie!" Michael exclaimed, smiling.

"You know one another?"

A strand of hair had escaped her perfect egg-shell coiffure. She tucked it quickly behind her ear.

"Michael helped me get my job at the market," Maggie replied. "He convinced Jake he should give me a try. You used to pop in to see Jake," she said to Michael. "You've not been round for a long time."

"Didn't seem right, after what Dennis did."

"Dennis is Michael's son," Maggie explained, addressing Eddie. "I always had a soft spot for him, but ... well, he made quite a mess of things."

Michael grunted. "You could say that. He went from bad to worse."

Eddie had walked over to a man standing near the entrance to a Records store.

Maggie patted Michael's arm. "Sorry to hear about Barbara."

Michael smiled, "Thanks, Maggie," he said.

She looked at him sharply. "I'd better go. Maybe we should meet for a cuppa?" It felt like an instruction.

"I'd like that," Michael replied.

"Your number will be in Jake's file. I'll give you a call."

"Ok, look forward to it. Oh, how come you two ...?"

"Oh, I used to baby sit. Knew his family." she replied, turning to catch up with Eddie.

Michael stepped through the cafe door, ducking to avoid the bell hovering above the entrance. It took a few moments before he spotted her sitting at a table wedged in a corner underneath a flight of stairs.

"Hello, Maggie. Thanks for this."

Maggie looked across the cafe and caught the eye of the waitress drifting towards them in a large black outfit. "We'll have tea and buttered toast."

That's the Maggie I remember, thought Michael. Likes to take charge. He smiled ...

"What's so funny?" she asked.

"Just you. I'd forgotten how bossy you can be."

"I tell it like it is, Michael." She took a sip of her tea. "Now — Dennis." Her tone was brusque. "Have you seen him lately?"

"Not since Barbara's funeral."

"At least he did the right thing," she said.

"I didn't want him there," Michael replied. "And I was right. He was obnoxious."

Maggie gave an exasperated sigh.

"Do you know what he's doing now?" Michael asked. "Someone told me he's driving a taxi."

Maggie nodded. "He was working for a real lowlife — Lee Hogan. Somehow, he's ended up with one of his cars."

"How do you know all this?"

"From, Amy. She's June Tiplady's daughter."

Tiplady? He was sure he'd heard that name before. Unusual — not one he'd forget.

"Amy works on June's stall at the market flogging cosmetics," Maggie continued. "She saw Dennis again in a bar, just after he got out of prison. She let him have a spare room in her flat, God knows why. I think there was always a bit of a spark between them. That's where he first met Lee Hogan. He was Amy's boyfriend."

"Was?"

"Lee Hogan's a nasty piece of work. He was smacking her around. He got beaten up and told to leave — ended up in hospital. He's still in a bad way."

"Dennis did that!?"

Maggie shook her head. "Doubt it. But somehow, he was involved."

"Where is he now?"

"He's still at her flat. Amy and I have our little chats. I think they're getting on ok."

"What about the taxi?' Michael said. "Wonder how he got that."

Maggie shrugged her shoulders. "Maybe he bought it; who knows."

"He's banned from driving," Michael said.

"I doubt if that's his biggest concern," was Maggie's pragmatic reply.

The waitress began clearing a table close to theirs. Maggie turned in her direction, "Two more teas."

Michael grinned at the blunt instruction. The waitress tutted as she walked off, scratching the order on a pad dangling from a lanyard around her neck.

Maggie adjusted her chair and leant forward, "I read the report in the paper about Billy Fisher. The coroner was harsh — laid the blame on you."

Michael shrugged his shoulders. "Some'll see it that way, especially the Fishers. They were there. It was what they'd come to hear — someone they could blame."

"Yes, Jake told me. He said there was nearly a courtroom brawl."

Michael nodded. "The bastards are out to get me."

"What's happened?"

"Trivial stuff — that's what the police called it. Gouged car, slashed tyres. Barbara was distraught."

"Doesn't sound like the Fishers. More like kids."

"You too, eh? That's what the police said. They aren't interested."

"What else?"

"A car outside, late at night. It looked like two men inside. They used to drive past very slowly. They wanted me to know. And someone smashed the back window of my car in the pub carpark after Barbara's funeral."

"I'm sorry Michael ..."

The waitress suddenly appeared, balancing a tray in one hand. The teacups rattled in their saucers as she placed them abruptly onto the table.

"Thanks," Michael muttered. Maggie simply arched an eyebrow.

"And then there was this." He smoothed out the crinkled piece of paper from his wallet.

Maggie bent her head over the ghoulish drawing of a face with a long thin neck and a hangman's noose, as if inspecting a rare stamp.

She leant on her elbows. "I think it's a bit weird. The Fishers aren't known for messing around like this."

She glanced around the cafe. "There's something else."

Michael noticed the waitress talking in hushed tones to two ladies, regulars he assumed, their heads twitching, nodding in conspiratorial agreement. They kept looking across as they sipped their tea. He wondered if they should leave.

Maggie seemed not to have noticed.

"It's something Eddie told me, he'd gone to the Doncaster races with some of his mates. He saw one of Lee's taxis pull up outside a pub near the main entrance. He knew all about Lee being in hospital, so he was a bit intrigued.

He got a good look at the driver. From his description I reckon it was Dennis. He saw two men getting into the taxi. He thinks they could have been Fisher's goons."

Michael felt his left eye twitch. "Could have been anyone. Maybe Eddie was mistaken?"

"About them being Fisher's men?" Maggie shook her head. "I doubt that's a mistake Eddie would make. He knows them too well, and not in a good way."

"You'd have known a few, growing up next to the estate? ... Brendan Fisher, maybe?"

Maggie glared at him. "I was just a kid," she replied, her voice a low whisper. Michael shifted uneasily in his chair. He wished he hadn't probed. He watched as she fought to regain her composure.

"Eddie showed me the scar across his stomach," he said. "It looked very nasty."

Maggie stiffened, "He nearly died. They ripped him open — it was touch and go. It's taken a long time for him to get the swagger he had before he got knifed. This gardening business has been the best thing."

Michael took a gulp of his now tepid tea. "Why did they go after him?"

"He told them he wouldn't do their dirty business anymore; he wanted out. It's not something you tell the Fishers. I told him to get away ... Canada, Australia ..."

"Why didn't he?"

"It's not that easy. He tried, but he has a record and no real skills. They don't make allowances for someone like that."

"I don't suppose the police were interested?"

Maggie gave a stifled laugh, "What do you think? Nobody talks, nobody wants to know. They'd love to get Brendan Fisher, but he's clever."

"You think that's who Dennis is mixed up with?"

"I hope not, Michael. I really hope not."

He looked up and examined her face. She was attractive: hard looking, but attractive.

"What are you staring at, Michael?"

"That scar on your lip ..." he said, pointing to the same spot above his own mouth.

Maggie touched it with the tip of her fingernail. "Oh, that ... a long time ago: it was someone I shouldn't have got involved with — prone to a bit of violence. Sometimes I try and hide it ... it's a reminder of how bad my life might have been if I hadn't had the strength to move on."

"I didn't notice it before."

"It's surprising what you can cover up, Michael," she replied.

Michael looked again at the scar on Maggie's lip. He wondered if it was any of the Fishers who'd hurt her. Brendan Fisher, maybe. He was well known for his vicious streak, even back then.

Chapter 22

Dennis parked on a rough patch of ground in front of the industrial unit. Owen was holding the office door open, as if he was waiting for Dennis to arrive. Leo rushed out, laughing, as if it was some schoolboy game. Owen winked at Dennis and held a finger across his lips, as if continuing the game. Brendan was standing at the far end of the table. The game, or whatever it was, came to a sudden halt. He sat heavily on a padded swivel chair. It creaked under his weight. They sat in silence while Leo made coffee. He carried over the cups on a small tray.

Brendan took a few sips and carefully returned his cup to the matching saucer.

"Welcome to the meeting, Dennis," he said.

Leo sniggered. Brendan stopped stirring his coffee and tapped the rim of his cup with his teaspoon. He placed it carefully in the saucer and glared at Leo. "This is a business meeting. No need for you to be stupid."

Leo mumbled something almost inaudible and stared down at his own coffee.

Brendan Fisher continued as if accepting Leo's incomprehensible remark as an apology. "You're one of us now, Dennis. You'll need to know something about our organisation." He paused and began to munch on a ginger biscuit. He took his time, swiped the crumbs off the table and then continued.

"We run several legitimate businesses mainly in scrap, waste, recycling." He pointed to a framed certificate on the wall. "That's from the Environment Agency. It's a certificate of approval for us to handle toxic waste. They're grateful for what we do, ain't that right?" Leo and Owen nodded, vigorously.

"Course, there's the problem of your dad." Brendan Fisher fixed on Dennis' face, his pale eyes searching, as if looking for something he'd missed. He continued his stare and began tapping his fingers on the table. "That's where we'll need your help."

Dennis' mind was a muddle of images; slashed tyres, gouged paintwork ... and pounding the back window of his dad's Volvo with a hammer and flinging a brick through their front window. His mother now dead — whose fault was that?

"Dennis, Dennis! Are you with us or not!" Brendan's aggressive tone snapped him back from the ghoulish thoughts pulsing in his head.

"Yeah ... sorry." That word! It crept up on him at the worst times.

Brendan Fisher smiled, "No need to apologise. You 'aint thick, Dennis. Just keep up."

He swallowed hard, sinking the word 'sorry' into his gut.

"Your dad's a lucky man," continued Brendan, his eyes glinting like granite.

"How come?" Dennis asked, tentatively.

"He's still alive, still in one piece."

Dennis stared at the table.

And my Billy's dead.""

Dennis' hand shook. He knocked over his coffee sending thin brown rivulets running like a mad, meandering stream. The four men sat and watched, as if mesmerised. Leo sprang up, grabbed a kitchen roll from the rack next to the sink and began mopping the table. Brendan pushed back his executive chair and swung it half round. He heaved himself up and rested his thick saddlebag of a backside on the edge of the table. He sat for some time, staring in the direction of a framed ink drawing on the wall.

"Limited edition, that is," he said. "Is that what you are, Dennis — a 'limited edition'?" He edged himself back into his chair, turned back around and glared at Dennis. "He's not your dad, not anymore. He's a murderer — got it!"

The slow rhythmical drip from the tap into the stainless-steel stink echoed in the tense silence. Dennis stared at the table. Words lodged in his throat. His head decided to nod, slowly, as if controlled by something remote.

Brendan leant forward, "A murderer needs to be punished — an eye for an eye." The shrill whistle of a truck's airbrakes interrupted his intimidating glare. "Ain't you got a taxi to run?" He said in a dismissive tone. "Dennis paused, briefly, and walked quickly to the door. Fisher called after him, "Remember what I said."

Dennis nodded. It wasn't a conversation; it was an order.

He drove slowly, letting his car amble forward, watching the industrial unit grow ever smaller in his rearview mirror. He had few bookings for the rest of the day, just a pick-up from the bus station and three runs to one of the supermarkets. The thought of helping one his regulars lift shopping from her trolley felt comforting, like a temporary analgesic.

He was glad when his last pick-up called to say she didn't need a taxi. Something about her daughter — he was too distracted to take in the details.

He was stretched out on the couch having taken several paracetamol for a thumping headache when Amy called from the hallway,

"It's me."

It always struck him as odd that she should announce herself, as though he might be expecting someone else to open the door to the flat.

"How's your day been?" she asked as Dennis stumbled groggily through to the kitchen. It was more of a greeting than an enquiry.

Dennis hugged her, crushing the bottle of milk she was carrying.

"Let me get this in the fridge."

She looked at him as she closed the fridge door. "Are you ok? Must have been a busy day."

"Just tired."

"I hope you aren't still angry at your dad."

Dennis turned quickly and thrust his face towards hers. "If it wasn't for him, I'd never have been in this mess," he said, tersely.

Amy sighed. "I wish you wouldn't talk like that. I think you should go and see him. At least talk to Lisa — your sister, remember?"

"Let's drop it, ok." Dennis replied.

Amy leant against the kitchen countertop. It was a minute or so before she spoke, as if waiting for the silence to have some sort of prescient intent.

"Maggie said Eddie — he's her nephew — saw you near the racecourse at Doncaster. He saw two men get into your car."

Dennis shifted uneasily. "So what? It was two punters who'd used Lee in the past, if you must know. Couldn't turn it down, could I?"

"Sometimes you scare me, Dennis. I just hope you aren't mixed up with the wrong crowd."

"Don't be ..."

Amy slapped her hand down on the countertop.

"What!? Thick! Stupid! Don't you dare ..."

"Sorry ... I didn't mean ..."

"Sorry! You're no better than Lee!" She threw a teaspoon at the draining board. It scudded across the surface and pinged into the stainless-steel sink. "Who were they, drug dealers working for the Fishers? That's what Eddie thinks."

Dennis shook his head. "No ... no, nothing like that. Please Amy, you've got to believe me."

"That's just it. I don't believe you. And do you know what? I don't trust you!"

She stormed down the corridor and slammed the bedroom door. Dennis stood, transfixed, spiked to the floor. The rifle-like crack of the door echoed in the bare walls of the corridor like the steel doors of a prison cell. It was only yesterday she'd told him, "You make me feel safe."

That's what he wanted — to make her feel safe. He wanted her to know he loved her.

Later that evening, he got a call from Brendan Fisher,

"I need you here tomorrow morning at ten, same place. Park 'round the back."

He set off early, just in case. He knew the traffic could be particularly bad at that time of day with trucks coming and going from the industrial park. He was stuck behind a large artic for the last few miles heading in the same direction. Bright, yellow indicators began their rhythmical flashing as the driver swung the rig onto the road leading to the warehouses. Dennis eased back, giving the driver space on the long, sweeping entrance road. Its brake lights flashed red as the driver dabbed his airbrakes before negotiating a sharp, righthand turn onto a spur road that led to loading bays at the rear of the units. He pulled up and watched as the driver backed into the loading bay for unit No 7, the one used by Brendan Fisher.

Dennis didn't want to risk being seen, snooping. He drove his car slowly round the back of the units and slipped into one of the parking spaces. He'd found a pocket-sized camera, a Canon, hidden under a battered and half-empty box of tissues and a few betting slips in the glove box. He reckoned Lee must have got it from one of his mates; they always had something to sell or to trade. It had a small image display, a zoom lens and slipped easily into his jacket pocket.

A footpath led along the edge of a high steel fence separating the loading bays from the other areas, mainly small offices and commercial buildings. He watched the truck driver climb down from his cab and move to the rear of the vehicle. He was lowering the tailgate as the roller-door at the back of the unit began to lift. He wasn't surprised to see Leo leaning his bulk against the side of the artic, talking to the driver.

A pallet truck, with Owen in its open-sided cab, moved towards the rear of the artic. Its long steel arms protruded forwards like tusks on some prehistoric animal. He manoeuvred the pallet truck and began moving square boxes from the truck's container and into the industrial unit. The crates were stacked three high, dwarfing the pallet truck, its hydraulics groaning under the load. Dennis waited until he was sure he couldn't be seen and then took out the camera. He forced himself to breathe slowly, catching his breath in the seconds it took to run off several images. He zoomed in as far as the camera would allow, aiming at the three figures; Leo, Owen and the driver, as well as taking several shots of the crates.

Dennis waited until the vehicle had been unloaded and the driver had climbed into the cab before walking back to his car. He slipped the camera back into the glovebox and hid it behind a box of tissues. The artic vehicle was almost out of sight by the time he'd pulled round into the parking spaces designated for 'Industrial Unit No 7'.

A single rap and Leo was there holding the heavy door open as if he'd been posted for a specific purpose.

"Mornin' Dennis." He sounded almost affable, even a grin.

Brendan Fisher gave the briefest of nods. He was wearing half-moon, designer glasses and scrutinising a sheaf of documents. Leo moved near the sink.

"Want one?" he asked, lifting a plain blue mug.

Dennis nodded, "Thanks."

"We've been busy, 'ain't we?" Brendan remarked, as if Dennis was in the 'know'.

For just a moment, Dennis felt he could relax and grab the seemingly, friendly words as if they were a precious gift. It was the pause that tipped him off. A pause punctuated by a groan from Leo. They were words laced with threats, the same language used in prisons, on the streets, even at school — delicate and dangerous, coded language that made him uncomfortable, put him off balance.

"Don't suppose you saw that truck leavin'?" Brendan asked, those pale eyes squinting above his half-moon glasses. Dennis took a sip of his coffee, a pause that stopped him jumping into a reply.

"Er ... Yeah. There was an artic pulling away as I drove up."

"That's one of ours. We handle two loads a week. They're kept here for a week — sometimes more," Leo said.

Brendan glared at him.

"What's in the boxes?" Dennis asked, nodding towards the rear of the warehouse.

"Stuff," Brendan replied. "Phones, mostly." He paused, "You can help Leo do an inventory. Don't want any mistakes. Our clients don't like mistakes."

Leo smirked and handed Dennis a clipboard with a yellow form attached. It was headed 'Communication Systems'.

"Let's go," said Leo, reaching out to a red push-button switch. Fluorescent tubes flickered, flooding the rear of the building in a spiking, blue brilliance that bounced off the dull containers giving them a sheen like polished wood.

Leo pointed at the form, "All you do is count the crates and fill in the form — easy."

Dennis quickly counted the stack; a row of six, four deep, three high. It seemed a pointless exercise. He scribbled the number in the relevant box on the form. Leo leaned over and stabbed a stubby finger at the bottom of the form.

"Sign it," he said.

"Me?" Dennis asked, surprised.

"Yeah. You checked 'em, you sign."

Dennis held the biro poised above the form; his fingers stiff, reluctant.

"Just sign it," Leo repeated.

Dennis sighed and scrawled his signature. Leo grabbed the clipboard and inspected the form.

"Got to print your name ... here," he said, pointing to a box adjacent to his signature ... "And the date."

Leo unclipped the form and slid it in front of Brendan. He scanned it quickly.

"Thanks, Dennis. You're an employee now, on the payroll. Not much; think of it as a token gesture for your support." He took out a single sheet of paper,

"You'll need to sign this. It keeps it all legit."

"What is it?"

"It's your contract of employment. Like I told you, you're one of us, now. You work for the company. You have a responsible job, Dennis, checking off loads, filling out forms, keeping our clients happy."

"I don't need a job, thanks. I've got my taxi to run."

"That! How much do you make running grannies around? A piddling amount. Besides, you can keep it. It's handy, having another job. Just remember, I know a thing or two — you 'aint got a taxi license, for one. And a cash business like that — I bet it all goes straight into your back pocket." He curled a smile, "You're a bit of a crook, really. Course, it goes without sayin' I expect complete confidentiality. Don't even think about doing anything stupid. Got it? That nice girlfriend of yours, what's her name? Amy ... that's it, quite a looker, she is. Be terrible if that pretty face of hers ever got disfigured. That's the right word, isn't it, Dennis, disfigured?"

Dennis felt lightheaded, his skin prickled, his face felt cold.

"What's the matter, Dennis? You don't look well." Brendan Fisher's tone was upbeat, as if he'd just been given good news. "I'm sure it won't come to that. I mean, who wants to see a nice girl like Amy with an ugly face ... What do you think?"

Dennis swallowed; the tang of incipient vomit filled his nostrils.

"Say something, Dennis. I want to hear you're not going to let that girlfriend of yours see an ugly face every time she looks in a mirror."

Dennis couldn't speak. He daren't even try. He just nodded. A brief, quick nod. It was all he could manage.

"Good. Nice to know you'll do the right thing. She'll be happy, very happy, to know how much you care." He raised his coffee cup, as if making a toast. "Here's to you, Dennis." His look suddenly changed. "Now piss off."

Dennis moved quickly towards the door. He needed no second invitation.

"There's the other business, o'course," Brendan Fisher growled, just as Dennis grasped the door handle. "Mr Michael Barrett ... "

Dennis shuddered. "Yeah, I know," he breathed, his voice almost a whisper.

"An eye-for-an-eye, Dennis. That's what we want. Think about it — Billy murdered ..." He paused, "And your mother dead," he added, slowly, deliberately ... "That can't be right, can it?"

The air outside was still cool. It tasted fresh, like a whiff from an ozone-filled sea breeze. His hands were shaking as he fumbled with the keys. His head was thumping, his heart pounding. Exhaling slowly seemed only to make it worse. He was startled by a white van heading at speed towards him. He panicked, wondering where he was. The white van was flashing its lights, its horn blaring. Dennis suddenly realised he was on the wrong side of the road. He swung his car over catching sight of the van driver shaking his fist as he sped past.

It took several minutes of careful driving before Dennis began to feel in control, not just of the car, but of himself. He glanced at the digital clock on the dashboard — 09:45. His head was clearer now, his breathing had slowed, the pounding in his head had eased. He remembered: a comforting, mundane task. He had to collect Mrs Rogers — another of his regulars. He hoped it would help push Brendan Fisher's menacing words to the back of his brain, at least for a while.

His thoughts turned to his dad,

An eye for an eye ...

He'd hated his dad — those stupid wrestling matches, his dad grinning from ear to ear at his squeals and cries. He remembered the thumps from his uncle, a headlock from his cousin and his dad always laughing and encouraging. "Grab his leg, Dennis ... Christ, can't you do better than that! ... Freddy, no eye gouging ..." He remembered cowering from his dad's huge boxing gloves in those enforced sparring episodes. He could hear him now, "Come on Dennis, hit me. Watch my eyes ..." And then a stinging smack from his dad's huge boxing gloves as soon as he lifted his head. Worst were the blows to his solar plexus ... "That's where you need to hit 'em. Bend 'em double, then a swift uppercut ..." It invariably ended with a swift uppercut.

Dennis clenched hist fists, "The bastard deserves what's coming," he muttered. "An eye for an eye."

Chapter 23

It was 6:30pm and no sign of Amy. She was normally home by 5:00 ... 5:30 at the latest. He checked the bedroom; nothing seemed out of place. Her clothes were neatly folded in the dressing table drawers, her nightie was tucked in behind her pillow, the small suitcase she used when staying overnight at her aunt's place was still in the back of the wardrobe. His brain raced;

Where is she? Working late? Sometimes, Maggie asked her to help clear up, especially when they'd had a busy day at the market. She went for a drink with a few of her pals once or twice a week — was that it? Maybe he should call? And say what? Where are you? Why aren't you home? She might get upset and accuse me of being possessive, jealous — like Lee.

The last thing he wanted was anymore comparisons with her ex. He didn't hear her come in. She was suddenly there, standing in the bedroom door, staring incredulously at the half-open drawers, her pillow askew, the mirrored wardrobe door slid open.

"What are you doing?" She pushed past him and began rearranging her clothes, sliding the hangers in the wardrobe so that they hung neatly. "You've no right to go through my things! What were you looking for? Money, jewelry, something to pay off your drug buddies?"

"No ... no, nothing like that. I was worried. You weren't home. I thought ..."

"You thought, what, I might leave? If I had any sense, I would. Anyway, this is my place. It's you that'll be leaving. If you must know, I was with Maggie. We went for a drink."

"Oh?"

"We talked about you, Dennis. I asked her what I should do. She's as concerned as I am. You either come clean and tell me what's going on, or you leave."

"I suppose that's Maggie's advice?"

"Yes, Dennis, it is. I thought we had something. I thought I could trust you. I need that more than anything. It's more important than ..."

"Love?"

"Don't give me that soft crap! It's an easy thing to say; flows easily off the tongue when you think you need it. I thought I knew you. You've changed. I should have realised prison would do that. You always get yourself in with the wrong crowd. I warned you about Lee, told you to be careful. You're still mixed up with the Fishers, I know you are. Maggie thinks so too. They're dangerous — seriously dangerous. They almost killed Maggie's nephew, left him for dead. If you are with them, I want you to get out of my flat, now!"

"I can't leave you, Amy."

"Can't! It's not your choice, Dennis. What are you — a lovesick leech!"

"Please Amy ... I only want to protect you."

"From what? From who? What makes you think I need you? Believe me, I don't."

Amy turned and walked quickly down the corridor. Dennis followed, striding after her, reaching out with his arm.

She spun round,

"Don't touch me!" She thrust her chin towards him, "This is your last chance, Dennis. You tell me what's going on, OR LEAVE!" Her voice was almost cracking, her eyes sparkling behind a slick of welling tears.

They were in the kitchen now; Amy was leaning over the countertop, rocking back and forth on her elbows. She looked up at Dennis,

"Well ...?"

Dennis paced round the kitchen, pausing to flick on the kettle. He took down two coffee mugs, got a carton of milk from the fridge and poured boiling water over the coffee granules. He felt calm now, almost relieved.

"Ok," he said, sliding one of the mugs towards her. "I'll tell you everything."

"I'm listening," Amy replied, her scepticism evident from the tone of her voice.

Dennis rubbed his palms together as if warming himself against the cold.

"It's the Fishers ..."

Amy groaned, "I knew it! You idiot!"

"Please Amy — you need to know — I'm scared, scared what they'll do."

"You should have thought about that before you went running to them. Look what they did to Lee!"

Dennis hung his head, "Yeah," he replied.

"What did you expect would happen — they'd just give him a slap on the cheek? You really are something else, Dennis. How the hell did you get yourself involved with them anyway?"

He fidgeted with his mug. "Prison was hell, I didn't think I'd survive, especially when they found out dad worked at the Young Offenders. I got the treatment; you've no idea. In some ways the days weren't as bad as the nights. In the day, there was a routine, there was order, of a kind. At night, every night, they'd shout and scream as we headed to our cells for lockdown, telling me what they had lined up, things they were going to do.

"The screws didn't care; they only intervened when it got serious. They just watched, smirking, laughing, as if I was the entertainment." He glanced at Amy, a furtive look as if expecting a rebuke of some kind.

"Go on," she told him.

"It was in the canteen. They were doing the usual, spitting in my food, making me eat stuff off the floor. This big ugly screw pointed to some eggs they'd pushed off my tray. I just lost it. I grabbed a handful and shoved it into his face. It felt great — I wasn't high or anything, but I could have been. It was as if it wasn't really me. I was just watching my arm shove a sticky handful of egg and mash into his face. He just stood there, not moving; I think he couldn't believe what I'd done. Next thing there was a full-on riot. I was put in isolation. That's when I tried to hurt myself. I just wanted to die. When I got back to my cell they came for me."

"Who?"

"Fisher's men; they run the jail. Many of the screws just stay clear. Some are blackmailed to do what they want. Danny Fisher is the main man. Brendan Fisher is a cousin, I think. I thought I was a dead man. A Fisher wanting to see the son of a screw — what would you think?"

"So, what happened? How come they left you alone?"

"He knew about me and Billy Fisher. We were school mates, sort of. Then there was the market break in ... I opened the back gate ..."

"We all know that!"

Dennis stared down at the glinting white counter. "Danny Fisher said he'd help me coz I'd done stuff for Billy. The word got out: no-one touched me, I could see the fear in their eyes."

"Oh, yeah. And then what? Don't tell me you were left to enjoy life."

"They got me to do some deliverin', collectin'."

"Drugs, I suppose."

"Fags and favours, that's why they called it."

"Very nice! It sounds like schoolboys in one of those posh, private schools."

"Sometimes a bit of violence — to make sure they understood …"

"Put the fear of God in them, you mean! I never thought you'd end up a thug."

"I didn't want to; I had no choice. A few days before I got out, Danny Fisher told me if ever I needed help … that's when he gave me Brendan Fisher's number."

"And you got him and his cronies to take care of Lee, that's right, in't it?"

"I did it for you, Amy."

"What! They nearly killed him!"

"I didn't think they'd hurt him like they did."

"You knew it'd have to be bad enough to make him leave me alone … and then there's his car. They were brutal, Dennis! That car is blood money!"

Amy took several deep breaths and grabbed the edge of the sink.

"You ok?" Dennis said in a soft, apologetic tone.

"What do you think! No, Dennis, I'm not alright; this isn't alright!" She turned and glared. "You'd better keep going. Tell me the truth. Those two men who got in your car; they work for the Fishers, don't they?"

"Yeah, for Brendan Fisher. He says I owe him for what they did to Lee."

"Why doesn't that surprise me? They'll never leave you alone, Dennis. What is it he wants?"

"Er ... to work for him ... for his firm. Something to do with imports and exports — mobile phones mainly."

"A job! Is that it! There's more, isn't there? Don't leave anything out. This is your one chance to be honest with me — your only chance!"

Dennis gulped, coughed and reached for a glass of water. "That's it — just a job."

Amy glared at him, "I'm not listening to anymore, Dennis! I'm going out. I'm meeting the girls in Gino's as soon as I've got changed."

Within minutes she was back in the kitchen. "I'm late ... get your own tea."

Dennis watched her tug at the zip on her black, knee-length boots." She grabbed a pair of high heels — I'll need these for later," she said, dangling them from her fingers.

"Want me to pick you up?"

"What, don't you trust me now?"

"No ... I just want you to be ok. Call me if you ..."

"We're going in Angie's car. Don't wait up, I'll be late. We're going clubbing."

A pang of jealousy hit him in the stomach, like a well-aimed punch. The door slammed shut leaving him feeling empty and lonely, her perfume lingering, slowly weakening, drifting off on some unseen current of air.

Angie waved, tapping her wrist, signalling it was time to go. Amy was in full flow — flinging herself around the floor, arms raised above her head, green and red strobes splashing her with colour — egged on by a ring of revellers, smiling, laughing, bouncing to the loud, thumping beat. There'd been plenty of drink: she'd been careful at first, watching what she drank, but other drinks were passed round, shots were laid out on side tables, each glass emptied in a single gulp and slammed back down onto the polished wood. By the time she'd queued and found her jacket, there was no sign of Angie, or any of her friends.

She staggered out of Sparklers Night Club, tripped on the bottom step and caught her spiky heel in a metal grating. It snapped as she fell, wrenching her ankle and sending her sprawling on the rough pavement. One of the bouncers lifted her as if she was a piece of limp cloth. Her shoes, one looking pathetically damaged, the other pristine in comparison, slipped off her toes and onto the street.

"Who're you with?" he said, propping her against the wall.

"Angie," she replied, looking round as if her friend would suddenly appear. Groups of clubbers were spilling out onto the street, some singing, others shouting and laughing. Amy tried to focus, searching the crowd for someone she recognised.

She swayed, unsteadily, and grabbed the arm of the bouncer.

"You need a lift," he told her. He pointed down the street. "There's a taxi-rank outside the Duke of Cumberland — take that alleyway across the road." He pointed, like a drill sergeant. "It's a short cut." He picked up her shoes, snapped off the other heel and thrust them into her hands. She leant against the bouncer's big frame as she thrust her feet into what remained of her shoes. She'd bought them earlier in the week; glossy shocking-pink with killer heels.

He took her firmly to the edge of the pavement and nudged her forward.

"Thanks," she muttered, hobbling across the street.

The alleyway was lit only by a few window lights set high on the gable-end walls sending out a muted glow from behind thin curtains. Amy hugged one wall, sliding her hands along the brick as she inched forwards like a mountaineer traversing a ravine, each dim window light providing a comfort, of sorts. Her uncertain float of inebriation had been replaced by a feeling of panic. Her fingers were scraping at the brick, her heart was thumping, and she was shivering, despite the warm night. She peered further down the alleyway, her eyes now adjusted to the dark. She could see a dim glow, like that from a nearly defunct torch, illuminating the far end of the alley. "Thank God," she muttered, quickening her steps, stumbling several times in her haste, but relieved as if she'd suddenly woken from a nightmare.

She only caught a glimpse of the figure lurking in the doorway as she hurried past, her fingers catching his jacket. She gasped and pulled her arm back as if she'd touched something repulsive. Her scream was stifled by a large, gloved hand planted across her mouth. A stubbled chin thrust into her cheek; her head pulled back hard against his shoulder. He was breathing hard, his nicotine breath filling her nostrils. He pushed her into the doorway, pinning her against a door, old bits of flaking paint smearing across her cheek and into her mouth. She could feel his heavy frame, his groin ramming against her backside, his free hand groping her breasts. Amy unclenched her teeth, letting one of his fingers slip into her mouth. She bit hard, her teeth penetrating the thin leather and into flesh. He jerked his hand free and thumped her head into the door,

"Bitch!"

He reached round, grabbed the front of her dress and tugged violently, ripping the thin material as if it were a sheet of wrapping paper. He leaned heavily against her, his hands searching, pulling, probing, his hips grinding hard against her, his chest heaving. He suddenly stopped, holding her with one hand while he tugged at his belt. He cursed and dropped his other hand from her shoulder. Amy screamed; a high-pitched, ear-splitting scream. Her attacker was still fiddling with his awkward belt, now using both hands. For just a moment, he seemed confused, numbed by events — his state of excitement, his uncooperative belt, her loud, shrill scream — and someone shouting from the end of the alley.

Amy willed her breathless lungs to scream again, a thin useless whine. And then voices. She shook herself free and tugged at the remnants of her dress as her attacker ran off, back down the alleyway. Three people rushed towards her — two men and a woman — all about her age. The young woman ran over carrying a man's bomber jacket and draped it over her shoulders. Amy felt her body tremble. She pulled the jacket tight, covering herself.

"You ok?"

"Yeah, thanks."

"Did he ...?"

Amy shook her head, "No ... you scared him off."

"My boyfriend's calling the police. We'll wait 'till they come."

"Thanks," Amy stammered, her body suddenly feeling cold. She felt unsteady, her head swimming. She reached out for the wall, wondering why it seemed to tilt away from her. Just as she thought she was about to collapse; she felt an urgent grab.

"Steady" — a man's voice.

His girlfriend slipped an arm round her shoulder, "You'd better sit down until the police get here. Where's Josh?" she said, speaking across Amy to her boyfriend.

"Gone back to the top of the alley — so they don't miss us," he replied, helping lower Amy to the base of the wall. "Anyone we should 'phone?" he asked.

She nodded. "In my bag ... my mobile," she replied, reaching out across the rough pavement as if it should be there, next to her. She began looking from side to side ... "My bag," she wailed. Anger replaced her threatening tears. "Where's my bag!!?" She continued looking around, patting the pavement as if it might be hidden under a slimy slab.

"Not here," said the young woman. "Ricky, go back and see if you can find it,"

Ricky illuminated the alley using his mobile phone. "Yeah, ok," he said, walking quickly down the alley.

"I think he must have taken it — the bloke who attacked you," said the young woman, crouching in front of Amy. "My name's Rachel, by the way."

Flashing blue lights lit the alleyway, bouncing off the high, gable-end walls. Josh was leading two police officers striding purposely towards them, bright light from their torches bouncing in the dark. A woman police officer knelt in front of Amy, "What happened?"

"He grabbed me ..."

"Who grabbed you?"

"I didn't see — he was hiding in a doorway."

"He ripped your dress?"

"Yeah," Amy replied, "He grabbed me from behind and shoved me against a door." Amy shivered and tugged at the bomber jacket. "Then he grabbed my top ... here," she said, pointing to the centre of her chest.

"Can you remember anything about him — what he was wearing?"

"Gloves ... he was wearing gloves. He had his hand over my face — he nearly smothered me —I couldn't breathe. He was heavy, I could hardly move. I bit one of his fingers ..." She tried to spit; a dribble that ran down her chin. "I can taste that glove," she said, wiping her mouth with the back of her hand.

"Did he rape you?"

Amy shook her head. "No; I screamed..."

"We heard her shouting," said Rachel. "We were walking past the end of the alleyway."

"You are?"

"Rachel, Rachel Burns. This is Josh," she said, turning to her boyfriend.

Josh pointed at a figure walking towards them, "That's Rick ... Any luck?"

Rick shook his head, "Sorry," he said, addressing Amy.

The other police officer flashed his torch down the alley, as if its light might reveal something. "What did he take?" he asked.

"My handbag," Amy replied.

"What's in it?"

"My mobile and maybe twenty pounds."

The woman police officer helped Rachel lift Amy to her feet.

"You sure you're ok?" she said.

"Yeah, I'm ok, thanks."

The policewoman peered closely at Amy's face. "Looks like just a few scratches and bruises. I think we should get you home. We can get a statement tomorrow." She signalled to her partner, "Get a blanket from the car," she said, taking out her notebook. She flipped it open and began taking names and contact numbers. A few minutes, and Amy was wrapped in a tartan blanket.

"Thanks," she said to the three friends. They stood, staring at Amy.

"Hope you're going to be alright," said Rachel. Her voice had lost its strong tone. She sounded hesitant and nervous. "It could have been me," she said, leaning into her boyfriend. He slipped an arm round her shoulders and slowly led her away. She was sobbing.

Amy was glad the porch light had been left on. She'd told the police officers she was alright — several times. She instinctively reached for her bag, suddenly realising it was gone, and with it her door keys.

"Oh, hell," she muttered. She stabbed at the doorbell several times, the familiar chimes giving her a feeling of security. It took several rings before the kitchen lights illuminated the glassed tympanum above the door.

Dennis gasped as she stepped into the flat, looking agog at the tartan blanket draped round her shoulders.

"Amy! What happened?"

She let the blanket slip off her shoulders. Dennis stood, transfixed, as if he couldn't comprehend what he was seeing.

"Oh, my God! Your dress! ..." He reached out, his hands barely touching her arms as if she was the most precious, delicate object he'd ever encountered. Amy moved closer slowly letting her body relax into his. Dennis picked up the blanket and wrapped it round her. He carefully led her into the bedroom and let her sit quietly on the edge of the bed.

"Thanks, Dennis. You are sweet." He blushed like a schoolboy.

She smiled, "I'm ok; just my pride. I was stupid."

"Who did this? Want to tell me about it?"

She shrugged her shoulders. "I couldn't find Angie. I fell — I must have been pretty drunk. One of the bouncers told me there was a shortcut to the taxi rank. I felt really nervous wondering why the hell that bouncer had told me to go down the alley. It was pitch black. I didn't see this man standing in a doorway. He grabbed me and shoved me against a door." She shuddered, "The bastard groped me. I managed to scream for help. I was lucky — they heard me, three of them. Rachel — that's it, Rachel — her boyfriend, and another lad. They shouted — I kept screaming."

"He ran off?"

Amy nodded. "They called the police — that's who gave me the blanket. They'll want me to make a statement."

"Maybe you should get some sleep?"

"Not a chance, Dennis — I'm wide awake now. I could do with a coffee."

They sat on the bed, slowly sipping milky-sweet coffee, her breathing soft, barely audible, his a slow exhale, their sounds deliberately numbed as if each wanted to converge to something they could share.

Chapter 24

Dennis couldn't sleep. Daylight seemed to be reluctant to show. The light changed almost imperceptibly as he lay watching the clock slowly and rhythmically deal its digits. He felt groggy and his head was thumping. He'd waited, impatiently, for the morning rays to appear and signal respite from his sleep-starved night. It did little to overcome his feeling of despair. Amy, his beautiful Amy, was lying next to him curled into a ball as if protecting herself from a further attack. He slipped out of bed and picked up his jeans from the small chair at his side of the bed, exposing the damaged wicker seat he'd promised to repair. He carefully opened the dresser drawer, lifted underwear and socks and sneaked out of the bedroom. His mouth felt dry and his breath had that stale morning odour he always tried to hide from Amy when they cuddled in the early hours.

His mind was racing. Did the Fishers have anything to do with this? Maybe it was a mugging; some scumbag looking for an opportunity? Why did she go down the alleyway — maybe it was a set-up? The bouncer had sent her that way — maybe he was in on it? His thoughts kept coming back to Brendan Fisher. Was it a warning? He'd threatened to hurt her if he didn't cooperate. But he was cooperating — sort of.

The shower provided a brief distraction. He scrubbed vigorously at his skin with the pumice stone Amy used for her feet, as if determined to scrape dirt-filled pores from his body. The shower gel stung where he'd scored the flesh on his arms. He wanted to hurt himself, inflict punishment and pain to counter his feelings of helplessness. For just a few moments, it felt good.

Amy appeared in her dressing-gown as he sat at the breakfast counter sipping his coffee, staring vacantly at the end wall, the one with a large clock mounted on imitation driftwood. She moved quickly, scuffing her pink slippers across the parquet floor.

Dennis grimaced at the red grazes on her face. "Sure you're ok?"

"Just a few scratches. My shoulder's sore; and my hip. I was wedged against the door frame ... it could have been worse, a lot worse."

"Maybe you should get checked over — see a doctor?"

Amy raised her head, defiantly. "I grew up seeing violence — it went with the territory." She spat out the words in sharp bursts. "The bastard took my bag — I only bought it last month."

"Maybe that's all he wanted?"

"Are you kidding!? He was looking for a woman too pissed to stop and think. If it hadn't been for that bloody bouncer, I wouldn't have gone near that alley. The bag was just coz he couldn't get what he wanted." She suddenly gasped, "I nearly forgot, he's got my phone ... and my keys!"

She grabbed a towel from the radiator. "I'm going for a shower," she said in a determined voice. "The policewoman is coming over to take a statement."

"Oh —what are you going to say?"

"Nothing much, I didn't see anything of his face ... I bit his finger." She scowled, "A big guy with a sore finger — I doubt if that'll help find him." Her eyes flashed, an angry, narrow-eyed stare. She kicked off her slippers, grabbed them off the floor and flung them down the hallway. "I'd prefer it if you weren't here," she told him.

"Ok," Dennis replied, hastily. "I've got a few runs to do anyway." He felt relieved. What if the police started asking him questions? . . . Where were you? Do you know anyone who might attack Amy?

"I'll head off, then," he said, quickly, concerned she might change her mind.

His car was his refuge. He could close the door, click in his seatbelt and drive, just drive. And he could think — at least turn things over in his head. Could it have been one of Brendan Fisher's thugs? It seemed weird to think of it as just a random attack. What about the bouncer?

"Dennis, dear, you've missed the turning — Sainsbury's — it's over there."

Mrs Robinson was tapping her finger on the window in the rear of the taxi.

He glanced in the rear-view mirror. She was clutching the handles of her large handbag, her hands tucked under her chin.

"Sorry, Mrs Robinson. I'll take the next right."

"It's not like you to forget which supermarket I use. Got lots on your mind, have you, dear?"

"I didn't sleep well," Dennis replied.

"Hot milk, Dennis. I always make myself a mug before bed."

Good for you, thought Dennis, his mind now devoid of anything other than an image of his passenger sipping her hot drink, wrapped in a pink dressing gown, her feet thrust into a pair of old slippers, her toe poking through a frayed end. He cracked open the window: the draught hit him like a stiff breeze.

"That better, dear?" asked Mrs Robinson.

"Yes, thanks," Dennis replied. "I was feeling a bit drowsy, that's all."

"You need to look after yourself, dear. We can't have you falling asleep at the wheel, can we?"

"No ... of course not. I'm fine, honestly." He pulled up outside the entrance to the supermarket. "I'll pick you up in an hour."

"Perfect," Mrs Robinson replied. Dennis stepped out and held the door for his elderly passenger. "If I were you," she said, as she checked her handbag, "I'd close my eyes for twenty minutes, or so. It does me the world of good."

Dennis pulled into one of the carpark spaces and sat staring out of the windscreen. He couldn't eradicate the thoughts in his head. They were more like accusations, the blame for what had happened pointing directly at him. He felt trapped, hopelessly snared in the grip of the Fishers. If nothing changed, he'd be back in prison, or dead. And any hint of betrayal? He knew what it meant. That's when you wished you were dead. It would be a slow, ugly death. And then an image of his father, taunting. 'Toughen up, Dennis ... '. That was always his dad's solution — act tough, be tough, never show fear. "You bastard," he said, loudly, his voice reverberating in the enclosed space. "You're as bad as the rest."

He felt his chest tighten; a sudden memory, like a panic attack, of being crushed in one of those wrestling bouts in their front room. At night he sometimes woke struggling to breathe, disorientated, his back sodden with sweat. He leant on his hands and let his forehead rest on the steering wheel. He realised, with jolt, that he was weeping. It was a feeling of powerlessness that made everything seem pointless ... useless.

He ignored Mrs Robinson as much as he could as he drove her back to her house, barely listening as she droned on about how concerned she was that he wasn't looking after himself.

"Thanks, Mrs Robinson," he muttered, as she took a five-pound note from her purse. Like all his regulars, she never queried why the fare was always the same round figure, even when he ran her round to her sister's house just a few streets away. It didn't seem like taking money illegally. They were simply compliant, grateful regulars.

He was supposed to go to the industrial unit after dropping off the old lady. He imagined himself bursting in, grabbing Brendan Fisher by the throat, demanding to know why they'd hurt Amy. He felt himself slump into his seat. It wasn't going to happen. There was no way he could attack a Fisher. Anyway, it might not have been them, he tried to tell himself, but without any real conviction. Maybe he'd find the courage to ask, demand perhaps? He had to know

Dennis took a longer route than necessary driving to Brendan Fisher's warehouse. It wasn't intended: he drove aimlessly down narrow streets, his brain a fog of indecision, eventually finding he'd driven in a circle, like a walker lost in a blizzard. Think! he told himself. He set off again, this time directing his vehicle to the roads he knew, roads that would take him to Brendan Fisher.

"You're late!" barked Leo. "Mr Fisher doesn't like to be kept waiting."

Dennis looked round. "Where is he?"

"Taking a piss."

Owen, stepped from the shadows at the back of the store, camouflaged by his slim build and soft sneakers. Brendan was just behind him, yanking at the zip on his large, flapping, chinos.

"Where the hell have you been!" he bellowed.

"Work. I had a regular customer."

"Work! Sitting on your 'arse. That's not work! Make sure you're here when I say — got it?"

"I need to keep my taxi business going. Makes it legit — you said as much."

"Yeah, well just don't think you can wander off whenever you like. Make sure I know when you're running your grannies to the hairdressers."

"If you say so."

"I do 'say so'. What's up with you?" He walked closer to Dennis, "I don't like your attitude."

Dennis willed himself not to flinch, "Amy was attacked last night."

Brendan Fisher stared at him. It was a look that conveyed all the menace of someone not used to being confronted.

"Bad was it?" he said, his eyes fixed on Dennis.

"Bad enough." Dennis replied. "She was lucky. A few cuts and grazes, that's all. Someone heard her shouting. The bastard ran off ..."

Owen smirked, "Before he shagged her."

Dennis glared, "Shut that stupid mouth of yours."

Owen took a quick intake of breath as if considering a sharp reply. All he managed was a scowl aimed at his feet.

"Did she see who it was?" asked Brendan Fisher.

Dennis shook his head, surprised at Brendan's apparent concern. "No, it was too dark. Heavy bastard, she said."

"Where?"

"Down an alley — opposite Springers nightclub," Dennis replied.

"What the heck was she doing down there?" Brendan Fisher sounded intrigued.

"One of the bouncers told her it was a short cut to a taxi rank," said Dennis,

Brendan Fisher shrugged, "That was her mistake. Sounds like a set up. What happened, exactly?"

Dennis gulped. "He took her bag when he ran off. Nearly ripped her dress off."

Owen sniggered and then swallowed whatever remark he'd thought of making.

"I don't suppose you lot know anything about it?" Dennis snapped. He had to stop himself from lunging at Owen. He wanted to smash his smug face, wipe that smirk off his ugly mouth. He clenched his fist, suddenly aware of a feeling of intense anger. In that moment, he felt no sense of fear.

"Cut it out," growled Brendan. "It wasn't any of my lads. It's not how we do things." He glared at Dennis. "Believe me, you'd know if it was any of us. I'll put out the word, see who was involved." He turned to Leo. "Have a chat to that bouncer ... he'll know something."

Brendan was suddenly all business. He glanced at his watch,

"Our truck should be here soon. Owen, get the forklift ready."

Chapter 25

Dennis thought Brendan had conveniently forgotten about the attack on Amy. It'd been a week since his confrontation with Owen. He wondered just how hard Leo would try to find the bouncer. They were all in the same club; big and bald, the younger ones pumped and muscled, others lazy, layered and large. Leo boasted that if he didn't know them, they knew him. He was surprised when Brendan suddenly asked Leo what he'd found out.

"Terry is the regular at Sparklers. I asked him about last Wednesday. He said there was another bouncer working there as well — works for that agency owned by Georgie Wilcox."

"Get a name?" Brendan sounded irritated. He was not a patient man.

"Sandy," Leo replied.

"Sandy? ... What kind of a name's that, for Christ's sake; Sandy who?"

"Terry didn't know ... he just called him Sandy."

"Next time I ask you I want more than just a name!" He strode off towards Owen at the rear of the warehouse mumbling angrily to himself, leaving Leo's head bobbing, apologetically, on his thick neck. Dennis thought better of thanking Leo. Instead, he followed Brendan Fisher, leaving Leo looking like a schoolboy who'd just been reprimanded by a stern headmaster.

The roller-doors rattled loudly revealing light from the early morning sun. Dennis blinked at the torch-like beam splitting the darkness at the rear of the unit. The truck was backing towards the unloading ramp, its lights flashing and a warning sound pulsating as it inched rearwards along the concrete pad. Owen manoeuvred the pallet handler onto the pad as the airbrakes hissed and the artic shuddered to a stop. Brendan began barking instructions;

"Dennis, get up there. Give 'em a hand," he shouted, gesticulating towards Leo and the driver straining to move the crates. It took an hour or so to unload the artic and for Owen to stack them carefully in the warehouse. There were twelve in total, identical in size. One was considerably heavier. It was badly scuffed and one corner had several broken slats. "What happened?" Brendan shouted. The driver didn't hear or didn't want to. He gunned the accelerator causing the vehicle's engine to roar in a plume of black diesel smoke.

Brendan stood waving uselessly at the rear of the artic as it disappeared behind a row of Robinson's Removal lorries parked along the exit road.

He kicked angrily at a tarpaulin laid out on the floor. "Need to get this crate fixed," he told Leo. He glanced at his wristwatch, "Got to go — don't leave 'till I say so. I'll be back around five."

Dennis instinctively glanced at his own watch. He had a taxi run at six. It'd be close.

Leo grabbed a toolbox set on a bench near the roller doors.

"Here," he said, handing a crowbar to Dennis. He rummaged further finding two more crowbars, a couple of hammers and a Stanley knife. He snapped the steel bands with a pair of tinsnips, slashed at the corrugated cardboard, and wrenched it away from the wooden packing crate snapping rows of metal staples holding the cardboard to the wood. The damage to the crate wasn't just at the exposed corner. Wood slats on the top and one side were cracked and broken as if someone had pounded the frame of the crate with a hammer. Leo ran his fingers over the splintered frame.

"Looks like it got dropped," Owen remarked. "Brendan 'aint goin' to be happy."

Leo grunted; "We'd better get it fixed," he said.

"There're some broken crates in the corner," Owen said. "Should be able to use the wood."

Leo held out one of the crowbars for Dennis, "Here ... be careful, don't want anything damaged."

Dennis levered one corner of the broken lid as Owen used his crowbar at the other end. It was well constructed. The top was secured with large four-inch nails hammered into a thick frame. It suddenly freed with a loud screech as the nails prised loose. Dennis couldn't help gasping at what he saw. His first thought was that it must be a mistake. He stared at the black rifle barrels layered between perforated-metal shoulder stocks and rows of curved ammunition magazines. They were sleek looking as if they were incapable of being used for anything more than a display. "AKM's" said Owen, lifting one out of the crate and attempting to assemble the folding shoulder stock. "Better than AK47's."

"Put it back!" barked Leo. "Don't be so bloody stupid."

Owen replaced the gun, carefully slotting it back between the rows of gun parts.

"Who are these for?" Dennis wasn't sure if he really wanted to know.

"Just get this crate fixed," Leo hissed, flinging his crowbar into the toolbox.

They managed to find a lid that was virtually intact from a pile of old crates stored in the far corner of the building. Dennis and Leo watched as Owen patched and reinforced the broken slats, handing him tools he needed like nurses supporting a surgeon in an operating theatre. They stood back and admired his handiwork. You'd have had to make a close inspection to see that the crate had been repaired. Owen was smiling broadly, running his hand over the edges.

Leo grinned. "Yeah, it's ok. That'll keep the boss happy."

Brendan came back early. They'd only just finished tidying up, sweeping the floor around the crate and returning the tools to the workbench. He flung the door open and shouted as he strode towards them,

"You finished?" He inspected the crate, tugging at the steel bands and examining the repairs they had made.

"Good job. Well done, lads." He turned to Dennis, "You've seen what's in this?" he said, wrapping his knuckles on the top of the crate.

Dennis stared at the crate and nodded, "Yeah, of course."

"Keep your mouth shut. The people we are dealing with don't like slip-ups. Just make sure you're here first thing on Thursday around eight."

Dennis checked his camera was tucked under the box of tissues in the glove compartment. He was nervous, very nervous. The sight of guns poking from the top of the damaged crate had shaken him badly. He was now part of something far worse than being involved with Brendan Fisher importing mobile phones. He liked to think he wasn't really a criminal. 'If I hadn't hit that idiot in the car ...' The thought that he might be the idiot was something he rarely considered. He was a victim of circumstance, of events beyond his control. He'd ended up in prison for something that wasn't his fault ... At least, that's what he told himself — and often. Phones and computers were bad enough — but guns! Who were they for — drug dealers? Crime bosses? He thought about an anonymous tip off to the police. Brendan Fisher would know it was him. He'd become embroiled in the whole operation — they had him — he was a part of whatever was going on. His name, his signature, was on documents held by Brendan Fisher. Nobody would believe he wasn't involved, especially given his obvious connection with the Fishers — Danny Fisher, Brendan Fisher, even Billy Fisher.

He suddenly thought about the camera in the glove compartment of his car. Would he dare use it? Would he get the opportunity? It was last week he'd given Leo a lift. Leo sneezed loudly, cupped his nose in both hands and wiped the glutinous drips with the back of his sleeve. Dennis had reached over without thinking and flipped open the glove compartment. Leo had delved in, grabbed a fistful of tissues, almost pulling the box out of the glove compartment. The camera had peeked out, like an unlit fuse. For a heart-stopping moment, Dennis waited for Leo to pull out the camera and dangle it, accusingly. Instead, he simply nudged it to the back of the glove compartment. He'd even apologised.

As he turned into the spur road leading to the industrial units, he noticed an empty cattle truck on the same road. Must be lost, he thought. This area is concrete, tarmac and cinder-block buildings, not a farm pasture. He chuckled to himself. One for the camera, maybe? He pulled into one of the car spaces at the front of Brendan's unit and watched the cattle-truck drive round into the loading bay at the rear of the unit. It had two decks painted dark green, slatted sides, a large cab — the sort that had a bed behind the front seats — and a tailgate splattered with dirt and grime kicked up from the tyres.

It looked well-used and in need of a good clean. Remnants of straw bedding were wedged between some of the side slats and the mudguards carried signs of dirt from wet fields. Brendan, Leo and Owen had already arrived.

"Get yourself a coffee," Leo instructed, "he'll be here any minute."

"A truck's just pulled in round the back," Dennis told him. "It's a cattle truck, though," he added, expecting they'd be surprised.

Brendan was suddenly out of his seat,

"That's our man," he said, walking quickly to the rear of the unit. He hit the button for the roller doors. The driver was already unlocking the tailgate. It swung down and clanged onto the loading ramp. "Alright, Frank?" Brendan shouted.

"Yeah ... I will be once that box of yours is loaded."

Brendan waved towards the pallet truck. "Owen ... get a move on!"

"Top deck," said Frank, directing Owen as he inched forward with the heavy crate they'd repaired.

Leo pushed Dennis towards a ladder at the front of the truck. "We need to attach the chain."

Dennis followed Leo up the vertical ladder, almost slipping on the greasy, metal upper deck. "Hook that end to the pallet," Leo instructed, dragging a second chain.

"Ok, Frank," he shouted. The chains stretched taut as the winching motor wound in the slack. The crate slid easily forward towards the back of the cab until it was tight against the frame of the truck, just under a curved wind deflector, painted red, like a cockscomb.

Dennis could hear Brendan and the driver talking,

"I need to get away asap," Frank told Brendan. "I'm booked on the night-ferry at Holyhead. Loading starts at nine and I've thirty store-cattle to collect from a farm near Coventry."

"When will you get to Limerick?" Dennis heard Brendan ask.

"The Ferry docks in Dun Laoghaire around three in the morning. My brother, Jonno, will be there. It's about three hours — we should get there about six, maybe six-thirty."

"What about the cattle?"

"That's the first job ... cattle first, then the crate. The farm's just outside Limerick, near Shannon."

"A long night," Brendan remarked.

"Yeah, well, you pay well. I've no complaints. As soon as the cattle are unloaded, I'll meet your lads. Their place is close."

"Still using that old potato store?"

"Yeah ... very quiet where they are. Have you been?" Frank asked.

Brendan laughed. "Many times. It belongs to a cousin."

"Got a lot of cousins, have you?"

"Enough," Brendan replied.

Leo approached from the rear of the truck.

"All sorted, Boss."

Brendan Fisher took out a wad of money wrapped in a thick rubber band. Frank flicked his thumb across the edges of the notes.

"It's all there," Brendan told him.

Frank grinned. "I just like the feel of it," he said as he climbed into his cab.

They stood and watched the cattle-truck driving off down the curved slip road. Brendan glanced at his watch, "This time tomorrow the boyos will be opening that parcel and distributing the goods. Nice work, lads." He peeled off some notes from a roll in his pocket. "Here, a bit of luck money for your troubles."

Dennis gave a mumbled "Thanks," and stared at the notes in his fist. With just a quick look he knew it was more than he'd earn in a week running his taxi.

Brendan told them to clear up the place and get rid of the stench — he'd be out the rest of the day, he told them. It was only then that Dennis realised his jeans were smeared with cattle dung.

"Where are they going with those guns?" he asked Leo.

"Limerick — you heard."

"I mean after that. Who's bought them."

"That's not our problem."

"Paramilitaries?" probed Dennis.

"Like I said, it's not our problem."

Dennis hadn't noticed Owen standing nearby. He had this ability to slither up, almost silently, and stand on the edge of a conversation with a barely perceptible presence and suddenly announce himself, delighting, it seemed, in the way he could take people by surprise.

"I've got some information," he told Dennis, "About that girlfriend of yours. It was Lee Hogan who set her up. His mates did it — spiked her drink, shoved her outside. That bouncer was in on it. They paid him a hundred. Big money for someone like Lee Hogan. Don't know which of 'em did the deed, I didn't ask!" he added with a big smirk on his face. "Don't worry ... I let 'em know we didn't appreciate what they did. They won't bother her again. Brendan doesn't like that kind of messing. We look after our own, don't we Leo?"

Leo grunted. "She's got a pretty face,'aint she?"

"Nice body too," Owen added with another menacing smirk.

Dennis suddenly realised how much he hated the Fishers. Fear was somewhere lurking, but only lurking, slowly ebbing — at least in the moment. He clenched his fists, digging his fingernails into the palms of his hand. He wanted to make that feeling of hatred last.

Chapter 26

Amy pulled out Dennis' jeans from the pile of washing she was sorting. She held them up by one of the belt loops,

"Dennis ... Dennis! What happened to your jeans? They stink!"

He was still half-dressed. He pulled on a t-shirt and a pair of black chinos.

"Oh ... I slipped," he tried.

"Slipped! On cow dung!?"

He forced a quick laugh, "Must have been from a muck spreader. There's a farm near one of the council estates. I was picking up a fare."

Amy sniffed at one of the legs of the jeans. "I thought these were a favourite pair."

Dennis shrugged. They'll wash ..."

"Hope so," Amy replied. "You off out again?"

"Dunno." Dennis replied. "Depends ..."

"On what?"

"If I get a call — what else?" Dennis wanted to bang his head against the wall as soon as the words left his mouth. He stood and gaped at Amy.

"Sorry ... I didn't mean ... I just can't think straight ... I'm in trouble, Amy, big trouble."

"Whatever it is, you'd better get it sorted! It's those bloody Fishers, isn't it?"

Dennis nodded.

She pointed to the scratches on her face, "Did they do this!?" she shouted.

Dennis shook his head. "No, it wasn't anything to do with them. It was Lee Hogan's mates. He put them up to it."

"What! You said he'd leave me alone!"

"It's been sorted ..."

"Sorted! You and the Fishers I suppose. Are you working for them? ... You are, I just know it!"

Dennis flinched. His telling silence made Amy gasp. Her arms flailed as if desperately trying to avoid drowning in an angry sea.

"Why, Dennis? Why are you still involved with those scumbags? What the hell are you keeping from me?" Her arms dropped to her sides as if she'd resigned to her fate.

"I hate the bastards," he said. "I got sucked in; I wish I'd never ..."

"Got involved? That was your biggest mistake! Mine was allowing you back into my life!"

"Please, Amy, let me tell you what's going on. I need help. You are the only person I can talk to."

"Bit late for that. I don't want to know about you and the Fishers. I don't want to be dragged in to anything to do with that lot."

"Look, Amy, If I don't do what they want, they'll come after you — that's the only reason I'm still involved."

"Come after me! What the hell's going on, Dennis?"

"You've heard of Brendan Fisher?"

Amy nodded. "Yeah. You can't live round here without knowing who he is."

"He runs this business out of a building on one of the business parks. Imports and exports of Walkmans, cd players," Dennis told her.

"Jake's involved in that — or he was. Maggie told me. Something to do with VAT fraud," Amy replied.

"Yeah, I know. That time they broke in and stole his stuff ... that must have finished Jake."

"Broke in — you let them in! What else Dennis? Don't stop now!"

"They got me involved; my names on documents they made me sign. I'm implicated ..."

"That's your problem. Go to the police ... tell them what you know. It's the only way you'll escape their clutches."

Dennis shook his head. "There's more. It's dad — they want me to get him for Billy Fisher's murder."

"To do what! 'Get him' — what the hell does that mean?" Amy gasped, "They want you to kill him — kill your own father!"

Dennis held his hands in front of his chest, as if in prayer,

"This wouldn't have happened if he'd done his job. Billy Fisher would still be alive."

"Your dad deserves to die, is that it? Is that what you think?" Amy's voice was loud, like a high-pitched wail.

Lines of smudged mascara made Amy look pale, ghoulish, as if her white face had been pressed against soot-blackened bars.

Dennis tried to avoid Amy's stare. He took a deep breath, "I owe them, big time. I was protected by Fishers in jail; and there was Lee," he added, as if this was a reasonable explanation. His tongue felt thick and useless. Every word seemed to issue as if spoken by someone else. "If I don't do what they want they'll come after you."

Amy clenched her fists. She stepped towards Dennis and smacked him hard in the face.

He dabbed at the blood trickling from his nose and wiped it on the side of his jeans. "They've threatened to ..."

"To do what?"

"Hurt you ..." He wanted to tell her about the threat to slash her beautiful face. He was afraid; he didn't want to see her give a look of pain, of hurt and betrayal ... "If I don't do what they want," he said, quietly.

Amy groaned, "Maggie warned me ... I should have listened to her."

"I hate them, Amy!" Dennis suddenly exclaimed. "I Hate them! I'll do whatever it takes ... I'll find a way."

"You!? How the hell ...?"

Dennis touched the trickle of blood on his top lip and straightened his back, as if the sight of his own blood had given him confidence. "There's more ... they're running guns to paramilitaries in Ireland. If I shop them, I'm a dead man." He paused; "And they'll come after you."

Amy flopped against the kitchen counter, resting her arms on the work surface. She looked dazed, as if reeling from a blow harder than the one she'd given Dennis.

"What are you going to do? What can you do?" Her voice was soft, a hint of resignation in her tone.

"Dunno, yet," Dennis replied. "I'm going to get evidence of what they're up to — the electronic stuff, the guns, paperwork. I don't care anymore. I don't want you hurt — or dad. I just want this all to stop."

Amy slowly pushed herself upright, "You better not lie to me, Dennis. No more half-truths, I want to know everything that's going on." She stared directly at him, a tear leaking from the corner of her eye, as if she was facing a bitterly cold wind.

Amy watched Dennis open the door, his leather jacket slung over his shoulder. He looked casual, almost carefree — it was only when he turned and tried to smile that she saw the strain on his face. Neither of them spoke, just a brief moment of eye contact as Dennis reached for the door. It wasn't the evasive, furtive look that signalled he had something to hide, it was a look of grim determination, a look of resolve. As Dennis quietly closed the door, she suddenly felt filled with alarm, a bit like one of those paralysing panic attacks she'd experienced in her early teens. There'd always been her mum, sometimes Maggie, to help her through it. She wished one of them was here now, standing close.

Amy felt a sense of relief when she left her flat and headed off to the market. It was as if all her troubles could be locked inside, once she'd closed the door. Wednesdays were usually quiet, but this particular morning the market was buzzing. Her stall had a stream of clients —mainly young women with toddlers and pushchairs, and a smattering of her older patrons — picking through underwear, rummaging in the boxes of lipsticks and liberally spraying the sample bottles as if they were a free gift.

The crowd thinned around lunchtime. Amy busied herself straightening and folding her display items, wiping down her glass display cases, sweeping up sweet wrappers and collecting empty Coca-Cola cans that had rolled under her stall.

She called out to one of the other market traders, asking them to watch her stall while she had a break. The curled sandwiches looked far from appetising. She opted instead for a chocolate-coated bar, a Danish pastry and a milky coffee which she laced with sugar.

Maggie was sipping tea, holding a mug as if it was porcelain china. She waved towards Amy, beckoning her over.

"What an earth are you eating, Amy!" she exclaimed.

"I didn't like the look of those sandwiches.'

Maggie laughed, "I know what you mean — well picked over. The soup's ok," she said, lifting her spoon. "Minestrone ... I think." She looked, pointedly at Amy's plate,

"That looks like comfort food to me."

"Yeah, well I need it."

"One of those days, eh?" Maggie probed. She watched Amy lift her coffee — her hands were shaking.

"Ok," she said in her no-nonsense tone. "What's up?"

Amy bit her lip, fighting against the ache in her throat. A couple of tears rolled down the side of her cheek. Maggie immediately produced a tissue, like a well-practised magician.

"Here," she said. "Now, what is it? — Dennis?"

Amy slowly nodded. She glanced round as if looking for an eavesdropper. "He's in big trouble."

"Maybe you should tell him to go, before it gets any worse. You've already had a bad time with Lee."

"I can't ..."

"Can't! Course you can. Don't let him ruin your life. He's a nice lad — or was — but trouble seems to follow him."

"It's complicated," Amy said, her voice barely audible.

Maggie looked at her watch. "Go and pack up your stall. You and I need to talk."

Chapter 27

Amy had agreed, reluctantly, to go with Maggie to 'The Quiet Man'. It was an old-fashioned pub that had changed little over the last sixty years or so and, as it name implied, was the sort of place suited to discrete conversations. There was no piped music and the landlord of this free-house had banned all things that emitted more than a hint of light. His only concessions were a cigarette machine next to the gents and a 1950s juke box that hadn't played a record for many years. A stained, wood counter stood in the centre of the room like a piece of bog oak that had emerged from the ground. It was ringed by a series of booths, each separated by panes of mottled glass and fitted with leather seats, weathered and polished by an unknown number of backsides.

Maggie ordered whisky and ginger-ale for them both. She nudged one of the glasses towards Amy,

"Here, try this," she said.

Amy grimaced as she lifted her glass. She took a sip and coughed as the peaty liquid touched the back of her throat.

Maggie was suddenly all business. She sat erect and took a small notebook from her bag.

"Right ... you'd better tell me what's been going on."

"It's Dennis," she said, slowly turning her whisky glass on the table, "He's in trouble — big trouble ... It's the Fishers."

"Why doesn't that surprise me," Maggie replied.

"I'm scared, Maggie. "He says if he doesn't do what they want him to do they'll come after me!" She instinctively touched her cheek.

"Is that who did that?" Maggie said, pointing to the scratches on Amy's face.

Amy shook her head. "Dennis said it wasn't them. They told him it was one of Lee's mates."

"Lee Hogan!? I thought you were rid of him?"

"He won't come near me again."

"Who says so — Dennis? The Fishers are vicious criminals, Amy. Far worse than Lee Hogan and his cronies."

"You think I don't know that!"

"So, why is Dennis involved with the Fishers — after all that's happened!?"

"He owes them. They protected him in prison, and he got them to beat up Lee. They've got a warehouse on that business park where Robinson's Removals keep their vans."

"I know it. They sometimes shift stuff for some of the traders." She took out a cigarette and let it dangle from her mouth, like a comforter. "Ok, what is it they want Dennis to do?"

"They want him to go after his dad. They want revenge for Billy Fisher's murder. An 'eye-for-an-eye' Dennis keeps saying."

"Attack Michael, is that it?"

"Worse ..."

"Oh, my God!"

"He says he doesn't want to do it, Maggie. He won't do it. He wants out. He said he'll get evidence of what they're up to."

"And you believe him?"

"I have to. What else can I do?"

"You could leave him, tell him to go."

"It's too late for that ... besides, I don't want to. And I believe him, he wants to protect me ... and his dad."

"How on earth is he going to do that!? And anyway, if he manages to get something on them, what does he do with it? He'd better be careful, very careful. If they find out they'll kill him."

"He knows that. For once in his life, he wants to do the right thing."

"You'd better get Dennis to tell you everything he knows. And I mean everything. Then you tell me ... Got it? I want to know what's going on. I want to keep you safe. If he slips up at all, if they smell a rat, you'll be in just as much danger ... maybe even more so."

Brendan was in a bad mood. He kicked out at one of the chairs near the table, sending it skidding along the floor. It clattered into the cupboards under the kitchen sink startling Leo who was pouring boiling water into mugs set on a plastic tray.

"What's up, boss?" he ventured.

"What's up! Guns, that's what's up! Those effin Ukrainians — two crates, I told 'em. The bastards are only sending one." He was breathing heavily, his pink face reddened with rage.

"When, boss?"

"When!? This Thursday." He looked round the building, "Where's Owen?"

"You told him to pick up those Sony Walkman's, remember?"

"Course I know!" bellowed Brendan, the suggestion he may have forgotten appearing to make him even angrier. Leo peered out of the window. "This is him now."

Brendan turned, quickly; "Dennis, don't just stand there looking like a spare prick! You and Leo go and help Owen." He snatched his car keys from the table and grabbed his black leather jacket from the back of his chair. "I'll be out for a few hours — got some business to take care of." He stormed out of the building, slamming the door behind him.

"Best keep your head down," said Leo. "When he gets like this you never know what he might do." Dennis realised he'd been holding his breath, hoping Brendan wouldn't suddenly return.

Leo leant over the sink and peered out of the window. He turned to Dennis, "Where did you park?"

"Round the back ... I'd better move it."

"Yeah ... ok."

Dennis had driven round to the parking space he'd used before — next to a small office building fifty metres or so from the mesh fence at the rear of the Brendan Fisher's unit. He reached into the glove compartment and slowly removed the camera. He rubbed its knurled casing, fingering the lens as if it were the barrel of a pistol.

What plan? He suddenly realised he had only a vague notion of how ... some opportunistic covert operation that was doomed to fail. And anyway, even if he managed to get some incriminating evidence what would he do with it? Go to the police? He remembered how much Jake hated the Fishers — would he help? The consequences of being caught, or not being believed, were too horrible to contemplate. They'd go after Amy, maim her, mark her for life. He'd have no life at all. They'd smash every bone in his body and dump him into a landfill. He gritted his teeth — he realised if he kept thinking about the consequences he'd be paralysed with fear. I have to do this, he said to himself. I've gotta protect Amy.

What about dad? he suddenly thought. This is what I always wanted, isn't it? ... to get back at him for all those years I'd wanted him to listen, instead of him telling me I wasn't tough enough. He'd have called me a wimp. He wasn't someone you could talk to, he did the talking, the telling.

But murdered!!?

Dennis rubbed the back of his hand against his forehead. He was sweating. His thoughts immediately returned to his dad. He deserves what's coming ... doesn't he? He'd make the bastard understand. He'd show him he wasn't a wimp! Dennis swiped angrily at the tears slipping down his cheeks. His throat began to tighten. Different thoughts; playing in the garden with his dad, building a den, the two of them sleeping out in a tent on the lawn. An acrid bile surged in his throat. Image of the Fishers — Brendan and Danny —filled his head "I hate the bastards!" he muttered. He needed this feeling of hatred, he suddenly realised. He didn't want to weaken — not this time. He needed that bitter taste. He wanted no more of their threats and intimidation. More than that, he wanted revenge.

Dennis spotted Owen swinging a white transit van into the yard. He glanced round and then aimed his camera. He took several shots of him getting out of the vehicle and opening the rear doors. He didn't have time to hang around.

"Where've you been?" barked Leo.

"Had to find a parking space," Dennis replied.

"Owen's just pulled in."

"Yeah, I just saw him," Dennis said.

Owen slipped through the front door, silently following his shadow. He was at their elbow before either of them realised.

"Get the effin door lifted will ya. I don't want to leave them boxes sitting with the van doors wide open."

Leo grinned. "Can't trust anybody these days. Come on, Dennis. Bring that clipboard," he said, pointing to forms lying on the table.

They climbed into the back of the transit and slid the boxes to the rear as Owen manoeuvred the loader into place. It took just a little under thirty minutes to unload and stack the eight boxes along a wall at the back of the unit. They were identical in size, each having three steel bands that dug into the edges of the ribbed cardboard packing. Leo had gone to look for tinsnips and Owen had driven off in the loader. Dennis could hear Leo rummaging in a toolbox near the workbench. This was his chance. He fumbled with his camera, it seemed to snag on the belt loop of his jeans. He tugged it free, glanced round, and then quickly took several snaps. He slid the camera back into his pocket just as Leo approached brandishing a large pair of tinsnips. Owen was suddenly there, like some reptile emerging from the dark. Dennis jumped.

"What's up with you Dennis? You're as nervous as a kitten." He smirked, "You 'aint been helping yourself to a few of those Walkmans?"

"Me? Course not," he stammered. "Just wondered where you were, that's all."

Leo began levering the tinsnips under one of the steel bands. "You two finished?" he said gruffly. "Mind yourselves ..."

The first of the steel bands snapped open with a loud crack, one end whiplashing across the box and just missing Owen. "Told you to move," Leo said with evident irritation. He snapped the remaining metal banding. Dennis pulled the broken strips to one side, as Owen slipped a Stanley knife through the packing tape securing the top of the box. Curls of white polystyrene foam spewed onto the floor.

"Leave it," Leo told Owen, who'd started pushing his hand into the packing material. "The Boss wants to check 'em first," he said, as if reprimanding a child. "Do something useful, go and make the coffee. Dennis, you clear up this stuff," he barked, kicking at the end of one of the metal strips. "I'll get some packing tape. We'll need to re-seal 'em after the Boss has had a look."

Dennis felt the same mix of fear and exhilaration he'd felt earlier. He heard Leo opening one of the toolboxes.

Where was Owen? He could sidle up in a near silence that was unnerving. Brendan and Leo didn't seem to mind, but it always alarmed him. He took out the camera and reeled off several snaps. Leo shouted as he approached. "Dennis, I told you to get this cleaned up. What the hell have you been doing?" Dennis felt himself gasp. He shoved the camera into the pocket of his jeans and grabbed a broom. "Couldn't find a brush," he replied.

Leo grunted. "Get on with it!"

Chapter 28

"We opened up one of the boxes," Leo told Brendan.

"All ok?"

Leo nodded. "Think so."

Brendan Fisher heaved himself out of his chair and scraped away some of the packing beads and inspected a few of the mobile phones.

"Owen," he barked, "Got the paperwork?"

"Yeah ... course. This lot came from Germany," he replied, handing over an A5 envelope. "Where are these going, boss?" Owen asked

"They're stayin'. Some bastard tipped off customs last week. This stuff'll have to sit here 'till things settle down." Brendan's phone buzzed. He glanced at the screen, "What the ...?" The call was very brief. Brendan hit the off button and thrust the phone into his jacket. He didn't look happy.

"Bit of business," he growled. "I'll be back in an hour or so. I want this stuff out of sight by the time I get back."

"Ok, boss. I'll get it sorted," Owen said, a little too cheerily.

Brendan glared at him. "You do that, Owen."

"What's the fiddle?" asked Dennis, as soon as he heard Brendan's car drive off. He hoped he sounded only mildly interested.

It surprised him that Owen was so keen to explain the scam.

"Easy. There's no VAT on imports from the EU. They're sold on through one of Brendan's businesses. The VAT stays with us and the business disappears."

"Owen's too smart for his own good," Leo remarked. "Dangerous to know too much."

"Brendan likes to have at least one smart guy around," Owen quipped.

Leo looked confused as if not sure if it was a slight against him. "Piss off" he said, raising a two fingered salute.

"Suppose you know about Jake Gould?" Dennis asked.

"Him! We put a stop to his interfering. He didn't want to cooperate; thought he could set up on his own. Don't worry about Jake. We put him out of business some time ago — 'aint that right, Leo?"

Leo grinned. "We took all his stock. His suppliers weren't very happy."

Dennis' stomach tightened. He could almost feel the beating Jake had given him and the look of anger and disdain.

"We'd better get these boxes sorted," Owen told them, "Before the boss gets back. He'll be pissed if we haven't got 'em tucked away."

Brendan was fuming when he returned. He flung the front door open, slammed it shut and strode over to a filing cabinet just behind his chair. He smacked the top of the steel cabinet with his fist and then fiddled impatiently with a key attached to his belt by a leather thong. He tugged at the top drawer, jerked it open and began flicking his fingers across the stack of hanging files. He took out a manilla folder, flung it on the table, sat heavily into his chair and began leafing through sheets of papers pinned in the corner with a red paper clip.

"That crate from Ukraine will be here on Friday morning," he said, tersely, continuing to thumb through the sheets of paper, as if looking for some detail he'd forgotten.

"When's Frank picking it up?" asked Owen.

"Not Frank. He's sick. It'll be his brother, Jonno. And it's not one crate he's collecting, it's two."

"Eh?" said Owen. "Is there another load coming in?"

Brendan slowly shook his head. "No. We've got to split the shipment. Those effin Ukrainians have us by the balls. We were supposed to get two crates. The lads 'ave done a deal with the UVF as well as the provos — the stupid idiots shouldn't have done it — they're both expecting a shipment. But we 'aint got two crates, 'ave we? That's why we've got to split this lot. I just hope it'll keep 'em both happy. If the provos ever find out we're supplying both sides there'll be hell to pay!"

"So, what're we goin' to do, Boss?" asked Leo, rubbing his hands together as if preparing for a fight.

"Get two smaller crates — and some more packing material. I don't want 'em to look like half a load."

"Maybe Robinsons Removals would have something?"

"Good idea, Dennis. You're full of surprises," Brendan remarked. "Ok, you and Owen bugger off in the van and see what they've got. Leo, I want a tarpaulin stretched out. We'd better start sorting the stuff."

Dennis was relieved, and in a strange way pleased with himself that his suggestion had been worthwhile. Robinsons were only too glad to sell them crates.

Brendan and Leo had unpacked several items by the time they got back. They were laid out looking like blackened bones from an archaeological dig. Short barrels were spaced in horizontal rows, shoulder stocks were lined end-to-end in vertical columns, curved magazines were clustered like spooning couples, and pistols were stacked in small boxes at the corners of the tarpaulin.

"Did you get the crates?" Brendan asked, his eyes remaining fixed on the array of disassembled weapons.

"Yeah," Owen replied. "They're in the van — plenty of packing as well."

"Good ... that's good."

Owen nudged Dennis. "We'll bring them through those double doors."

It didn't take long. The two crates were easy to slide out of the van and onto the concrete floor in the building. They lifted them onto wood pallets and unloaded the rolls of bubble wrap and barrels of polystyrene pellets. Brendan came over and began inspecting the crates. "They'll do," he said. "I want 'em waterproof."

Owen pointed to several sheets of bitumen matting. "Got this stuff as well. Robinsons use it for the floors of their vehicles. We can staple it to the inside of the crates."

It took most of the day to cut the matting and fix it in place. Brendan began circling the crates, his mobile phone clasped in his hand.

"Jonno'll get here sometime tomorrow," Brendan remarked, as if speaking to the two packing crates. "I don't trust that thick idiot!" His mobile phone buzzed. He stared at the caller ID,

"Liam," he said as he walked off. "You'd better get 'em shifted quickly at your end. No slip-ups. Make sure the UVF don't trip over the IRA lads." Dennis could just catch the odd few words. "And 'ave a word with Frank. He'll need to meet Jonno in Dun Laoghaire. I don't care if he's on his deathbed — his brother's an effin liability!"

He seemed to have calmed down when he walked towards them, about fifteen minutes later. "Owen, go and get some pizza and a few beers. It's going to be late when we finish. I'm trying to get hold of Jonno." He pointed towards the weaponry laid out on the tarpaulin, "Dennis, do a count. And get it right!"

Dennis watched Owen leave the building. He could hear Leo firing staples into one of the crates and Brendan shouting into his phone as if Jonno was partially deaf. He felt for the camera, took several shots of the spread laid out on the tarpaulin, and then knelt down and took some pictures of individual pieces; automatic rifles, cases of ammunition, high powered pistols. It was when he stood, camera in hand, that he realised Brendan was no longer barking into his phone. He began counting out loud as Brendan approached and quickly tucked the camera into his pocket. "Dennis, you idiot. Get a notebook to write the numbers down. There's a stack on those shelves next to my file cabinet." He sounded more at ease, even affable. "Got hold of Jonno. He'll be here around ten in the morning."

Dennis moved quickly; his arm held stiffly against the bulge of the camera. He grabbed a notebook from the bookcase, selected a pen from the stack in an empty coffee jar, and rejoined Brendan, who was on his knees, nudging the armaments into neat rows.

"Should be all here; fifty AKMs, fifty magazines, fifty shoulder stocks, a hundred pistols ..." He looked round at Dennis who was gaping at the array of weapons. They looked even more sinister laid out, ready to count. "You writing these down?"

Dennis nodded, quickly drawing headed columns in the notebook. "Just getting sorted."

Brendan grunted, "Got to be right, Dennis. No mistakes. You ready?" He repeated the numbers, and then resumed the count; "Eight boxes of small arms ammo, eight of 303s ..."

They'd just finished when Owen appeared carrying three pizzas and a sling of beers.

It was like a picnic from some bygone era. The four men perched on stools, pizza boxes and beers placed on the edge of the tarpaulin; a cache of arms laid out where you might have expected hampers of teacakes and sausage rolls. There was an air of joviality; Brendan squeezing a reluctant smile, Owen tapping his fingers against an empty can of lager, Leo stuffing a large slice of pepperoni pizza into his mouth. Dennis was thinking of little else than of his camera, imagining it to be a grenade capable of taking out the lot of them, including himself.

Brendan made them scrub their hands again before they touched any of the weapons. They had to be kept clean, he told them. Each item was then individually wrapped and laid carefully on beds of protective pellets. Dennis ticked them off ensuring they were divided equally between the two crates. He was relieved when it was clear he'd got the counts exact. It was nearly half past ten that evening by the time they'd secured the lids in place. Brendan stood back and admired their handiwork. He had a broad grin on his face.

"We start early tomorrow," he said. "Be here by eight —got it?"

They all nodded.

"Not a word, not even to your deaf grandmother," Brendan told them.

"She's dead," remarked Leo, in all innocence.

Owen groaned. "For Christ's sake ..."

Chapter 29

Amy said very little when Dennis got in. She didn't want to know when he tried to explain he'd had a couple of late fares.

"Don't," she said. "No more lies. If you don't want to tell me the truth, don't say anything."

She told him it'd be best if he slept on the couch. "It's there, or nowhere," she said. Dennis knew he was in no position to argue. He took a pillow and a blanket from the linen cupboard and attempted to get comfortable on the small couch. His feet hung over the end, despite bending his knees towards his chest. He eventually discarded the pillow and stretched out with his shoulders resting on the arm rest. Sleep seemed impossible. Lying uncomfortably on the couch, unable to sleep, he no longer felt convinced his plan would work. What plan? he asked himself. What if he couldn't convince Amy? What if Owen caught him? ... it'd be Owen. What if Brendan got suspicious. Anyway, what would he do with his precious information? The wallet of photographs was in his jacket pocket. Several Lee must have taken, there were even a couple of Amy.

He was glad when the first light began to creep into the room. He felt exhausted, robbed of sleep, bombarded by grotesque images of Leo beating him senseless, of Amy being raped by Owen, of Maggie and Jake pointing at him, their fingers almost touching his face, shouting at him for getting them mixed up in all of this; and his dad, telling him he was weak, telling him to toughen up. He woke from his nightmare with a jerk, disorientated, convinced that everything he'd dreamt had actually happened. It took a few moments for him to realise he was in Amy's flat. He lay back, waiting for the morning light to seep into the room thinking of the futility of even imagining he could do anything meaningful. He slowly pushed himself upright and reached for the hoodie he'd thrown onto the floor and then crept into the kitchen. He splashed his face with cold water, dried himself on a tea towel and carried his shoes as he left the flat.

He was early. He parked his car round the back and sat waiting for the others. It'd become his usual spot, out of the way, unnoticed. He checked his camera was secure in the left pocket of his jeans. He'd removed the wrist strap in case it dangled. He peered through the viewfinder, took several snaps of the rear of the building and then swung his camera round to the entrance road. Slowly filling the lens was Brendan's silver Mercedes and, almost in tow, Owen's blue Ford.

Dennis walked round to the front of the building as the two cars pulled to a halt. Brendan had the key to the front door poking out from his fist. Owen was out of his Ford in a flash, bouncing on his thin legs. Leo let his door swing open and heaved himself out of the passenger seat, the front of the car leaning on its soft suspension. He was carrying a paper bag — McDonalds. He looked pleased with himself as he placed the burgers and fries onto the table. They ate in silence — save for the odd grunt of appreciation and slurp from the mugs of coffee Owen had prepared — as if they were old friends.

Brendan wiped his fingers on one of the paper towels and began punching a number into his phone.

"Where are you, Jonno?"

The reply was clearly not what Brendan wanted to hear. "When!?" he shouted, "You're supposed to be here early!"

There was a reply, which must have been an apology, of sorts. "You do that, Jonno." He slung his mobile onto the table. "About eleven-thirty," he says. "I'll cut his bollocks off if he's any later."

They spent the morning tidying up. Brendan wanted all the stray polystyrene pellets swept up and the bubble wrap rolled and stacked.

He sat at the table, the mobile rarely leaving his hand. It was around twelve when Jonno's cattle-truck finally appeared. Brendan ran out, brandishing his mobile like a night-stick. "At last!" he shouted as the truck shuddered to a halt.

Jonno lowered the driver's window and leant on his elbow. "Dropped off a load of calves."

"That's bloody obvious," Brendan remarked, waving towards the dank straw hanging from the slatted sides. "This thing stinks!" Jonno was focused on grinding the gear lever into place. The truck suddenly jolted forward. "Pull up round the back."

Leo appeared with three sets of overalls. "We'll need these," he said, flinging a pair to Dennis, and a second pair to Owen. They were all the same size, extra-large.

Leo helped Jonno drop the tailgate and the ramp to the upper deck. It had been raining and streams of slurry were washing along the ribbed-metal flooring. Owen cursed at the slippery surfaces as he attempted to drive the forklift onto the truck.

"Go and help him," Brendan told Dennis as Jonno climbed the vertical steel ladder onto the upper deck. Leo followed, nudging Dennis every time he hesitated. They threaded chains along the channels in the flooring leading from the winch, hooked them round each pallet, slowly dragging them along the upper deck. Leo grunted and cursed, Brendan, directing from the ground, added his own stream of profanity, most of it directed at Jonno. Owen had taken his forklift to a hose at the corner of the yard and began spraying its wheels and frame. A thin sludge quickly developed and ran along the cracks in the concrete pad and into a drain.

By the time they had the two crates secured and suitably hidden under a tarpaulin, it was almost three in the afternoon. Jonno had started to complain about the time, which served only to annoy Brendan.

"You'd better not miss that Ferry, Jonno. You should've got here on time."

Dennis and Leo were smeared in mud and muck, most of it on their legs and arms. Jonno was wearing a bib overall which he simply climbed out of and threw into the cab. Leo didn't look or smell so bad once he'd discarded the old jacket he was wearing for one in the boot of Owen's car.

"Bloody hell, Dennis, look at you — you're a mess," exclaimed Brendan. He glanced at his watch; "You might as well go. Suppose you'll have some taxi runs?"

Dennis nodded. "Got one at six — one of my regulars."

"Won't need you much tomorrow, just the morning. I need this place cleaned up," he said, pointing to the muck and straw dropping in gloops from the sides of the cattle-truck.

Dennis didn't wait to see if Brendan had anything else to say, just in case he changed his mind. He forced himself to walk slowly, casually, as if leaving a group of workmates he'd known for years. Once out of the building he walked quickly to his car. He could see Jonno climbing into the cab of the cattle truck. He shoved the camera into the glovebox and drove back up the entrance road, ahead of Jonno. He pulled into a parking space and waited for the truck. It was moving slowly, spewing snorts of black exhaust. Dennis pulled out so that he was immediately behind the vehicle. At the first set of lights, he reached across for his camera. He took several shots through the windscreen and then turned left when the lights went green onto a street he knew well. It ran almost parallel with the main road.

A few of his regulars lived in the area. He drove as quickly as he could, weaving between parked cars and several builder's skips, eventually turning into a service station some three miles ahead. It was a busy section and a set of lights just before the service station slowed the traffic to a crawl. Dennis fidgeted with his camera and paced along the busy road, looking for signs of the cattle truck.

He didn't have to wait long. Jonno's truck ambled along as if delivering a full load of cattle to a remote farm. He lifted his camera and took several shots of the truck leaving the stop lights in plumes of blue-black exhaust.

Dennis smiled to himself. This was easy.

Despite the overalls, his shirt and jeans, even his socks, were smeared and damp and had a rank, overripe smell of soft cow clap. He slipped out of his shirt, jeans and socks, balancing on the door mat, tiptoeing into the flat. He showered, smothered himself in deodorant and got changed into a clean pair of jeans and a pale blue button-down. He stuffed the clothes he'd discarded into a bin-liner and dropped the bag into the boot of his car. On his way to pick up Mrs Johnson, he stopped at a local Co-op car park, one of those with rows of recycling bins, and dumped the bag into a hatch below a sign thanking people for their donations.

He pondered, as he drove Mrs Johnson to her regular meeting at the Mecca bingo hall, what his next step should be. Tell Amy? Show her his evidence? And then what? He searched aimlessly for other scenarios as he drove towards the bingo hall. He soon realised he had little option other than go to Amy with his account of Brendan Fisher's operations.

If I can't convince her ... It was a thought that wouldn't leave. *She'll listen ... She's got to.*

He said very little to Amy that night. She was ice-cold. Conversation was virtually non-existent, save for a few perfunctory and direct remarks — they needed milk, hadn't he noticed? Where's the remote?

"You'd better order a pizza, I suppose." Her eyes were fixed on a magazine she was leafing through.

She was watching tv when he got back carrying a vegetarian pizza. Not his favourite, but it was the one she preferred. They ate in silence, a Wednesday night murder serial providing the excuse needed to avoid any stutters of embarrassment. Dennis' jacket hung over the chair. The edge of the wallet of photographs was peeping out from his jacket pocket. He felt exhilarated at having held his nerve, pleased with himself for having snatched the opportunities to get the evidence. He needed a sign, a signal from Amy, something to suggest she'd listen.

"I'm off to bed," she suddenly announced. It was said without warmth, just a blank glance as if she couldn't care if he was there or not. For Dennis, it would be another night on the couch. He munched on one of the remaining slices of pizza and opened a can of coke. He felt calm, pleased that he'd managed it — got the evidence he wanted. It was as if he'd past the most difficult stage — having the courage to start. If everything went wrong, at least he'd tried. Sitting, sipping his coke and picking at the last piece of pizza, he allowed himself to think about the repercussions. Fear was his greatest enemy; it always had been. When he was young, he'd wondered why school bullies had frightened him. They seemed to be without fear, as if nerves were something they'd never had to conquer. He guessed they had to be tough — showing weakness wasn't an option. Is that what his dad wanted — for him to be more like them? A thug? He'd sometimes imagined himself as a protector of the others who were bullied on an almost daily basis. Instead, he'd become one of the gang, doing what they wanted. And yes, he'd become a thug. It took only a few kickings of anyone the Fishers decided needed the 'treatment' for him to revel in his role.

Is that when it started, is that when his life was changed? He nodded to himself. He knew it was. It had continued; they had him; they could use him for whatever they wanted. He'd kidded himself they were his mates, that he was one of 'them'. He'd be used by the Fishers for whatever they wanted.

He still felt fear. But it was different. He was disgusted with himself for what he'd done, for what he'd become. And he was angry, angry that they wanted him to murder his dad, angry that they were able to wield such violence without giving it a second thought. Most of all, he was angry with himself for being weak and living in the lap of the Fishers. He was angry with himself for wanting to punish his dad, and for what? Some ugly thought that his parents didn't deserve him, as if they'd no right to interfere in his life. They'd tried, he knew they had.

He no longer saw himself as a victim of circumstance. He was a victim because he thought it was the only option he had. But now, there was something more powerful than fear — It was hatred, hatred of the Fishers. Dennis smiled to himself. The bastards had made a mistake, a big mistake. This was his chance.

Next morning, Dennis ate a bowl of cereal and made himself a strong coffee which he drank black, laced with sugar. He'd spent another uncomfortable night on the couch. Snatches of sleep were fretful, his t-shirt was soaked, his hair matted with sweat, his mind racing randomly, through images of his parents, of the Fishers — Danny, Brendan, — of prison inmates wagging accusing fingers, and Amy turning away from him, hiding a hideous scar on her face. They were thoughts he couldn't simply dismiss. He didn't want them tucked away to be cleansed and hidden in some deep recess in his brain. There was a rage hardening in his head which seemed more than capable of overcoming the feelings of impotence that dogged him whenever he encountered the Fishers.

He drove off slowly, tailing an older model dark-blue Ford Mondeo. It was being driven very carefully, an older man sitting low in his seat. Dennis gave him room and crawled forward to a set of traffic lights on red and waited for the green filter onto the industrial park.

He watched Brendan, and then Owen, pull up shortly after he'd parked in his usual spot. When he entered, they were sharing a story, a tale, a joke, perhaps, their heads leaning forward listening to Leo. They laughed in concert, smiles all round, smiles that disappeared in an instant when they noticed Dennis standing hesitantly at the open door.

"Close the door will 'ya. That's a hell of a draft you're bringing in." Leo and Owen laughed at Brendan's remark, as if it was a continuation of their banter.

Dennis strode over to the sink and began making a coffee.

"Help yourself, Dennis. Don't mind us."

He had an apology on the tip of his tongue, but he was practised, now, in suppressing words that put him on the defensive. Owen was baiting him, looking for a reaction. It didn't bother him, not anymore. He filled his mug, sniffed at the milk in a small metal jug and added just enough — not the dollops that Owen splashed in a row of mugs as if watering a window box. He felt calm, immune from their stares, protected by some invisible shield.

He glared at Owen, "Get your own."

Owen stared back as if testing the scene. The other two were silent; spectators waiting for fighters to come out of their corners.

Brendan broke the tension,

"You'd better not mess with him, Owen. Not this morning. What's got into you, Dennis?"

"Nuthin'" Dennis replied. "Just pissed off, that's all."

Brendan's voice raised a notch. "Oh, yeah?" There was a long pause, a dull, deep void. "That girlfriend of yours — been rationing it, has she?"

Leo sniggered. Owen added his own high-pitched cackle.

Brendan spun round on his chair. "Enough! There're things to do."

He slid a folder across the table. "Dennis, you check these shipments. I want to know dates —when they leave, when they load, when they dock in the UK — got it?"

Dennis reached for a pad and took the documents out of a folder. He watched Brendan rifling through the drawer of his filing cabinet, mumbling something about Jonno. "I'd better call the lads, see if they've got those guns ok."

He slammed the file drawer shut with a force that rattled and rocked the cabinet and started towards the door, phone in hand. He stopped abruptly and pointed at the file, still unopened. "Dennis, wake up!"

Dennis slowly and deliberately pushed the file to one side.

"I don't want to do this anymore," he said, the quiver in his voice betraying his nervousness.

Brendan leaned on the table, knuckles down, and glared at Dennis, his fat belly brushing the polished surface. "What are you sayin'? Nobody leaves, not in one piece. Think very carefully. There's that girlfriend of yours, Amy. If you're so weak as to let that girlfriend suffer, then suffer she will. And you'll watch, got it? You'll have a front row seat."

Dennis' face blanched, his hands began to tremble.

Brendan leaned in closer. Dennis could feel the heat of his breath, stale and acidic. "I hope you haven't forgotten your dad," he hissed. "The murdering bastard! It's simple — it's him, or you." He pushed himself upright. "I'd say that's only fair. It doesn't have to be him. Just someone in the family; you, I mean. Your dad has his life back, your girlfriend keeps her looks. They'll thank you. You'll be an ugly wreck, if you survive. But then, that'll be your choice. And a very noble one at that. Courageous some might say. Foolish others would say."

Dennis felt a mix of paralysing fear and intense hatred, resisting the urge to fling himself at the barrel of lard leering at him with dismissive smugness and plunge his thumbs into his eye sockets. He gripped at the edge of the table, concerned for just a moment it was exactly what he was about to do.

"You'd better decide — and quick," Brendan Fisher told him. "Or you can get a grip and get on with sorting those files and do what I say."

Dennis nodded. He suddenly felt unable to do or say anything else.

Brendan gave Dennis a withering look. "I'll be watching you closely, very closely."

Dennis nodded again. He placed his hand on the yellow file and watched as Brendan charged out of the front door.

Chapter 30

Dennis didn't wait for Brendan to return. He shouted to Leo that he was off and had a taxi run.

"Probably won't be back," he said, testing himself with the thought he might mean forever. He knew, of course, he'd have to return. There was no way he would leave Amy, or his father, to face the kind of animalistic retribution that the Fishers could dish out. Threats, fear, intimidation, violence — they were normal currency for the Fisher clan. You paid a price.

He found himself on a straight stretch of dual carriageway, letting the smooth ride eat up time and distance. Fisher's threats didn't feel as close, cocooned as he was in his cockpit, gently caressing the steering wheel. He was armed with evidence in the small camera tucked under a box of tissues in the glove compartment. But how to use it? It might prove to be nothing more than a damp squib in his hands, and dynamite in the hands of the Fishers. He shuddered at the thought.

Dennis saw Amy entering the flat carrying several carrier bags from the market. He waited until she'd stepped inside before parking his car and following her, camera in hand. She gave him the briefest of glances when he walked into the kitchen and continued unloading tins of food, packets of rice and boxes of cereals onto the counter. He stood silently watching her, his back straight, head erect, like a sentry. He felt calm and strangely self-assured as he placed the camera on the corner of the counter.

"What's that?" Amy asked.

"Evidence," Dennis replied. He spoke deliberately, and with a deeper and stronger tone than usual, as if he was auditioning for a part in a Shakespearean tragedy.

She turned, a can of baked beans in each hand, clearly surprised by the timbre of his voice. "Evidence — what evidence?"

Dennis placed the brightly-coloured wallet on the table, "Photos of what the Fishers are up to."

Amy stood holding the two tins clutched to her chest. "The Fishers? What do you mean?"

"I've got photos of their operations," he continued. "I need to show you," he said, sliding the pack towards her.

"I don't want to know!" She said, angrily. "This is your problem, not mine."

"I'm protecting us, Amy. This might be my only chance."

"And that's it? You think a few snapshots will stop them?"

"It's all I've got —but it's something — look."

Dennis slowly spread the images on counter, as if dealing from a pack of tarot cards. "This is the back of the unit where they unload. That's a couple of his men, Leo and Owen."

They stared at the photos, heads almost touching. "This lot came in from Germany."

Amy peered at a blurred image of a stack of mobiles in an opened crate layered on piles of polystyrene foam, like fish in a box of ice. "Maggie told me the Fishers knew all about Jake," she said, tapping her manicured fingernail on the photo. "And you let the Fishers in! Maggie told me Jake had a hell of a time paying off his suppliers. It was all your doing!"

"I got sucked in. I didn't think ..."

"That's you, isn't it? You never think! You were stupid, stupid to get involved."

Dennis stiffened. "I can't change what's happened. I'm done with being used."

"And just what do you propose? A few photos are not going to stop them."

"There's more," he said, continuing to lay out the photographs.

Amy gasped — a delayed intake, as if she'd suddenly realised what she was looking at.

"Guns?"

Dennis nodded. "That lot's from the Ukraine."

"Then what? Sold to drug gangs?"

"They're sent to Ireland," Dennis told her. "Limerick. Brendan Fisher has cousins there."

He pointed to a photo of a large vehicle.

"What's that?" Amy exclaimed. "Looks like an old car transporter."

"It's a cattle truck. The guns are hidden under a cover on the top deck, just behind the cab. I've got to do something. If I don't murder dad they'll come after me. I'll be a dead man." He spoke calmly with no hint of fear in his voice. "And they'll come after you."

"What the hell have you done!?" Amy exclaimed.

Dennis' voice was firm. "I'm done with all of 'em."

"What can you do? They're too powerful. You don't stand a chance."

He shrugged his shoulders, "Maybe. But I've got to try."

"What good is this stuff anyway? You think it'll bring 'em down? I don't think so. Not a chance. What are you going to do with it? Go to the cops? Doubt if they'd do much. Too many of 'em are happy to leave the Fishers alone."

"I need people who hate the Fishers."

"Uh ... there's plenty, but nobody who'll take them on. Intimidation goes deep. Most people just deal with it as best they can."

"I want you to set up a meeting with Maggie. I need her to see these."

"Why should she listen to me? As soon as she hears your name and the Fishers, she'll tell me to shove off."

"I've got a gut feeling ... she needs to know ... These guns are for paramilitaries in Ireland. And they've made a mistake. They've slipped up ... and Brendan Fisher knows it. That's why it's got to be now, Amy."

"I wouldn't hold your breath. She won't want to be involved ... she's seen what happens to anyone stupid enough to cross the Fishers."

"That's exactly why she'll want to help, if she can," he replied.

Amy sat at the table they liked to use and beckoned to Maggie who had a mug of tea in one hand and an incongruously thin china plate with a slice of Bakewell tart in the other. She gave a quick nod in Amy's direction and slalomed through the maze of tables and chairs. Amy's heart was pounding,

"Got something to tell you," she said.

"Let me guess — Dennis?"

"Sort of," Amy replied. "It's complicated."

"Most things are," Maggie said. "You'd better tell me what's bothering you. You're not pregnant, are you?"

"Me! I'm not that stupid."

"Serious, is it?"

Amy leaned across the table, "It's about the Fishers," she whispered. "I need to talk to you — somewhere private — today if possible."

"Not sure I want to know ..."

"Please, Maggie. This is important."

"Ok ... We'll go to the 'Quiet Man'." She glanced at her watch. In about an hour ... it'll be empty — the graveyard shift."

The Quiet Man was, as Maggie predicted, all but empty. There were just two old ladies occupying one of the booths.

"Think you can stomach a whisky and dry?" Maggie asked. The old wooden floorboards creaked as the barman approached and delivered their drinks.

Amy took out a folder containing the photos Dennis had taken and glanced round, as if to reassure herself they wouldn't be overheard. "What's this?" Maggie asked. "I thought it was just a chat?"

"Dennis is working for Brendan Fisher."

Maggie groaned. "Not sure I want to know," she said, touching the thin scar on her lip. "That bastard is evil. One day I'll get even ..."

"Because of what he did to Jake?"

"Because of what he did to me," Maggie replied.

"There's stuff I should know?"

Maggie forced a laugh, "There's lots you should know ... not now. What's this about Dennis and the Fisher lot?"

Amy tapped the folder "He took some photos of what they're up to ..." She slowly handed a couple of the prints to Maggie. They were of an opened crate layered with mobile phones.

"You think I don't know about their scams?" Maggie replied. "There's nothing me, or Jake can do. Anyway, he's out of all that, and I'm glad. It was stupid to get involved."

"It's not just mobiles ..." Amy slipped a group of prints to Maggie. "Look ..." Maggie slowly leafed through the photos. There were shots of Leo and Owen at the rear of the unit, a large truck backed into the unloading ramp, the same truck being driven away, Owen in the pallet handler. Amy handed over the last of the photos — guns and ammunition laid out on a tarpaulin.

Maggie leaned in closer and ran her long finger along the rows of armaments. "So, he's supplying drug gangs. What do you want me to do," she said, dismissively, "tip off the cops?"

Amy shook her head and glanced furtively across to the empty booth across from theirs. "They're not going to any crime gangs, these are for paramilitaries in Ireland." She showed Maggie shots of a cattle truck. "This is what they are using. They hide the crates then pick up cattle and take 'em across on the ferry. Dennis says they've messed up. The Fishers are supplying the IRA and the UVF. They were both expecting a shipment, but only one crate of arms got to Brendan Fisher. They had to split them and repack the lot into two crates." She pointed to the photo of the guns laid out on the tarpaulin. "That's how Dennis got this photo."

Maggie slipped the photos back into the folder. "Dennis better be very careful. I'm amazed he managed to get these," she said.

"He says he doesn't care anymore," Amy replied. "He wants to do what it takes to stop them. That's why he wanted me to talk to you."

Maggie sighed, "Nothing would please me more than to see those bastards in jail, but this stuff will only put Dennis in danger — and you, probably. They have long tentacles. Look at Eddie — he could well have been a laid out on a slab in a mortuary."

"He knows this. He says he's got to do something ..."

Chapter 31

Maggie waited impatiently for the afternoon to amble slowly on, chain smoking, creating a pile of lipstick-tipped, half-finished cigarettes smoldering in a glass ashtray on the corner of her desk, pausing occasionally to remove a shred of loose tobacco from the tip of her tongue. She hadn't rehearsed what she wanted to say to Jake, she just hoped he was in the mood to listen. She wondered how he'd react on hearing the name 'Dennis'. His anger at what had happened hadn't abated. He could still launch into a tirade of accusations, as if she was the one responsible for hiring him in the first place. And in his darkest moods he didn't hold back. There was door slamming, fist thumping, curses and more than a fair share of expletives. The traders had learnt, very quickly, not to mention Dennis within earshot. Jake lost thousands of pounds when his shipment of mobile phones was stolen. Several of the others involved had demanded he cover their losses. He had threatening phone calls, a bullet sent through the post wrapped in silver foil, a 'get well' card from the Fishers and a visit from two large Frenchmen exhibiting a sufficient range of gallic expressions to leave him in no doubt as to what they'd do if he didn't pay up. Maggie knew what had upset him the most. It was the way Brendan Fisher had stepped in, as if he was an incompetent, and taken over the entire operation. The irony that in doing so, the crime bosses had left him alone wasn't lost on Jake, or the Fishers. He received a note,

No Need to Thank Us.

The Fishers had saved him. It was an ugly truth that didn't sit at all well.

"Jake, can I have a word?" Maggie was busying herself shuffling papers that didn't need shuffling, and rearranging her desk, sparse as it was.

"Yeah, of course. What's up?" He grabbed a chair and pulled it closer to her desk. A broad grin spread quickly across his face. "Man trouble?"

"No! Even if there was, you're the last person I'd want to talk to."

Jake held up a hand in mock surrender. "Just thought I'd offer." Maggie was relieved he seemed in a good mood. It wasn't likely to last. She sat up erect and spread her fingers against the top of her desk, as if admiring her polished fingernails. "This is important, Jake. We've known each other long enough to be able to speak our minds."

"You tell it like it is, Maggie. I'd expect nothing less from you."

Maggie nodded. "This isn't easy. All I ask is you let me finish and not go off like a bottle of pop."

"Of course not. You can discuss anything with me, you know that."

Maggie touched her top lip; she could feel it quivering under the tip of her finger. "It's about Dennis ..."

"What! I want nothing to do with him!" He pushed his chair away from the desk. "If that's what this is about, forget it!"

"Please, Jake ... hear me out ... you promised."

He tugged his chair back towards Maggie's desk, "This better be good, Maggie. It's bad enough knowing he's shacked up with Amy!"

"I'll ignore that remark," she said, seeing it as an opportunity to establish a tentative hold on the conversation. "It's information you might want to hear. If you can keep that temper of yours in check ..."

"Ok, ok ..."

"It's Dennis is working for Brendan Fisher."

Jake snorted. "The bloody idiot! I thought he was running a taxi?"

"He still is. And they want revenge for what happened to Billy. "

"Michael, you mean?"

Maggie nodded. "They want Dennis to get him."

"What, help Fisher's goons beat him up?"

"Worse ...They're also threatening to hurt Amy if he won't do what they say. You know what those bastards can do. I haven't told June ... I daren't."

"And what do you expect me to do, ask them to be nice?"

"Just listen, Jake. They're importing guns and selling them to the provos in Ireland. Dennis took photos — Amy showed me."

"He's playing a dangerous game, Maggie. He'll slip up. They'll butcher him. Skin him alive."

"He's had enough, Jake. Amy says he just wants to bring the bastards down."

"He hasn't a chance, Maggie. Best thing you can do is tell him get the hell out —take Amy with him."

Maggie shook her head, "They'd put a contract out on him, you know they would."

"Then he's only one option," Jake replied. "Stay working for them."

"You don't mean that, Jake."

"Course I don't, but he doesn't have much going for him. There's nothing I can do, much as I'd like to get the evil sods. And I doubt there's anyone willing to take 'em on — drug dealers who want part of the action, maybe, but I doubt it."

"They've slipped up, Dennis says."

"Dennis says ...? Huh ..." Jake sounded dismissive.

"He knows they're selling to both sides," Maggie continued. "The UVF as well as the provos."

"Oh, yeah — getting greedy, are they?" Jake scratched at the back of his neck. "The Fishers won't give a damn who uses the stuff."

"But the Provos might ..."

Jake sat back in his chair. "The Fishers will be careful."

Maggie leaned towards him, her eyes glinting. "That's just it. There were supposed to be two crates coming from the Ukraine, one for the provos, one for the UVF. They only got one. They had to split the stuff and repack it. They'll be getting half what they paid for."

"How do you know this is true?" He smirked, "What's Dennis got — a couple of invoices?"

"He took photos; all the stuff they had to divide — rows of it — guns, automatics, pistols ... grenades, I think. They had to get two smaller crates and repack. They hid 'em in a cattle truck and then took 'em across on the ferry. He's got photos of the truck."

Jake gave a dismissive snort.

"At least have a look ..."

Jake sat staring at Maggie. "Then what? Make him photographer of the year?"

She shrugged her shoulders, "You always said if you ever got the chance ... this might be it."

He pulled a large handkerchief from his pocket, smothered his nose and blew loudly.

"Getting a cold, Jake? You should look after yourself."

"Oh, I intend to Maggie ...Ok," he said, "you and Amy bring the photos here, tomorrow — just before we pack up. Make it look like a normal meeting. I don't want Dennis to know — got it."

"Thanks, Jake," Maggie replied as he ambled towards their adjoining door, rubbing the back of his neck. She heard his chair give its familiar reluctant squeak, followed by several loud sneezes. "Get something for that cold!" she shouted.

The next day was unusually quiet. Heavy rain pinging off the corrugated iron roof had given way to sharp bursts that sounded as if metal pellets had been thrown from the sky. The few that had come to the market, wet and bedraggled, smelling of damp wool, left as soon as they'd found what they were looking for. Amy kept watching the second hand on the clock above the entrance door ticking round in jerky steps. She tried to stay busy, but as the thin stream of customers slowed to a trickle the only thought in her head was of Dennis' photographs. Apart from Bateman, still scrubbing his cutting tables and meat counter, and Doris, washing the last of her mugs in a plastic bowl, she was the only person in the hall. Maggie waved from the window of Jake's office. Amy had the photos in her backpack which she'd carefully hidden under a table at the rear of her stall. She grabbed her bag and quickly climbed the metal steps to Jake's office. He beckoned her to take a seat next to Maggie. He eased himself into a larger chair at the end of the table, "Right, Amy, let's have a look at these photos."

She placed the folder of photographs on Jake's desk. Jake leaned forward, peering intently.

"I know those two," Jake remarked. "He's the muscle," he said, pointing at Leo. "The other one's Owen Connors. Dangerous, he is. Likes to use a knife."

"Is he the one who slashed Eddie?" Maggie asked.

"I'd put money on it," Jake replied.

He paused on the images of the guns and ammunition spread out on the tarpaulin. "This is serious stuff." He drummed his fingers on the table. "Clever," he remarked, "hiding the crates behind the cab. Who'd want to climb over that stinking rig?"

"Dennis thinks they pick up a load of cattle before taking it on to the ferry."

"I'm sure they do," added Jake. "Dennis did well, getting these. Better than I thought."

"What now?" Maggie said.

Jake grunted. "He's got to stay working for the Fishers. I don't want him doing anything that might spook them."

"You'll help, then."

"I'll think about it, talk to some people I know. No promises."

"Thanks, Jake."

"Don't thank me yet, Maggie." He tapped the top of the images, "You'd better look after these, Maggie." He reached towards Amy and gripped her arm "Don't let Dennis talk to his dad, not yet. I'll talk to him first. I might need his help —that's if I decide something can be done." Amy nodded.

Jake looked directly at her. "You be careful, Amy."

Chapter 32

Michael was in the bathroom when the doorbell rang. He finished as urgently as he could, quickly rinsed his hands under the cold tap and hurried downstairs. He swiped his damp hands down the sides of his trousers and opened the front door. Jake was standing half-turned towards the street as if checking for something, or someone. He spun round, stepped past Michael and quickly closed the door.

"Everything alright, Jake?" Michael asked. Jake didn't reply, he simply headed down the hall and into the kitchen.

"Beer?" Michael asked.

"A whisky, if you've got it," Jake replied, pulling out one of the kitchen chairs.

Michael returned carrying two glasses, a bottle of whisky hooked under his arm. He poured a good three fingers into each of the glasses, placed the bottle in the middle of the table and sat across from Jake. They clinked glasses,

"What's up, Jake? You look serious. This isn't just a chat, is it?"

"There are things you need to know."

"The Fishers?"

Jake nodded. "And Dennis."

Michael took a slug from his glass, "Now what?"

"I need you to listen, it's important. There's likely to be trouble."

"And this involves me?"

Jake nodded. "It involves me as well. And then there's Dennis ..."

"Why am I not surprised!"

"Yeah, well, I've certainly nothing to thank him for." He let his glass rest on his lip and sipped carefully. "He's working for Brendan Fisher," he said, "at a warehouse on one of the industrial parks."

Michael looked away. "I'm sorry to say this about my own son, but I don't trust him. He's been nothing but trouble."

"Hear me out, Michael." He rubbed the palm of his hand across the table and balled it into a fist. "I haven't spoken to him, not yet. It's his girlfriend, Amy; she has a stall in the market with her mum. Maggie's like a surrogate mother — they're close, have been for years. She was never happy that Amy took up with Dennis."
"Huh ... don't blame her. So why are they still together? It's not like Maggie to hold back," Michael commented.

"The Fishers have him by the balls," said Jake. "They've threatened to harm her if he doesn't do what they say. There's other stuff as well ..."

"Always is with those bastards."

"Yeah, we both know that." Jake took a breath and exhaled loudly. "Dennis has had enough. He wants out. He wants to bring 'em down."

"Dennis!? I hate to say this, but he's a wimp, Jake! There's no way he could get to the Fishers. What the hell are you talking about?"

"He's taken photos of what they're up to. Takes guts to do that Michael."

Michael looked across at Jake, "Then he's as good as dead. They'll find out ... What's he got, anyway?"

"They're running guns — supplying paramilitaries in Ireland."

"So what? It doesn't surprise me, not in the least."

"They've slipped up big time," Jake told Michael. "They were supposed to be sending two shipments, one for the Provos and one for the UVF."

"They're suppling both sides!?"

Jake nodded. "Guess what? They had to split a shipment. Both of 'em are only getting half what they're expecting."

"How come?"

He told him about the guns from the Ukraine. Michael listened with obvious incredulity at how Dennis had managed to take photos of the guns laid out on a tarpaulin so they could be divided into two crates, one for the Provs, and one for the UVF.

"And I suppose the Provos don't know they've lost half their shipment to the UVF?"

"Not yet they don't," Jake replied. "Imagine what'd happen if they did."

"Dunno, Jake. It's hellish dangerous. Can we trust Dennis? Not sure I can. And just what do we do with these photos — show them round a bar in Dublin? We've no contacts. Who's going to listen to us? Try anything and the Fishers would hear about it."

"Look, don't you think I haven't been asking myself the same questions, ever since I saw the photos? We'll never get an opportunity like this again. They don't make many slip-ups." He drained the last of his whisky and tapped his glass on the kitchen table. Michael took the hint and poured out shots for them both. They took small, serious sips as if the whisky would aid concentration.

"How do we know this isn't some trick?" said Michael. "He could have even been set up without realising."

Jake shrugged his heavy shoulders. "That's why I need you to talk to him."

"Not sure about this, Jake. I doubt he'd want to meet with me, anyway."

"Amy reckons he wants to see you. He's got things he wants you to know."

Michael pushed hard on his thick-rimmed glass as if attempting to screw it into the table. "When?"

"As soon as you're ready. But don't leave it ..."

"Now, you mean?"

Jake nodded. "Now, Michael."

Michael thought he heard the doorbell. He opened the door, half expecting to see his bridge partner, Barry. For a split second he didn't realise it was Dennis. He looked cleaner, taller than the surly, scowling, hunched figure he'd last seen at Barbara's funeral.

"Hello, Dad."

It was a calm voice, a normal voice, nothing aggressive, no hint of rancour in his tone or demeanour. Just for a moment, Michael hesitated. "You'd better come in," he said.

Dennis followed him down the hall and into the kitchen.

"You've kept it nice," he said, eying the gleamingly clean sink and the kitchen dresser displaying rows of crockery.

"Jake said you wanted to see me," Michael ventured, motioning for Dennis to take a seat.

"Thanks," Dennis replied, moving cautiously, as if he was a visitor, a guest.

Michael made them coffee and then, almost as an afterthought, took out a half-opened packet of digestive biscuits and two small plates. "Good to see you, Dennis."

"Thanks, Dad. I wasn't sure if ..."

"I wasn't sure myself. Jake convinced me I should."

Dennis helped himself to a digestive, catching the crumbs in the palm of his hand and tipping them carefully onto his plate. He took a gulp of coffee.

"That job at the market — it was the best time. I loved the place," he said.

"So, what happened?"

"Billy Fisher, that's what."

"Nasty little runt, he was."

"He was at the same school, him and his cousins."

"Can't have been easy," Michael said. "I suppose I knew you were having a tough time. I should have done something."

Dennis shrugged his shoulders. "Don't think there was much you could have done ... probably made it worse."

"You got pretty angry in those days ... I just wanted you to ..."

"Be the good son?"

Michael hung his head. "I never tried to understand why you got so angry ... especially with me."

"You remember that time ...?"

Michael ground his teeth, his jaw pulsed. "When I hit you? I'll have to live with that for the rest of my life. It thumps me in the gut every time I think about it."

"Don't think I helped," Dennis said. "I was so mixed up."

"Finding out you were adopted probably didn't help."

Dennis nodded. "I wanted to make you proud of me, but it nearly always seemed to go wrong. And then I gave up trying."

Michael took several sips of his now tepid coffee. "I'd seen too many kids end up in the Young Offenders. I didn't want you to end up like them." He paused and looked directly at his son; "I didn't want the embarrassment. I went about it the wrong way. I should have stood up for you. Maybe if I had, none of this would have happened."

Dennis fumbled with his coffee mug. "You got me the job at the market, though."

Michael nodded. "Jake's a good friend. He took a bit of convincing. You were doing such a great job. What happened?"

"Like I said, Billy Fisher showed up, all threats about what he'd do if I didn't help. He wanted me to steal some copper pipe — said it'd be just that, nothing else. It didn't stop there ..."

"Never does, not with scum like the Fishers."

"He wanted me to leave the back gate unlocked. He said he'd get me shopped for stealing. I was so stupid."

"Jake found out."

"He knew it had to be me. He kicked me out ... I lost a job I loved. The stall holders — they are the best people. And Maggie — she was great, helped me get a place, even gave me some money. That's where I met Amy, she has a stall at the market."

"So I heard."

"She let me have a room," Dennis continued. "Her boyfriend lived there as well — Lee Hogan."

"Lee Hogan ... I've come across him."

"He gave me a job driving, taking cars to a chop-shop, mostly."

Michael pushed his chair back and walked over to the kitchen counter and refilled the kettle. "That's when you drove into Lisa's boyfriend's car," he said, fiddling with the lid of the coffee jar.

Dennis nodded, slowly. "Prison was hell — worse. They found out about you. I thought about suicide, many times." He pushed his empty mug towards the end of the table. "You heard of Danny Fisher?" he said.

Michael nodded and picked up Dennis' empty mug. "Yeah. One of the king-pins in that extended family. Nothing much happens without his say so, even if he is in jail."

"I got into trouble for attacking a guard ... I just couldn't take it anymore. They put me on suicide watch. When I was put back in my cell, one of Danny Fisher's goons said he wanted to see me. He claimed he wanted to help."

"Why?"

"He wanted me in his pocket. And I knew that, but I didn't care. I wanted protection. He had me collect from other prisoners — and worse. I did some bad things in there. He said if I needed help on the outside ... That's when he gave me Brendan Fisher's number. I was grateful. Grateful for helping me survive."

"I know enough about life in prison to know most just want to survive."

Dennis' jaw twitched. "I liked being able to do what I wanted. I got back at those bastards who'd made my life hell. Sometimes I bruised a few that didn't deserve it. I didn't care, not at the time."

Michael stared at his son. There was a hardness, a mean look he'd seen many times. If he didn't know it was his son, the man across the table could well have been just another vicious thug.

"You were one of Fisher's enforcers ..."

"Yeah. What of it? I owed him, big-time. When I got out ... you remember I came here ..." Michael nodded ... "You told me to go... and Mum did. She was right, I'd messed up big time. I went to stay with Lee Hogan; he gave me a job of sorts — taxi driving. I found out he'd been hitting Amy, threatening her after he'd moved out of her place. I called Brendan Fisher — I wanted Lee scared off. They nearly killed him. He ended up in hospital for several weeks. That's when I took one of his cars, started running a taxi business on my own." Dennis swept his right hand through an arc, as if caressing a steering wheel. His hand hovered, "Part of me was glad they'd done that, beaten him to a pulp." He leant on his elbows, "I was scared they'd do the same to me."

"You got yourself in deep," said Michael.

Dennis gave him a quick glance, a look suggesting Michael was close to saying something stupid.

"Brendan Fisher told me I owed them for what they'd done to Lee. He made me work for him at a warehouse, moving mobile phones." He slowly raised his head and looked directly at Michael.

"There's worse, Dad. A lot worse. They want me to do their dirty business."

"Oh...?"

"An-eye-for-an-eye ..."

Michael understood, immediately. "It's me, isn't it? They want you to ... to do what, kill me? Is that why you're here Dennis, is that what you've come to do? This is all a trick, isn't it?"

Dennis shook his head, vigorously. "No, Dad. Nothing like that, you've gotta believe me."

"Oh, and how do I know you, or one of Fisher's goons, won't just be waiting for the opportunity."

"Please, Dad — I want to make it right — I want to stop them. They're threatening to slash Amy if I don't do what they want." He looked across at Michael, his eyes pleading, "I've gotta get out of this. I don't want you hurt, and I don't want anything to happen to Amy."

"Oh yeah, just how do you propose to take on the Fishers?"

"They're running guns ..."

"Jake told me. "These photos — you think that's all we need to get at the Fishers? Those bastards are ruthless. It'll take more than a few images."

Dennis shrugged his shoulders. "It may be our best chance — our only chance."

"So, we're all in this together are we, you, me and Jake? Whatever we decide — if we decide — there'll be consequences."

"I know that," Dennis replied, quietly.

Chapter 33

"Maggie, what are you doing here?" Michael assumed it was just a meeting with Jake. "I don't want you to be involved."

"Like it or not, I am involved, Michael. It's not just you, or Dennis, there's Amy. They'll start with her; I know they will."

Jake shouted through the kitchen hatch, his voice rising in anger. "Maggie's right: It isn't just you, Michael. There'll always be some other poor sod who gets the treatment for looking at them the wrong way." Michael heard the soft whoosh of the fridge door. "Look what happened to Eddie," he said as he walked into the room carrying three beers and a stack of glass tumblers squeezed between his big hands and his belly.

"You sure Dennis hasn't been told to do this?" said Michael. "I want to believe him ..."

Jake shrugged his shoulders, "Could be a set-up, but I don't think so. Those photos he took look real to me."

Maggie reached into her handbag, "See for yourself, Michael. This is potent stuff. He was brave to take them."

Michael peered intently at the photograph of the guns on a tarpaulin. He felt a cold shiver inching slowly down his spine. He slowly poured his bottle of Guinness, his eyes still fixed on the images laid out on the table. "Now what?" he said.

"That's why we're here," Jake replied, with a hint of irritation. "First thing is to agree that we can trust Dennis, and that these photos are real."

"Well, Michael?" said Maggie.

He nodded. "I've got to believe him." He paused and looked at them both. "I just hope we're not wrong."

Maggie and Michael watched as Jake took several gulps of his Guinness and then swiped at the white froth that had gathered round his mouth.

"What are you thinking, Jake?" Maggie asked as Jake carefully placed his glass on one of the cardboard coasters.

"We need to stir things up — get word to the Provos and maybe the UVF."

Michael nodded, "Yeah, I can see that," he said, as if Jake was stating the obvious. "But we know nothing about them."

"They hate each other's guts," Maggie remarked. "But we've got to be careful. They think all Brits are ignorant — know nothing about Ireland."

"That's probably true," Jake added. "But these aren't politicians, they're paramilitaries. The one thing both of 'em hate is a betrayal." Jake tapped on the computer, "Supplying both sides is a betrayal they'll not forgive."

"What! You think we should somehow contact both of them?" Maggie queried with some alarm.

Jake shook his head. "No —just the Provos, I reckon they're better organised, especially over here."

"I'm not sure about this," said Michael.

Jake leant forward resting his forearms on his thighs. "You got any better ideas?"

There was a tense silence with both men avoiding eye contact, as if doing so might provoke a confrontation.

"No point in you two getting out of sorts. Let's just chuck in ideas — anything — no matter how absurd it seems."

"Sorry, Maggie," Michael mumbled. "You're right. It's solutions we need."

"Try this," she said, quickly. "There's a priest at the catholic church on the edge of Marshbrook estate … "

"Didn't know you were a church goer," Jake remarked.

"I don't tell you everything," she replied, sharply. The two men glanced at each other. Maggie appeared to ignore them. "Father Carey — he must be in his seventies — he was supposed to retire but they can't find a replacement. He's a staunch republican — he often slips in a remark about a united Ireland. It's rumoured he was a bit of a rebel in his day."

"Very nice," Michael commented. "So what?"

"If anyone knows who might be a contact, it'll be him. I'd put money on it — and he's no fan of the Fishers."

"What do you think, Jake?" Michael asked.

Jake shrugged his big shoulders. "It's worth a try. You trust him, Maggie?"

She nodded. "He preaches a long sermon, but he's a man of few words. I reckon it'll either be a nod of his head, or a quiet 'no'."

It was after Maggie left that Jake confided in Michael that he wasn't sure about Maggie's scheme. He wasn't at all convinced Maggie's priest would have any useful contacts and even if he did, Jake knew the Provos wouldn't want anyone to be able to identify them. If they decided to take care of the Fishers, it might not end there.

If Jake had been able to read Maggie's thoughts, he'd have been even more concerned. Almost as soon as she stepped into her car, she began to wish she'd never mentioned Father Carey. It seemed foolish to assume he'd know anyone within the higher echelons of the republican paramilitary. It seemed equally foolish to expect he'd listen to her, let alone offer to help. It was not as if she was his most loyal parishioner. Her faith was based on a sense of guilt. When she was a child, she'd gone with her mother and grandmother to mass almost every Sunday. When her grandmother died, she'd decided, in her young mind, that it was the church's fault and made it plain she didn't want to go. Eventually her mother gave up trying to cajole her reluctant daughter. She often wondered if it was simply homage to her grandmother that nudged, sometimes nagged, her to follow her code and take the sacraments on something approaching a regular basis. If she was honest, she knew the appeal was that it was the same priest she'd briefly encountered at Beech House. There'd never been any flicker of recognition. But then why should there be?

The following morning, she paced around her kitchen, chain-smoking her way through a full pack of cigarettes and drinking more cups of black coffee than usual, rehearsing in her head what she wanted to say. By the time she set off to the church to attend morning Mass her brain was buzzing from caffeine and nicotine overload. The acidic feeling in the pit of her stomach didn't help. The service dragged. It was as if time within the confines of the church was slowed to accommodate the deliberate movements of the priest and his congregation.

Maggie hung back waiting for the last of the aged parishioners to shake the hand of the priest and leave through the main gothic arch. She walked towards him as he began lifting a blackened stub of candle from an ornate candle holder in front of the altar.

"Father Carey, can I have a word?" The priest turned as Maggie approached,

"No altar boy," he said, sternly.

"Probably at school?" Maggie ventured.

Father Carey stood erect and peered up at the statue of the Virgin Mary, which appeared to be balanced precariously on a plinth fixed high on a pillar adjacent to the altar. "School?" he mumbled, as though it was an excuse he hadn't considered. He turned to face her,

"You'd better come through to the rectory."

Still a charmer, thought Maggie.

He waved a loose arm and led her into the vestry. She watched as he lifted his stole from round his neck, folded it in half, then half again, and gently kissed the gold lamia cross embroidered into the green silk. He slipped quickly out of his surplice and hung it carefully on a coat hanger on the back of the door.

Father Carey seemed much taller without his priestly garments. His pink face looked scrubbed and recently shaven. His thinning white hair had been tugged across his scalp and held in place with what Maggie guessed was Brilliantine. It reminded her of the scented oils her father applied before tripping off to the local pub.

The rectory was attached to the vestry by a corridor lined with a row of chairs and a couple of tables displaying religious booklets and magazines. It had the appearance and feel of a doctor's waiting room. Father Carey ushered Maggie into a study. It had a Victorian fireplace with ornate tiles, a polished brass grate and a marble mantlepiece with an imposing crucifix in the centre. The walls on either side had mahogany bookshelves filled with books, most lying askew, some dangling precariously over the edges of the shelves. He sat in a well-used armchair and motioned for Maggie to sit in a chair opposite his.

"Maggie, isn't it? Maggie Harrison? I remember now. You knew that lad who was stabbed ... Eddie?"

Maggie nodded.

"I was grateful for what you did, Father."

"Your son?" commented the Priest. It was said as if he knew something of her past.

"No, Father. I knew the family."

"You gave him the last rites. It was touch and go."

Father Carey nodded. "I was delighted he pulled through." He steepled his fingers in front of his chin. "I hear he's ok, now."

"It's taken a while," Maggie replied.

"Now, what's this about?" the priest said, abruptly.

Maggie stretched her neck and sat upright on the edge of the uncomfortably soft chair.

She took a deep breath, "You heard what happened to Billy Fisher?"

The priest sat back and nodded, "Yes, I remember. Anytime the name 'Fisher' comes up, it gets my attention. I read the report in the paper. They blamed the prison officer."

"Michael Barrett," Maggie told him. "The Fishers are out to get him, Father. He took the blame, and the prison governor didn't help." She gulped; words lodged in her throat. For just a moment, she wondered if she was doing the right thing, involving this priest in their troubles. "Dennis Barrett, Michael's son; he's got himself mixed up with the Fishers."

"How?"

"You know how events sometimes spiral in the wrong direction?"

"Unravelling those tangles has been my life's work."

"He knew Billy Fisher from school."

"Can't have been easy, especially given his dad's job."

Maggie nodded. "Dennis left school as soon as he could. His dad got him a job at the market. Michael, and Jake Gould — he owns the place — know each other."

"And that's where you met young Dennis?"

"Yes, Father, I've worked there a long time. He loved that job, worked like a trojan."

"What happened?"

"Billy Fisher, that's what. He got Dennis to unlock one of the security gates. Jake found out and ... you can guess the rest. That's when it really went wrong."

"Events spiraling ...?"

"Yeah, and not in a good way. He found a job, of sorts, driving for another low life. He was high on drugs and drink when it happened."

"What ... what happened?"

"He ploughed into a car — killed the driver."

Father Carey slowly nodded and stared at the empty grate. He gripped the armrests on his chair. "Think I'll need a drink. I think we both do. Whisky, ok?" Maggie watched him wipe two cut glass tumblers with a small cloth lying on the sideboard, polishing each carefully, as if cleaning the chalice after Mass.

"Thanks," Maggie said, as she took the glass from Father Carey's hand. She let the warmth build in her stomach as she sipped from her glass.

"Dennis got a prison sentence. You can imagine how tough it must have been."

The priest held his glass away from his lips, "They found out about his dad?"

Maggie nodded. "It was inevitable, I suppose. He got the full treatment; they even had him on suicide watch."

Father Carey put his whisky to one side, "He got help, I presume?"

"From the Fishers — Danny Fisher. He gave him protection in jail."

Father Carey nodded, sagely. "They're cute, those Fishers. There's always a price, and usually it's a big one."

"He was given Brendan Fisher's number," Maggie continued. "He was foolish enough to think he could trust them."

"And what happened to Dennis?"

"Brendan Fisher wanted payback. He's kept Dennis close, very close."

"Oh?"

"Dennis is working for him at an industrial unit."

"I don't like where this is heading," said Father Carey, staring at the crucifix on the mantlepiece and slowly shaking his head.

"They want him to go after Michael — take care of him."

"Kill his father!?"

Maggie nodded. "They won't rest until Michael's dead."

"Dennis can't go to the police, I suppose?"

"Who'd believe him?" Maggie replied. "And anyway, the Fishers have too much on him. He's working for them — he's as good as one of them."

"I don't really see how I can help, Maggie. I know a few of the police, but I doubt it would do anything other than warn the Fishers. Some of them are in the Fishers' pockets."

Maggie took a deep breath. "Dennis has got information; evidence about gun running."

"Gun running!? There were always a few rumours — I'd heard about their Limerick clan. You say he's got evidence?"

Maggie nodded. "He wants out, Father."

"And he thinks this evidence he claims to have will bring them down?"

"Not claims to have ... he took photos of the guns they shipped."

"He's either very brave or very stupid. One hint and they'll have him killed. Does he realise?"

"He says he doesn't care, not anymore. And it's not just his dad — they'll go after his girlfriend if he doesn't do what they want."

"I still don't see what I can do to help, Maggie."

"They've slipped up, Father. They've been supplying the IRA ... and they've been supplying the UVF. They had to split a supply of guns and send them off in two crates, one for the Provos and one for the UVF." Father Carey stared fixedly at a small photograph mounted on the wall next to the mantlepiece. Maggie followed his gaze. It was an old black and white of a woman standing in a full skirt with a wicker basket on her arm and a small child stretching his fingers up towards her hand.

"That's me; I was six years old."

"With your mother?"

Father Carey smiled. "She was a wonderful woman. My father died the previous year. She reared me, and my younger brother, on her own," he said, the quiver in his voice betraying the raw emotion he was feeling. "She was very strong, very determined."

"She must have been very proud of you, Father."

Maggie caught the glint of a tear in the corner of his eye. "Yes, I suppose she was. Always do the right thing, she used you say. Listen to your heart."

They sat staring at the cold fireplace, letting a blanket of silence settle.

"Well, Maggie, you haven't come to listen to me being nostalgic." He was beaming, as if thoughts of his mother had given him a reaffirming sense of who he was. "This thing with Dennis and the Fishers — what is it you're hoping to do, exactly?"

"We want a contact, Father. Someone in the Provos."

Father Carey hesitated, briefly. "You want the IRA to know about the shipment of arms being split between them and the UVF?"

Maggie nodded. "For starters, yes."

"There's more?"

"It'll depend on the provos."

The priest sat stroking his chin, "Just a name?"

"Yes, Father, just a name."

Maggie watched as he stood and rested an elbow on the corner of the mantlepiece. She wondered if this was the signal for her to leave.

He held out his hand as she stood. His large hands engulfed hers in the way practised politicians might greet their supporters. "I'll see what I can do. No promises."

Before Maggie quite realised, she'd been ushered out of his room and to the door leading back into the church.

Chapter 34

A week now, and Maggie hadn't heard from Father Carey. She wondered if she should go round to the church and see him again. Jake had expressed his frustration more than once.

"We need to know, Maggie. If he can't — or won't — help, that's the end of it."

Maggie felt guilty that she might have pressured Father Carey into doing something he might later regret. He'd know that anything involving the Fishers and the Provos would lead to some form of violent confrontation. That's what she wanted, it's what Jake wanted; but was it something Father Carey was willing to sanction? Maybe he'd go to the police? Hadn't he said he had contacts? Her head buzzed with thoughts that kept her awake into the small hours.

The sound of her mobile took Maggie by surprise.

"Maggie?" Father Carey's soft Kerry lilt sounded much stronger over the phone.

"Father Carey ..." Maggie held her breath, waiting for the priest to speak.

"I have a contact," he said, as if talking in code. "But it comes with a warning ... my warning. They're very wary of using information from sources they don't know. Any mistakes, any leaks and you'll all be in trouble, serious trouble."

"It's a risk we have to take, Father."

"Just as long as you're sure. Make it very clear to the others. They've got to realise what they're getting into. And it's got to be you, Maggie. No-one else."

"Yes, Father," Maggie stuttered. The enormity of what she, they, were about to undertake suddenly hit her, as if potential repercussions were only just becoming a reality. This wasn't just risky, it was potentially suicidal.

"Come round tomorrow night at seven."

It was almost dark when Maggie reached the priest's house. She was glad she'd shoved a pair of leather gloves into the pocket of her coat. It wasn't particularly cold, not for mid-September, but she'd felt clammy and chilled even before leaving her house. She pushed the doorbell and listened to the chimes pealing from somewhere in the building. A hall light shone through a window in the centre of the door, just above an ornate doorknocker, long since redundant. Maggie could hear the shuffle of feet and a slipper flapping against the hall floor. Father Carey opened the door. He urged her to step inside and then quickly closed the door.

"It's the housekeeper's night off," he said. It reminded Maggie of his bemoaning the absence of the altar boys. "Got to look after myself on Thursday evenings."

He held up a hand, like a policeman directing traffic. "Wait here," he said. Maggie looked round at the paintings on the walls as he set off towards his study. There was a photograph of elderly priests at an ecclesiastical gathering of some kind, each looking as though they'd attempted to outdo the other in the layers of garments they were wearing. None of them looked like Father Carey.

When he returned, he was carrying an envelope.

"This is the information you need," he said. "It's a phone number. I'm not sure who'll answer, probably Tom, Tom Delaney, though I doubt that's his real name." Father Carey held the envelope tight in his fingers before releasing it into Maggie's hand as though it was a last chance for both of them to put a halt to events. He moved past Maggie and slowly opened the front door. "Be careful, Maggie," he said, staring intently into her eyes. "For my mother's sake — God rest her soul — be careful."

"I will, Father," Maggie replied, shoving the envelope deep into her coat pocket.

Later that night she called Jake. "I've got a phone number," she said, and then paused, "I wish now I hadn't suggested going to see Father Carey. It seems wrong, somehow, to get him involved."

"It was your idea, Maggie. It was the only idea we had."

"Yes, yes, I know ... He's a good man, Jake. I just feel I've pressured him to do something he probably regrets."

"Best not to worry about that now, Maggie. By all accounts, he'll be glad to see an end to the Fishers."

"But the Fishers and the Provos? He knows what that will mean. It won't sit comfortably with him."

"You think he might do something stupid? Go to the police?"

"Not a chance. It'll just be his own conscience, and maybe the thought of his mother ..."

"His mother?"

"Forget it, Jake. It doesn't matter, not now."

"You sound a bit upset, Maggie. I'll take things from here; I can make the call."

"No, it's got to be me. And listen Jake, not a word to the others, not until I've talked to the contact."

There was a loud hrmmph from Jake. "Ok, Maggie, if that's the way it's got to be. Just be careful."

Maggie forced herself to breathe slowly.

"You ok, Maggie?"

"Of course," she replied, doubting Jake would be convinced.

Maggie took the single sheet of notepaper from the envelope and re-read the scrawled instruction written in pencil, each large rounded letter spanning two lines of the ruled paper.

'Call Thursday at 8pm. Get prepaid. Use the SIM card in the envelope.'

The SIM card had spilled onto the kitchen table when she'd first opened the envelope. The instruction to get a pre-paid phone hadn't surprised her. She knew immediately it was a 'burner' SIM. Jake used them in many of his dealings.

She took the back off the tiny mobile she'd taken from Jake's supply and slipped the SIM card into its slot. It felt like a loaded weapon. She sat with the phone held between her fingers watching the digital clock in the corner of her sitting room flick through the numbers ...19:59. She turned on the phone and hit the dial button.

The response was almost immediate. "Hello, Maggie."

For just a moment, Maggie felt irritated that someone, a stranger, should call her by her first name.

"Who's this?" It was an instinctive reply.

"No games, Maggie. We need to meet."

"Sorry ... I didn't mean ... Yes ... where?"

"Been to confession, recently?"

"Confession? Not for years."

"It's time you made a visit. Tomorrow night at 9. Use the booth nearest the altar. Confession normally ends at 8, so there'll be no one else there."

"Ok," Maggie replied. She wondered just how involved Father Carey was.

"Bring the evidence in a brown envelope. And the phone you are using."

Maggie sat staring at the blank screen. She reached for her bag and thrust the phone into one of the zip pockets. For some reason, she hadn't expected the meeting would be this soon. What about Jake, and the others, should she let them know? She shook her head, as if responding to her own question.

Not now, not yet.

Maggie's heels echoed off the flagstone aisle leading to the four confessional booths along the right-hand wall of the church. She wished she'd worn more sensible shoes. Apart from an old lady chanting the prayers of the rosary, the church was empty. Maggie was relieved to see the old woman tuck the rosary beads into her fist and heave herself out of the pew.

The curtain across the confessional booth nearest the altar was pulled across, as if someone was receiving the sacrament. Maggie hesitated and then slid back the heavy red curtain. The booth was empty. She knelt, her knees sinking into a cushioned hassock. She could see a man's silhouette through the metal grill in the confessional. He spoke without turning his head, keeping his face in profile. A long straight nose, small chin, high forehead; it was an image that reminded her of a schoolteacher, not a Provo.

"Tell me what you know." A smooth, clear voice.

"The Fishers are sending guns to the UVF as well."

"As well as the IRA?"

"Yes," Maggie replied.

"How do you know?"

"Dennis Barrett works for them." She said, holding the envelope in front of the grill.

"And he is?"

"He was in jail. One of the Fishers gave him protection. He's paying the price."

"That's it?"

"His father, Michael Barrett, was a prison officer in a Young Offenders. One of the Fisher's lads was killed. They blame him for what happened."

"Yes, so I heard."

"They want Dennis to kill him. They're threatening to attack his girlfriend if he doesn't do what they want." Maggie paused. "Dennis wants out. He doesn't want his father killed. He doesn't want anything to happen to Amy."

Maggie watched as the silhouetted man nodded. "You trust him, Maggie ... this Dennis Barrett." The man had a polished English accent. It took her by surprise. She'd imagined it would be someone sounding more Irish than the Irish. Public school? Maybe, she thought — or an ex-army officer, a Sandhurst man, perhaps.

"Yes, I believe him. He knows what's going on. The Fishers slipped up. The supplies from the Ukraine had to be split, one half to the UFV and the other to the IRA."

"If this is true, Maggie, the Provos will certainly be interested." He referred to the Provos as if they were a group he knew by reputation rather than personal involvement.

"Leave the photos in the confessional ... and the burner phone."

"Ok," Maggie replied. "What happens next?"

"Nobody likes to be double-crossed," he said, as though a short preamble was required before he replied. "Especially the Provos." He turned towards the mesh screen. Maggie could smell tobacco smoke on his breath. "I'll do some checking," he said. He leaned closer, his face almost touching the grill. "You be here next Tuesday — same time — got it?"

"Yes ..." she replied.

"And Maggie — not a word to anyone — not a whisper. Is that clear?"

"Yes ... I understand."

Jake wanted to know if she'd made contact. She told him she had, and that's all he needed to know. "So don't ask, Jake," she'd said in a tone that bordered on confrontation. He'd backed off, but she knew he wasn't happy.

"This better not go wrong," he'd told her. "Otherwise, we could all be killed."

"Who by, the Provos, or the Fishers?" she'd said. A remark, rather than a question.

"Does it matter?" he'd replied in a testy voice. "They're both dangerous. Anyway, it's too late now. The Provos might start asking around. There won't be any protection for us, not if the Fishers find out."

"We discussed all this, Jake. We agreed, it's a chance to finish the bastards. We'll never get another opportunity. You're just pissed because it's me talking to the Provos. You don't think I'm up to it, is that it?"

Jake stood, sullen and silent.

"You've got to trust me, Jake," Maggie told him. "You've no option. Just accept it."

Jake smiled. "Ok, Maggie."

The following Tuesday, she walked to the church. She'd left a few minutes later than she intended, not wanting to be seen hanging around in a place she felt she didn't belong. She felt breathless and hot by the time she reached the lychgate set in a stone wall. She hurried along the path and pushed open the heavy door. The church looked empty. The clock had just finished striking as she hurried along the aisle towards the confessional booths. She hesitated before reaching up and pulling back the drape, its curtain rings sliding easily along the well-worn rail. She tugged the drape closed and knelt on the hassock, recalling the traditional chant; "Bless me Father ..."

"Not needed, Maggie," came the military voice from the other side of the grill. "Nice touch though."

Was he mocking her? She berated herself for being stupid.

"We've looked at your photos and done some checking. We got confirmation from our contacts in the UVF. Needless to say, they are equally concerned. They're leaving it to us to deal with the matter, at least for now."

"Now what?" Maggie asked.

"It's not 'what', it's how. That's my particular strength," he remarked. "I'll need to talk to Dennis," he added.

"Here?" Maggie asked.

"I doubt he's a church goer," the silhouetted man replied, a hint of laughter in his voice. "He has this taxi," the voice said. Maggie found herself nodding, "He'll get a call from one of ours — Eve. The pick-up will be outside the Apollo cinema on the High Street at nine tomorrow night. She'll know his car, and what he looks like. We do our background checks, Maggie. She'll address him by his name."

"I'll tell him," Maggie replied.

"You'll do more than that." The voice was menacing. Pleasantries had been dispensed with. "If he doesn't show, we'll treat him like one of the Fishers. We don't play games."

"I understand," Maggie replied, catching her breath.

Chapter 35

Maggie called Dennis. "Come round to mine tomorrow morning," she told him. "Be here by eight, ok?"

"What is it?" Dennis tried to ask.

Maggie's tone was sharp, unmuted by the mobile. "Just be here."

The door opened quickly, as if Maggie had been waiting. Dennis followed her into the kitchen. He pulled out one of the chairs and sat at the table. Maggie took a cigarette letting it dangle, unlit, from her lips. She stared intently at Dennis' face as if searching for something she'd prefer not to see, looking for a blemish that might signify a frailty of some kind. She held the cigarette by her fingers, rested her elbow on the table. "Things are moving Dennis."

"You've made contact?"

She nodded. "You can't back out, not now."

"Yeah, I know," he replied.

"It's you they want to see — tell you what you've to do."

He nodded. "Where?"

"You'll get a call tomorrow evening at nine. A woman will book your taxi. Eve — that's the name she'll use."

Dennis smiled, "Very appropriate."

Maggi dismissed his remark with a wave of her hand. "She knows your car, and what you look like. She'll call you by your name. That's the first thing she'll say."

She leant towards him and scrutinised his face for the second time. "Not the time to be flippant, Dennis. Just remember, you can't say a word to anyone."

"You mean Amy?"

"Especially Amy. I don't need to spell it out. This has got to work, Dennis."

Dennis nodded. "I know, Maggie," he replied. "I know."

Dennis was relieved Amy wasn't home when he left the flat. He didn't want to try and explain why he'd be working late, or to have yet another difficult discussion about what was going on. She'd told him some of them were going for a drink later.

"You'll tell me as soon as you know something?" she'd said, as though it was a mantra she had to repeat.

The digital clock in his car showed 19:50. Dennis drove along the streets he now knew like old friends. At the end of the high street there was a row of tenements, then a tower block, a swimming pool next to a comprehensive school and, just before the park, a McDonalds. He ate slowly, licking his fingers between mouthfuls of burger and bunches of fries, interspersed with slugs of ice-cold milkshake. It was a meal to fill a void — a comfort meal.

He'd drained the last of his milkshake, threw the wrappers and plastic cup into a bin just outside his car, and brushed the crumbs off the front seat when his phone rang. His car clock had just flicked to 21:01.

"Dennis?"

He hesitated, just for a moment, and then answered the call. "Yeah, it's Dennis, Dennis Barrett."

"This is Eve. Pick me up outside the Apollo cinema in fifteen minutes."

The phone went dead.

The Apollo was at the opposite end of the high street near the old county library — now used as a centre for pre-school children. The pavement arced round the front entrance of the cinema with its art-deco features. It had survived by showing old movies to film clubs.

Dennis saw a slim, dark-haired woman wearing jeans and trainers apparently scrutinising one of the posters on the wall of the cinema. He drove up in front of the building and parked his car. The woman was standing less than five metres away, still looking at the billboard. She glanced at her watch and then walked quickly over to his car. He lowered the passenger side window. She bent down and stared into the car, her eyes scrutinising his face.

"Dennis?"

"Yes," he replied. "I got your call."

She opened the car door and got into the rear seat. "Fountain Road," she told him, as she buckled her seatbelt. "Number 39."

Dennis watched her in his rearview mirror. She stared out of the window for most of the journey, as if interested only in the architecture on display. Taxi driving had taught him a thing or two about passengers. Some wanted to chat; the weather, the neighbours, decorations, their pets. Women, usually. Men were much less forthcoming — unless they'd had a drink or two. He sensed Eve would maintain her silence. He caught glimpses of her in the rearview mirror: thirty-ish, he reckoned. Her dark hair was cut short, and she had a small oval face, very pale, and dark, intense eyes, with just a hint of mascara.

"On the left," he heard her say. Dennis slid his car along the kerb coming to a halt adjacent to a garden wall built of the same brick as the semi-detached house. The front garden appeared well kept. There were several bushes that screened the front window and ornamental shrubs growing against a fence shielding the house from next door.

Eve was out of the back seat before Dennis realised. She stood by the driver's door waiting for him to unclip his seat belt. "This way," she said, pointing Dennis to a wrought-iron gate. The front door was being opened as they approached. A man held the door ajar.

"Come in." He stood, intimidatingly close, eying Dennis. He was tall, strong looking, with dark hair cut short at the sides and swept back, a loose long quiff hanging over his forehead. He rubbed at his jaw, thick blue-black bristles rasping against the palm of his hand.

"This way." He led Dennis down the hallway and into a dining room. Dennis was surprised to see a second man, squat, heavy set, standing in the corner of the room. Eve followed; a hint of her perfume caught on a draft of air as she closed the front door. "Take a seat," he said, nodding to a chair tilted against a table. Dennis watched as the man and Eve sat on similar chairs across from his. The pug-faced, squat man grabbed a third chair and shuffled towards the end of the table.

The silence — their silence — made him feel uncomfortable. He tried to focus on the woman, Eve. Was that her real name? A glance told him there wasn't a hint that might suggest a connection of some kind. She was staring at him, expressionless.

And the two men: it was clear they had no intention of introducing themselves. "These photos," the tall man said, tapping an A4 folder, "it's not what we like to see, not from our partners." There was a grunt from the end of the table. He spoke clearly, head erect, his eyes fixed on Dennis'. " What is it that's made you decide to turn against the Fishers? You work for them. Surely you understand the consequences of what you've done?"

Dennis gulped. "I want out," he stammered.

"That simple, is it? You just want out?" We know all about you in jail — got a bit of protection from Danny Fisher. And as soon as you're out, you get in touch with Brendan Fisher. Bit strange that, don't you think?"

"They want me to get at my dad."

"Kill him. Is that it?"

"Yeah. They blame him for the murder of this kid in prison."

"Billy Fisher. Yes, we've done our checking. And then there was that waster you had beaten up — Lee Hogan."

Dennis nodded. He was startled by just how much information they had.

"We just want to make sure," he continued, leaning closer to Dennis.

"I've had enough," Dennis told him. "I don't want anything to happen to my dad. Or Amy ... my girlfriend. They're going to slash her if I don't do what they want."

"So, someone thought we'd be the ones to take 'em out, that it?"

"Yeah ... Maggie. She hates the Fishers. And Jake ..."

"Jake, we know all about Jake. Running a nice little VAT scam before the Fishers saw him off."

Dennis stared at the table, gripping the edge with both hands. It felt sticky with grease, as if a coat of varnish hadn't quite dried.

The man opposite shoved his chair away from the table and leaned back, balancing the chair, his head rubbing against the yellowed wallpaper. It seemed to take an age before he spoke. His voice was deeper, sterner.

"We'll need your help," he eventually said. "But before I go any further, I need you to understand, any slip ups, and you'll be on your own. Those Fishers are mean bastards. This ain't just knocking a few heads together — know what I mean? But I'm assuming that's what you're expecting?"

Dennis felt the blood drain from his face. This was condemning three men to die, to be murdered. "Yes," he replied, his voice starting to break. "Yes," he repeated, this time staring back at his inquisitor.

Dennis stared at the tufts of black hair sprouting from his thick fingers. His fat hand looked like a black spider. "There's another shipment of guns coming in tomorrow."

"Yeah," Dennis remarked. "Brendan wants us all in early. Says the crate should be arriving around nine."

The man nodded. "That's what we've been told. Jonno's one of ours. He's to be there around 10:30. You just be there, on time. I don't want Brendan getting twitchy. You do everything as normal. He'll want to get the stuff onto Jonno's cattle truck as quickly as he can. We want Jonno to get the guns away before we take action."

He leaned forward on his chair. "This is where you come in. Get yourself back into the building, somewhere near the front. Act normal. Offer to make 'em coffee ... just get yourself somewhere where you can see Jonno." He slid a small phone across the table. As soon as you see his truck turning onto the main road, you use this phone. That's it. Just two rings."

"Then what?" Dennis asked, alarmed that one of them, Brendan, Leo, maybe Owen would see him. He had a sudden image of Owen appearing silently from the shadows.

"You get out, Dennis. Through the emergency exit."

"It's alarmed,"

The heavy man smiled, "You'd better move fast. There'll be two of us through the front door, two through the back and one watching the emergency exit."

"That'll be me," the tall man said. "It'll be quick. Our shooters won't have time to sort out who's who. Anyone in the building will be killed. Got it?"

Dennis was relieved it would be the calmer, less intimidating man covering the emergency exit. Crashing through the exit door and coming face to face with one of the other goons shooting at everything that moved filled him with dread.

"You sure you can do this?" said the military looking man, his back ramrod straight. "Anything that alerts the Fishers and this could all go wrong. That's what we don't like."

Names were suddenly thrown around, as if he was now one of them — a Provo.

"Gerry here's not too happy. He's worried you might not have the guts."

"It's your plan, Tommy. I'm just a foot soldier," he said, lifting his arms as if holding a rifle.

The tall man — the one Gerry had referred to as 'Tommy' — leant forward, his forehead almost touching Dennis'. "That's why we've taken another precaution, one which might strengthen your resolve." He moved slowly back into his seat, "Eve …"

Eve stood and walked quickly out of the room. Dennis heard her walk down the hall and then a single rap and a door squeaking on its hinges. There were mumbled voices; feet shuffling, muffled groans, a stifled cry.

Dennis gasped. Amy was being half dragged, half carried by Eve and a stout woman who could well have been Gerry's sister. He sprang to his feet, Amy looked at him wild eyed, a look of terror.

"Amy!" he shouted. Her head lolled to one side and her body slumped into the arms of the Gerry look-a-like. Before he could take a step towards her, Tommy's large hands were gripping his shoulders. Amy moaned, and then shook her head as if trying to clear her befuddled brain.

"Dennis … help me, Dennis …"

Dennis reached out, his hand almost touching her face. He could feel Tommy's powerful fingers digging into the nape of his neck. He kicked back with the heel of his shoe, catching Tommy's shin. In what seemed an instant, Tommy cursed, grabbed Dennis even harder and thumped him hard on the back of the head with the heel of his hand. Squat Gerry was suddenly there. He unleashed a blow deep into Dennis' solar plexus. Dennis sank to his knees, his body shaking and convulsing in breathless gasps.

Tommy hauled him to his feet. "No need for this, is there Dennis? Nothing's going to happen to Amy, not if you do what we've asked. She's just had a sedative, that's all. She won't even remember a thing; it'll just seem like a dream."

"Or a fucking nightmare!" Dennis exclaimed.

"No need for bad language," Tommy said, in his clipped English accent. "Gerry doesn't like bad language, do you Gerry?"

Gerry snorted; "Just like people to be feckin' pleasant."

That's Gerry for you," said Tommy. "Feck this, feck that. Never hear him swear, not really swear." He strengthened his grip, "Got to be careful, Dennis. We're in dangerous territory."

"Cut the crap!" Eve sounded angry. "All he needs to know is if he doesn't do the job right, then his girlfriend's in trouble, big trouble." She glared at Dennis. "Got it?"

Dennis clenched his teeth, stared back at Eve and slowly nodded.

"The girls'll take good care of her," said Tommy, as they pulled Amy towards the door. Dennis watched her attempting to struggle looking like a marionette, her legs and arms splaying in all directions.

"She'll be ok," Tommy said, as the three of them shuffled out of the room, Amy now hanging limp as if the fight had gone out of her.

"She'd better be," Dennis exclaimed.

"That's rather up to you Dennis. "I take it you are fully on board?"

"Yeah," Dennis replied, gritting his teeth at the anger welling up inside him. "You do your bit, take care of the Fishers."

"Bit of spirit, that's what I like to see," said Tommy. "Don't you worry on that score."

Chapter 36

Dennis' heart suddenly raced. His phone was buzzing like a large fly. He looked at the screen, it was Maggie. She never called, what did she want? Why now? He felt cold and clammy, his mind a whirl of indecision. There were two options; answer, or let it ring out.

He didn't like either of them. It was just 7:00am and he'd been up since six, going over and over what might happen in the next few hours. It'd been a relief to get up and take a shower. He'd hardly slept. His head had been filled with nightmarish images — Amy dangling from the arms of the two women like a rag doll; Brendan Fisher's face leering at him; guns popping, spitting fire, silent blasts that had him twitching as if he were riddled with bullets.

He grabbed the phone.

Maybe, just maybe it was nothing? Maggie's tone told him something different.

"Dennis, where are you?" She spoke like a mother reprimanding her teenage son for staying out late.

"Just leaving ... got an early pick-up."

"Where's Amy?"

"Not here," he managed, hoping he sounded convincing enough.

"Where is she? I tried calling her last night. No reply."

"She went clubbing."

"Clubbing! After what happened! Is she mad!"

"I think she wanted to do something ... you know ... something normal."

"Normal! And you let her go!?"

"She said she'd stay over with one of her mates."

"Who? Got a name? Surely, she told you!?"

"... Erica something. Can't remember. Nothing to worry about ... honest."

"'Nothing' and 'honest' are two words that don't sit comfortably with me, not with everything that's going on," she hissed. "You call me as soon as you hear from her, got it?"

"Yeah, course."

"There's nothing else I should know, is there?"

"No, no ... It's all ok."

The phone suddenly went dead. Dennis wanted to get out of the flat as quickly as he could. Confronting Maggie at the door, on the warpath, was the last thing he needed. He patted his pockets, checked he had the burner phone stuffed under a rag in his jeans, slipped on his old denim jacket, grabbed his car keys and headed out of the flat.

He decided to fill an hour or so with another trip to McDonalds, this time parking his car and going inside, drawn by the comforting familiarity of the bright lighting, white formica counters and red plastic bench seats. Apart from a few cars lining up for coffee to go, the only other customers were a couple of men in work overalls idly nursing paper mugs of coffee and picking at the remnants of their food. They took little notice of Dennis. One of them glanced in his direction and then continued staring out of the window at a white van parked directly opposite. It had the same blue logo as those on their overalls.

Dennis ordered a coffee and a sausage muffin and waited for his order to appear. They'd added a small portion of fries in a red envelope. The girl behind the counter smiled. He felt himself blush.

"The first customers always get free french-fries."

'Free french-fries,' he repeated in his head. It sounded like a tongue twister. He wondered if it was company policy, a deliberate technique to get the yawning early morning servers to exercise their tongues.

"Thanks," he said, taking his tray over to one of the cushioned benches.

He ate carefully, retrieving crumbled pieces of muffin from his paper napkin. It was easy-eating, a meal with an immediate satisfying hit. Thoughts of the Fishers, the Provos, his dad, Maggie, even Amy, seemed a fog away as if reality had been suspended in some surreal eatery. A feeling of gloom began to fill his head as he finished the last remnants of food. He drained his coffee, glanced across at the workmen clearing their trays, and followed them towards the exit.

He could see Leo and Owen in conversation with Brendan as he parked in front of the unit. Brendan looked in no mood for idle chat. He was stabbing a finger into the palm of his hand, as if making a point. He spun round as Dennis opened the door and pointed through the front window, "Get that thing out of sight. I don't want any cops wondering what the hell your so-called 'taxi' is doing parked in front of my unit! I just got a call, Jonno's coming early, he'll be here in thirty minutes." Brendan didn't like sudden changes. He always went off on one if things weren't going as he expected. It struck Dennis, as he drove his car round the back, that it might be the Provos deliberately trying to disrupt things.

Brendan wanted the crate of guns loaded on the pallet and the rear doors lifted, ready for Jonno. He helped Leo clear the yard and open the gates that led onto the concreted area in front of the loading ramp. They were rushing around, cleaning and clearing, not that there was anything much to shift. It seemed to soothe Brendan's temper, as if activity of some sort was essential. Leo began hosing down the concrete apron in front of the loading ramp. He motioned for Dennis to grab a brush and sweep the excess water into the drain. They both glanced at Brendan walking back towards the front of the building, muttering to himself. Leo winked at Dennis. "Bit on edge this morning."

Dennis nodded. "What's got him so pissed?"

"It's Jonno. He's usually late coz of traffic or summat. This is the first time he's called to say he'll be here early. Better look busy and stay out of his way." He grinned and winked again at Dennis. "Least we'll be finished early. Owen brought some beers —stacked 'em in the fridge. Reckons we'll need a drink." He gestured towards the cloudless blue sky. "Going to be a hot one."

Jonno's cattle truck ambled into view just as they finished cleaning the yard. Brendan stood, hands on hips, watching as Jonno slowly backed his battered truck towards the ramp. Crusted cattle dung hung from the slatted sides and dank, blackened straw trailed from the tailgate. Brendan stood back, letting Leo and Dennis guide Jonno as he edged closer.

"How come you're early," Brendan shouted up to the cab, as the rig came to a shuddering halt.

"Had to drop off some steers. Went quicker than I reckoned; roads were quiet."

"Brendan grunted, "Ok, let's get this lot loaded," he said, motioning towards the warehouse. "Where to next?"

"Got to pick up some calves, then on to Hollyhead. Should have the stuff in Limerick before it gets too dark, if I get the early ferry." He hopped down from his cab as Dennis and Leo moved to the rear of the truck. It took a few minutes of Leo pounding at the slide bolts with a hammer to release the tailgate. It suddenly dropped, the steel door slamming onto the concrete apron. Leo jumped backwards.

"Hell, Jonno. You need to get this thing sorted."

Jonno smiled, pointing to the rusted springs on either side of the tailgate. "Need to replace 'em sometime," he said, tapping one of them with a spanner. The loose spring shook, uselessly.

"You do that, Jonno," Brendan hissed. "This thing's a bloody death trap."

Jonno appeared to ignore him. He pulled on a hydraulic lever on the side of the truck and began lowering the ramp for the upper deck. It moved slowly, jerking on leaking hydraulic rams. He then climbed onto the back of the truck and hooked the ramp to the lower deck. Brendan waved to Owen, who was sitting in the pallet handler watching proceedings, his forearms resting on the steering wheel. He raised the crate just sufficient to clear the ground and drove slowly along the concrete platform towards the truck's tailgate.

"That thing safe?" he shouted. Jonno didn't reply, he just waved Owen forward, a huge grin revealing a row of misshapen teeth. The tailgate creaked under the weight of the pallet handler, its rear wheels spinning on the greasy metal surface. If Owen was alarmed, he didn't show it. He seemed to be enjoying this as a test of his driving skills. He nudged at the controls, lifting the crate just enough to put pressure on the rear wheels and inched forwards onto the truck. Brendan looked relieved. He gestured towards Leo and Dennis,

"What're you waiting for?" he growled.

Leo tugged at Dennis' jacket and led the way up the ladder and onto the top deck. It stank of rotting straw and fresh dung spread around as if it had been deliberately run under a muck spreader. Despite the muck, it was a relief to be working with Leo on the upper deck, well away from Brendan and Owen. They worked quickly, now familiar with what needed doing. Jonno stood back to admire their handiwork. "It'll do," he said in his rattling Irish brogue. He hopped down off the tailgate landing cat-like on the concrete yard.

"You two ready?" he said, looking up to the upper deck. Without waiting for a reply, he tugged at another set of hydraulic levers. The winch motors groaned, their latches bouncing over the cogged gears as the chains began to tension. Leo and Dennis secured the crate behind the cab, just under the wind spoiler. Satisfied, they covered the crate with a tarpaulin and cinched it tight with bungee cords.

"Well done lads," Brendan shouted, as Dennis and Leo climbed down from upper deck, the relief evident from the tone of his voice. He grinned and pointed at their filthy denims,

"Get yourselves cleaned up, for Christ's sake."

Dennis followed Leo into the building towards a toilet block tucked in the back corner, close to the roller doors. It was just big enough for a urinal with a toilet cubicle, two showers and four metal lockers along one wall. Dennis had learned from Leo to keep a spare set of clothes hanging in one of the lockers. There were no locks, not on the metal lockers or the toilet cubicle, and the adjacent showers were three-sided with a partition of sheetrock between them. Dennis took his time, struggling out of his soaked top at the same time, keeping an eye on Leo, waiting for him to get into the shower. He pulled off his jeans and glanced over at Leo's fat backside and broad shoulders wedged into the shower. It was only when Leo had turned on the shower and water was splashing out across the floor and into the drain that Dennis delved into the pocket of his soiled jeans, took out the burner phone and shoved it into the pocket of his dry denims hanging on a hook in the locker.

He quickly stepped into the adjacent shower, letting the water flow over his head and down his chest. Dirt puddled round his feet as he scrubbed at his face and rubbed his arms, scratching at hardened layers with his fingernails. He turned off the shower as soon as the rank-looking water had begun to turn a lighter shade and had floated towards the drain. He wanted to be out before Leo. He dried himself quickly, rubbing his hair and wiping off what remained of the dirt on his face and neck. He was dressed in his dry clothes by the time Leo had finished scrubbing.

"You were quick," Leo remarked, stepping out of his shower, one hand cupped round his cock as if to hide his modesty.

"Not as much to wash," Dennis replied.

Leo laughed. "Suppose a couple of minutes is enough for skinny runt like you."

Dennis pulled on a pair of socks over his still damp toes and slipped his feet into a pair of old trainers. He couldn't avoid the sight of Leo toweling vigorously, pulling rolls of fat from hip to hip as he sawed across his bum, his tiny cock bouncing off his inner thighs.

"What're you staring at?" said Leo, grinning broadly as if proud of his display.

"Nothing much," replied Dennis, returning the grin. Leo was grunting as he continued drying, patting his skin as if looking for some damp patch his vigorous toweling had missed. Dennis rubbed the palm of his hand over his scalp and walked back into the warehouse, oddly pleased at the banter with Leo.

He's not all bad, thought Dennis. The best of an ugly bunch. He'd nearly forgotten about Jonno. He hurried anxiously towards the loading ramp and then a flush of relief at the sight of the cattle truck still parked in the yard. Jonno seemed in no hurry to leave, leaning out of the cab, chatting to Brendan.

The diesel suddenly roared, the thick cloud of blue-black exhaust ending the conversation with Brendan Fisher. He slowly backed his rig and then swung round to the gate, waving back towards Brendan and Leo, and then a wave towards the roller doors where Dennis was standing. Dennis' head was spinning with excitement and fear. Brendan suddenly shouted across the yard. He looked pleased.

"'Ain't you cleaned up well. Where's Leo?"

"Still in the ..."

Leo was there, at his shoulder, smelling faintly of aftershave.

Brendan laughed. "Where're you goin'? Got a hot date?"

Owen joined in, pointing at Leo, as if he'd never seen him so scrubbed. "You great fat ..." he stopped in mid-sentence as Leo took a step forward.

"Cut it out!" said Brendan, sounding irritated. He pointed to the pallet-handler. "Get that thing back into the shed. And hose it down, I don't want that stink trailed across the yard."

Dennis could feel the sweat gathering under his armpits and in the small of his back. The sun was bouncing off the concrete pad and the building was beginning to feel like a furnace.

Owen shouted across the yard as he rested against the pallet-handler. "There's some beers in the fridge," he said.

Brendan seemed interested. He rubbed the palm of his hand against his forehead, "Ok, it's bloody hot."

"Even hotter in there," remarked Leo, nodding towards the building.

"What ya waiting for, then?" Brendan said, plonking himself on a bench at the side of the loading ramp. "Go an' fetch 'em."

"I'll go," said Dennis, tripping in his haste to get into the building.

"Steady," shouted Brendan. He laughed, "Don't want an accident claim!" Leo grabbed Dennis' arm, tugged him upright, and gave him a shove. "Ok, Dennis; you go."

The building was stiflingly hot. He hurried towards the front of the building, banging his hip against a stack of boxes and almost slipping on a patch of oil left by Leo's pallet handler. He tugged hard at the handle of the upright fridge. The door flew back on its hinges, bouncing off an adjacent bench and rebounding into his arm as he reached for a carton of lagers on the bottom shelf. He elbowed the door back, grabbed the carton and plonked it on the bench. Sweat dripped over his temples and down both cheeks. Time seemed to be racing, bleeding like a gashed wound, his brain begging him to do something ... anything!

He plunged his hand into his pocket, his fingers searching for the burner phone. It felt slimy, slippery, seeming to wriggle in his hand like one of the pet goldfish he used to keep. His eyes fixed on the mobile as if it was being held by someone else's hand. He willed himself to stop shaking and then hit the call button. Two rings, and then it went dead. He tried to remember; Was that the signal? Should there have been a reply? He stared at the phone, wondering, in that moment, if he should hit the call button again.

"What are ya' doin'!" Owen's voice. Dennis looked round to see Owen walking quickly towards him. He shoved the phone in his pocket and took a glance at the emergency door in the corner of the building. Owen was running diagonally across, slaloming around boxes, chairs, stanchions. Dennis sprinted towards the door. He sensed Owen getting closer like a shadow about to engulf him. Owen launched himself, hitting Dennis' shoulder and slamming him against the door. The emergency latch sprang open, sending the two of them sprawling out of the building, the door alarm blaring like a klaxon, a red light flashing above their heads. Before either of them had time to react, there was the sound of gunfire. It sounded remote, as if they'd got the wrong building. Owen glared at Dennis, grabbed his jacket and smashed his forehead into Dennis' face. The pain was intense; his nose spouting blood, his jaw spearing against his eardrums. Owen was on his feet, head up, swiveling like a startled deer. Just as he took a step, Dennis kicked out, sending him sprawling. Owen rolled and sprang to his feet, a knife blade glinting. He flung himself at Dennis, thumping the blade into Dennis' stomach.

Gunshots rang out. Owen's body convulsed as bullets sprayed into his body. Dennis screamed as a bullet smacked into his thigh, splintered bone bursting out of his hip. And then a numbing silence and blackness, as if his brain had emptied.

Chapter 37

Maggie stood staring out of her office window, her phone glued to her hand.

The ring tone startled her. "It's done," said a man's voice. She exhaled a sigh of relief, catching her breath. Wild thoughts began to organise into a list of concerns. The fate of the Fishers seemed of no consequence. "We've got the girlfriend," the voice continued.

"Amy, you mean Amy!"

"She's ok. Pick her up at 39 Fountain Road."

Maggie felt the blood drain from her face. "You bastard! If you've hurt her ..."

The voice seemed to dismiss her outburst. He continued in a calm, measured tone.

"Fountain Road," he repeated. "Number 39."

"What about Dennis?"

There was a pause, a hesitancy that made Maggie gasp.

"He got caught in the crossfire."

"He's dead!?"

"Not sure. There were police, ambulances ... we didn't have time to hang around."

"Why?" shrieked Maggie. "He wasn't supposed to get hurt!"

"One of Fishers' gang got to him as he left the building. They were both down."

"Down? What the ...? Killed you mean!"

"Maybe ... don't know — our shooter isn't sure."

Maggie thought he'd ended the call, it seemed like a final remark, the bad news delivered. An image of Dennis collapsing in a blast of gunfire slammed into her brain.

"Listen, you stay silent, you and your mates. It's a gangland hit — that's what the cops will assume."

"What if they don't?"

"We've people on the inside, high up people. They'll steer it the right way."

"And Brendan Fisher?"

"Dead. The Fishers are finished. One more thing — a reminder — ditch the mobile."

Maggie nodded, staring at the phone as if it was something that had inexplicably found its way into her possession. Brendan Fisher, dead. For just the briefest of moments, she felt euphoric.

Amy! It was if her brain had suddenly snapped into gear. "Fountain Road," she mumbled to herself. "Number 39." She shoved the mobile into the bottom of her bag and ran down the hallway, grabbing her keys from the small table next to the front door …. What about Dennis? She dithered, just for a moment. Get going, her brain reasoned. Amy first.

Maggie pulled into the kerb, scraping the front tyre as her car jerked to a stop. The news report on the radio grabbed her attention, just as she opened the car door …

'A shooting … early this morning … First reports are two men were killed, another two were seriously injured. Both are in intensive care … A police source said it had all the signs of a gangland attack …'

She tried to process the news report as she ran along the pavement, searching for the house. He's alive … Dennis is alive …

She stopped at the numbers '3' and '9' fixed just above the letterbox of a Victorian semi-detached house, threw open the gate and glanced at the net curtains hanging across the window half expecting the curtains to twitch, like a warning. She thumbed the doorbell with her left hand and pushed at the door handle. The door swung open — a dark, uninviting hallway; dank, stale smelling.

"Amy ... Amy!" Maggie's shouts reverberated off the walls. A noise coming from upstairs, then a series of muffled groans. Her shoes clattered on the wood stairs, her heart pounding. The sound came from one of the bedrooms. Maggie flung open the door and gasped. Amy was lying stretched out on a bed. Her hands were bound and tied to the bedhead. A chord wrapped round her ankles was looped through the frame. For a brief moment, Maggie stared, as if she'd found something unexpected. Amy's mascara was smudged round her eyes, her hair was loose and matted against her forehead. She groaned, flinging her head from side to side. Maggie moved quickly, pulling the gag away from Amy's mouth, stretching the cloth over her chin. She was staring, vacantly,, as if she could hardly believe it was Maggie. She coughed, grabbing air into her lungs.

Maggie tugged at the cloth wrapped around Amy's wrists. "Thank God! Thank God!" she repeated as she struggled with the knot on the bedhead. It suddenly loosened. Amy freed her hands as Maggie grappled with the chord at the foot of the bed. Amy pushed herself up over the edge of the bed, flung her arms wide and wrapped them round Maggie's neck, her body trembling as she sobbed in loud, grunting, breathless, gasps.

"You're safe, now," Maggie whispered as Amy's sobs weakened and her breathing became more regular.

"Is it all over?" Amy asked. "Where's Dennis?" she said in the next breath, looking round as if she expected he'd be waiting at the front door.

Maggie just wanted to get her away from this hell hole. "Let's get you home," she said.

They drove off in silence. Maggie glanced across at Amy. She hadn't spoken since they'd left the house. She'd slumped into the passenger seat, her eyes red and rheumy, her face blanched white. She was now sitting upright, stiff, rigid looking, her breathing was slow and measured.

"What happened," she asked. "The Fishers are they ...?"

"Finished," she replied."

"What about Dennis? Is he ok?"

Maggie felt her hands tighten on the steering wheel. "He's in hospital," she replied.

Amy gasped. "What! How come? What happened?"

Maggie pulled over and gripped her arm. She was shivering. "He got caught in the shooting."

Amy gasped. "He's ok? Tell me he's ok!"

"He's alive, that's as much as I know." Maggie wanted to keep it as simple as she could. She just hoped Dennis would survive.

"I need to see him! Please, Maggie, take me to the hospital."

"Not yet," Maggie replied, in a firm voice. "Sorry, Amy. We can't do anything that might arouse suspicions ... Look, I'm going to take you to my place. A hot shower, a cup of tea."

They drove back in silence, Amy staring out of the passenger window, occasionally dabbing at a tear leaking down her cheek. Maggie guessed that's what she needed, a bit of quiet to let her try and make some sense at what had happened. She'd been through a lot, and there was still more to come. She's a tough kid, thought Maggie.

Amy spent a long time in the shower. Maggie had given her a large fluffy towel, clean underwear, a tee shirt and a pair of tracksuit bottoms.

"I'll make us some tea," she said. "Hot and sweet."

Amy sat on one of the kitchen stools, rested her elbows on the counter and stared, zombie-like, out of the large window overlooking the back garden. Maggie pushed the tea in front of her, "Here Amy, this'll help." She gave a dismissive look, her eyes narrowed, "You think a cup of tea will sort this mess!?"

It was late afternoon when Maggie decided she had to call the hospital. Amy worried her. She looked like some Victorian waif, pathetically pale, consumed by an anguish she didn't understand. Maggie eventually got through to a senior nurse she knew.

"Dennis, Dennis Barrett? Yes, he's in surgery. How come you're interested?"

Maggie hoped she sounded only mildly concerned. "I thought it might be him. He used to work at the market, then got hooked up with the Fishers. He's family," she added, immediately wondering why she'd said that.

"I probably shouldn't be telling you this, Maggie ... He's got a serious knife wound and a bullet shattered his hip. He's in surgery. He'll be in intensive care for some time, I reckon." There was a pause. "I don't suppose you are interested in the other man?"

"He's alive?"

"Just, he got shot in the head ... Look, I've got to go."

"Thanks ... thanks," Maggie replied.

Amy seemed dulled, as if the remnants of the drugs they'd given her were still coursing through her system. "He's ok?" she managed.

Maggie looked intently at Amy. She wanted to blink and see her smiling face and bright-eyed infectious charm. Instead, she was blank, unresponsive.

"Amy ... Amy! Are you alright? Amy ..."

"I need to see him ..."

Maggie instinctively decided on a sanitised response. "They are operating right now. We'll be able to see him soon — maybe tomorrow."

Amy gave a weak smile. "That's good, isn't it?"

"Yes, Amy. He's safe. They'll look after him."

Maggie slipped an arm round Amy's shoulder, "Bed, I think."

Maggie got a call mid-morning the following day. It was the nurse she knew, the one she'd contacted earlier.

"He's out of surgery," the nurse told her. "The other man's more serious," she said, as if assuming the two injured men were both of concern to Maggie. "You won't be allowed into intensive care, but there's an observation window. I should warn you — it can look a bit scary seeing someone hooked up to the monitors."

"Thanks," Maggie replied. "I'll warn Amy. When?"

"Come around seven this evening."

Amy poked her head round the door. "Who was that?"

"The hospital. We can go and see him at seven tonight."

The outburst from Amy was immediate. "Seven! That's hours away!"

Maggie shrugged her shoulders. "Nothing we can do. Look, I need to call Michael, and Jake and tell them what's happened. Amy nodded as if it was something that hadn't occurred. Maggie decided to make her calls from the other room. She passed Amy the remote. "Bit of mindless tv." She was pleased when Amy raised a smile and began flicking through the channels.

Jake picked up on the first ring. "Well?" he said. "How's she doing?"

"Bit shaken up, but otherwise seems ok."

"Is she hurt ... they didn't do anything, did they?"

"Drugged her and tied her to a bed. But alright, I think."

"That's all! Hell, Maggie. You sure she's ok?"

"She's pretty strong, Jake. It's Dennis ..."

"She knows, then?"

"She knows he's pretty bad. I told her he's in intensive care."

Jake grunted. "That's more than they told me."

"We can see him tonight, at seven," Maggie said.

"I'll let Michael know. He's out of his wits with worry."

"What about the Fishers?" asked Jake.

"The Provos killed Brendan Fisher and one of his goons. The other one's unlikely to survive — took a bullet in the head. He's in a coma. Right now, it's Amy and Dennis we need to worry about."

"And Michael," commented Jake.

Chapter 38

They dashed across the hospital tarmac and up a flight of steps. The large entrance doors slid open as they approached. A receptionist was giving directions to an anxious-looking couple confused by the maze of corridors and coloured arrows painted on the walls.

"Dennis Barrett," Amy said, in a demanding tone.

"He's in intensive care," Maggie added, leaning over the counter.

The receptionist scanned her computer. "Intensive Care is third left," she said, pointing down the main corridor. "Check in at the nurses' station." Amy turned and began walking quickly down the corridor. Maggie caught up, her heels clipping loudly. Michael was already there, sitting on the edge of one of the chairs rubbing his hands over his thighs, staring at the floor.

Maggie called over to Michael. He glanced up; a startled look as if he hadn't expected to see them. He raised a weak smile, "We can't see him," he said, "not yet."

Maggie patted his arm. She didn't even attempt to say anything, she simply smoothed her hand against his forearm as if applying a lotion. Amy stood at the reception desk, fiddling with a bracelet hanging from her wrist. "Sit down, Amy, for God's sake." Maggie sounded irritated. Amy slid onto a seat across from Maggie and Michael, staring at the doors marked 'Staff Only'. The three of them sat, barely moving, the only sound an occasional loud sigh. The ringing of Michael's phone broke the silence. He struggled to take it out of his pocket. He glanced at the screen, "It's Jake," he said, holding up the phone as if providing evidence of the caller. It was a brief call. "Course, Jake, I'll let you know as soon we hear anything."

Jake expected a visit from the police. The taller man introduced himself as Detective Inspector David Burton. He was polite, polished and well-dressed. In Jake's eyes, he looked more like a well-groomed executive than a police officer. "This is DC Slinger," he said, turning to the short squat man whose eyes were fixed on Jake's.

"Been a while," the Detective Constable said, his eyes hardly deviating from their intense stare.

"You two met before?" asked the DI.

"Yeah," DC Slinger replied, still looking directly at Jake, "We grew up on the same council estate, 'aint that right, Jake?"

Jake nodded. "Never thought you'd end up a copper," he said.

Archie Slinger peeled a reluctant smile across his pugnacious features. "And I thought you'd end up a crook. Look at you now, a respectable businessman."

"Enough of the pleasantries," said the DI in a tone that was every bit as smooth as his well-pressed suit. "I presume you've heard about the shooting?"

"Yeah," Jake replied, "Word travels fast in this neighbourhood, especially if it involves the Fishers."

"Brendan Fisher and one of his gang killed, two others in intensive care— quite an outcome," DI Burton remarked.

Others? Jake hadn't thought of Dennis as one of Fishers' mob. He wasn't meant to get shot, he wasn't meant to end up in hospital on life support.

"Any bad blood between you and Brendan Fisher, was there?" asked the DI.

Jake shook his head. "You must be joking. I stay well clear of that lot."

"Takes a brave bunch to go after the Fishers," said DC Slinger.

Jake shrugged his shoulders. "Suppose," he said.

"No 'suppose' about it," said the DC. "What's your theory, then?"

"You're the ones doing the investigation," Jake replied.

"I don't suppose there was any way you were involved? Maybe you hired a few hitmen? You had that break-in at the market a few years back, just kids, you said. Could have been the Fishers?" DC Slinger looked pleased with himself, as if he was about to strike a rich vein of information.

"The Fishers; what would they want with a few market stalls?" Jake replied.

"I remember at the time thinking there was more to it. Course we had no hard evidence, but a couple of sources told me about computers, Walkmans, phones," added Slinger.

"VAT fraud," interjected DI Burton. He tutted, "Serious crime, Jake. Could have got you a long stretch."

"Seems the Fishers were involved in the same stuff," sneered Slinger. "Maybe that's what happened. Maybe they wanted to send you a message. They wouldn't like competition."

"It'd give you a motive," added the DI.

"Look, I'm no fan of the Fishers. But it wasn't me. As for fraud — I run a market, that's all."

Archie Slinger looked out of Jake's viewing window. "Flea-market, more like."

The DI turned to Jake, "So, you've no idea who did this? What's the word on the street?"

"Nothing ... Probably a gangland hit — one of them big crime bosses from London," Jake replied.

"We've no doubt it was a professional hit. Well organised." The Di gave his nails a quick inspection. "Course, two of 'em got out. Not sure about one of 'em, he's in a really bad way ... the other's likely to survive."

"Dennis Barrett," Archie Slinger remarked. He rapped his knuckles on the viewing window. "He used to work here, didn't he?"

"Just for a while. I had to give him the sack. I only gave him a job coz I knew his dad."

The DI looked up. "His dad — yes — Michael Barrett. Quite a coincidence, that. We did a bit of checking. He was a prison officer at the Young Offenders. He was on duty when a kid got murdered — a Fisher — Billy Fisher."

Archie Slinger nodded. "The coroner wasn't impressed. Laid the blame squarely on him." He sniggered. "And Guess what? Years later, his son, Dennis, survives a spell in prison and then ends up working for Brendan Fisher. Apparently, he got cosy with Danny Fisher and his goons when he was inside. Maybe he worked for them — probably had no choice."

Jake forced himself not to take a step back. "Might have run a few errands for them, that's all."

"You could be right, Jake. He was a bit of a wimp, by all accounts. I'm surprised he came out in one piece," Slinger remarked.

Jake bit his tongue. "He was lucky, that's all."

"The DI resumed the inspection of his nails, "We'll want a little chat with Dennis, of course."

"If he lives," added Archie Slinger with a self-satisfied smirk.

Chapter 39

Jake called Michael the following day. "How bad is it?"

"He took a bullet in the hip," Michael replied. "Shattered his pelvis. Lots of bone fragments, but the bullet went straight through. He'll have to learn to live with a limp, the doc says."

"Glad it's not worse."

Michael grunted. "It wasn't just the bullet; he took a knife in the gut. They've operated. The knife caught his lower intestine and punctured his stomach. They reckon he'll need at least one more operation before they can get him stabilised."

"He'll be in there for a while?"

"Yeah. They've got him on a morphine drip, hooked up to monitors. He's still pretty much out of it. The nurse reckons he'll be in intensive care for a least two more days."

"But they think he'll be ok?"

"Yeah, seems so," Michael replied.

"There's something you should know," Jake said. "I had the police round asking all sorts of questions. I'm pretty sure they'll want to talk to you, and Dennis, when he's able."

"Somehow, I didn't think it would end without them getting involved," Michael replied.

"We need to meet up — you, me and Maggie — before they start taking statements."

Michael sighed into the phone. "Yeah, ok. When?"

"Tonight, it's got to be tonight. I'll tell Maggie we'll meet at her place. We've got to get our stories straight. Sounds like they won't be able to talk to Dennis for a few days."

"What about Amy?" asked Michael.

"I doubt they'll have any idea of her involvement. Might be best if we keep her out of it — for now."

Michael mulled things over as he drove to Maggie's house. The autumn weather carried a chill in the air and trees had begun to shed their leaves. He had an almost overwhelming sense of relief that Dennis had survived, but now he'd begun to realise that the next few days would be difficult and dangerous. Jake was right: they had to get their stories straight. Any slip-ups, any mention of the IRA, would be a death sentence. He drove carefully down the street, unsure of the house he was looking for. He spotted Maggie's car and swung into her drive. She opened her front door as he approached;

"You found it ok?" she asked, without waiting for a reply. "What's this all about?" Jake wouldn't say much."

"He had a visit from the police, asking questions," Michael replied.

Maggie offered no sign of alarm. "It's what I expected," she said in her matter-of-fact way. "Maybe not this soon."

Jake tapped on the front door and let himself in. The two men sat at the kitchen table as Maggie closed the Venetian blinds on the window overlooking her garden. The stainless-steel sink gleamed under a bank of overhead spotlights.

She poured coffees and set a small jug of milk on the table.

"The police called," Jake said.

"Michael just told me," Maggie replied.

"We need to make sure we've got our story straight," he said. "No mistakes. We keep it as simple as we can."

"That's exactly what the guy from Provos told me. Our story is that it must have been a rival crime gang. He said they have someone in the police who'll try and steer it that way."

"Try?" said Michael, his voice rising. "What does that mean?"

"No guarantees, I guess. It's up to us. As long as we don't slip up, they'll do their bit. The last thing the police will want is a big public exposure about the provos murdering people on the mainland — even if it is the Fishers."

"There's going to be press interest, given the Fishers' reputation," Jake told them. "Let's hope they jump to the conclusion it's a rival crime gang."

"What about the police, Jake?" Maggie sounded a little exasperated.

"Two of 'em," he replied. "DI Burton — not from round here. He's got a local DC helping — Archie Slinger."

Maggie groaned, "He's dangerous."

"Is he the one from the Marshbrook estate?" asked Michael.

"Yeah, grew up there — always was a nasty piece of work," Maggie replied. "He's more muscle that brain."

"Don't underestimate him," Jake said. "He's like a dog with a bone. And him and me 'aint exactly mates. It's the DI that worries me. Smooth, he is. You wouldn't know what he's thinking."

"I could ask around?" Michael offered. "I still know a few from the old days."

Jake was quick to reply. "No, Michael! Too risky. This DI is clever. It'd be stupid to talk to anyone in the force. It'd only raise suspicions."

Michael nodded and retreated behind his coffee.

"This is what they've got," said Jake. "Archie Slinger knows all about the Fishers threatening you at that coroner's hearing. He's clearly filled in the DI with every detail. Then there's Dennis' time in prison. They know about the protection he got from Danny Fisher. And then he ends up working for Brendan Fisher's mob. Too much of a coincidence for the DI — you, and Dennis, both with a connection to the Fishers. They know about Dennis working at the market, and the break in," he continued. "Archie Slinger reckons the Fishers were involved, somehow."

Maggie sat back in her seat. "If I were the DI, I'd be suspicious, very suspicious."

"Archie Slinger would love to get one over on me," Jake told them. "He'll be paying his snitches to get any info that's out there." He tapped his ring finger against the edge of the table. "Slinger's bound to find out about Amy. You go through it with her Maggie — make sure she knows not to mention the IRA."

"Apart from that, I guess she can just tell the truth, more or less," Maggie replied. "Dennis is living with her, they've known each other for a few years, met at the market. She just thought he was running a taxi business. Had no idea he was involved with the Fishers; that ok?"

"Nothing else they might dig up?" asked Jake.

"Oh, I nearly forgot. She got attacked one night after leaving the Sparklers nightclub. There'll be a police incident report."

"Dennis wasn't with her?"

"No, they'd had a bit of a row. She went with a few of her mates, she thinks someone spiked her drink. She ended up being groped in an alleyway across from Sparklers."

"She was ok?" said Michael, sounding concerned.

"Yeah. Someone scared off the attacker. The police took her home."

Jake paused. "Don't think that's anything to worry about. In fact, it might help — gives her a bit of credibility. Just tell her to make sure she doesn't fall into any traps. Go over it with her, Maggie. Several times."

Maggie nodded. "Will do. She's upstairs, asleep. She's pretty exhausted."

They sat in silence straining to find something they had missed.

"You ok, Michael?" Maggie eventually asked.

He nodded. "Just thinking about Dennis. I hope he's ok."

Maggie reached across and patted his arm. "Me too," she replied. "He doesn't deserve to ..." She stopped in mid-sentence. "You've got a brave son, Michael. Very brave."

Chapter 40

"The police keep asking to interview him," the matron confided to Michael.

"Can't you hold them off? Just a few days, that's all I ask," he implored.

"I'll do what I can," the matron replied.

The headline in the newspaper caught Michael's eye as he walked towards the exit door of the hospital. He felt utterly drained. Staring through the observation window at the array of monitoring equipment and the green line on a heart monitor spiking like peaks on wind-blown waves had sapped his energy. He'd watched and winced at the sight of blood-soaked dressings the nursing staff lifted from Dennis' thin torso.

His phone buzzed. It was Jake.

"Get the evening paper — front page. We'd better meet up at Maggie's later."

Michael grabbed a paper from the shop at the entrance to the hospital. The headline hit him as he unfurled the newspaper. The lettering was big and bold, as if the editor had deliberately set the font and type size for maximum impact.

'Gangland Attack'

The recent shooting at a local business park has all the hallmarks of an attack to kill by a major London crime gang, according to an anonymous source within the police.

Michael skipped forward.

A spokesman for the South Yorkshire police confirmed they were working in close collaboration with the London Met.

The Chief Constable has issued a statement to the press. He said given the information they had received, valuable police resources can now be targeted in the right area.

"Who told the paper it was London crime bosses?" asked Michael, waving the paper he'd purchased.

"Who do you think?" Maggie replied. "The provos —or at least, one of their contacts working in the police."

"The police top-brass will be happy," added Jake. "It's the Fishers, for Christ's sake. There'll be some very pleased senior officers. And having this shooting linked to a London crime syndicate is a nice way to close the file."

"You think they'll still want to talk to Dennis?" asked Michael.

"Of course they will!" Maggie told him. "He was in the building; they know he was working for Brendan Fisher — he's one of the Fisher gang, as far as they are concerned. They'll want to know if he's any idea who did it. All he has to say is that he heard gun fire, and that he and Fisher's goon made it out through the emergency door."

"What about the knife wound?"

"He can tell them Fisher's man went berserk and accused him of being in on it."

Michael's hands worried the glass tumbler of whisky Maggie had poured. "Bit thin, isn't it?"

"Look, all the police will want to do now is close the file," Jake said in a voice that betrayed his doubts.

Michael got a text later that morning. It was from DI Burton.

'Given recent developments, and the nature of Dennis' injuries, we won't be interviewing him until he gets out of hospital.'

He forwarded the text to Jake and then called, wanting to hear Jake's opinion.

"You got the message from the DI?"

"Yeah, just read it."

"That's good, isn't it?"

"Think so," Jake replied. "You never know with those bastards. We still need to be careful. It gives us time to make sure Dennis has his story straight."

Jake was still thinking about the text Michael had received from DI Burton when there was a rap on his door.

"Come in!" he shouted.

It was Archie Slinger.

"What brings you round?" he asked. It wouldn't be a social visit.

Slinger pulled a chair closer to Jake's desk. He sat and looked past Jake at the large viewing window. "Nice little business you've got here,' he said. "It'd be a pity if we ever had reason to take a closer look."

Jake leant forward, "You threatening me?" he said. "Hope you're not one of those coppers who make wild allegations."

"I know you from the old days, before you became supposedly respectable. You haven't changed, not that much."

"Neither have you, Slinger. Once a thug, always a thug."

Archie Slinger sneered. "Maybe that's something you should remember."

"Don't you worry, it's never far from my thoughts," Jake replied, wondering in the moment if he'd prodded a dangerous snake.

Archie Slinger rubbed the top of Jake's desk with the palm of his hand. He made an inspection of the wood, as if expecting to find ingrained dirt.

"I don't believe a word of this crap," he suddenly remarked, baring his small, pointed teeth. "This shooting — it wasn't anything to do with crime bosses from London; what do you think, Jake?"

"I've read the papers. Seems there was a tip-off."

"A tip-off, eh. How very convenient. So, tell me this; how come Dennis Barrett wasn't killed? Ok, he got shot, but I reckon that was an accident. Professional hit men don't usually miss. The other fella took a bullet to the head. They were out to kill him. Not so sure they were trying to kill Dennis."

Jake shrugged his shoulders, "He was lucky, I guess."

"I'm not stupid," Slinger replied. "They wouldn't leave any survivors. So, maybe he wasn't working for Brendan Fisher. Maybe he was a plant. It got me thinking, who else wanted the Fishers sorted. Someone desperate enough to hire some hitmen. I'll tell you who..." He pointed a stubby finger. "You, Jake. You and the rest of those so-called businessmen you deal with. And Michael Barrett, of course. He must be delighted." He slapped his hand onto the desk.

"I'll tell you what really pisses me off — someone high up thinks this is all a nice opportunity to wipe the Fishers off the books."

"Seems reasonable," Jake suggested.

Archie Slinger sneered. "They haven't lived round here. I know this patch. I know the villains. Someone round here will know something. The top brass might want this all swept under the carpet, and the DI might have to accept the version in the papers, but not me. You just remember that."

"Thanks for the warning," Jake said as Archie Slinger scraped his chair across the wood floor.

"Think you're clever, don't you Jake? You've got a weak link, though — Dennis Barrett. Squeeze something soft and it gets messy, very messy."

Slinger stood and glared, hunching his shoulders into a boxer's pose, taunting his opponent to come out of the corner. Jake sat, head erect, and returned the stare. "That it?" he said. "That all you've got?" He was back again to those times they'd boxed in the school gym.

Slinger was a dirty, street fighter with hard knuckles, gouging thumbs, head butts, sharp elbows, teeth that bit. Win any way you can, that was Archie Slinger.

The DC grabbed the edge of the door and slammed it closed. Jake exhaled slowly and listened to the scuff of Slinger's shoes fading down the corridor.

Dennis was off the danger list. It was four days since he'd had abdominal surgery, and he was now deemed fit enough to tackle his shattered hip.

Michael had been there when the consultant warned he would need several operations to remove the fragments of splintered bone before they could consider a hip replacement.

Word had got around about the improvements Dennis had made. DI Burton had made a number of requests for an interview. "Just to tidy up the loose ends," he'd told Michael.

What none of them had anticipated was that Archie Slinger would take it upon himself to approach the matron and say he wanted to interview Dennis. He told her that Michael had agreed, provided she was happy. It didn't occur to the matron that a detective constable would tell a blatant lie.

"I suppose," she'd said.

"Let's get it over and done with," he remarked, as if it was nothing more than a tooth extraction. "About twenty minutes," he said, tapping a small recorder he'd taken from his jacket pocket.

"Do you know who I am?" Slinger asked as he pulled up a chair next to Dennis' bed.

"No ..." He glanced at the recorder Archie Slinger held in his hand. "Police?"

"Yeah, that's right, Dennis. Just want a brief word, that ok?"

Dennis nodded. The matron glided past as if to provide reassurance that this had all been agreed.

"Just twenty minutes, detective," she said. "I'll leave you alone while I have my break."

Archie Slinger creased his pug-face into something resembling a smile. "Ok, matron. You go and have your tea."

Archie Slinger leaned in close. "Now, Dennis, tell me what you know. Who did it?"

Dennis pushed himself up against his pillows. "Don't know," he replied, cautiously. "It all happened so fast."

"What happened, exactly?"

"I was at the front of the building, where the office is. Brendan Fisher told me to get some beers from the fridge."

"And it was while you were there that the shooting started?"

Dennis nodded. "I heard bursts of gun fire ..."

"How did you know it was gun fire, heard it before, 'ave you?"

"Only in the movies," he replied. "I remember the noise, it was deafening. That tin shed amplifies every sound."

"Then what?"

"Owen came running up. He shouted to get out. That's when I ran."

"To the exit door — you and Owen?"

"Yeah. We both got through at the same time. He was more or less on my back."

"And ...?"

"Don't remember much after that. More gunfire. We both got hit."

"You've missed out a bit. You got stabbed." He smirked, "You didn't stab yourself, did you, Dennis? So, it had to be Owen. Why would he suddenly pull a knife and stab you in the gut?"

"Freak accident —must have been. Maybe he wanted to protect himself?"

"From what, gunfire — with a knife? You don't seriously expect me to believe that. You know what I think? I think he stabbed you deliberately. He thought you were involved, somehow."

"I got hit, just like him."

Slinger smiled. "Something you should know, Dennis. He's still alive. In a coma, but when he comes round, he'll talk, and I'll know. It should have been you," he hissed, "He took a bullet through the brain."

"Look, they were firing at both of us. I was just bloody lucky."

"Language Dennis! No need for that, is there?"

Archie Slinger moved closer to the bed, resting his hand on Dennis' hip. "Why don't you try telling me how you were involved?" He pressed down, his knuckles digging into Dennis' bandaged torso. Dennis gasped and gritted his teeth. "Hurt, does it? I bet it does. Nothing like a bit of truth to numb the pain." He pressed down harder. "You were involved, somehow. Who're you working for? Somebody paid you, did they?"

Dennis shook his head. "No!"

"Was Jake involved? He had a few grudges, maybe more than we realised. And then there's your dad. They were mates, right?"

Dennis stared anxiously towards the exit door. "I was working for Brendan Fisher."

"You had no choice. They'd done you favours, protected you in prison. You owed them, 'aint that right? Them dead — well it gets you off the hook." He aimed a fist at Dennis' wound. "I want the truth. Don't think I'm finished with you yet. I'll get you and Jake ... I've wanted to get that bastard for years, and now I nearly 'ave 'im. I just need you to start talking."

He thumped Dennis even harder, just as the swish of the matron's skirt announced her imminent arrival. "Are you alright, Dennis,' she called.

Archie Slinger patted Dennis' arm, "He's fine.'aint you, Dennis. Nothing a few aspirins can't fix."

The matron looked anxiously at Dennis. "I think he's had enough, for now."

"For now," Archie Slinger replied. "Thank you, Dennis," he said. "You've been most helpful."

The matron plumped up Dennis' pillows as the detective left. "You look uncomfortable. I'll get you something for the pain."

Dennis closed his eyes and let his head sink back against the pillows. Archie Slinger's ugly, threatening face seemed to loom over him, leering. The pain in his hip was intense and he could feel the ooze of blood beginning to stain his bandages.

Chapter 41

"That creep, Archie Slinger; he's been to see Dennis in hospital!" It had become a regular meeting, the three of them at Maggie's house, like a company of conspirators. "The matron told me," said Michael, turning first to Jake, then to Maggie. "He told her I'd said it was ok."

"What!" Maggie exclaimed. "You didn't ... give permission."

"Course not!" he shouted. "What a stupid thing to say! The last thing I want is those bastards to go anywhere near him; especially in hospital!"

"Ok, cut it out!" Jake sounded irritated, as if having to separate two squabbling teenagers. "Think about it — there's no way Slinger would have got permission; not from the DI, and certainly not from you, Michael. I told you he was dangerous, but he's also stupid. Once the DI gets to hear of this, he'll be on a charge sheet — maybe taken off the case. We need to know what Dennis told him — hopefully nothing. Talk to him, find out what happened. And have a word with the matron. See if there's anything she can add."

Maggie handed Michael a mug of coffee. "Sorry," she said. "That was stupid of me."

"It's easy to get a bit edgy," Jake said. "Doesn't help, though. No good jumping to conclusions."

"Sorry," Maggie repeated. "I just don't want anything to go wrong."

"Right," said Michael, clearly wanting to end what had become an uncomfortable discussion, "I'll see Dennis as soon as they'll let me. What about Amy?" he asked.

"I've kept her out of the way. The room upstairs is big enough — and there's a tv, a fridge and a microwave. But she's jumping the walls, wanting to go and see him."

"I think she should," Jake said. It'll start to look odd if his girlfriend doesn't show up. Just make sure you see him first, Michael. I don't want her hearing stuff she might let slip."

Michael nodded. "Ok," he replied.

"You'd better go with Amy," said Jake, turning to Maggie. "Make sure she knows it's just to see how he is — she's not to go asking about what happened. That can come later."

It was almost ten on Monday evening when Maggie got a call from Father Carey.

"You haven't been to confession recently."

"No, sorry, Father." For just a moment she was surprised. She'd been ten years old and about to take her first communion when a priest had last asked her to attend one of the sacraments.

"Tomorrow night,' he said. "The last booth."

The last booth? She suddenly understood.

She decided not to tell the others. Whatever it was that Father Carey wanted, it was unlikely to be good news — or anything to do with her spiritual wellbeing.

She always felt nervous about going to confession. She put it down to not going very often. When she was a teenager, it always felt as if she was being probed to admit that some casual fondling with a persistent boyfriend constituted a sin that must be admitted. She still went a few times a year, usually because of some compelling feeling of guilt that had long been embedded in her psyche. But this, she suspected, had nothing to do with saving her soul.

The church was cold and empty. The aisle leading to a line of four confessional booths was lined with the Stations of the Cross and pictures of saints welcoming, perhaps judging, sinners seeking contrition.

She heard the sound of Father Carey's irregular breathing from behind his side of the confessional booth. She drew back the heavy red curtain and knelt on the hassock. Her knees settled in the depressions made by an indeterminate number of the faithful.

Father Carey spoke in a soft voice, "Thank you for coming, Maggie. There's something you need to know."

"I thought it must be important, Father."

"Yes, my child," he said, in a deep voice.

His words made Maggie tremble. To be referred to as a child, a child of the church, made her realise just how much faith she still had.

The deep, resonant voice continued. "You could be in danger," he said. "My contact in the Provos thinks someone in the police is involved with these arms deals."

Maggie felt the blood drain from her face. "Any idea who it might be?"

"Sorry, Maggie, that's as much as they were able to tell me. My guess is it's someone close to the investigation, someone who wants to cover up their involvement."

"Or someone wanting revenge," she whispered to herself.

"Eh ... Please be careful, Maggie."

"Thank you, Father, I will."

She trudged slowly past the idols and icons hanging from the walls of the church. Her head felt heavy, her brain numb. She shook herself as she approached the large oak doors. It was pitch-black beyond the century's old graves that arced in front of the church, most with headstones tilting at odd angles as if uncomfortable in the settling earth. She headed quickly towards her car parked in the black shadow between adjacent streetlights. She drove slowly, thinking about what Father Carey had told her. There was the other man, Owen Connors; but he was still in hospital in an induced coma. And then there was Archie Slinger. She couldn't envisage him being anything other than a quasi-legitimate thug. What about DI Burton? Smooth as silk and bright. He was a possibility. But somehow, she couldn't imagine him being involved in gun running. Was she being stupid? And then there was the possibility it was someone they didn't know, someone higher up in the police?"

She didn't remember much about the drive back to her house. She was relieved to see Jake's car parked behind Michael's. It'd been agreed that Dennis would stay at hers, at least until he was stronger. And having Amy living with her as well made it feel safer, somehow.

Dennis' walking frame was in the hallway. Amy was gently closing the door to her front room, her finger touching her lips.

"Shush," she whispered on exhaled breath. "He's asleep."

Maggie nodded, took her elbow and led her towards the voices in the kitchen. She took a couple of ice-cold cokes from the fridge and passed one to Amy.

Michael took a gulp from the beer he was holding and gave her a second look. "What's up, Maggie? You look upset."

"I've been to see Father Carey," she told them. "His Provo contact says someone in the police is involved."

"Involved? Involved how?"

Maggie shrugged her shoulders. "That's all he could tell me — other than to be careful —maybe someone involved with running guns?"

"A bent copper — or coppers. It's possible," Jake replied. "It could be someone chasing the Provos for all we know. Nothing else?" said Jake. "That's it?"

"It's a warning, Jake," Maggie replied. "They wouldn't tip us off unless it was very serious."

Owen heard a voice calling his name. "Mr Connors, Mr Connors ..." The voice got louder, more insistent. "Mr Connors ... Owen ... open your eyes."

A woman was leaning over him, her face barely discernible through the fog filling his brain. She seemed to be floating around his bed, suddenly appearing at one side, then the other, and now hovering as she repeated her instructions.

"Owen ... Owen."

Things were clearer now. The woman was a nurse, all smiles as if thrilled to see him. The last thing he remembered was being carried on a stretcher and being lifted into the back of an ambulance. An intense, sharp pain pierced his brain somewhere on the side of his head. He screwed up his eyes and let out a squeal he didn't recognise.

Her instructions were different now.

"Lie still, Mr Connors. You've had a bad head injury. I'm going to give you a shot of morphine. It'll help with pain."

It — the pain, his excruciating pain — gradually subsided into a dull thud as the nurse floated off on silent shoes and the light above his bed found its soft rainbow of soothing colours. He let his eyelids descend, like a heavy curtain closing a stage performance.

"You've got a visitor," the nurse announced. Owen felt the backrest slowly lifting. His intense headaches had largely subsided, just an occasional sharp twinge that seemed to have escaped the narcotics swimming through his veins.

"Hello, Owen." Archie Slinger's voice set him on edge. He blinked at the blurred figure approaching his bed. "Just wanted to see how you're doing." He looked over his shoulder. "I told the nurse I'd keep it brief. Nice room they've given you," he remarked looking round at the bare walls. "Mind if I close the door?" It swished closed with a nudge.

Archie Slinger leant over the hospital bed and put his ear close to Owen Connors' mouth. His wheezing breath was musty and stale.

"Your breath stinks," Slinger whispered, wafting his hand in front of his nose.

Owen Connor's eyes focused on Slinger's. "What do you want? Not like you to make social calls."

"Just visiting a pal," he replied, baring his needle-point teeth. "Looks like you're going to recover."

Owen tried to look away. Archie Slinger pulled up a plastic chair, "What happened?" he asked, "Who were the shooters?"

"Dunno," Owen said. "Dennis Barrett was involved, somehow."

"He was in another ward, took a bullet in the hip."

"Huh ... that doesn't mean nothing. I saw him on the phone, just before the shooting started. I reckon he was sending a signal."

"How come you made it?"

"He ran to the exit. I grabbed him just as we crashed through. They were waiting. I heard a few bursts — that's when I pulled a knife and stabbed the bastard. Next thing I remember was waking up in this place." Owen looked at Slinger, "I didn't kill him, then?"

Slinger shook his head. "Came close,"

"Pity."

"Yeah, well there's a problem. They want you on a charge of attempted murder."

"What!"

"Could have been worse — he might have died."

"I can't go to jail! Not again! I'll get it rough, specially if they learn about my involvement with a copper, especially a bent bastard. I'll want to plea bargain, I'll have to."

"Oh yeah, and just what does that mean?"

"I'll tell 'em about you, Slinger, about you getting cash from Fishers for years."

"You can't do that," Slinger hissed. "I won't let you."

"Look, Slinger, if I go down, I'll make sure you're in the next cell. I reckon Dennis Barrett will know a thing or two. Whoever did this was well informed. And given he was a stooge for the gunmen, I reckon he'll back up what I tell 'em."

Slinger leaned closer, his chin almost touching the bandage on Owen's head. "It's a shame you're taking that attitude. You ain't exactly in the right place to be making threats. Me, on the other hand, I can ask you very nicely to keep your mouth shut, or ..."

"Or what? You don't scare me, Slinger."

Archie Slinger ran his fingers up and down the saline drip above Owen's head. He yanked hard, pulling the cannula needle out of the back of his hand. Before he could scream for help, Slinger grabbed one of the pillows and covered Owen's head, his strong arms and large hands pushing hard — squeezing, kneading — sweat dripping off his forehead as Owen's body began to convulse. It was a useless struggle. Owen's arms went limp and dangled over the edge of the bed. The line on the heart monitor gave a final few kicks and then straightened. Slinger removed the pillow as amber warning lights flashed and a buzzer sounded. Two nurses rushed into the room and ran over to the bed, pushing Archie Slinger out of the way. Another nurse arrived with a defibrillator and began attaching the pads to Owen Connors' chest. They seemed to ignore Slinger, their efforts concentrated on saving their patient. They tried three times, each time Connors' body arcing stiffly, as if jerked by a rope tied round his waist. Connors was lifeless and limp. A nurse removed the paddles and began coiling the leads. One of the other nurses wiped a tear from her cheek and stifled sobs with the crook of her arm. Another nurse handed her several tissues and slipped an arm round her shoulder. The senior nurse turned to Slinger,

"What happened?" There was more than a hint of accusation in her voice.

"He said he couldn't breathe. He suddenly went into convulsion. I thought his face was going to burst. It was over before I had a chance to do anything."

Slinger leant over the body. "Poor bastard." He turned to the nurse, "Maybe you should have watched him more closely?"

The nurse stammered; "I ... we thought he was out of danger, detective."

"Hard to tell with head injuries," Slinger said. "You should know that. The DI isn't going to be pleased."

Slinger smiled to himself as he left the hospital. Nothing like a lecture to put 'em on the back foot.

DI Burton glared at Archie Slinger. "Next time you go and interview a witness you clear it with me first! What the hell were you playing at? I'd only just heard he was no longer in intensive care!"

"Just wanted to see if he'd be able to say anything, sir. As it was, I didn't get a chance to even ask him a question. He went into spasms just as I pulled up a chair. The poor bastard died right in front of me."

"Where were the nurses?"

"On a break, I think. The sister said I could have a few minutes."

"And in that few minutes, he suddenly went into convulsions and died?"

"Can sometimes happen with head injuries, so the nurse told me."

The DI took a deep breath, as if trying to compose himself. "Looks like we'll have to rely on Dennis Barrett to tell us what happened."

"He was let out of hospital a few days ago," Slinger announced.

"Yeah, so I heard," said the DI. "He's staying with some family friend." He consulted his notebook. "Maggie Harrison. "

"That bitch," remarked Slinger, suddenly all snarls and surly. She works for Jake Gould at the indoor market. She's been seen around with Michael Barrett."

"Dennis Barrett's father?"

Slinger nodded. "Quite the little friendly bunch, 'aint they? They've all got history with the Fishers. Can't be just a coincidence, can it?"

In the six months since his assignment, DI Burton had watched the snarls and sneers that punctuated Slinger's grunted comments — even the ugly smile that wrinkled the lines around his mouth into dark, stubble-filled grooves. And his flaunted displays of arrogance, as if to say I'm untouchable, you stupid bastards. He could almost feel the disdain in Slinger's voice when he addressed him as 'sir'.

Burton's assignment was to find out just how much Slinger was involved in the Fisher clan's illegal operations. That he was a bent copper was a given.

He'd received word from one of his informants that Slinger was seen, on several occasions, meeting with one of Fishers' mob — Owen Connors. But proving Slinger was smoothing the way for the Fishers to conduct their crimes without police interference the DI knew wouldn't be easy. It needed, at the very least, information from someone on the inside. Owen Connors could have been, should have been, that source. And then there was Dennis Barrett; he'd served his time in jail and almost immediately began working for the Fishers. But why? Maybe he'd be the break Burton needed? He'd been so consumed with proving Slinger's involvement, he'd almost forgotten that the Fishers were a bunch of dangerous, violent criminals. The shooting had come out of the blue. There was nothing from his contacts in the Met. They had tentacles into most of the big crime families; if it was one of them, they were being very tight-lipped. There was usually someone who'd know something. Some even liked to boast about their involvement, or feed info on those who'd done the job. Burton knew that honour among thieves was a myth, especially in the competitive and lucrative worlds of drugs and gun-running.

Within a few minutes of a well-organised attack, the two men who might have known something about Slinger's involvement had somehow survived. Was that a mistake? These were professional assassins. Why hadn't they made sure everyone was killed? Brendon Fisher and the other gang member had been gunned down and then finished off at close range —a double tab to the head. Maybe the attackers didn't have time to mess around.

Burton was very sceptical that Owen Connors had died of his injuries. He was gob-smacked when he got the call to say he'd suddenly died. And then to learn that the last person to see him alive was Slinger. Something told him Archie Slinger's days were numbered. The Fishers were gone, Owen Connors was dead. Slinger would be nervous, very nervous, that one of the other Fishers, someone like Danny Fisher, would assume Slinger had a hand in the attack. It wouldn't take much, just a word.

And all it needed was a whisper. Burton couldn't resist a smile. It was the sort of street tactic Slinger would have used.

Chapter 42

Slinger lived alone in a flat on the edge of the Marshbrook estate. His wife had taken their two young kids and left with another man several years earlier. His flat was in a 1970's building that had a reputation for housing petty criminals; loan sharks, prostitutes and heavy thick-set men who plied their trade in protection or some brand of enforcement.

He'd apparently left in a hurry. An unfinished cup of coffee stood next to the sink and the remains of a pizza lay on a table. A shelf was littered with the contents from an upturned drawer. DI Burton picked through the items, smoothing out bills and leafing through a pocket-sized diary.

"What are we looking for, sir?" asked a young detective constable.

"Not sure," DI Burton replied. "Got to be something here he's missed."

"You think he's in trouble?"

"I'm sure of it," Burton replied, in an exasperated tone. He turned his attention to the diary. It seemed to have been used to record what looked like phone numbers. A number of the pages were marked with the letter 'F', circled in red. Others had the letter 'O', again circled in red. It was easy to jump to the conclusion that 'F' meant the Fishers, and that 'O' referred to Owen Connors. Pages at the back of the diary had numbers that appeared random; '200', '150' '300'. The same numbers were repeated on several pages. What were they? he wondered; drug shipments? gun types? container weights?

The young DC called from the bedroom. "This is interesting."

DI Burton walked through to the bedroom, still holding the diary, "What've you found?"

The DC held out a wad of notes wrapped with a wide rubber-band. "Fifties," he said. "They were in a box under the bed." DI Burton ran his finger over the edge of the bundle. "Got to be five grand here. I reckon this is one bundle he missed."

"Lot of money to leave," commented the DC, eying the notes in DI Burton's hand.

"He's got a lot more of these," Burton replied. He suddenly realised: the numbers referred to amounts of cash. The DI remembered hearing him talk about a villa in Spain, somewhere near Alicante.

"Put out an alert," he ordered the DC. "He could be heading to Spain — check departures from Birmingham, East Midlands, Manchester. You know the drill. I want him found."

Three kids riding bikes along a trail through a copse of trees and bramble bushes spotted a body floating half submerged under a shopping trolley in a drainage ditch at the back of one of the supermarkets. They'd run, panic-stricken, into the supermarket and blurted out what they'd found to one of the cashiers.

Archie Slinger's hands were tied behind his back with a cable-tie and a partially burnt rag was stuffed into his mouth. His lips and face were badly blistered and most of his hair had been singed.

"What the hell!" exclaimed DI Burton when he was told of DC Slinger's murder.

He quickly organised a team to search the area. There were broken branches and signs of a body having been dragged to the edge of the drainage ditch. A burnt-out transit van was found later in the week behind a redundant factory building that had long since been reduced to a brick shell and rusted steel rafters. The blackened van had nothing to offer as to what had happened, or who the perpetrators were. He grimaced as he read through the report the DC had produced.

"Looks like he was given the rough treatment," the DI mumbled to himself. "Tortured the bastard."

He'd thought earlier about having Archie Slinger arrested, but reckoned there wasn't enough evidence, and besides, he was useful. He thumped his desk in frustration, alarmed at his own naivety. There were no rules, not for a bent copper. In his mind he could see a bunch of thugs grabbing Slinger and throwing him into a vehicle. And then the rest … "Maybe you were a bent bastard …" the DI muttered to the empty chair opposite his desk. "No-one deserves to be murdered like this."

News of Archie Slinger's murder came as a surprise. It was Michael who'd received a call from his old mate, DI Peter Clark.

"Got news for you, Michael. It's Archie Slinger — they found his body in a drainage ditch at the back of the shopping centre. Looks like another gangland hit."

It took a few moments for the information to sink in. "One of Fishers' lot?"

"Don't think so, they're about finished, at least in this area. It's more likely to be a gang taking over from the Fishers, maybe eastern Europeans. There've been rumours about Slinger taking backhanders to do with gun-running."

"Poor bastard," Michael exclaimed.

Peter Clark grunted, "Some say he had it coming."

"All the same …" Michael replied.

Jake was less sympathetic. "Good riddance," he said, on hearing what had happened. "It'll be a very quiet funeral."

"What about the DI?" Jake asked.

"Apparently he's on the rampage," Michael replied. "He seems to have set the entire force on finding out who did it. Maybe it'll take the heat off us."

"Maybe," Jake said, "at least for a while."

Three weeks earlier, Detective Sergeant Sandra Andrews had transferred, at the DI's request, to South Yorkshire. She insisted on seeing all the files on Archie Slinger. A little reluctantly, DI Burton had agreed. He'd been her boss, her mentor, when she'd joined the Met. She was just as impressive, perhaps more so. She moved slowly, deliberately, as if every move she made, every physical gesture, had been planned in advance. There was a sense of precision about her, and she treated every detail, no matter how insignificant it seemed, as something that might be important. That was what had sometimes irritated him, the way she could get stuck on a line of enquiry that appeared to be a side issue, spending an inordinate amount of police time chasing puffs of dust that appeared to be of no consequence. He'd seen her in action often enough to know when she was onto something. That's when her dark eyes narrowed, as if shutting out the light, and her skin became mottled and bright, as if she'd been exercising. In the debriefing sessions, he'd seen her suddenly move from being quiet and watchful, to being centre stage, revelling in the spotlight, playing her audience of fellow officers and detectives as if they didn't stand a chance. In many ways, they didn't.

"I'm amazed he wasn't drummed out of the force years ago," she said, tapping the pile of manila files. "All these dodgy, one-man interviews, informants he kept to himself; he was even up before a disciplinary and given a final warning!"

"Law unto himself," Burton remarked. "But you can't deny he was effective. His conviction record is one of the best in the force."

"He certainly had some interesting ways of getting evidence," she replied. "Sometimes I despair at the way we protect our own."

Burton didn't comment. He prided himself on his ability to analyse, to rationalise, and on his attempts to determine what lay behind the actions of a criminal. What he lacked was the background. He wasn't reared, like Slinger, in neighbourhoods where crime was about the only option. He had a very poor 'nose' for something being wrong, someone ducking the truth; not like Slinger who had a reputation for 'extracting' information from the most reluctant of sources. That was something they didn't teach at university. It was forensic science and psychology.

He envied men like Slinger, socialising easily and freely with other coppers. There was often a quick nod or a handshake on the streets, and an innate understanding about which door to open, which hood to slam against the wall, and which scared druggie was carrying more information than was good for him. He made his own, unique, assessments of what made the criminal world tick. 'Knowing too much — that's what's dangerous', Slinger often remarked. Maybe, thought Burton, Slinger held too much information. Maybe what happened to him was inevitable.

With both Slinger and Owen Connors dead, the only person who knew what happened was Dennis Barrett.

Chapter 43

"That's Maggie Harrison's place, next house on the left," DI Burton told DS Andrews as they approached a row of semi-detached houses. The DI pushed the doorbell. A two-tone chime sang through the hall window.

"Maggie Harrison," he said, holding the police badge attached to a lanyard around his neck, "meet Detective Sergeant Andrews." It was the briefest of introductions. "We want a few words with Dennis Barrett."

"And with the others," added DS Andrews, gesturing towards the cars parked nose-to-tail in the drive. They followed Maggie into the front room. The Detective Sergeant did a slow, deliberate scan, first of Michael, then Jake, her eyes then hovering over Dennis. The DS appeared to be enjoying the discomfort they were all clearly feeling. It was as if she'd had training in interrogation techniques from the military.

"I may be new to the case," she said, "but I've read the files, I've read every word I could find that has anything to do with you lot and the Fishers. And do you know what? It reeks of something very unpleasant." She paused; "None of you would've been unhappy to see the Fishers taken care of, in fact, I'd be surprised if you didn't celebrate a little. I can't help but come to the conclusion this is what you all wanted." There was a clink of cups coming from the kitchen, "I presume that's Amy getting us some tea ... she's your girlfriend, right?" she asked, staring intently at Dennis. He barely had time to nod before she turned to Maggie. "And you're her guardian angel. A relative, is she?"

"No ... not exactly," Maggie replied.

Amy appeared, hesitantly carrying a tray of cups and a pot of tea. "We were just talking about you," DS Andrews remarked. "You're Amy?"

She nodded, the cups rattling in their saucers as she placed the tray on a coffee table.

DS Andrews continued as if the tea-tray was nothing more than an ornament.

"Now, let me get this straight. You, Jake, look after Maggie ... or is it the other way round? And you, Michael ... we could say this mess started with you and what was said by the coroner at Billy Fisher's inquest. Wasn't exactly complimentary, was he? And then there's you, Dennis," she said, glaring at him stretched on a reclining chair, "you're the one at the centre of all this, working for the Fishers and somehow surviving the shooting. Is there a lot more to this that we don't know? Maybe there are things that have gone on that you haven't revealed to any of the others? Lots of secrets in this room, I suspect."

"Dennis got shot, along with Owen Connors," said Jake. "He was lucky to survive."

"It seems Owen Connors wasn't quite so lucky," she remarked. "But Dennis here, sitting here in the lap of luxury being looked after by his girlfriend in Maggie's nice house, he's come out of this relatively unscathed."

"He's been badly injured." said Amy, finding her voice. "He'll probably have a limp for the rest of his life."

"It's going to make it harder for him to carry that cross." She smiled as if pleased with her remark. "Do you know what I think, Dennis? There are things that have gone on that don't add up, petty things ... like an attack that left that hoodlum you were working for fighting for his life. And how come he gave you his car? Says in one of the reports you've been running an unlicensed taxi service."

"I want to know what was going on at the warehouse," interjected DI Burton, his voice loud and determined, as if wanting to take control. "What the hell were they up to?"

Dennis had been squirming in his seat at the implications of DS Andrews' questions. This was more comfortable territory. This was the sort of questioning he'd expected.

"They were into imports and exports of electronic equipment."

"Claiming the VAT, is that right?"

Dennis nodded. "It was on a big scale. Probably some crime syndicates involved."

"Probably?" said Burton, his tone heavy with sarcasm. "No probably about it. So what do you think happened? Why were they gunned down?"

"All I can think of is that something went wrong ..."

"Oh, come on, Dennis. You can do better than that. It wasn't just mobiles and Walkmans, was it? You forgot to mention the guns — you know, those things that go bang and kill people."

Dennis glanced anxiously at Jake who returned a blank stare as if to say 'you deal with this.' "That started a few months ago," Dennis replied. "They came in from the Ukraine ... then taken to Ireland on a cattle truck."

"Oh, very clever," commented the DI. "Where to? ... who to?"

"There's a Fisher clan in Limerick, I think that's where they went."

"And after that?"

Dennis attempted to shrug his shoulders, "That's all I know."

There was a long silence.

"Were you involved in the shooting, Dennis?" said Burton.

"Me?" Dennis replied, his voice squeaky with guilt. "No-way."

"Somebody had to be close enough to know what was going on. The shooters got a tipoff, they had to. Maybe it was Owen? Or Leo? But

I reckon they'd be too loyal, or should I say, too scared —just leaves you?"

Dennis shook his head.

"Could have been Archie Slinger," said Jake. It was a remark that seemed to take the two detectives by surprise. DS Andrews glanced at DI Burton and closed her notebook with a sharp snap.

"He's one of ours," remarked Burton.

"He lived very well for a copper," Jake replied. "Maybe you should start looking closer to home."

The DI glared at Jake, his jaw muscles clenching as if chewing hard. He then turned to Dennis,

"Maybe we'll never know the truth. Too many criminals involved. This may slip off the front pages, but I'll keep digging."

DS Andrews let the tension build before intervening. She took out a card and placed it on the edge of the coffee table. "Just in case one of you wants to have a chat," she said. The DI turned to leave and marched quickly out of the room. DS Andrews followed, but not before looking slowly round the room, as if wanting to ensure she remembered every detail.

"What do you reckon, Jake?" Maggie asked. They were standing at the bay window, eyes on the two detectives as they approached their car. She took a deep drag from her cigarette and exhaled as if deliberately aiming at DS Andrews.

"They'll be watching us," Jake remarked. "A pretty sharp pair, they are. We need to be careful. It'd be stupid to think they'll just pigeonhole a report and forget all about us."

Michael nodded. "Jake's right. They'll dig deep to find out who murdered Archie Slinger. It won't matter how bent he was; he was one of their own."

Jake grunted. "Yeah; one slip, and they'll come back hard. Burton doesn't believe for one moment we weren't involved."

"Then there's the Press ..." Maggie remarked.

Jake nodded. "They'll be itching to get an inside story. It won't just be the local papers; the tabloids will come knocking."

He turned to Dennis. "You're the one they'll want to talk to. The word's out that you survived. They'll want to know how you were involved."

"Just like those cops," Dennis replied.

"Oh, they can be much more dangerous," Jake said, glaring at Dennis. "They're not bothered about rules and procedures. Only takes some zealous reporter with contacts in the police and a bit of cash to loosen a few tongues." He looked across at Amy, "They'll try and get a comment from you, Amy. It'll be soft stuff at first. 'Did you know your boyfriend was working for the Fishers?' 'How was he involved?' If you give them a hint of something, they'll sink their teeth in hoping you'll squeal." He let his words hover ... "They'll want to know how come he wasn't killed, like the others ... and then the line they'll drop in when you least expect it — It'll seem nothing — 'is he a hero?', 'Is your boyfriend a hero?' A nod from you, even a smile, and they'll smell a story."

Amy felt like an observer, sitting in the corner of the room listening to Jake and Maggie. Dennis seemed lost in his own thoughts, lolling back against the headrest on his chair, staring at the ceiling. She decided to go to the bathroom, just to get away from them all. She exhaled as she closed the door. She peered at herself in the mirror. "Oh, God ..." she muttered, leaning her hips against the edge of the wash-hand basin. She pushed a forefinger at the shadows under her eyes and raked her fingers through her hair. It fell around her chin, straggly ends touching her neck and shoulders. She felt in her pocket for a hair band and tugged her hair back against her scalp into a short ponytail. She checked the bathroom door was locked, stripped out of her denims, lifted her blouse over her head, kicked her underwear across the floor and stepped into the shower. The water massaged her back and neck and ran down her breasts. The lather from the dispenser fixed on the wall of the shower smelled of coconut oil. She took her time, reveling in the warmth of the pummeling spray. The ceiling fan sucked the steam into a vent as she toweled herself dry and the mirror began to clear. She glanced at herself; pink, glowing, her shoulders bright red. Maggie's face cream felt cool and soothing. She put on her underwear and pulled on her jeans, pushed her toes against the denim, and adjusted her bra. "Right," she said, peering into the mirror, pleased at her now bright-eyed, glowing reflection. She sprayed herself with one of Maggie's more expensive brands of deodorant, penciled in eyeliner, gave herself a last inspection, and winked at the mirror.

Dennis looked up as soon as Amy entered the room. His eyes hung on her in a way that made her skin tingle.

Maggie waved her forward; "Is that my perfume?" They both laughed. "Go and sit next to that pining boyfriend of yours." Amy grinned. They were all looking at her now, as if they'd just realised she was there. She had a feeling of being on equal terms with the others and an inexplicable sense of her own importance, as if she'd been nominated and elected into some secret society. She walked over to Dennis, her head held erect, the others parting to let her through.

Jake stood and manoeuvred his big frame and stood with his back to the door. He turned his attention to Michael. "The press will know all about the coroner putting the blame on you for Billy Fisher's murder. They'll try and get a comment. They'll probably ask if you're pleased the Fishers have been killed."

"I've had to deal with the press a few times. I can handle 'em," Michael replied. "I'll say I don't like to hear of anyone being murdered, not even the Fishers."

"They'll ask about Dennis; might even ask you to confirm a rumour they've made up —just to get a reaction."

"Even something made up!?" Amy queried in alarm.

"Tricks of the trade," Maggie commented.

"You'd all better be prepared for the 'hero' question," said Jake. He spoke as if he was the only one who wouldn't be caught out.

They sat in silence, heads nodding. Michael broke the silence.

"I'm proud of what you did, Dennis," he said, staring at the beige carpet. "Very proud."

"We all are," Amy added.

"Yeah ... took guts," said Jake in a low, hushed tone.

Maggie looked across at Dennis and smiled; a pleased, glowing smile as if her protege had achieved a prize; the highest accolade, against all the odds.

"Thanks," Dennis replied, glancing across at his dad beaming with pride and fiddling in his pockets as if looking for a medal to pin on his son's chest.

Dennis felt an urge to take one of the painkillers he'd been prescribed. He didn't need their words, not with the black thoughts circulating in his head. He grimaced and clenched his teeth. Was this the time? Was this the time to tell them what he'd done? — smashing the back window of his Dad's Volvo, slashing the tyres on his mother's car, that drawing of a noose he'd shoved through the door ...

"What's wrong, Dennis. You ok?"

"Yeah," Dennis replied. "Course I am." It was a curt, abrupt reply.

Dennis had a sense of watching something surreal being played out in Maggie's front room: they were actors on an intimate stage wanting him to be pleased with their performance. It seemed as much for their benefit as his. There was guilt to be shared, but it was as if they were intent in absorbing his, like sponges.

Dennis thought about his dad — he'd thrown him out, ignored the hell he went through at school, and Billy Fisher's murder had tattooed a target on his back.

"Guilty, your honour," he muttered under his breath.

And Jake — lots of criminal activity behind that goody-goody image. And as for being shoved out by Jake, Dennis knew it was his own fault. "Guilty, your honour."

He looked across at Maggie — she was involved in Jakes's scams, happy to take his money. She wasn't really bothered about him, all she cared about was her precious Amy. Guilty? Certainly complicit. He liked that word ... 'complicit'.

Oh, and Amy. If it hadn't been for Lee, her bollocks of a boyfriend, he wouldn't have ended up in jail. Guilty? Maybe not. A victim? Certainly.

Yes, there was guilt to be shared. They were all smiles now. Didn't they realise how much he was hurting? His brain was a scramble of thoughts, his body stabbed with pain. He was a freak, a wreck.

He pulled himself forward, his hands shaking as he gripped the armrests of his chair. Amy looked alarmed. "What you did was the bravest thing I've ever known!" she exclaimed, as if shocked by his dark looks,

He shook his head and stared at the floor. "Had no option," he muttered.

Jake gave Dennis a determined look. "This isn't the time to feel sorry for yourself. You were lucky to survive; just remember that." He moved closer, his manner almost threatening, "And if there's stuff you haven't told us," he said, as if reading Dennis' mind, "this isn't the time." He leaned closer, "It never will be."

Dennis looked away, breaking Jake's intense stare.

Something took Dennis back to his early years, in his bedroom, reading comics filled with stories about super-heroes. He remembered the thrill of imagining he too was one of them, someone who'd always fight the bullies and the criminals, and always come out on top. It hit him like a brick. He didn't need their pity and certainly not their forgiveness; he wanted their admiration. Nothing would be served by telling his dad what he'd done. To his dad, he was courageous and brave, and he wanted it to stay like that. The boy he'd adopted had turned out well — hadn't he? Not too bad for someone picked up from the nuns.

Maggie would adore him like a son. He looked up and studied her face. 'Nah,' he said to himself. She returned his stare. Just for a moment he felt something strange between them. It was possible ... It was a thought. Did he didn't really want to know? Maybe It was better like this, Maggie full of admiration. It would be weird — too weird if she had anything to do with his adoption. He couldn't envisage himself a baby in Maggie's arms. He wondered if Maggie had similar thoughts?

There was only Jake. He had the feeling Jake would never see him as a hero, not in the way the others would. He'd maybe admire him for his courage, but would Jake ever really trust him? It didn't matter. He could live with that.

As for Amy: she was beautiful; she loved him, of that he was certain, and she wanted to be with him. That's what she'd told him — and it's what he wanted ... wasn't it? It could be perfect. He smiled to himself ... the hero and his adoring girlfriend. Clark Kent and Lois Lane. Maybe it would be too perfect. Maybe she wasn't enough, not for someone like him. He was bigger than all of them now. Fear ... what fear?

He lay back on his reclining chair and let his thoughts drift back to his comics and to the superheroes, giving him their applause. They'd all know who he was. If he was left with a limp, so what? It'd be another marker, like the scar on his forehead. They'd know, those bastards who'd made his life hell.

He felt light-headed. He had options, and he would decide. He smiled to himself; ok, I'm not some comic freak. He looked up and called her, a soft voice that didn't sound like his.

"Amy ..." She was all smiles, looking bright, radiant. A hero's girlfriend. Perfect.

Maggie sat at her office desk and buried her head in her hands. She couldn't help herself: gulping sobs were followed by a stream of tears. She covered her eyes with her handkerchief and forced herself to swallow hard against spasms of grief. Guilt, relief, fear— these were feelings that made her feel uncomfortable, even vulnerable. The relief that things were over, that Amy and Dennis were ok, had been replaced by an intense sense of guilt. The thought of what might have happened to Dennis had upset her more than she would ever have expected. It brought back the sense of loss she usually kept well hidden. She thought about that time in Beech House, of that bed, Janine's bed, stinking of bleach. Maggie hated the smell, the acrid tang of bleach.

Who was it that had taken her baby boy that awful day when she'd watched out of the window? She remembered the young couple, the woman carrying a baby, the man helping her into the front of their car. Her baby? It must have been. The man had briefly glanced in her direction; tall, dark haired, well built. She didn't get a good look at his face, but there were occasions, in those first few years, when she thought she recognised him.

She felt an intense emptiness, like a hunger that filled her with an intense sadness. Jake rapped on her door and poked his head round,

"Maggie, you alright? Not like you to ..." he stopped himself as Maggie looked up at him. Her reddened eyes were weeping tears, mascara streaking down her cheek.

"Been a bit of a shock, this business with the Fishers," he said.

Maggie blew her nose loudly and nodded.

"Not like you to get so upset. They're safe now ... we all are, come to that."

"I know, I know," Maggie replied. "We were lucky. Dennis was very nearly killed and I dread to think what might have happened to Amy."

"Is that what's got you so upset? It's shock, Maggie. It hits us all in different ways."

"It's not just that, Jake."

"What then? You'd better tell me what's up. I hate to see you so upset."

Maggie took a deep breath. "It's made me realise how precious life is. Can't take it for granted."

Jake nodded. "There's more, isn't there."

Maggie reached for a tissue and dabbed at the streaks of mascara on her cheeks. "When I was very young, I got myself pregnant."

"I didn't know that," Jake replied.

"Why would you. I was forced to have my baby adopted. It broke my heart, but I was determined not to let it ruin my life. I was Patricia Byrne, then. I changed it to Harrison when I got married and I started using my middle name — Maggie."

"What happened ...?"

"To the marriage? Didn't last. He was a bad-tempered bastard. He did me one good favour — gave me his name."

"And your baby?"

"A son. He was taken away — and given away. All for the best, they said. Maybe it was; I don't know. I was just a child."

"You want to find him, is that it?"

"More than anything, Jake. It's suddenly become important, very important." Maggie looked up and smiled, "I don't want to die without trying." She stared intently at her boss, "I need help, Jake. I need to know if he's alright."

Jake pulled up a chair, "I'm listening."

Words rolled quickly out of Maggie as if they'd been held in a corked bottle, waiting to be released. Jake made no comment as she told him about the nuns, the forced adoption. She told him about her friend, June, and how her family had simply accepted Amy into their family. Jake nodded when Maggie told him her parents would have none of it. "They just wanted the baby, and me, out of the way — as quickly as they could."

It was when she told him about seeing the couple carrying a baby and getting into their car that he sat up and leaned towards her.

"You think it was yours?" he asked. "Tell me what you can remember. The car, what colour?"

"Oh, pale blue. I'll never forget the colour. It was big, foreign looking — not that I knew much about cars. Oh, the front, the grill, it reminded me of a pair of nostrils. Weird what sticks in your head."

"What about the couple? You said you got a look at the man."

"I was watching him — he had a big stride —I remember his stride — and heavy shoes. They were crunching on the gravel. Funny what you remember ..."

"Could have been boots ... work boots?"

"Heavy shoes, I'd say. He was tall, I think, solid looking. He walked a bit like a soldier — straight back."

"What about his wife?"

"Don't remember much about her. I suppose I didn't want to know who she was. I think I'd have gone mad if I'd seen her face."

"What about a birth certificate?"

"Must have been a record ... but I wasn't given anything. I suppose it must have been given to the couple who adopted."

Jake grunted. "Where ... where were you?"

"A place called Beech House. It's still there. It's offices now, an insurance company, I think."

Jake took out a notebook from his jacket pocket. He pushed his biro hard onto the paper as he wrote, underlining some of the words. He paused, looked up and eyed her. "You haven't told me when your baby was born?"

Maggie felt a wave of panic. She reached for a cigarette and took a deep drag, exhaling the tobacco smoke towards the ceiling light. "I'm not sure," she replied, her voice whisper quiet.

"Not sure?"

"I was young, upset, confused. All that bothered me was what was happening to my baby. I remember feeling sick when I saw they'd taken him from the cot next to my bed. There wasn't even a clock on the wall, never mind a calendar. No one told me. All I know is that it was late Summer, maybe into Autumn."

"September?" Jake queried.

Maggie took another drag of her cigarette. "Could have been ... must have been."

"And the year?"

Maggie forced a smile. "I was fifteen," she replied. "1972."

Jake made a few quick scribbles. "Not much to go on," he said.

"Please, Jake. There's no one else I can ask."

Jake took a cigarette from the packet lying open on Maggie's desk. He lit up and stood to leave, patting his notebook as he did so. "I'll make some enquiries. No promises ..."

"Thanks Jake," Maggie replied.

Chapter 44

It was a distraction, but, as Jake soon realised, it was not unwelcome. Thoughts of the Fishers, DI Burton, DC Andrews and even the death of Archie Slinger eased themselves into the recesses of his mind. It was Maggie he wanted to help, if he could. He thought it would be easy — there'd be a record of her son's birth, and something to show who'd adopted him. Someone local, he reckoned. Yeah, it'll be easy.

He was wrong.

He'd called the bishop's office. "Beech House? I'm not sure ... let me check with Mrs Fraser, she's been with us the longest ..."

It was several minutes later ... "I'm Mrs Fraser. I believe you're enquiring about Beech House?"

"Er ... yes. It was an adoption agency ..."

"Not an adoption agency. My understanding is it helped young girls who got themselves pregnant," Mrs Fraser replied, in a cutting Edinburgh accent intended to define her as coming from the 'right side' of the city. "It was closed down several years ago — in the late 1980's, I believe."

"I'm enquiring about a birth in 1972."

"And you are?"

"Jake Gould. I'm a friend of the mother. She works for me."

"I'm sorry, Mr Gould, we don't have any records from Beech House."

"None? Are you certain? Surely, there must be records of births, adoptions?"

"There's nothing here. I archive documents for the diocese. I suspect all the paperwork would have been destroyed prior to the sale of Beech House. We wouldn't want such information to get into the wrong hands, would we?"

Jake grunted, "Surely there must be something ...?"

Mrs Fraser sighed. "I wish I could help you, Mr Gould. I suggest you try the registry office.

"What about the nuns who worked there?" probed Jake.

There was an audible sigh. "It was a long time ago. If any of them are still with us, we wouldn't allow any form of interrogation and besides, it's more than likely anything they'd recall would be unreliable, at best."

Jake felt his anger surge. He gripped his mobile and hit the 'end' button.

"Bitch," he muttered to himself. He lit a cigarette from the packet he kept for emergencies. His regular stockpile had depleted fairly quickly in recent weeks. He'd always loved the ritual associated with a good smoke. Sometimes it was in just sliding the cigarette from its packet that he enjoyed — and the tease of the unlit cigarette dangling between his fingers. And sometimes it was holding the cigarette with his lips and slowly lifting his lighter, the one with a flip-top and knurled strike wheel. The first drag hit the back of his throat. It filled his lungs and warmed his nostrils as he exhaled. He sat for a moment, letting the nicotine find its way into his blood stream and then returned his attention to the mystery of Maggie's child. He thought about storming over and confronting Mrs Fraser. Somehow, he doubted it would do much good. And anyway, he thought, she might be telling me the truth. Maybe the records had been destroyed. Something told him this was unlikely. She clearly enjoyed her role as a keeper of secrets.

The lady at the General Registry Office was more helpful. "There'll be a record," she told him. "1972 —It'll be more than likely an adoption certificate. They were common in those days. What's the mother's name?"

"Maggie," Jake replied, without thinking. "Sorry ... Patricia Byrne," he said, correcting himself. "She changed her name."

"Where was the baby born?" he was asked.

"Beech House. It was for unmarried mothers."

"Never heard of it," she replied.

"It was run by nuns. It closed down and the building was sold. That's when all their records were destroyed — least, that's what I've been told."

"Ok, I'll see what I can do. We'll need a letter from the mother ..."

"That's not a problem," Jake replied.

Ten days later, Jake got a call from the Registry Office. It was the same lady he'd spoken to previously.

"We found a record —it's on microfiche and pretty hard to read. It's as I feared, there's not a lot of information. It shows the mother's name, the place of birth, the baby's sex and date of birth."

"Does it say who adopted the baby?"

"I'm afraid not. And there's no record of the father."

"What about the baby's name?"

"Nothing. The family adopting would probably have named the baby."

"Is that it?" Jake asked, his voice rising in disbelief.

"I'm sorry ... It's likely it would have been a local family, but they could have moved, or simply don't want to be traced. It's never straightforward."

Jake inhaled. "Thanks," he managed.

He sat and pondered what, if any, progress he'd made. He knew, at least, that Maggie —Patricia Byrne — had a baby in Beech House and, as she'd said, the baby was adopted. He also had a date of birth. The only other titbit of information was that Maggie had seen the couple she thought had made the adoption. A large car, sky-blue with a metal grill that looked like flared nostrils? It wasn't much to go on. A grill with a vertical section down the middle? Is that what she meant? How many cars had grills like that? It'd be a 1970's car ... Rovers were often sky-blue. 'Foreign looking', Maggie had said. Could have been German — a Merc, maybe? Swedish ... a Volvo? A slither of something formed in his mind. Michael — he'd had that old sky-blue Volvo of his for as long as Jake could remember. He'd sometimes teased him about getting it changed. Jake began trying to work out if it would have been possible. "Over twenty years old," he remembered Michael telling him.

Just a coincidence? He chuckled to himself. Michael would have a fit if he knew he was giving any consideration to the idea he and Barbara might have adopted Maggie's baby.

The colour was right, the age would fit. Jake thought about Maggie's description of the man. Big ... heavy boots ... strong looking. There was too much to just ignore. And besides, he had nothing else to go on.

He called Michael later in the day. "I need to see you, Michael — it's not something I want to talk about on the phone ..."

"You sound serious, Jake. Nothing to worry about, is there?"

"I'll come over around seven," Jake replied, ignoring Michael's query. He hung up before Michael had the chance to ask any more questions.

Michael's Volvo was in the driveway. A big, lumbering, sky-blue sedan. Jake walked slowly to the front and stared at the grill.

Jake turned as Michael opened the front door, "Just admiring your old Volvo," he said.

Michael stepped forward and leant on the bonnet and smiled. "I reckon I'll be on the scrapheap before this beauty packs in. Still looks good, despite the dents," he added, enthusiastically. "I bought it new in 1972. It was a surprise for Barbara — a new car to bring home the new baby."

Jake rapped his knuckles on the roof of the car. Michael looked irritated, as if Jake was intent on damaging his precious car. "That must have been Beech House," Jake said. He spoke slowly, deliberately.

For a moment Michael stood, transfixed. "Well, yes," he stammered. "That's where ..." He paused and stood erect. "Dennis is adopted. Barbara couldn't have any more children, so it was the only option. We did the right thing. These were unwanted babies. Some youngster stupid enough to get herself pregnant. Beech House gave these girls a chance to move on, put what had happened behind them. I sometimes wished we hadn't gone anywhere near the place. Dennis was bloody difficult."

"What about the young woman who had the son you adopted. How do you think she felt?"

"What's this about Jake. You accusing me of something?"

"No ... course not. You're a good man, Michael. I've no quarrel with what you did."

"What's your problem then?"

"It's the young mother who gets lost in all of this, especially if her own family forced her to have the baby adopted. It was a cruel process. Seems to me that Beech House had little concern for the mother."

"It's not like that now, Jake. Things have changed."

"Yes, that's why places like Beech House have closed down.

"There's something you aren't telling me, Jake. Why this sudden concern about unmarried mothers?"

"I think I know who's Dennis' mother."

"What! No way. This was a legal adoption — he was ours — the mother has no rights ..."

"A mother always has rights." He tapped the car. "The only memory that mother has is of a couple arriving in a sky-blue car. She was watching from an upstairs window ... I think it was you and Barbara she saw."

Michael made no attempt to refute Jake's allegation. He clearly didn't want to know who the birth mother was.

"It was a long time ago, Jake. I'm just glad Barbara isn't with us to hear this rubbish. And as for Dennis, think what he's done? He's saved our lives, Jake. He's a different person. I don't want anything to upset the relationship between us. I've longed for a son I can be proud of, and now I have one. Digging up information on his birth mother is the last thing he needs — and the last thing I want."

Jake resisted the urge to tell his friend it was Maggie who might be Dennis' mother.

"How do you know, Michael? Maybe this is just the right time to tell him?"

Michael raised his voice. "It isn't! It never will be!" He suddenly smacked his hand on the roof of his car, walked quickly to the front door and slammed it behind him.

Jake climbed quickly into his own car, cursing under his breath. What had he expected? That Michael would be overjoyed?" He'd decided, whatever happened, he needed to talk to Maggie. He drove slowly, aimlessly navigating through the suburbs and eventually finding himself in the Marshbrook estate. Two youths attempting to dislodge a picket fence that fronted one of the few well-kept gardens ran off as his car approached.

At least the Fishers won't be around, he told himself. Maybe those kids will have a better chance? He shook his head ...

Chapter 45

Maggie sounded breathless. Jake heard her cough into her phone, "Can you come round to my place?"

"Now!? Have you got some information? ... I'll be right over," she added, without waiting for a reply.

Jake paced round the living room of his flat. Unlike his office, the place had an ordered neatness. The doorbell buzzed. Maggie looked wide-eyed and nervous. He couldn't tell if she was excited by the prospect of finding out what Jake had to say, or wary of what might be revealed.

She sat at the dining table, "Well, Jake ...?"

He took his time, pouring two of his more expensive malt whiskies. Maggie stared at hers as if it might contain something unpalatable. He sat opposite and took a sip, inviting her to do the same. "Well, Jake," she repeated, "You've not asked me here to sample one of your expensive malts ... good as it is."

Jake looked directly at her. "I've an idea who might have adopted your baby,"

"You know! Who, Jake?"

"Just so you understand, they wouldn't have known who the mother was."

"I know that! Come on, Jake, tell me ... tell me!" Her eyes were wide and wild, as if fear and exhilaration were competing emotions.

"I think the man you saw was Michael."

Maggie gasped, "Michael!? Michael Barrett!? ... Michael and Barbara?"

Jake nodded. "Michael admits they adopted from Beech House. The dates fit — it was a baby boy, a few days old ... and then there was the car ... that was the first clue. And your description of the man. Weak, I know, but it added a bit of credibility."

Maggie's hands were shaking as she cradled her whisky. "He could be your son," he said.

"Could?" Maggie sounded alarmed.

Jake leant towards her, "Look, Maggie, I was gobsmacked as well. I think you need a talk with Michael."

"You've told him about me?"

Jake shook his head. "All I've told him is that I think I know who the mother is. The rest is up to you."

Maggie leaned back and drained her whisky. "Thanks Jake. I can't thank you enough ..."

"Just be careful, Maggie. Michael is already worried. He wasn't exactly pleased when I left. He thinks this will turn Dennis against him. After all that's happened, that's the last thing we need."

"What about Dennis?"

"He knows nothing of this. He knows he was adopted — maybe that's why things were difficult between him and Michael. Talk to Michael, but be very careful, Maggie. Just accept it won't be the best news he's heard."

"And Dennis?"

"God knows how he'll take it." Jake paused to take a slug of whisky. "That's if you decide to tell him."

"What? I've no option. He's my son!"

"That's up to you, Maggie. It'll be your decision."

Michael found it odd that Maggie wanted to meet him "somewhere away from the rest," she'd said. "It's private, just between us."

"Sounds personal," he'd replied.

She'd paused, briefly, "It is, Michael."

They'd agreed on 'The Star'. "After the lunchtime regulars have gone," Maggie told him.

It was as she'd hoped — virtually empty. There was a convenient booth at the far end. She hadn't slept well, and her early morning coughing spasms weren't helped by her first cigarette.

Michael was suddenly there, easing himself onto the bench-seat opposite hers.

"You alright, Maggie? You don't look too good."

"Bit of a cold," she replied. "I need a coffee."

They sat in silence, waiting for the barman to deliver two black coffees.

"Well, Maggie, what's this all about?"

She warmed her hands on her cup and took several sips. Michael was staring at the table, as if anticipating an uncomfortable conversation. She took a deep breath and exhaled, slowly.

"When I was a teenager, I got myself pregnant. My parents were, to put it mildly, furious —they were embarrassed at having a pregnant daughter, and probably very ashamed. They made me have my baby adopted."

Michael jerked back, spilling some of his coffee on the table.

"You!?" he said. "It's you Jake was talking about!"

"Don't be mad at him, Michael. I needed to find my son ... I asked Jake to help."

"Your son! He's not your son. We brought him up, me and Barbara. We're his parents."

"Look, Michael, I don't want to argue with you. Of course, you and Barbara were ... are ... his parents. But I'm his mother. I gave birth to him."

"Just to be clear — it was Beech House?"

Maggie nodded. "They treated us horribly."

Michael's voice softened," I'm sorry to hear that, I had no idea."

"It was a long time ago …" she replied.

"Twenty-five years."

Maggie smiled, "Twenty-six," she corrected.

They ordered second cups of black coffee, waiting in an uncomfortable silence, avoiding eye contact. Maggie was relieved when the coffees arrived. She sensed Michael wanted some sort of confirmation, but the moment passed.

"You want to tell Dennis?"

"He's a right to know, Michael."

"What if this is a mistake? What if we adopted someone else's baby?"

"I've thought about it. There's a slim chance he's not my baby — very slim."

Michael was nodding. It was clearly a thought that had crossed his mind.

"He looks like me; same colour eyes, slim build, long hands, thin fingers." She spread her hands on the table, as if to demonstrate the similarity. "He's mine … I know he is."

"And just how do you think he'll react? I've finally got the son I always wanted. I don't want to do anything that might …"

"Think I don't know that, Michael! I need you to accept he's my son."

Michael agreed, eventually, they should approach Dennis together. Maggie made it clear; she was quite prepared to talk to him on her own, if he continued telling her 'this isn't the right time'. She could understand his reluctance. He was scared, she knew that. Why wouldn't he be? she thought, when her rational self allowed her to look at it from his point of view. He's scared of how Dennis might react. So was she.

It was a surprise when Michael suddenly announced he'd had 'a word' with Dennis — told him there were things they needed to discuss, "You, me and Maggie." What he didn't tell Maggie was how nervous he had been. He'd expected a surly reply, the 'old' Dennis, telling him to 'piss off'. Dennis had taken a few moments before agreeing. His sudden, "ok ... where?" had filled Michael with a sense of relief.

Michael suggested a pub a few miles away.

The cleaners were still finishing clearing up from the previous night when Maggie arrived. She spotted Dennis sitting, nursing a pint, just as Michael came through the door.

"Morning, Michael," Maggie said, almost in a whisper, as if not wishing to disturb the sanctity of the moment. They joined Dennis after Michael had ordered from the bar. Maggie instinctively took out a cigarette, her lip twitching in anticipation — at the whiff of sulphur from a lit match and the faint crackle as the first drag ignited the strands of tobacco. Dennis reached across and flicked a lighter with his thumb. "Thanks," she said, slightly surprised.

"What's going on?" asked Dennis. "Why all the secrecy?"

Maggie looked at Michael, wanting him to say something. He sat, staring at the floor. She hoped he hadn't changed his mind. She took a quick drag from her cigarette and then stubbed it out, grinding the tip into the ashtray. It broke in half.

"When I was young — a teenager — I got pregnant. My parents went mad, especially my dad. Things were different then; I had no option, they made me ..."

"Made you?" Dennis asked.

"I was taken to a home for unmarried mothers."

"What!?" said Dennis, sounding alarmed. "They wouldn't let you keep it — the baby?"

Maggie shook her head. "It wasn't like June's family."

They were words she regretted as soon as they left her lips. Involving June was never her intention.

"June ... June Tiplady ... Amy's mum?"

Maggie slowly nodded. "Her dad wasn't around. He wandered in and out of their lives ..."

"Heard he was a bit of a free spirit," Dennis remarked.

"Not how I would describe him," Maggie replied, sharply. "Amy was brought up in the Tiplady family. They looked after June and Amy as if it was the most wonderful thing that had happened. 'She's a gift from God,' June's mother often remarked."

Dennis slid his elbows further onto the table. "I never knew," he said.

"I wished I'd had a family like June's," Maggie said, tapping her finger on her cigarette packet. Things might have been different. As it was, my baby was taken after just a few days. It was adopted."

Dennis sat back on his chair. "Is that why I'm here?" he said. "Is it because I was adopted?"

"You were born in Beech House," Michael replied.

The three of them sat as if in a trance, not a word, as if waiting for Dennis to process what he was hearing.

Maggie finally broke the silence.

"It's you, Dennis," she said, softly. "You are my son."

Maggie sensed Michael shifting uncomfortably. She glanced across; his face was blanched white; a tear was leaking down his cheek.

"You were just a few days old when your mum and me collected you," Michael said, swiping at the tear with the back of his hand.

"My mum?"

"Yes, Dennis, your mum," Maggie said. "Michael and Barbara adopted you, they are your parents, they reared you."

"She wasn't my birth mother," he replied, sharply.

"We were never told who your real mother was," Michael said. "We weren't allowed to know."

"And I wasn't told who'd adopted you," Maggie added.

"You didn't ever try to find out?" Dennis said, with a questioning incredulity.

"I was told there was no way I'd ever know. Things were different, then. And I was young, just a girl."

"And that's your excuse?"

Maggie hung her head, "I should have done something ... It was when you nearly got killed, I suddenly felt I had to know where my son was. Jake banged hard on a few doors and got some answers. Without him, I'd never have known."

Dennis fidgeted, nervously twisting his fingers and then pulling at each in turn. "What about the man, my real father?" he said, watching Michael's face. "Who was he? Where is he?"

It was a few moments before Maggie replied, as if she was rehearsing her reply. "I lied about who he was," she said. "I told my parents he was a soldier from the barracks. I said he was married and didn't want to know."

"They believed you?" asked Michael.

Maggie shrugged her shoulders. "It was a convenient story. My mother just said I'd have to go to Beech House and have it adopted."

"Who was is it?" Dennis asked. "Someone local?"

Maggie nodded. "He just wouldn't stop. I couldn't breathe. I was stupid ..."

"You were raped?!" Dennis' fists were clenched, his face was white.

"Doubt if he'd have seen it that way."

"Who was the bastard?" said Michael. "Did you know him?"

"Oh yeah, I knew him alright." She took a deep breath. "He was from Marshbrook."

"One of the Fishers?" Michael asked, hesitantly.

Maggie nodded.

"Who was it?" he pressed.

Maggie reached for her broken cigarette and crushed it into the glass ashtray. "Brendan Fisher."

Dennis gulped. "He was my father? That bastard was my real father!?"

"That's what I said," Maggie replied, in an exasperated tone.

"Did he ever find out?" Dennis had his head bowed, as if in prayer.

"Of course not!" Maggie retorted, her eyes wild, like those of the teenager who'd screamed her lungs out when she realised her baby had been stolen, as if her only purpose was to produce the goods. "You are the only ones I've ever told. Not even June." She was suddenly breathless, exhausted by her outburst. They sat, avoiding eye contact, waiting for words that had to be spoken.

They'd excluded Michael, she suddenly realised. It was as if she couldn't quite find a place for him. One day I'll thank him for being a father to Dennis, she thought to herself. One day ...

Dennis hugged Maggie; a tentative hug that developed into a full embrace. She kissed his cheek and rubbed a finger over her red lipstick smeared across his cheek, as if he was a ten-year old. "A lot to take in," she said as she stepped back, still holding his arms. He tensed when Michael stepped hesitantly towards him and put an arm around his shoulders. It'd been a long time ...

Dennis was glad when they left. His head was pounding, his throat felt dry and his tongue seemed to have swollen. He ordered a coffee and sipped, slowly. He was muddled and confused by what he'd just been told. In his fantasy world, he'd often imagined finding out who his real mother was. He'd even hoped it might be someone like Maggie; someone he admired. He thought of her kindnesses; that note with a kiss, and the extra money pinned to the corner. He cringed, remembering the look on her face when she realised he was the one who'd opened the back gate and let Billy Fisher and his gang into the market.

Fishers ... they were the curse of the place, a feral bunch who'd run and ruined his life right from first encountering them at school. And now he knew, he was part Fisher. He was one of them. Was it a stain? An imperfection? They'd wanted him to kill his father, they'd wanted revenge for what happened to Billy Fisher. They'd threatened to slash Amy's face ...

He smiled to himself. I can be a tough bastard if I want to be ... Brendan Fisher's in me ... a bit of him. It was a thought that felt strangely comforting.

And anyway, his brain reasoned, I've done what Brendan Fisher wanted ... killed my father ... Not Michael, but the thug who raped my mother.

He couldn't help himself, he laughed, laughed out loud ...

Epilogue

Four months later

Jake told Dennis there was a job for him at the market. "You'll be working with Maggie I'm afraid," he said with a grin. Dennis wasn't sure that's what he wanted. Working with someone who he'd only recently discovered was his mother seemed odd. It proved much easier than he'd imagined.

"Look, Dennis, just call me Maggie. I'd prefer it that way," she told him. Dennis was relieved. It seemed to do something to their relationship. She wasn't just the Maggie the traders knew — although a number commented she was different, somehow — she conveyed a warmth rarely seen, if at all. Most had noticed her quick smile and eyes that shone whenever Dennis was around. Nobody said anything to her, or to Dennis. It was as if in doing so they might see Maggie revert to her former self. The hard, unforgiving woman had become a nicer version of herself.

Amy sat at the breakfast bar, tipped a few cornflakes into her bowl and began adding milk from a carton.

"That's not much," Dennis commented. "How about some toast?"

Amy shook her head. "I'll have something later."

"You look a bit pale," Dennis said. "You sure you're alright?"

"I've been feeling a bit sick in the mornings," she told him.

"Maybe you're coming down with a bug."

Amy shook her head. "It's nothing like that, Dennis ... I'm pregnant. I just got the results from the clinic."

"What?! Pregnant!"

"Is that pregnant — oh, no ... or pregnant — wow."

Dennis beamed and hugged her. "It's great news," he said. "Us ... parents ... wow!"

"You sure, Dennis, it's not too soon, is it?"

He wrapped her in his long arms and kissed her. "We want a future together — all those hours making plans ..."

"With the help of a few glasses of wine," Amy replied. "It's been more giggling than talking seriously. This isn't just a few ideas about where we should go on holiday, this means a commitment from us both. Surely you need time? I love you, Dennis, I know you'll be a brilliant dad — but only if you don't feel trapped."

"I don't ... feel trapped, I mean. I want to spend the rest of my life with you, Amy; you and our baby." He hugged her tightly and gently kissed her. He then knelt, lifted her loose t-shirt and kissed her naval.

She stroked the top of his head. "I love you too." She laughed, "That tickles."

Dennis stood, held her close and stroked the back of her neck.

"We'd better tell June, and Maggie," Amy told him.

"And Michael," Dennis added. "How long ... before ...?"

"Think I'm about 3 months," Amy replied. "I'm going to check myself in at the clinic."

Dennis laughed, "We'd better start some serious planning!"

"You're sure you're not worried about ..."

"No ... no," he replied. "We even talked about getting married ..."

"When it feels right."

"I think this is the right time."

Amy laughed, "Are you proposing!"

Dennis nodded. "If you two will have me."

Amy giggled. "I couldn't be happier. Yeah, hell, let's do it."

"Something else to tell the grandparents!" Dennis replied.

"Grandparents!" Amy exclaimed. "I hadn't thought of them as grandparents."

"I doubt if they thought it'd happen this soon," Dennis said. "This'll give 'em all a shock!"

June wasn't as enthusiastic as Amy had hoped. "I love him, mum," she said, "and he loves me, I'm sure he does."

"Sure ... sure? You think he does, is that it?"

"No, mum, I know he does. He wants this baby, he wants to be a father, and he wants us to get married. I thought you'd be delighted."

"All I want is for you to be happy, Amy. He's had a chequered past, to put it mildly."

"It wasn't always his fault ..." Amy tried.

"Never is," June retorted. "There's always a reason; there's always someone else to blame."

Amy fought back the tears that threatened to betray her resolve. "If it hadn't been for Dennis, the Fishers would still be putting the fear of God into anyone that crossed them. They've run this area like their own kingdom. No-one did anything — not even the police!"

"He was brave — foolish and brave. But I can't get over the danger he put you in. It could have all gone very wrong."

"But it didn't, mum. He's a hero in my eyes."

June nodded. "That's what Maggie and Michael keep telling me. Look. Amy, I don't want to argue with you, I just want you to think about it. I want you to be sure you're doing the right thing — for your sake and the baby's."

"I have, mum. I want to spend my life with this man, and I'd really like your blessing."

June smiled. "I just want you to be happy, and if that means marrying Dennis, then yes, you have my blessing." She paused, "If he ever puts a foot wrong, he'll have me to answer to."

Amy grinned. "Thanks, mum. It means a lot."

June reached out and tilted Amy's chin with the tip of her finger, "We're family ... we're Tipladys!" she said, emphatically.

Amy flung her arms around June's neck, "Thanks, Mum. Thanks for everything."

Maggie couldn't hide her delight. "My two favourite people ... getting married!"

"Three of us," Amy said, rubbing her belly.

"What!? Oh my God, you aren't ...?"

Amy nodded and smiled.

"When?"

"She's three months or so," said Dennis, as if wanting to get in on the conversation.

"This is wonderful news! Have you told June? I bet she's thrilled."

"She wants us to be very happy," Amy said, not wanting to elaborate on her mother's reaction.

"I'll let Jake know ... you'd better phone Michael."

"I called him just before we came over,' Dennis told her.

"And ...?"

Dennis grinned. "What do you think? He's thrilled ... looking forward to being a grandfather."

Maggie laughed, "Two grandmothers and a grandfather. This baby of yours will be spoilt rotten."

It was the following day; Maggie gripped his elbow and greeted him with a wide smile, "Jake and Michael want to organise a 'do' for your wedding," Maggie said.

"A 'do' ... a meal, a disco. That'd be great. Thanks Maggie."

"A celebration," she said. "It'll be in here. The traders want to be involved."

"What, all of them?"

"All of them," Maggie replied. "They'll do it right, you'll see."

Dennis laughed. "This'll be something different," he said. "Amy will be delighted."

"Oh ... don't tell her," Maggie told him. "Keep it as a surprise."

Amy and Dennis left the Registry Office and climbed into the polished Mercedes that Jake had provided. It was festooned with white ribbons and had a 'Just Married' banner flapping from the aerial on the roof.

"Where are we going?" Amy asked. "She stared out of the window clutching a floral bouquet. "What are we doing here?" The car inched onto the gravel at the back of the indoor market. As the car pulled to a stop, the roller doors began to lift. Balloons were fixed around the entrance and a thick red carpet was unfurled to within a few paces of the car. Dennis quickly opened the car door, lifting her train as he did so. "Step this way," he said, his face beaming. Amy took his arm as she stepped onto the red carpet.

The traders had lined up the stalls and made an aisle with ribbons, bunting and flowers. The butcher had laid on a hog roast, trestle tables had been decorated and there was new crockery Jake 'purchased' from someone he knew. He'd set up a bar at one end and a small stage for a DJ. Amy, arm-in-arm with Dennis, shrieked with delight. They strolled slowly down the makeshift aisle, the traders applauding and shouting.

Mrs Tiplady had supplied her grandchildren with packets of confetti which they threw in all directions. The moorish lady stepped forward and draped an embodied silk scarf around the couple. "It's a tradition," she told them, before giving each a kiss on both cheeks.

Michael and Jake were standing at the end of the aisle, just behind Maggie and June. They clapped their hands in applause as the couple walked forward and within seconds everyone in the building had joined in. Maggie and June had linked arms, as if leaning on one another for support. Maggie kept dabbing at the tears that wouldn't stop.

There was something of a quizzical look on June's face. She'd told Jake she still wasn't quite sure about her daughter marrying Dennis. "What if it goes wrong? What about me and Maggie? We've been friends for a lifetime."

"It's Amy's happiness that's important ..."

"Exactly!" June replied, her tone full of exasperation.

Jake ushered Amy and Dennis to the table at the end of the red-carpeted aisle. Jake waited for the guests to take their seats at the carefully arranged trestle tables, and then invited Dennis to lead his bride to the buffet table. Their view was partially obscured by a large wedding cake the tea ladies had made. Mrs Tiplady was surrounded by her daughters and grandchildren. June had three sisters; each having produced two grandchildren for Mrs Tiplady to spoil. They ignored whatever protocol Jake had intended and one of them, a three-year old girl in a shocking-pink dress, insisted on sitting between Amy and Dennis. Amy mouthed 'it's ok' to her grandmother who, in any case didn't seem remotely concerned.

The plates had been all but cleared when Jake handed Michael a microphone. They were standing on the small platform where the DJ had set up his equipment. Most of the guests were seated, having filled and replenished their plates from the huge buffet the traders had provided. All the tables had been lavishly adorned with flowers and coloured ribbon, magnums of champagne, and boxes of streamers itching to be set loose.

Michael raised the microphone and tapped the end causing a deep thud to reverberate through the speakers. The buzz of conversation eased almost instantly.

"Please ... please raise your glasses in a toast to Amy and Dennis."

They all stood, held glasses aloft and clinked with those nearby. There was a spontaneous cheer that echoed throughout the building.

"I don't want to tell stories of when they were young, or tell daft jokes," Michael said. "I just want to us to revel in the warmth and delight I know we all feel for this wonderful couple. I owe you an enormous debt of gratitude for the way in which you stallholders have welcomed them into your lives. I will be forever grateful to you all, and of course to Jake."

There was loud applause as Jake raised his hand in acknowledgement.

"You all know Maggie," Michael continued ... "and we all know that without her this place wouldn't be the success it is today." Jake was nodding, vigorously, and the traders murmured their agreement. "She's one very special lady." He paused and turned to look at Maggie. She gave a quick nod as if giving her assent for what he was about to say.

"There is a special and unusual bond you may not be aware of — although some of you may have guessed — Maggie recently discovered Dennis is her son."

There were gasps and then a crescendo of applause as Maggie was urged to stand. Dennis blew her a kiss.

"Here ..." whispered June as she passed tissues to Maggie.

"And June" — Michael motioned for her to stand — "Without her ... well, there'd be no Amy!" Laughter rippled round the building. "As you know, she's been a part of this business since the beginning, and she passed on her knowledge and nouse to her successful daughter."

He paused and waved to Dennis and Amy.

"And there's more," he said, teasingly. "I've been given permission to announce Amy is expecting. In a few months, Amy and Dennis will be parents." There was a loud cheer, several of the men banged rhythmically on the tables, Mrs Tiplady's brood grabbed handfuls of streamers and let them go in a succession of percussive bursts.

Michael waited for the laughter and shouts to settle and for Mrs Tiplady to move the last of the streamer cartridges out of reach of her enthusiastic grandchildren.

"I nearly forgot," he said. "I've got some messages of congratulations." He opened the first card. "It's from Father Carey. He wishes the couple a happy marriage ..."

"With my full blessing!" boomed a voice from the entrance to the building. "I didn't think I could make it ... "

Maggie waved to Father Carey, pointing to a chair on their table. The priest's dog collar shone like a white band against his charcoal suit. He waved back and walked along the red carpet as if it were an aisle in some splendid cathedral. Michael waited for the priest to take his seat next to Maggie and then lifted the microphone,

"I have some cards — mostly from some of the traders who couldn't be here. He quickly read out their congratulatory words. Michael grinned and shook his head. "This one's from our tea ladies," he said, waving the card in their direction. "I don't think I can read it out loud, not with children present, not to mention Father Carey!" Michael waited for the giggles to fade before opening the last card. Unlike the others, it was addressed and postmarked. He read out the message, it simply said, "Congratulations to you both — someone forgot to sign their name," he said laughing. As he waved the card in the air, he noticed something written in pencil on the back. He paused, and then quickly pocketed the card.

"A final toast," he announced. "To the happy couple. This is the proudest day of my life," he added. And then hurriedly sat down. The couple took their cue and walked down the carpeted aisle to cheers and shouts. Mrs Tiplady dug out a few more boxes of confetti for her enthusiastic grandkids. They needed no encouragement.

Jake turned to his friend, "What is it Michael, you look as white as a ghost. You ok?"

Michael pushed the card he'd slipped into his pocket in front of Jake. He tapped his finger on the writing at the back of the card.

'Congratulations! Quite the hero!' And then, 'Take care' followed by initials, 'DF'.

"Danny Fisher," Michael said.

Jake nodded.

"Now what?" Michael hissed.

Jake took the card and slowly tore it into small pieces. "He's a lifer. It'll be a long time ... he'll be an old man before he gets out. The Fishers are finished." He looked directly at Michael. "It's not the same Dennis. He's different ... strong, tough ... he's had to be. He's the bravest man I've ever met. Forget those bastards."

"Hope you're right," Michael replied.

The two friends stood and watched the couple, Dennis all smiles, Amy on his arm, radiant. They kissed and stared at one another, the guests cheering, Mrs Tiplady's grandchildren giggling and pointing.

Michael turned to Jake. "A great day ..."

Maggie tapped Jake on the shoulder. "What's up with you two? There's a wedding to celebrate!"

Michael smiled at her, "Sorry, Maggie." He picked up the microphone; "Clear the floor ... Amy, Dennis, please lead us off with the first dance."

They stood watching the happy couple. Jake put his arm around Maggie's waist, "Our song."

Maggie hesitated, "Next dance, Jake, got to dance with my son first."

Maggie slipped her arm in Dennis' and led him onto the floor. "I'm so proud of you," she said as they swayed to the easy beat. "We've done things I never imagined we were capable of. You stood up to those Fisher bastards."

Dennis hugged her close and kissed her cheek. "And I found my mother."

"We're family," she said, her eyes wet with tears. "Amy, the baby, June, Michael, Jake ... we all share something very special. We'll look out for one-another — always."

Dennis held his mother in his outstretched arms. "At last, I know who I am, and where I belong."

They embraced, hugged and laughed. "I couldn't be happier," Maggie said, wiping at the tears on her cheek.

Printed in Great Britain
by Amazon